A PRAVERIAN SERIES
BOOK THREE: THE DARKWOODS TRILOGY

THE
BALLAD OF ARAMEI

J.A. REDMERSKI

ISBN-13: 978-1480264526
ISBN-10: 1480264520

This book is a work of fiction. Any references to real people, historical events, or real locales are used fictitiously. Other names, characters, places and incidents are products of the author's imagination, and any resemblance to actual events, locales, persons living or deceased, is entirely coincidental.

Cover Design by Michelle Monique Photography
Models: Amber Coney & Yuriy Platoshyn

DEDICATION

This book is dedicated to all of the book bloggers/reviewers and the many readers out there who embraced The Darkwoods Trilogy with more love than I ever thought it would have. Without all of you, Darkwoods would never have gotten as far as it has.

Also, to my dear friend, Kristen Dome, who runs my Facebook page because I simply can't do it myself! *Muah!* She is an awesome friend who has stuck around for me since the 'MSN Days', and believe me, that's saying a lot!

Table of Contents

1

I WAKE UP TO an earthy smell rising headily into my nostrils, and the cool, prickly feel of grass blades cushioning my naked body. At first, I think I'm dreaming, but as my heavy eyelids slowly break apart I realize the warm slivers of light crisscrossing my skin are the sun's rays beaming down through the tree branches above me.

A few black dots move through the blue sky, followed by the caw of a crow. My sight is blurry, my eyes glazed over by moisture and a very fine amount of sentience.

I smell blood. *A lot* of blood. And it's so potent, almost chemical. I taste it in my mouth, lingering heavily on my tongue in a thick, briny layer of copper and salt and bile.

Gross.

I doubt I'll ever get used to this.

The realization hits me in this moment and I jerk my body upward, my eyes popping open wide. Where the hell am I and what exactly did I eat last night?

Oh God, please let it have been animal, or better yet, something already dead from the grocery store. Yeah, that's not likely. The image of me busting into Finch's Grocery in full-fledged werewolf form and tearing my way straight to the meat aisle makes me laugh a little. But the humor of the moment quickly fades and I'm back to pulling the pieces of my mind together.

My sight comes into focus; the view of the mountain covered by fog and thick clouds only looks like a backdrop. It's too far away to seem absolutely real. I'm surrounded by trees and grass and soil. The sunlight glistens on the tiny stream of water out ahead and on a spider's web dangling precariously between the branches of a low-lining tree. Everything is deep green and full of life.

I really am naked...

Instinct causes my arms to come up across my chest, covering what I can of my breasts. I pull my legs toward me, closing them tight and letting my knees fall to the side. I should be cold, but I'm not. My body temperature is very warm, but not uncomfortably. In fact, I feel better than I have ever felt. Last night was only my second time shifting and much in the way after the first time, my body feels new and revived, as if I have been reborn. But this time, I feel even better than the first. I wonder if it might feel better each time. Something tells me that it will, that each transformation is destined to make me stronger.

I hear everything. The song of early morning birds and the water moving in that seemingly calm stream are amplified in my ears. I hear the heartbeats of animals and the soft padding of movement on the forest bed all around me. I even hear insects burrowing through the earth and the wispy fluttering of butterfly wings that no human would ever be able to hear. The butterfly lands on a leaf nearby and I watch it for a long time before it feels strong enough to flutter away toward the small sunlit clearing out ahead.

The scent of pine trees and maple trees and wildflowers is so strong that I feel like it could easily intoxicate me.

The insistent smell of blood raises the hairs on my arms.

Finally, I look down at my naked body, allowing my mind to grasp the true measure of the situation. Fresh blood is moist in my hair, weighing it down and sticking to the skin on my chest and arms. Blood is smeared down the length of my ribs and across my left leg. My hands are absolutely covered in crimson, darker underneath the bed of all ten fingernails. I can only imagine how my face looks. I feel it all around my mouth, the blood, and along my cheek toward my ear where it's already starting to dry and crust.

I visibly shudder at the thought of what, or who I might have killed last night, what or who I might have...eaten.

My heart is heavy with remorse and guilt. I can live with killing an animal—though I don't particularly like the thought of that either—but I could never forgive myself for killing a human being.

How did I get out here?

Panic envelops me from the inside out. The last thing I remember was being in the basement with Isaac at my side. I remember several days of hell and pain and burning and delusions. I remember Isaac's face, looking down at me with tortured, loving eyes as he swabbed the cold, wet cloth across my forehead and my face and my neck and my chest.

I remember seducing him.

And he never hesitated to give in to me. Never. He wanted me as badly as I wanted him.

But he was supposed to keep me restrained down there. I wasn't supposed to be able to get out. I vaguely recall when he unlocked the shackles around my wrists and ankles on the night of the full moon so that there would be minimal damage to my body as I transformed. So that my transformation wouldn't rip the shackles completely from the old dank stone wall, but I wasn't supposed to break free from the basement.

I'm not supposed to be out here.

Where is Isaac?

I crawl across the forest bed just a few feet until I realize that I don't need to crawl at all. My legs feel strong and powerful. I rise to my feet, pressing my palm against the nearest towering tree and look all around me, searching for any sign of Isaac, while at the same time trying to hide my nakedness with my hands and my moist, dark hair. Maybe he hasn't awoken yet. He could be around here anywhere, asleep in the high grass in the clearing, or under any one of a thousand trees.

And I still have no idea where I am. I sense that I know which direction to follow that will take me home and that I could never really be lost, but I still don't know where *here* is.

I've never seen that mountain in the background this close before.

Wow...I have to be far away from Hallowell. Somewhere north.

My panic levels are rising higher. I'm completely naked, covered in blood and dirt and my hair is a tangled rat's nest. I don't need a mirror to know that I look like a crazed girl, even like some psycho backwoods cannibal straight out of a Rob Zombie film. My animal instinct tells me I can find my way home, sure, but that doesn't mean no one will see me on the way there and call the police to pick me up. How would I explain *that one* to Uncle Carl and Aunt Bev?

"Isaac?" I say just above a whisper. If anyone out here hears me, I only want it to be him. "Isaac!" I whisper harshly, looking all around me in every direction.

I step softly over the debris in the forest bed and practically tiptoe around tree after tree, using each one as a shield and avoiding going anywhere near that small clearing which has nothing to shield my nakedness.

But then it hits me: with these new animal senses, it should be nearly effortless to hear his footsteps, no matter how quietly through the woods. I should be able to detect his heartbeat, hear the blood pumping through his veins. I should be able to hear his thoughts, smell his toothpaste and the natural scent of his skin.

I stop behind another tree and shut my eyes, trying to take it all in, to block out the obvious and let my senses guide me to something farther away. I inhale deeply of the cool, morning air and open my ears to the sounds that had lain buried underneath everything else so close to me.

Isaac taught me how to control my thoughts and how to block out the uninvited intrusion of others, but I still have a lot to learn. The time he spent teaching me was all devoted to this; because of a traitor, a Praverian gone Dark that lives among us. There wasn't time to teach me much about how to block out the things around me, to tame the voices that I hear or to turn the volume down on all of the noise. I don't yet know how to do these things to full capacity. Unlike him, I can't just *do it*. I have to concentrate. I have to focus. And it's not easy.

I hear something rustling far off in the distance behind me and I hold my breath for a moment to keep it from drowning out the sound. With my eyes still closed, I take a step backward and then turn around. I listen closely and hear it again. Something is moving on the ground, the distinct sound of leaves shuffling underneath movement is heavy and localized to the same spot. I hear a heartbeat but I can't tell if it's human. I try to reach out to Isaac telepathically, but I get no response.

Hunched over slightly, still trying to cover my nakedness, I pick up my pace and move quickly through the forest in the direction of the noise. My human instinct compels me to watch my footing, to step over sharp twigs and small branches and rocks that may shred my feet, but my animal instinct is what helps me to actually avoid these things. As my pace quickens I realize how easily I miss everything without even thinking about it. And when I start to run, I begin to leap over objects that somehow my animal mind knows are out in front of me before my human mind is aware of it.

As the noise gets closer I slow down. But I'm confused because I'm having trouble blocking out the noises all around me to be able to focus solely on it. Trickling water somewhere to my left is so magnified that I feel like an insect next to a waterfall. The birds flying overhead sound as though they have enormous wingspans flapping with heavy force. Everything is amplified times ten and I can't block any of it out. I press my hands against my ears and don't even notice that I'm walking backwards.

I fall over something and when I land in an upright sitting position my back is pressed against something firm and warm. Blood seeps from underneath my butt and my thighs, and my hands are planted in a mound of disgusting, squishy, rubbery entrails.

My breath catches and my arms come up quickly and I practically slip on the entrails as I try to pull my body out of the cavity of the carcass.

I finally get away and stumble backward, falling yet again, but this time against the cleaner ground a couple feet away. The dead moose's elongated head lays haphazardly, the long, grayish tongue lolled out of its opened mouth. Its giant antlers are still in-tact, jutting up from its massive head, but its stomach has been completely torn apart. The ribcage shows through underneath the ravaged fur; most of the ribs have been broken and some lie in the pile of innards spilling out from the body and onto the ground.

Bile rises up in my throat.

I pick myself up, bracing a hand against a small tree and cup the other over my mouth and nose in an attempt to cover the smell. Flies and maggots are already starting to gather, but this is a fresh kill. It was my kill. I know because as I gaze across at the endless depths of its glazed-over black eyes, I glimpse little pieces of memory from when I took it down last night. I try to block it out, but when I shut my eyes, the blackness only gives way to a more vivid visual.

A branch snapping behind me and the sound of a low, guttural growl is what pulls my head out of the hunting visual.

I turn around briskly at the waist. A large black bear is making its way toward me about a hundred feet through the trees, probably attracted here by the scent of my kill.

I suck in a sharp breath and start to panic, until I see another figure coming in behind it.

It's Isaac. Isaac!

I want to be happy and relieved, but why is he walking so slowly? He clearly sees the bear and I sense that he knows I'm standing here even though it's possible that from his angle my body might be obscured by the forest. Surely he knows. But why hasn't he started running to help me?

The bear draws closer and my body locks up out of fear. I don't want to run. They always tell you never to run when you come face to face with a bear. But everything in me is screaming at me to run. I keep looking to and from Isaac and the bear, expecting him to pounce on it from behind any second now, but instead, Isaac falls back and keeps a still position near a tree, letting its massive trunk partially conceal his naked form. My heart is hammering against my ribcage. I'm hunched over slightly with my knees bent and hands out in front of me, arms bent at the elbows. Instinct now tells me to be ready to fight. Wait…fight a bear? This is insane.

The bear rises up on its hind legs and begins to sniff the air, its clawed paws dangling down near its belly. It grunts and sniffs and grunts some more.

And then it sees me.

My preternatural eyes, shifting black of their own accord, catches the bear's eyes boring into mine. I don't know whether to be terrified, or…territorial. The moose's blood rises up into my nostrils heavily, but for some reason unknown to my human mind, this time my throat doesn't retch at the scent of it. My stomach doesn't swim in a poisonous lake of bile. No, it smells good and my stomach *aches* for it.

My black claws come out and the skin on my forearms begins to turn gray.

I move toward the bear, my back arched over as my body molds itself into a battle-ready stance. The bear growls and jerks its head abrasively side to side. But it begins to back away and then it runs in the opposite direction. I watch as the mass of black fur bounds through the forest and out of sight.

Isaac steps away from the safety of the tree and moves toward me, a grin spread across his beautiful face.

I catch myself pushing my hair back down over my shoulders so that it covers my exposed breasts and I turn my body at a sideward angle and press my thighs together.

"Like I haven't already seen all of that before," he says just a few feet away.

He is right, after all, but it just feels weird. I mean really there's nothing sexy to me about standing here in the nude, covered in blood and dirt with wild woman hair.

"Actually there is," he says having fished around inside my head, still grinning the grin of the Devil. I love that grin. It usually means he's up to no good, and Isaac being up to no good usually means I'm going to like it.

No! Not here like this! I cover myself even better, pushing my hands down below my pelvic area to hide as much as I can.

"Thought you weren't going to read my mind?" I snap, though there's a trace of humor in my voice.

His hands come up as if surrendering. "Closed off now. I swear."

"Okay," I say looking at him more scoldingly, "what *was* that? That bear could've killed me, Isaac."

He smiles and looks downward for a brief moment. "Ummm, no it couldn't have," he says. "And I wanted to see how well you handled it—that's why I was reading your thoughts."

"You were testing me?"

He nods. "And you did well," he says. "You gave in to your animal side quicker than most newbies do."

Of course, I have not at all forgotten the fact that he is standing here talking to me butt naked. It doesn't matter one bit that we've already seen each other in our birthday suits and that we've consummated our relationship; there's just something uncomfortable about talking to *anyone* while completely nude. It's not natural…well, I guess in a sense it sort of is, but I easily keep my eyes looking at everything above his waist.

"And besides," Isaac goes on, "a black bear would never attack a werewolf. A grizzly, on the other hand, would without hesitation. They never win, but they're a formidable opponent."

"Well, what if that would've been a grizzly?" I say, now crossing my arms and tilting my head to one side. "Huh? Tell me that—would you still have left me to fend for myself?"

Isaac laughs under his breath and moves to stand right in front of me. He presses his forehead against mine, cupping my arms in his hands below. "Good thing there are no grizzly's in Maine," he says and pecks me on the tip of my nose. "But yes, I'd still leave you to fend for yourself."

My mouth falls open. I playfully push him away and let out a spat of air. "Seriously! I can't believe you!" I'm still sort of laughing through my poor attempt at being offended because he's still sort of grinning behind his poor attempt to be serious.

He grabs me and pulls me toward him, crushing his lips against mine. He kisses me long and hard and I press my naked body against his, grabbing his hair in my fists.

The kiss breaks and the first thing I notice is that Isaac looks clean. I step back and look him up and down.

"Why aren't you gross like me?" I cross my arms to look reproachful, but really it's more to cover my breasts. And I still stand at sort of an angle so that my thigh covers my private area below.

He tugs his head back. "This way," he says and reaches out his hand.

I take his hand and walk alongside him toward the sound of water.

"I feel like Adam and Eve," I say, "well, Adam and Eve written by Seth Grahame-Smith, anyway."

Isaac smiles over at me, but doesn't say anything.

"What is it?" I say.

"Nothing."

I narrow my eyes at him and he gently grips my hand as we make our way over a large fallen tree branch.

"Isaac," I say, though watching my footing more than looking at him now, "I'll just start digging around inside your head if I have to—Oh! That's right! I can do that now, which means you can't hide anything from me anymore."

His lopsided grin deepens.

"I already told you that I don't care if you ever listen to my thoughts," he says.

He reaches out and pushes away a dense patch of low, thin tree limbs that jut out over the path so that I can walk through them.

"But you know I don't want to," I say.

He walks in behind me, letting the limbs snap back into place afterwards.

I see the creek out ahead now.

"It's just that I'm glad you're taking to this so easily," he says.

We make our way to the edge of the creek and I step right in, letting the water come up to my waist and I begin to wash. Isaac sits on a large tree limb sitting low near the ground. The tree that it comes from is awkwardly shaped, rising over the top of a small ridge that surrounds the creek.

It really doesn't feel so weird bathing in a creek. Not that I've ever done it before, but I spent my childhood swimming in ponds and creeks and rivers and lakes, so it doesn't bother me. Of course, I'd love some soap, shampoo and conditioner. *A lot* of conditioner.

I look over at Isaac sitting on the limb as I scrub the blood from my elbows and say, "Define easily."

God he looks good naked...I force myself to look away.

2

I HEAR ISAAC JUMPING down from the limb and I wait to look up when I hear the water move as he steps into it. He comes up behind me and guides my body back so that he can wet my hair.

"I tried to prepare myself for this," he says, combing his fingers gingerly through my wet, tangled locks. "I expected you to be completely traumatized by the whole experience, to wake up after a shift like right now, and maybe hate yourself, hate me for what you've become."

He works his fingers through another section of my hair, never pulling it.

"I told you that I would never hate you," I say, "I promised you the night you changed me."

I feel his breath on the back of my neck as he sighs deeply.

I turn around to face him.

"Isaac, what's wrong? And don't lie to me."

He gazes into my eyes, searching for something, though I'm not sure what, but he seems concerned. I study his face for a moment and then it hits me. I don't need to probe his thoughts to know what he's thinking.

I let my head fall slightly to one side and I reach up and rest my fingertips on his cheeks, water drips from my hands and runs down the length of my arms.

"You think I'm forcing myself not to hate you because of my promise?" It discourages me that he would even consider that, but I can't bring myself to criticize him for it.

Isaac looks right into my eyes, but doesn't answer.

I lean up and kiss his lips softly and he knows that words aren't needed to assure him now. He knows that I would still love him even if the promise was never made.

"So," I say, looking around at the trees on all sides, "exactly how do we get back...you know...being naked and all?"

Isaac turns me around again and scoops water into his hands, pouring it on my shoulders and neck and gently scrubbing the blood away that I had missed.

"That's the tricky part," he says, "but it should be fun."

"Fun? How could anything about that be fun?"

I hear him laugh softly behind me and then he leans around and kisses my cheek.

I don't like that mischievous feeling I'm getting from him right now. Okay, maybe I like it just a little bit, but something tells me this is going to be an interesting morning.

~~~

Apparently, we ended up nearly three hours away, north of Hallowell and when Isaac told me this on our trek through the mountain, I could hardly believe it. I just couldn't understand how I had traveled so far away on foot (as a werewolf, but *still*) and hardly remember anything but bits and pieces of my kill.

We walk for an hour before I finally see and hear signs of human life and it all starts coming at me like a whirlwind of noise: the sound of traffic, the thumping and rapping of something trapped inside a wooden box trying to get out. I hear someone humming and someone else whistling in the shower.

I hear two people having sex and I instantly reach up to plug my ears with my fingers.

Isaac stops in the forest before we make it onto a trail that leads into a small town.

"You didn't hear anything unnatural when we were at the creek," he says, placing his hands on the sides of my neck.

Now that I think back on it, he's right. I look up at him, searching for answers.

"You were able to block it all out because your mind was only on me," he says. "It's all about focus and discipline. You have to *know* that you're the one in control of your mind and not the things around you."

I nod heavily, fully understanding yet at the same time not so sure of my ability to pull it off.

"It'll come natural to you soon enough," he says, "but you have to stop fighting it."

"How am I fighting it?"

"You're trying too hard. Just let it go. Don't think about how you *need* to do it; just don't think about it at all."

I nod once more.

It's true; when we're having a conversation the noises around me seem to naturally fade into the background unless I'm *trying* to push them into the background.

He takes my hand again and says with an I-hope-you're-ready-for-this sort of expression, "Just follow my lead. Don't say anything if we're spotted, alright?"

I swallow hard and nod. "Okay." I'm hoping he's going to explain exactly what we're about to do, but as he starts to walk away, pulling me along beside him, I realize I'm not going to get an advance briefing.

We head down the path and when we come to the end minutes later, instead of stepping out into the wide open of someone's backyard, we stay hidden in the veil of trees on the outskirts. The back of the old house comes into view. There's a high deck perched against it and a sliding glass door covered by thick, long curtains. I catch the scent of bleach and Pine-Sol from the raggedy mop that hangs stiffly over the deck railing. The house sits on at least two acres of land where just outside of it, off in the distance, a few other houses are scattered about the hilly landscape.

Isaac pulls me farther around the back of the house and we come to a barn, fairly new. I can smell the heavy scent of freshly cut wood and paint which the red door had recently been painted with.

"Do you hear anyone inside?" Isaac says, crouching with me still in the cover of the trees.

"In the barn?"

"No," he says with a hint of laughter, "the house."

I listen for voices and movement, but all that I can hear this closely is the purring of a cat.

I shake my head no.

Isaac points toward a part of the back of the house, just off to the side near the deck that looks like a small add-on room.

"Do you smell it?"

I look at him confusedly, wishing he would start elaborating his questions more.

"Coming from that room," he says, "do you smell the detergent?"

I inhale deeply and shut my eyes, thinking only of that room and I do smell detergent strongly, along with fabric softener and dryer sheets. Normally, stuff like that always gives me intense headaches, but not this time. It's as if I'm immune.

"Yeah, I do smell it," I say and I'm starting to understand what his plan is.

"Come on," he says, taking my hand again.

My heart is pounding in my chest as I follow him out into the open and toward the back of the house where the laundry room waits for us. We duck behind a large tractor, stop to look around to make sure no one is outside and then when Isaac feels it safe to continue, we dash across a long stretch of yard and make it to the high deck. I hear the cat purring inside more clearly now and I look up to notice a white fluff-ball curled up inside next to the window, sleeping. We inch our way around the deck and make it to the laundry room. He tries the knob, but it's locked. I hear both the washing machine and dryer humming inside.

I start to say something about needing a key, but just before the suggestion leaves my lips, the doorknob cracks and falls into Isaac's hand, broken.

"Isaac!" I whisper harshly. "Why'd you break it?"

He turns at the waist to look at me. His gaze strays up and down my naked body, the grin on his face getting bigger. "As much as I like what I see," he says, "if we don't hurry and get dressed we run the risk of being found like this."

"Oh, right," I say, now wanting to speed this theft up.

The laundry room door creaks open and we slip inside the tiny room barely large enough to contain both of us at the same time. Isaac pulls open the dryer and a mound of clothes tumble round and round before coming to a full stop. A few pieces of clothing fall out and onto the floor. We both crouch low and start sifting through the items, which I'm glad are fully dry already.

Isaac jerks out a pair of tan slacks and holds them up, but he doesn't examine them long before he's slipping his naked legs down into them.

"Hurry up," he says, motioning toward the dryer.

Gah! It's mostly old lady clothes! One by one I pull out something hideous and flowery, not to mention oversized by at least two sizes. Holy shit, is that a *moo-moo*? Embarrassed to even be holding something so un-sexy in front of Isaac, I shove it deep into the dryer.

"Someone's here," Isaac says peeking around the door. "Hurry up!"

My heart beats even faster now and the nervousness is starting to make me a little nauseous. I'm not sure which scares me more: getting caught stealing someone's laundry, or getting caught butt-naked stealing someone's laundry.

"Adria," Isaac says from above, still watching from the door, "this isn't a fashion show. Doesn't matter what it looks like, just grab something, quick."

Without thinking about it, I reach inside and yank out whatever my hand touches first, hoping like hell it's not the moo-moo.

A cream-colored granny slip-gown. Great. Just great. It's almost as bad as the moo-moo, but Isaac's right, there's no time to be picky.

I practically throw the gown over my body and feel how it literally engulfs me, falling past my hips and stopping just above my ankles.

Isaac glances back at me. "Damn, you're sexy," he says, trying to hold in the laughter.

I glare at him, letting him know I won't forget that and he'll be paying for it later.

As we go to leave, the back door opens up onto the deck and an old lady with bluish-purple hair steps out, looking right at us. I sort of freeze and so does Isaac.

"What—Hey! What are you doing with my clothes?" The woman's eyes dart around the deck and then she waddles quickly over to the mop and takes it into her hand.

"Time to go," Isaac says, dragging me along.

We take off running across the yard and back toward the forest.

"Stop! Bring those back! I'm calling the police!"

I can hear the old woman trying to run after us, but she gives up and stops once we dart into the cover of the trees.

I'm laughing manically. I can't help it, but that kind of rush does weird things to a person.

We run a good distance through the forest and I realize that I should be out of breath by now. I should be sweating, or feeling something to indicate I'm overworking my body, but minutes later and I still feel the same as I did before I started running. Finally, we come to a stop near another makeshift trail that looks to lead right toward a highway; the sound of cars passing over an exit bridge seems closer. And with my keener sight I can see a set of railroad tracks far out ahead.

"Never thought I'd be the one to figure it out first," I say, holding the thin fabric of the ugly gown at my back hoping to make it look tighter around my form.

Isaac looks at me curiously and I just grin.

"Werewolves have been the cause of missing clothes on laundry day all this time," I say. "All of those frickin' socks!" I shake my head.

Isaac rolls his eyes and laughs under his breath.

"I don't think socks are going to help cover much," he says, "so I doubt that explains the Great Sock Disappearances."

"Oh yeah?" I say, cocking my head to one side. "I take it you've never seen a Red Hot Chili Peppers concert before then?"

"Can't say that I have," he says, and judging by the grin, he's fully aware of the sock-wearing-capade I'm referring to.

We leave the path and make it to the railroad tracks. The highway stretches southeast out ahead and it's obvious we're closer to a town by all of the houses, churches and various other sorts of buildings I see just past the highway. Cars buzz by every few seconds.

"We can't walk two more hours back to Hallowell dressed like this," I say, looking down at myself. "Well, *you* could get away with it, but me…not so much."

Isaac is still trying so hard to hold back his laughter, but he might as well let it all out and get it over with because he couldn't be any more obvious, really. And he does look hot, even wearing some old guy's khaki slacks. They fit him perfectly and rest at just the right measure down low on his hips, revealing the sculpted curvature of his waistline, six-pack abs and bellybutton where a little happy trail hides below the top button.

But me, on the other hand, I am about as mortified and embarrassed as I've ever been dressed in this gown and looking like I just spent a rough night in the woods.

"You stay here," he says and instantly my brows crease with objection, "and I'll go over to that gas station and call Nathan to come pick us up."

An hour and a half later, Nathan is pulling up along the side of the road and we're hopping in the back seat of his FJ Cruiser. Harry is with him, as I had a feeling he might be.

"Damn, girl," Nathan says after turning around in the front seat to see me sitting in the middle next to Isaac. "Not even you can do *that* gown justice."

"Shut up, Nathan," I say, gently hitting the back of his seat.

Nathan grins back at Isaac. "We were starting to get worried, bro." He puts the Cruiser in gear and we pull away.

"That's an understatement," Harry says from the front passenger's seat. "How did she get out, anyway?"

Isaac sighs heavily next to me and I feel his arm tighten around my waist.

"She just did," Isaac answers and I can hear the irritation in his voice.

Harry was sort of overprotective of me even long before he found out that he's a Praverian and that I'm his Charge. But now, ever since he went through his Becoming not even a month ago and everything was revealed to him, that overprotectiveness has definitely gone up a few notches.

"You all know I'm sitting right here, right?" I say. "How did I get out—you're talking about it like I'm an animal or something."

All three of them look right at me with grins and raised brows—Nathan from the rear-view mirror—and I shrink back into the seat. An animal. Of course. Talk about sticking my foot in my mouth.

Oh my God…I'm an animal. I'm a *werewolf*. It's already my second time shifting, but I think I still have a long way to go before all of this will completely sink in.

Isaac pulls me closer. "How do you feel?" he says, and I can sense the gentle smile in his voice because he knows I must feel fantastic.

I tilt my head to see his eyes. "I feel…powerful." It seemed a little weird to say that word, almost as if it were ridiculous, but it's absolutely true. I feel like I can do anything: scale a high wall with ease, rip a phone book in half with my bare hands. I feel like I can fight anyone with no fear, but instead with complete and total confidence that I will win…well, humans anyway. I'm nowhere near confident when it comes to other werewolves. But I'm not the slightest bit afraid of the prospect. And that in itself is amazing to me.

Fear. That's it…I have absolutely no fear. None….

"Powerful *and* crafty," Harry says with a little playful mockery in his tone. "It's only her second time and already she's outwitting the Alpha boyfriend."

I notice Isaac's eyes narrow and I squeeze his hand, looking up at him with eyes that say, *Baby, it's just Harry. What do you expect?*

He smiles faintly back at me, knowing I'm right.

"While we're all alone," Nathan says, "we need to get this whole thing about who Adria can talk to straightened out before we get back."

"Yeah," Harry says, "they're all starting to talk—most of them aren't buying the story about how Adria just needs time alone to deal with her new existence."

"Rachel, for example," Nathan says, "is coming up with all kinds of crazy stuff."

"Like *what*?" I say, raising up and holding onto the back of his and Harry's seats.

I hate Rachel. The feeling has always been mutual, but before, back when I was just a 'weak, ghastly freak of a girl with a fantasy' (that's what Rachel called me the day I caught her with her tongue in Isaac's mouth), I couldn't say anything because she might try to kill me. Now that I'm on her level, I can defend myself and I'm looking forward to it.

You know what they say about paybacks.

"Something about you getting knocked up," Nathan says and he's grinning hugely in the mirror at me.

"But the main rumor," Nathan adds, "is that the Blood Bond is still making you loco." He swirls his finger around the side of his head in a circular motion.

"Let's not elaborate on the details of Rachel's rumors," Isaac says next to me, already sensing the anger it's causing me and the inevitable retribution.

"No, I want to hear this," I say, leaning up between the front seats even farther. "What has she said, Nathan?"

He glances back at me once before putting his eyes back on the road.

"It's just Rachel," he says, "and they're just rumors—don't stoop to her level on account of childish rumors."

"Oh, but they're not childish," I say, "and you know it. Harry just said that most of them don't believe our excuse anymore. This could cause problems."

I feel Isaac's hand rubbing my back, trying to soothe me and it's working. He switches from his palm to his fingertips and chills attack my body all over.

"Let them believe what they want," Isaac says, now moving his fingers to the back of my neck and I practically wilt.

"I agree," Harry says. "This could buy us some more time."

"But I can block my thoughts," I say, though my tone isn't as abrasive as it was seconds ago.

"Yeah, doll, you can," Nathan says, "but you're still new and it might be easy for a Praverian to penetrate your thoughts regardless of how strong your mind wall is."

"Well then let's put it to the test," I say, rising up fully again.

Isaac's hand stops in the center of my back.

I look over at Harry. "Try it. Read my mind."

Harry just looks at me for a brief moment, shrugs and then gets down to business. I actually feel his mind trying to penetrate mine and it's very different from another werewolf. A wave of heat energy begins at the top of my head and spreads down the back of my neck leaving my skin feeling warm and tingly. My right eye begins to twitch, but I manage to calm it only to have all of my focus concentrating on a tiny growing spot of painful cold in the very center of my forehead. The spot begins to spread outward and my vision doubles, but I still manage to hold Harry's intrusion back. I'm struggling, but the longer I hold it, the less I feel Harry's power and eventually it fades away completely. When I feel my mind is light again, I release my focus and just stare at him, hoping he won't tell me that he still got in regardless of my efforts.

I look at him, waiting impatiently.

"*Well*?" I urge when he doesn't answer fast enough.

"You have a strong wall," Harry finally says and then he puts his back against the door of the Cruiser so he can see Isaac sitting behind him. "I couldn't get in."

Isaac nods absently a few times as if in deep thought.

"I'm not saying that I should go back to being the social butterfly," I say, "but I think getting back to some normalcy is better at hiding our secret than keeping me away from everyone and giving anyone reason to wonder what's really going on."

"She's right," Nathan says. He pulls onto an entrance ramp and the Cruiser speeds up as we hit the freeway. "But you have to be careful," he adds looking at me through the mirror again.

I rest my back against the seat and snuggle up closely to Isaac.

"I know," I say, "and I will."

"So...any clues as to who might be the traitor?" I say.

Harry turns around to face the front again, but it seems more out of disappointment than for comfort. "Nothing," he admits. "So far, everybody checks out. I haven't stopped invading their minds since this all started and still nothing."

Isaac reaches over and pulls my legs onto his lap and I curl up even closer to him, resting my head in the wedge of his arm.

"But this situation is a lot different than the one with Genna," Harry goes on. "Genna was hiding her presence from everyone. The traitor I doubt is doing the same thing because Adria would probably have seen him or her, too. This person is right out in the open and considering the fact that there are no humans in your house," he looks over at Nathan briefly, "I think it's safe to say that the traitor is a werewolf."

"Wait," I say, "you mean like an actual werewolf? No illusions or anything like that?"

Harry leans slightly around the seat to see me and he nods. "Yep," he says. "Our bodies are human; we can still become what you become. Being what we are doesn't make us immune to anything but disease and old age."

Nathan laughs. "Apparently, you're not immune to old age, either—who do you feed on anyway, Harry?"

"That's a good question," Isaac says.

I just look back at Harry without verbally adding my own obvious interest in his answer.

"I go to the hospital," Harry says and then looks right at me and adds, "And the nursing homes—you'd be surprised how many elderly people are willing to let us drain them."

I shudder at the thought of it and then I say, "You *tell* them?"

"Sometimes," he says with a slight shrug, "can't hide from them because they're already so near death and I personally don't want to lie to them and tell them I'm an angel—most of them think that at first."

But then Harry cuts the conversation off abruptly and I get the feeling it was bothering him a little.

Harry goes back to the important matter, "But since disease and old age are also two things that werewolves are immune to, if one of us were to become werewolf, we wouldn't need to feed as often to stay young."

"So what are you saying?" I ask.

"Just that if the traitor is also a werewolf, it knocks out another tool I might've been able to use to find out who he or she is."

"Leaving you no bread crumbs," Isaac says.

Harry nods. "Exactly. Two of the ways in which I would've been able to pinpoint the traitor—feeding patterns and someone Adria could see that no one else could—are useless."

"So then what's left?" I say, feeling more and more defeated and exposed.

"Sheer luck if we want to smoke it out safely," Harry answers with heavy abandon. "And we *have* to smoke it out safely."

I sigh heavily and meet Isaac's gaze. He looks as concerned as I know I do.

3

BACK AT ISAAC'S HOUSE, the first thing I do is hit the shower. We had gotten all of the blood off my body in the creek, but by the amount of reddish-brown flowing into the shower drain, we only managed to wash away about five percent of the blood from my hair.

I think about my two transitions as I stand in the shower and let the hot water batter my skin. I remember the excruciating pain, the way my skull literally split in half. How my ribs each snapped one by one in fast succession and how I thought I was going to pass out from the pain. But I couldn't. I remember trying, holding my breath for so long, hoping to cut off the flow of oxygen to my brain so that I could just collapse and not feel the pain anymore. But I know now that I'll never be that lucky.

And I also know that I'll do everything in my power to keep from shifting between moon cycles. I'll be damned if I ever let anger or lust get the better of me, sending me right back into that violent and cruel and unforgiving transformation. I may not be able to control a full moon shift once a month, but I won't let it happen when the rest of the month it's all in my hands.

Of course, I say that now, but deep down I know it won't be easy, to hold back the rage, to refrain from being seduced by lust. If it were easy, everybody would be doing it. This makes me wonder just how much easier it will be for me to stay calm in angry situations. I know there's more to it than just doing Yoga or converting to Buddhism.

This worries me a great deal.

I get dressed, thankful to toss that hideous granny gown in the garbage and head to Isaac's room to find Daisy sitting with him. It's obvious that I walked in on a conversation because their words cease in an instant and Daisy's face lights up when she sees me.

I try to act nonchalant, but at the same time I'm way too curious to let it slide.

I hug Daisy back as she slips her arms around me and at the same time I say, "What were you two talking about?" I'm looking right at Isaac standing next to the bed.

Daisy pulls away and smiles at me, tilting her blond head gently to one side, which makes her look all the more innocent. "Oh, honey," she says, letting her fingers fall away from my elbows, "it's nothing really to worry about."

I smile back at her, but I'm not giving up that easily and she knows it. "Well then there shouldn't be any reason to keep it from me then."

The two of them glance at each other as if to say quietly, *Guess she got us on this one.*

Isaac moves over to me and he's half grinning, half concerned and I don't know whether to be worried, or not.

He nods toward the bedroom door and hooks his hand around my elbow. "Come on, we'll show you."

I look back at Daisy once, hoping her expression might reveal something more telling than Isaac's, but she's even better at hiding the severity of a situation than he is.

What is this all *about*? I really hate this….

I walk with them down the stairs and into the large den where Rachel and five of her minions meet us halfway having come from outside. Rachel sneers at me as I pass, but I ignore her as usual. She really isn't worth my time and now that I have to discipline my anger more than ever, I probably should just stay away from her altogether. I'm not scared of her. I'm scared of the transformation.

Isaac takes me past the kitchen and into the back hallway where the door leading into the basement sits. I catch the scent of funky moisture and mildew and rotting wood before Isaac even opens the door. I hate it down there. It's like being locked in an eighteenth century dungeon, complete with shackles and rats and thick rock walls dripping with filthy water and every creepy-crawly one can imagine.

The wooden stairs creak and moan underneath our steps as we descend into semi-darkness. The air is always cooler down here, but I would take the sticky heat of a Georgia summer over this dank, raunchy air any day. It's not until we make it down the last step that I realize it's not as dark as it should be. There's an out of place swath of light coming from somewhere in the large basement far behind the staircase, bathing the partial stone and wooden floor in a dense, eerie gray glow.

Daisy comes around in front of us and smiles at me sort of…apologetically. But before I have the chance to make my impatience known any more than it already is, we step farther into the room and I see where the strange light is coming from.

"What the—?" I start to say, but I just cut myself off and stare out at the massive hole in the back of the basement, the massive hole in the so-called thick rock wall that I always thought of as the equivalent of reinforced steel. The hole is…well, probably about my size in werewolf form and leads right outside into the back area of the house. It's the only spot in the basement wall not surrounded by earth.

I look at Isaac and Daisy back and forth, my mouth slightly hung open.

"I'm just going to assume I'm the one that did that?"

Isaac's eyes crinkle around the edges and his mouth stretches marginally into a hard line. "Yeah, you sort of did that," he says carefully.

I cringe. "*Sort of* did it?" I say. "There's nothing sort of about that." I point at the hole as if they don't already know that it's there. I let my hand drop to my side and walk over to the new basement exit, stepping around chunks of rock scattered all around the floor.

At least the view is nice. It's a beautiful summer morning and the breeze is cool filtering through the trees that surround the house. The sun is shining and only a few white cumulus clouds hang in the sky.

After studying the jagged edges in the giant opening and letting the stun fade from my head I turn around to face Isaac and Daisy.

Isaac is grinning faintly again, enough that I can detect it, but it's almost as if he's trying to hide the fact that this somehow humors or delights him.

"And what's so funny about this?" I say looking directly at Isaac.

Daisy is smiling too, but at least she's trying to be understanding because clearly I'm not finding anything about what I did humorous or delightful.

"Well, it's not exactly *funny*," Isaac says, his lips lengthening into a smile even more evidently. "It's just that...well, it's hot."

My head feels like there's a spring in it as it jerks inward and my eyes crease under wrinkles of perplexity. "Hot?" I say. "Hot as in hot-hot or sexy-hot?"

Daisy is suppressing a giggle behind me, but I don't take my eyes off Isaac who has some serious explaining to do. I put my hands on my hips and I'm sure I look like my mother did when I was little, but I don't care.

"Sexy-hot," Isaac says. He moves in close and places his hands on each of my shoulders, cocking his head to one side. Oh great; there's that irresistible grin of his that causes me to fold every time. "Obviously, this is how you escaped last night. It's hot because you're stronger than any girl I've known who was Turned and not born a werewolf."

He must be mistaken. That's absurd.

I look back at the wall opening and say, "It was just a weak wall." Then I turn to see Isaac again. "This is an old house."

He kisses my cheek and says afterwards, "I told you about this, remember?"

"About what?" I say, and I really can't recall just yet what he's referring to, but somehow I know it's about to be an *Oh, that!* moment.

"About females often turning out stronger than males," Isaac answers.

"Oh, that...," I say, stepping away from him.

I'm not as laid-back about this news as they clearly appear to be and Isaac detects it right away. I turn my back on him and walk back to the opening in the rock wall and step out into the partial sunlight.

I hear Daisy and Isaac whispering to each other, but I'm too involved in my own thoughts to wonder about what they're saying. Besides, when Isaac joins me outside and I hear Daisy's footsteps fading as she goes back up the basement steps it's sort of obvious they were agreeing that Isaac should 'take it from here'.

I turn to look at him immediately, letting my arms fall back at my sides. "Okay, so where am I supposed to go every month if there's no basement to shackle me to?"

Isaac lets out a sigh and his shoulders relax. It's as if he had been trying to figure out exactly what was bothering me and realized too late what should've been obvious in the beginning.

"We have a month to figure it out," he says. "It's really not an issue."

"Isaac, I could've hurt...*killed* someone last night."

He steps back up to me, raising my chin with his fingertip. "We'll fix it," he says. "And before you say it, I mean the situation, not the basement wall." Another grin creeps up at the corner of his mouth and I can't help but smile a little.

I go to kiss him until the sound of rocks and earth grinding under several sets of tires funnels around to us from the end of the driveway at the main road. Isaac's gaze is solely fixed on the back of the house as if he's staring right through it to see who's pulling into the drive. That intense look etched in his expression instantly has me on edge.

I feel his fingers slip through mine and then his grip tightens around my hand. Before I even think to ask what's going on, we're walking around the side of the house and into the front yard where three 4-wheel drive SUV's and one massive black Escalade are pulling up to the front of the house. My heart is hammering inside my chest and I don't even know who's inside the vehicles yet. I have this feeling in my gut, twisting my insides into knots and it's telling me that I probably don't want to know.

Standing just at the edge of the front of the house, Isaac reaches out his hand and carefully pushes me to stand behind him instead of at his side. I don't argue.

"Who's that?" I whisper harshly.

"It's my father," he says quietly, never taking his eyes off the vehicles.

Figures pile out of the SUV's; tall, brute men that I know aren't really human. I count twelve of them who each take up a position in the yard and around the house. One in particular walks right past Isaac and me to stand watch at the back of the house. My eyes lock on him as he walks by and for a moment I can't look at anything else, my mind is lost in theories of what this could be about. Trajan doesn't come here often and I can count the times I've seen him at this house on one hand, but never has he come here with an entourage. And I'm a little discouraged that Raul, the ancient werewolf soldier whom Isaac is good friends with, isn't among them. Seeing him might have made me feel better about this. Maybe. Okay, probably not.

The driver's door opens on the Escalade and another guard steps out wearing average clothes like the rest of the guards: dark jeans, tight-fitting t-shirt and black biker boots. He moves to the back door and opens it and Trajan steps out. He is always more handsome and intimidating and frightening than anyone in his company. I can never understand how someone can seethe so much power, how he can put fear in the hearts of men simply with the turning of his gaze or the solemnity of his expression.

I said before that I don't fear anything, but that was a lie. Trajan Mayfair, or rather Lord General Vukašin Prvovenčani, is the one I fear.

But why is he here?

I step up closer behind Isaac, watching the scene from the view around his shoulder.

Isaac bows his head as Trajan locks eyes with him, but Isaac doesn't take his hand from behind his back which holds onto my arm protectively. Trajan stops only a few feet from the Escalade and folds his hands behind him on his backside. And suddenly I feel his gaze on me. I don't just see it I *feel* it, like he's under the surface of my skin, raging like a fever. I swallow hard but the knot in my throat just won't go down.

"Father." Isaac says in greeting.

I hear the front door of the house open and several people from inside come out onto the porch, but I find myself focusing on something…some*one* else. I hear a delicate, steady heart beating, the rise and fall of soft breaths. I can smell the sweetness of musk oils and vanilla and lavender heavily on the air. My heart falls when I realize that Aramei is somewhere inside that Escalade. It's like I can feel her inside of me, I can taste her on my lips and hear her heartbeat underneath the sound of my own. My throat begins to close up with tears, but I'm stronger now and I force them back into the deepest part of my chest.

Then I hear a voice in my head:

"We need to talk," Trajan says to me and apparently to Isaac at the same time. *"Isaac, you will go inside and instruct your pack to* remain *inside. All of them. Adria will join me in the vehicle."*

Isaac's hand tightens around my arm and his body stiffens. The link stuns me at first; I shouldn't be able to hear anyone's thoughts or telepathic communication other than Isaac and Harry's.

Isaac must've opened his link with his father to me.

"But father," he says telepathically and I can hear the unease in his words, *"I mean no disrespect, but I cannot leave her. Not alone with you."*

My eyes feel bigger all of a sudden and I turn my head robotically to look up at him, stepping around his side just a few inches so that he can see the worried look on my face. The thought of sitting alone anywhere with Trajan is alarming, but I think Isaac refusing to do what his father commanded is more-so.

"You will *leave her alone with me,"* Trajan says and I see that his solid, emotionless expression never wavers. *"I will not harm her."* It was an intolerant demand spoken in the calmest of words, yet at the same time I could sense that Trajan was also doing right by his Alpha son by giving him his word that he won't hurt me. Trajan would never feel the need to give *anyone* his word, or the need to explain himself. I know that he would kill someone first before ever offering such an accommodation as this.

And Trajan isn't the type to lie or use manipulative tactics like Viktor Vargas would. Trajan doesn't need to. This alone gives me reason to trust in his words and so I step out the rest of the way from behind Isaac.

"I'll be fine," I say aloud, putting my hands on Isaac's hand before he can grab me. "I believe him."

Isaac's chin rolls outward, the look on his face unsure, concerned, but he knows as well as I do that we have to give in to what his father commands or else the situation will quickly take a violent turn.

"Leave your mind open to me," Isaac whispers and I nod once, agreeing.

I peer deeply into his bright blue eyes and let our thoughts sync. Instantly my head feels slightly heavier as Isaac's mind wanders through mine and latches on the same way he had been physically latching onto my body just seconds ago.

His jaw moves as he grits his teeth harshly behind his tightly closed lips.

Isaac looks back at his father, nods and reluctantly lets go of my hand. I soften my eyes on him, hoping to calm him even more and then I walk toward Trajan, feeling every one of my steps pulling me farther and farther away from the safety of Isaac's arms. The last time I stood face to face with Trajan was the night I was rescued from Viktor Vargas. Trajan looked down at me that night from his massive height and body; he is the biggest and deadliest werewolf in the world and I stood up to him. I didn't fear him an ounce. He had just thrown Isaac through the wall of the Vargas house and out into the snow, saving Viktor from being killed by Isaac's hand. Something in my mind clicked when it happened and fear was the last emotion that I could evoke in that moment. Rage, anger and hatred were all that I could feel and I had let Trajan know it.

And he didn't kill me.

But right now, I'm not feeling those vengeful emotions which had helped to smother the fear in the past and as I stand before Trajan now, I can't help but be immensely nervous and exude a childlike timidity in front of him. I fold my hands together in front of me and bow my head once out of respect. I don't know if I'm doing it right, but hopefully Trajan will overlook it if I'm not. Just give me points for trying, please. Thanks.

Trajan nods, opens the back door on the Escalade and motions for me to get inside with his hand palm up. Nervously, I look back at Isaac one more time as he's walking up the porch steps, taking his time so that he can use what's left of it to watch me.

"I'll be listening," he says telepathically, *"and if I sense the slightest bit of alarm I'll be out here before you see me coming."*

"Okay."

"Leave the link open," he adds. *"Even if my father tells you to close it off. Do you understand?"*

Easy for him to say that, but I'm the one outside with Trajan. Alone. If Trajan tells me to shut off the link I might have to cave and do what he says.

"Yes," I answer.

Isaac walks inside the house to the voices of a dozen concerned people:

"Isaac, what's going on?" Isaac's sister, Camilla, says restlessly.

"Why is he here?" Daisy says. *"I sense something is wrong, terribly wrong."*

"You left her with him?" Harry snaps.

"Shit around here just keeps getting better," Zia says and I always find it amazing how she can be so sarcastic in even the most traumatic times, or maybe she's just better at hiding her fears than some are.

The flurry of voices snaps out of my head like turning off a light switch when Trajan speaks.

"Please get in."

I finally do as he wishes and climb inside the backseat of the massive vehicle. The first thing I do is look around the seats for Aramei and I'm baffled to see that she isn't here.

I sit down and the noises from outside close off as the door shuts behind Trajan.

"I assume you're wondering why you can feel her?"

It takes me a second to understand his question because, quite frankly, I'm sitting in a close, confined space with the world's most feared werewolf and I have every right to be pushed up on the level of stupid and it not count against me.

"Uhh…yes, I am as a matter of fact," I say, forcing the nervousness down some so that I can at least retain a bit of dignity. "Where is she?"

"Aramei is in the cabin," Trajan reveals, "and why you can hear her and sense her is the reason that I am here."

He speaks so calmly that one might presume he isn't capable of violence if they didn't already know who and what he was. But truthfully, the calm in his voice is what intimidates me the most. It translates as confidence and dominion; he doesn't have to raise his voice or use threatening words to get his point across because that eerie calm does it for him.

Trajan, as always, is handsome beyond words, with dark, flowing hair and matching facial hair that grows perfectly on his chin, under his nose and upward along the lower half of his cheeks, buzzed short so that it's not too bushy. But he's dressed differently than I've seen him before in the cave when he looked much more savage and ancient, wearing no shirt and an old leather coat split down the sides. Today he looks more like the men he brought with him, except that he wears his black jeans and tight black t-shirt better than they do. There's something about a man with power that makes him look better in his clothes than everyone else.

I straighten my back and fold my hands together in my lap. I try to look him in the eyes as little as possible because it feels disrespectful of me.

"Would you mind telling me first why I can sense her at all?"

Trajan rests his back in the comfort of the seat and lets his extremely long legs splay, folding his strong hands together adorned by thick silver rings that look like something bought from a gothic shop. The only difference is that his rings are, I know, very real and very priceless. But more than their worth, the fact that they're solid silver shows even more how powerful this werewolf is because silver burns like hell.

Isaac told me this. The necklace that he gave me in June is silver, but now that I'm werewolf I can't wear it for long periods of time or else my skin will start burning. I have since put it away safely and I don't wear it at all.

Trajan looks out ahead of him and says, "You were once bonded to Isaac when you were human. Becoming a Black Beast dominates a Blood Bond and you no longer have to drink his blood to stay alive, but it is still in you and it will always be."

I turn my head to look directly at him so that I can focus solely on his words as they fill my mind with wonder. But he keeps his gaze focused out ahead, not appearing to look at anything in particular, but not lost in his thoughts, either.

And I continue to listen with the greatest intent.

"Anyone bound by our blood," he goes on, "can be eternally linked to all who are bound in the same way. You are connected to Aramei because of this and it will never change."

I feel Isaac's heart fall tremulously as he hears his father's words in my mind.

"But this connection is so rare, Adria," Trajan says, now looking right at me, which makes it feel mandatory that I look at him too, "that it is a miraculous thing, you must understand."

I am caught off-guard by the sliver of hope in his voice that at first I thought I was making up. But there was definitely hope in his words, an emotion that I never would have otherwise associated with someone like him. Why would he care about something as petty as hope when everything he wants and needs tends to fall right into his lap?

"How rare?" It's all that I can say. I'm still trying to feel him out, to understand where this meeting might be leading, to figure out of I need to be concerned.

"You and Aramei are the only two to be connected since the Asvald sisters seven hundred years ago. They were daughters of a Viking warlord, both bound by blood to my father." There is a sudden knowing glint in his eye now and his tone shifts for a moment to indicate a faint layer of wit. "As you can see, Blood Bonds run in the family."

He looks away from me again and goes back to being completely serious.

"Aramei has changed," he says and silence fills the dense air around us.

An announcement like this one might not seem so extraordinary to some, but those three little words are truly worth giving my full attention to.

I just look at him, hoping he won't stall to divulge the details that I desperately need and want, yet at the same time in a way, fear.

"For two hundred years," he goes on, "Aramei has only ever spoken to me, only ever spoken my name aloud. She has not shown an ounce of understanding the world around her, but has been trapped in a world of her own, some strange world inside her mind that I've never been able to comprehend. It seems so real to me, Adria." He looks over at me and his face reveals even more of that hope I saw before, which has now also become determination. And it shocks me a little that he used my name, speaking to me as if I were a friend and he is taking advantage of my ability to listen. But the determination suddenly dissolves from his face and there's a sort of sadness left in its wake.

He sighs and I glance down to notice his fingers moving along the contours of his rings.

"In two hundred years Aramei has never spoken my name and it felt like she never even knew who I was anymore. She calls out to me, yet my heart tells me she doesn't really know me, that she has not the slightest inclination of my presence. It is as though my name resonates inside her head as an echo from long ago before the blood took her mind and when she loved me." His face has hardened, but this powerful being I know is incapable of tears. His sadness and despair can only come out as anger and rage. And I feel it laying there dormant in his heart, a storm of emotion that he has let build up inside of him for two centuries.

I try to swallow that knot in my throat again, but another one just forms in its place.

Trajan turns to me again and I raise my eyes to his without hesitation.

"She spoke your name two days ago," he says and my heart locks up in my chest because I already know what he's about to say next. "And when she did, there was absolute life in her eyes. She *knew* you, Adria...she knew you."

I shift uncomfortably on the seat and look toward the window next to me rather than at Trajan anymore. I can't bear to look at him because I feel so guilty. How can she know me, but not him? This can't be happening....

Isaac's mind is swimming with realization and panic. I can see through his eyes as he stands in the den in the center of the floor, pacing back and forth across the carpet as everyone watches all around him. I see Nathan standing near the den entrance leaning against the wall with his arms crossed and there's an equally concerned look on his face that I know, just by feeling Isaac's emotions, is pretty much how Isaac looks right now, too.

"I need you to communicate with Aramei," Trajan says and my heart falls into my stomach, "and I will not take no for an answer."

4

SO MUCH FOR THINKING Trajan might have a kind bone in his body. I should never have let myself believe that were remotely possible. I think about putting my hand on the door handle and helping myself out, but decide against it. Where would I go and how would I get there? I'm trapped inside this Escalade with nowhere to run.

But just as Isaac promised, he's running down the front steps of the house and towards us.

I'm positive Trajan knows that he's coming, but he never takes his eyes off me. Seconds before Isaac makes it to the window, three of Trajan's men step in front of him and stop him in his angry rush.

My whole body stiffens when one of the guards is sent flying over the hood of the Escalade and crashing into a tree about fifty feet on the other side of me. And then the Escalade shakes and jolts as Isaac and another guard crash against the rear. I hear the covering over the brake lights shatter and then a loud *bang* as the guard's body is forcefully pressed against the back window, the sound of glass snapping and cracking as he's pushed further and further into it and it's barely withstanding the weight. The vehicle jerks side to side and I find myself gripping the back of the seat in front of me, my fingers digging abrasively into the leather.

Trajan is absolutely calm and motionless.

"My guards cannot defeat my son," Trajan says looking directly at me, "but once he gets past them, the only one left is me."

My hands begin to shake and sweat, my eyes dart from the fighting going on outside the vehicle and back to Trajan, who just threatened his son's life in so many grim words. And by the resolute look in his eyes, I know the ending to the inevitable outcome rests solely in my hands.

I take a deep breath, grip the door handle and step calmly outside the Escalade.

Isaac throws a fourth guard off him and rushes over to me, breathing heavily and already bleeding.

"Stay away from her!" Isaac says as Trajan gets out and closes the door softly. "You're not taking her with you! DO YOU FUCKING UNDERSTAND ME?" The demonic undertones in his voice send shivers through my body. He pushes me behind him aggressively.

Trajan doesn't move and his expression doesn't shift an inch from the composed, emotionless state it has remained in for most of his visit. Instead, in reaction to Isaac's disrespect Trajan simply lowers his head just enough so that his dark blue eyes appear hooded underneath the lids, giving his face an even more intimidating and intolerant appearance.

I move back around and stand in front of Isaac, placing the palm of my hands on his chest. He's trying to keep his eyes on both of us, but finally he can't help but look only at me, realizing without having to read my mind what my face reads.

"You're not going anywhere with him," Isaac says in a harsh, desperate whisper. Creases form and harden at the corners of his eyes. He reaches out to grab me, but I gently push him away. And then I shut my thoughts off to him so that he won't know the lies I'm about to tell him, are lies.

"Isaac," I say softly, "I want to help. I can communicate with her...I...," I let my breath catch; "...I could feel her emotions as plainly as my own that night we stayed with her in the cabin. They were *so* strong...I-I didn't completely understand it then, what had happened, but now I know. She's reaching out to me. She needs my help and I *want* to help."

Everything that I said was true except the part about wanting to help. Make that two things that I still fear: Trajan and being in Aramei's presence. She nearly brought me to my knees that night. Her two hundred-fifty-year-old imprisoned emotions are too much for me to bear, too potent for my much younger mind to contain.

Isaac's face is besieged by fury and conflict, his breathing still heavy from the fight just moments ago. He looks back and forth between Trajan and I, a swarm of emotions lay in his eyes.

"I go with her," Isaac demands.

"You can join her later," Trajan says. "You are Alpha here and your duty is to your pack."

"My *duty* is to *her*," Isaac snaps, pushing the words fiercely through his teeth. "You know that more than anyone, *Milord*," he adds, putting grave emphasis on a word that would normally be replaced with 'father', but he refuses to address him in that way.

I feel something else seething off Isaac's skin other than anger and defiance. I sense something triggered in him far more dangerous and I look over at him, studying his angry eyes and the change boiling inside of them.

From the corner of my eye, I see Harry step out onto the front porch. He has probably been listening this whole time, too. Being my Guardian, it's going to take as much convincing to keep him away as it is for Isaac. I glance across the yard to see Harry and I shake my head no. *"Stay on the porch,"* I say in my mind, hoping he will hear me as easily as Isaac does. *"You'll make it worse if you interfere."*

Harry, apparently hearing my thoughts, stops before descending the porch steps. And he waits.

I turn to Isaac, placing my fingers gently on one side of his face and I soften my expression. His hand comes up to hold my wrist and he leans inward, kissing the base of my palm.

"Isaac please," I whisper, "let me do this. I feel like I need to do it. I'll be okay. Your father has no reason hurt me and I'm under his protection so you have to know that no one else would."

I hope I'm convincing enough. If I don't do this, this might not end well for Isaac and I can't let that happen.

"You take care of business here," Trajan says from behind, "let her and Aramei be alone for a time and then you can join her."

"For how long?" Isaac says, his voice still heavily laced with disdain.

"That will be for me to decide when I am ready."

Isaac doesn't move or speak for several long, tense seconds, but I feel his entire body harden like stone against mine. The air around the three of us is rife with hostility, barely contained by Isaac. I'm surprised that his eyes haven't shifted black.

He hates his father right now. I know that he loves him, but this is a different sort of hate and I can only tell what it's fueled by, not what outcome it will inevitably cause.

Somehow, this realization worries me more than where I'm going….

I step carefully away from Isaac and his hand falls away from my wrist, his fingers lingering until they reach the tips of my own. As I make my way to the back passenger's side door where I had been sitting before with Trajan, I hope that Isaac will contain his anger until we're gone. Every muscle in my body is stiff with trepidation. And I try not to make eye contact with anyone; not Isaac or Trajan or even Harry who still stands at the top of the porch steps watching me from afar and I know holding back his own dire sense of urgency to accompany me. But Harry knows more about what will happen than Isaac could ever know. Because Harry knows my future. And everything that is happening right now is certainly part of the design, that road my life must follow in order to fulfill my destiny as a Praverian Charge.

If I was in any danger, Harry would know it.

What he's doing right now is an act. I'm sure of it. Because he still must do everything he can to make those around us believe he is only human, my overprotective human best friend that knows nothing of destinies or futures or wars to be made.

I am destined to start a war. And it's Harry's job to make sure that I do it.

When I think of this, I'm sure to close my mind off to Harry because…I don't want to be the cause of any war.

And I refuse to be.

~~~

The first half of the drive is completely suffocating. No one speaks, which means there's nothing to distract my keen senses from all of the petty sounds and smells around me. The stench of gasoline burns my nostrils and my lungs. I can even smell the blood on the driver's teeth from whatever animal…or man that he ate during last night's full moon. I can't seem to block out the constant grating and humming of the tires burning across the highway or the roar of the engine and the thunder rumbling in some distant thunderstorm. But worst of all, I feel suffocated because I'm trapped in this tin can with Trajan sitting next to me and every now and then I hear Aramei in my mind, struggling with whatever kind of life she is living inside that lost and lonely head of hers.

I don't know what Trajan expects me to get out of her. More than that though, I'm afraid of what I might see. If I see anything at all.

"You're hearing her now mostly through me," Trajan says, facing forward.

I look over carefully. "Aramei?" I know he meant Aramei, but really I'm so nervous sitting here with less than three feet between us that I'm not confident in my own voice around him yet.

Trajan nods subtly.

"You'll be able to connect with her fully on your own once you get there," he says.

"Well, how am I doing it now?"

He glances over at me. "Her link is very powerful," he says. "I believe you're hearing her through me."

"But I thought you said I was connected to *her*?"

"You are," he says looking back in front of him again, "but so am I and I believe she's using me as a bridge. I imagine once you are standing face to face with her, her emotions will flood your mind."

I look away too, recalling how this very thing happened the last time I visited her and how much I didn't like it. "They will," I say softly.

I feel his eyes on me from the side. "Explain."

"When I saw her last," I begin, "I think she tried to communicate with me then—no, I *know* she did."

"Yes," Trajan says, still looking right at me which makes me all the more nervous, "Evangeline told me of your visit. That was the night in which my beloved began changing."

I feel his eyes move away from me finally and then I turn my head to see him.

"Evangeline?" I say. "Is that Eva?"

"Yes, Eva has been my most trusted caretaker for Aramei for many years. But she grows weary and I expect she will die soon."

My eyes widen a little as his strangely casual words catch me off-guard for a moment. But I can't bring myself to say anything in response. Not sure what to say about something like that anyway.

"Well then," I say, "What do you expect of *me*?"

"Whatever you can give me," he says looking directly into my eyes which sends shivers through my arms. "I expect you to tell me everything you see in her mind, everything no matter how insignificant it may appear to you. Do you understand?"

The diminutive amount of confidence I had acquired over the course of our short conversation fades away in an instant with his demand. And I realize in this crucial moment that Trajan Mayfair, regardless of being Isaac's father and regardless of needing my help to communicate with the love of his life, will never hold me in high enough regard to spare my life if I do anything to displease him. I know that our 'conversations' can never be mistaken for Trajan growing to care for me, or that he will ever see me as anything more than a tool to help give him what he needs more than anything. I can never let my guard down with him because the second I do, the second that I feel comfortable in his presence might be the time in which he turns on me and kills me.

I turn away from him, unlocking our gaze and I stare out ahead through the windshield and watch the landscape fly by.

When we finally arrive at the cabin, I'm as anxious as ever to get out of the vehicle and away from Trajan. The last thirty minutes of the drive he spent scanning the pages of a thick, old notebook, jotting down things that I assume had something to do with business and his leadership. Maybe it was about conquering packs and killing off rogue bloodlines. I don't know, but seeing as how it's Trajan Mayfair, I know he wasn't writing poetry.

I step out of the Escalade and at first I'm afraid my head will be engulfed by Aramei's emotions, but I sense nothing. The soft wind funneling through the surrounding trees is cool on my face. I hear the sounds of nature all around me and the familiar rushing of water crashing against the rocks in the nearby waterfall. It's so peaceful here and I want to just stand here forever and bask in the comfort of it, but I know that in just moments there will be nothing comforting or quiet about my visit at all and I dread going inside.

Raul, the big werewolf guard who is a friend of Isaac's, stands watch at the foot of the steps leading up to the porch. He looks different in the daylight, his smile more radiant and trustworthy, but the second Trajan steps out of the vehicle moments after me, Raul straightens his back, gripping the handle of his sword at his side and his smiling face stiffens into something much more military.

Trajan approaches and Raul and the other four guards standing nearby, all bow low at the waist and hold it for four seconds before rising back up into a straight position. Trajan doesn't even look at them, but walks by them all without a word and slips inside the cabin. He leaves me standing out here among the guards, but I'm pretty sure he knows I'm not going to try running away or anything.

Raul's posture loosens and so does his expression. A huge grin spreads across his face. "Finally tossed that pup out did you?" he jokes about Isaac.

I grin right back at him and, of course, play along because it might break his big, scary heart if I don't.

"Yeah, I did, Raul," I say stepping right up to his giant form. "I just couldn't get you off my mind."

Raul's grin deepens and he rolls his chin upward a little, looking proud and feeling sexy. I swear the big guy is blushing. But he's not as talkative as I've seen him in my brief encounters with him in the past. Trajan is inside and I was brought here for a purpose, in which Raul probably feels it's better not to delay. I step up and around him, letting his soft smile comfort me for a very brief moment before I head inside.

The cabin is unsurprisingly spotless, except for high up in the rafters where the servants can't reach. The space smells richly of lavender and honey. I can hear water dripping from another room and the sound of the servant's soft, bare feet shuffling throughout the cabin. I count five women dressed in long, sheer black gowns as always, tending to duties downstairs.

As I walk by, each of the servants stops what they're doing and bows their heads to me. It feels awkward and I do wonder why they would feel the need to do that to me, but I didn't come here to question the actions of servants.

I stand at the base of the wooden stairs that lead onto the vast open floor that overlooks this room below. And I take a deep breath before I place my foot on the first step.

I still can't feel her, which strikes me as odd. But I soon find out why as I take the last step and enter the top floor. I look across to see her lying on the giant bed against the far wall, sleeping soundly.

Trajan stands in the center of the room with his powerful hands clasped in front, resting on his pelvis.

Evangeline, or Eva for short, approaches me and bows once in the same way the servants had downstairs.

"Tis' good to see you again, Milady," Eva says as she comes out of her bow.

I feel my eyes furrow with confusion, but still, I don't spend any time inquiring about my own curiosities while Trajan is here. It just feels wrong and…unacceptable. But 'Milady'? This just keeps getting weirder.

I nod to Eva as if to acknowledge her greeting, but really I have no idea how to go about all this formal stuff; it's so completely foreign to me.

It may be early morning still, but the upstairs space is quite dark having only one small box window and it's covered by a thin, white curtain. The light funneling in through the downstairs windows only spreads so far up here where the balcony seems to cut off most of the light, leaving the top floor bathed in semi-darkness. A few candles are lit throughout the room.

Feeling completely uncomfortable, I take a seat on the chair next to the little round table near the balcony and fold my hands nervously in my lap. To my utter shock, Trajan walks over and takes the empty seat.

I shift on the chair, straightening my neck and allowing my shoulders to stiffen. I feel his eyes on me, but at first I can't bring myself to look directly at him. He feels so dangerous and everything about this entire series of events is unimaginable to me. I am a new werewolf, having suffered only two full moons. Trajan is…I shouldn't be here.

A flash of the man's face that Trajan killed in that cave so long ago sears through my mind.

I swallow air and look up to meet Trajan's gaze, who looks back at me with such solid calm and deafening silence that I want to drag my nails across the tabletop just to invoke some natural noise.

But I sit as still as a statue, until finally Trajan breaks that silence.

"You are right to think me cruel," he says in a composed, yet compelling voice.

I don't say anything.

"I would never deny that," he goes on, "but our ways are different than yours. They always have been. Humans are weak and those like you who were human before gifted with this power will always be human. You will never understand our ways, nor will you ever know the true depth of our existence."

"Why don't you enlighten me, then?" I say, and I don't sweeten the poison in my voice. Surely he knows that he's seriously offended me and despite being who I am and him being who he is, I can't sit here and let him completely turn me into his submissive little tool.

A small part of me hopes he doesn't kill me though.

"It cannot be told," he says simply.

I lick the dryness from my lips carefully and look over at Aramei sleeping. The quiet starts to fall across the room again and then I say gently, "But what about Aramei?" And when I'm not thrown onto the floor with Trajan's massive hand around my throat, I continue:

"She's only human. Do you think of *her* as weak?"

"Yes," he says and his frankness stuns me, causing my head to snap around to face him again. "Aramei is weak because she is human, but that does not mean I cannot love her."

Maybe he's right in saying that humans are weak. I think I may have in a small way just proven his point by assuming he had been trying to anger and offend me all along when that wasn't the case at all.

I lower my eyes away from him and gaze back at Aramei.

"Humans are unnecessarily violent," he says, "and vile and treacherous and foolish."

"And werewolves aren't violent?" I say. "And I'm sorry, but there seems to be a lot of treachery among your kind, too."

Trajan crosses one leg over the other and rests his right arm on the table. His eyes stray toward Aramei who still hasn't moved since we got here even though we aren't making any effort to lower our voices.

"Only small pockets of our kind are treacherous," he says, still looking out ahead. "All races of life harbor treachery. Violence? No, Adria, violence is hatred and callousness and folly. We are none of those. What you consider violence in our case is merely honor and survival."

I really could go on and on about this with him, delving into why they have death-match fights and things like that, but I think I'm walking enough of a thin line with my defiant questions already. And something deep down tells me that he will easily have a worthy justification for anything I throw at him.

I hope he'll drop it, too.

Trajan stands from the table and pushes the chair back underneath it.

"But I did not bring you here for conversation," he says walking toward the bed where Aramei lay sleeping. "At least not with me."

"What am I supposed to…I mean how exactly am I supposed to communicate with her?"

Eva has been standing near the wall all this time, so quiet and still I forgot she was even in the room. With her hands folded gently in front of her she takes two steps forward and bows her head in Trajan's view. He simply nods and she leaves the upstairs floor, the sound of her soft bare feet shuffling quietly down the wooden steps behind me.

I look back at Trajan as he sits down on the side of the bed next to Aramei with his back to me. I pause for a moment, thinking long and hard about my next move and then I rise to my feet. Slowly, I approach them and make my way around to the side so that I can see both of their faces. Trajan reaches out his hand and brushes the length of Aramei's cheek with the backs of his fingers. She stirs, but remains sleeping.

Trajan doesn't look at me when he says, "I do not know," and his admission numbs me. He tilts his head gradually to face me now, "But I'm sure you will figure it out." He leans across Aramei and touches his lips to her forehead.

I just stand here, flummoxed. I want to say: What the hell do you mean I'll figure it out? But the actual words never escape my lips.

Trajan rises from the bed and absently I move to the side to let him walk past.

"I will leave you now," he says, looking back once, "if you should need anything, Eva will assist you."

"But…." I can't get the question out.

And just like that, Trajan makes his way down the steps into the vast room below and leaves me standing here. I didn't expect any bonding between he and I, or much in the way of conversation, but I really didn't expect to be left on my own without an inkling as to how I'm supposed to go about this, either.

5

IT'S NOT UNTIL I hear the front door shut after Trajan walks out, do I let myself snap out of the disbelief.

"He always leaves," Eva says coming up the stairs.

My chin draws in slightly. "Wait…," I say, putting up my hand, "did I just become Aramei's new babysitter?"

A faint smile softens Eva's face as she walks over to me. The long, see-through black gown she wears clings softly to her naked hourglass form; her dark auburn hair rests freely against her back like a wave of silk between her shoulder blades.

"I suppose you have, Milady."

"Please don't call me that."

She stops in front of me.

"I mean…well, it's just weird, y'know?"

Eva nods softly; her delicate hands are cradled just below her belly. "Very well. I will call you Adria."

A failed attempt at a smile barely cracks my face. "Thanks."

I let out a heavy breath and approach the bed, sitting down on the side of it where Trajan last sat. I reach out my hand and tuck my fingers under a long lock of Aramei's light-colored hair. It feels so soft against my skin, the way I expected it to feel. I always did think of her as an angel and the way she lays here now, covered by a thin, white satin sheet and enveloped by her fluffy pillows so that her soft hair can lay feathered upon them, makes her appear even more angel-like.

I brush my fingertip across the bridge of her nose.

"I don't know what I'm supposed to do, Eva." I never look away from Aramei.

Eva steps up behind me and I feel her hand rest on my shoulder.

"Wake her," she says, "and then perhaps you will know."

There's more in her suggestion than what she is letting on. It feels like Eva already knows what I'm supposed to do, or what might happen.

I stare down at the sleeping angel for a moment, admiring her beauty and innocence, forgetting that the only emotion I should feel for her is sorrow.

"Aramei?" I say softly.

She doesn't move and so I say it once more, raising my voice a notch. "Aramei, please wake up." I comb my fingers through her hair and I can smell the lavender shampoo that it had been washed with recently.

Her eyes gently crack open, revealing a slither of iridescent green hiding underneath the delicate lids. She's looking right at me, like she did before, on that night Isaac brought me here last and I felt her emotions within me. Her eyes open the rest of the way and she never seems to blink. I sit here frozen, my breath caught in my lungs. As always, I'm afraid I'll scare her with any sudden movements. But at the same time, I'm mesmerized by her and what is slowly happening between us.

"Just let it happen," I hear Eva's voice whisper behind me and for some reason unknown to me, the advice puts me completely on edge.

Aramei's eyes lock intensely on mine and suddenly I feel like I can't breathe. My hands begin to shake irrepressibly. I can't move my body. It's as if I'm no longer the one in control of it.

"Don't fight it…." Eva's voice says though it sounds so far away that I want to turn to see if she's even still standing in the room.

But I still can't move. Aramei's gaze sears into mine, holding my body and my head solidly in place. Sweat begins to bead on my forehead and the more I try to look away, the more forcibly my head is held still.

Aramei reaches out both of her hands to me and my body leans toward her of its own accord.

"You see me…," she says without moving her lips, *"…Find me…."* There is nothing but pain and desperation in those two words, which shakes my heart to its bitter core. Tears are streaming down my hot cheeks, my entire body shudders and trembles, but I still can't look away from her.

As her hands get closer it feels as though time is slowing down.

Her fingers touch my face and it's like being hurled off the top of a skyscraper. I feel like my body is falling a thousand miles per second. I try to scream out, but I can't. My voice is locked inside my head along with any control over my own muscles. And when I see the ground hurtling upward at me, I try to prepare my mind to brace for the impact. But instead, once I'm at the bottom, my body stops abruptly and is then heaved violently out ahead, horizontally through some series of rapid-moving pictures…no…*places*. I see trees whipping by me. Darkness and then light and then darkness again. I catch glimpses of the recent past: Aramei standing near the waterfall in my dream, the vision of her lying next to me on the floor, Trajan making love to her, Eva and the servants bathing her. I see even further back in time: Sibyl's face glaring in at Aramei from the shadows, the dangerous face of Nataša watching over Aramei. I see Viktor and the faces of people I have never met. Time moves faster now and it's getting harder to see with much detail, but I always see the darkness and the light as the days fade into the past in and out of my mind like blips on a screen. I see the landscape turn white; vast, treacherous mountains covered by snow and then the landscape turns green again as the season changes.

Finally, just when I feel like my body has breathed its last breath and that death has come to take me, time stops abruptly and I'm looking in at a life once lived as if it had been my life.

As if it's happening all over again....

The valley stretches boundlessly in the distance, tucked deeply between a vast mountain range on all sides. At the foot of the mountain, scattered about the valley is a small village where hay-covered roofs and wooden structures dot the landscape. A small herd of sheep stand amid the ocean of grass just at the top of one hill, tranquil in the early morning sunlight which filters down through a layer of mist cascading across the landscape. Every now and then a baa echoes between the mountains and fades amid the sound of a waterfall.

It's a village of poor farmers and sheep herders and fishermen, but a village untouched by the outside world. The only world that infiltrates this hidden valley is the dark world of the Black Beasts, a myth to some, but to others a danger they have feared for more than a thousand years.

Aramei, daughter of a farmer, walks behind her cottage carrying a basket filled with yesterday's laundry, tucked underneath her arm and pressed against her hip. She wears a long russet-colored dress and a pair of worn leather sandals on her dainty feet. A piece of cloth holds her hair behind her, tied against her back.

She makes her way past the barn and slips into the forest behind it where the stream snakes in from the nearby pond. As she leans over the water, washing her father's shirt, the sound of footsteps shuffling through the leaves behind her causes her to turn around. A tall and handsome man with a full moustache and long, braided dark hair smiles down at her. She has seen him before in her village, but knows he is no resident, nor any resident of any village within four days walk of here. His accent is odd, more like a mixture of her native Serbian and something more guttural like that of the Germans.

She had heard him speaking to a fisherman just yesterday.

But he seems harmless enough and she knows by the way he looks at her that he must have her in his sights. She is unmarried, after all, and it was but a matter of time before suitors began seeking her out. But why this strange foreigner? She thinks quietly as she stands to her feet, drying her hands on her apron. Her smile is soft and pretty and inviting, but not so much that she is giving in to his interests. Just enough to be polite and cordial. But it does make her uneasy that he followed her out here by the stream while she is alone. It gives her comfort that she can see the back of the large barn behind her house from this distance.

"Milord," she greets him and half-curtsies with the coyness of a young girl.

The man, dressed in fine garb that reminds Aramei of something royal yet casual, like the noblemen from the north, bows his head gently and reaches out his hand to her. A thick silver ring with an engraving across the band adorns one finger. She notices that his hands are dirty, unbecoming of the rest of his appearance. Hesitantly, Aramei offers her hand to him and he takes it between his thumb and fingers, leans over and touches the top of it to his forehead.

"I am Viktor Vargasavić," he says after raising his head again, but he keeps her hand gently clutched in his fingers. "Have I offended you with my curiosity?"

Gently, she lets her hand slip from his.

Even more bashful now because of his intimate introduction, Aramei turns and bends over to retrieve the basket from the ground, tucking it back against her side. She bows her head slightly. "No, Milord, but it is inappropriate to be here alone with you."

Viktor smiles and bends one arm behind him across his lower back. He bows once more and holds it longer than the first time; a gesture of submission. "Forgive me," he says and rises upright, "I mean no disrespect."

Aramei blushes and lowers her eyes.

"Sissa! Sissa!" her older sister, Filipa, shouts as she runs toward them from the back of the barn. She's waving one hand in the air above her, the other holding her dress at the legs to keep the ends from dragging the ground.

Aramei smiles at Viktor. "I must go," she says. "Good day to you."

Aramei meets Filipa halfway.

"Who is that man?" she says, eyeing Viktor from across the yard. She takes the basket from Aramei and carries it for her and fits her arm around Aramei's back, clutching her shoulder.

"His name is Viktor," Aramei whispers, "but that is all I know."

Filipa looks at Aramei warily in a sideward glance, helping her farther across the yard and out of Viktor's sights. "Did anyone see you?" Filipa asks sternly. "Sissa, he is not from here." She stops near the east side of the barn, drops the basket and moves around in front of Aramei, grasping her shoulders in both hands, shaking her. "He feels dark. You must stay away from him. Do you understand?"

"Yes, I understand."

Aramei has no intention of defying her sister's orders. Viktor is handsome, but like Filipa said, he is an outsider and their father would never approve of their marriage. And Filipa, taking the place of their mother nine years ago after she caught the fever and died, Aramei would never consider disobeying her. Aramei is only nineteen, Filipa twenty-five, but Filipa has been as much of a caretaker as their mother was and Aramei often forgets that Filipa is her sister.

"You trouble me sometimes," Filipa says, taking Aramei's hand. "I cannot decide if you are fearless or just plain heedless."

Aramei lowers her head shamefully. Filipa is right after all; Aramei has always gotten herself into trouble and in tight situations while growing up. Instead of running from a snake, she stopped to study one when she was five and it nearly bit her. Filipa pulled her away just as the snake went to strike. And when Aramei turned twelve, she went out alone to look for one of their sheep lost in the valley though it was known that wolves had likely claimed it. They could have claimed her, too, but Filipa found her and brought her back before the sun slipped behind the treacherous mountains. Aramei had always been very smart, having surpassed Filipa in learning to read and to sew and to cook—Aramei is still better at all of these things than her sister—but she has always been slow to judge when it came to recognizing danger when it stood in front of her. Curiosity and a heart bigger than her head, they were Aramei's greatest weaknesses. Little did she know that they would also one day be the death of her.

"Come," Filipa says and she leads Aramei back inside their cottage.

~~~

A storm blew through overnight, leaving the valley in a blanket of cool, misty air and rain-soaked earth. Aramei is up before the sun helping her father and Filipa find Vela, their skittish horse that had burst free from the stable spooked by the cracking thunder and lightning. For nearly an hour they searched for the horse, finally splitting up just as daylight creeps over the horizon, bathing the valley in warm light.

Aramei pulls her coat tight around her form and heads toward the North Hill, where the sheep often graze. When she makes it to the top of the grassy hill and looks down at the base of the other side, there Vela stands, alone and calm, drinking from a water hole.

"Oh, Vela," she says many minutes later when she makes it down the hill to where the horse is. "Father will have your hide one day if you keep this up." She pats the horse on its thick, muscled neck. A low whicker shudders through its body and its chestnut-colored tail swishes back and forth. Aramei goes to fix a loop of rope around its neck when the horse starts to appear agitated, its ears perking and a few whinnies rattle its chest.

"Okay, girl," Aramei says, patting Vela's neck once more. "What is it?"

Without warning, Vela rises up on her hind legs, knocking Aramei onto the rain-soaked grass and mud. The hooves come down hard against the earth as Aramei rolls through the mud to get out of the way.

"Vela! Where are you going?"

The horse whines and takes off back toward the village, the sounds of its hooves beating heavily against the ground.

Aramei pushes herself up and goes to dust herself off, but gives up when she realizes it will take more than that to wash these muddy clothes. She sighs heavily, thrusting her slim arms down against her sides. Feeling that the mud has taken a hold of her left foot, Aramei gently pulls her sandal from the mess and steps over onto a mound of grass. "That *awful* horse!" she says exasperated.

"They can be fickle creatures at times," says a man's voice.

Aramei turns around, startled, to see Viktor standing in the shade of a nearby small cluster of trees. She presses her hand to her chest as if that might help to calm her heartbeat.

She lowers her eyes and pretends to be straightening her dress and dusting more mud from the fabric, although it only makes her hands messier. She closes her dress robe tighter around her body, her gentle fingers clutching the fabric together at her chest.

"You are not from my village," she says, but doesn't make eye contact.

Viktor's body moves closer, but he stops at a comfortable distance of five feet.

"No," he says and she can hear the pursuit in his voice, which makes her slightly uneasy. "I am just a traveler of these lands. I set up camp east of here—could smell the fires and something like sweet bread cake."

"You came here for bread cake?" Aramei tries to hide the smile in her voice. She's weary of him, but isn't ready to dismiss him just yet.

Viktor's charming close-lipped smile widens as Aramei finally looks at him, but her eyes dart off here and there every few seconds to keep from meeting his.

"Bread cake," he says, "and a beautiful young woman."

Aramei's body stiffens and she gazes downward at her muddy sandals.

"I do apologize, Milord," she says, "but I believe all of the women who make bread cake here are too old for your tastes."

"You do not make bread cake?" he says with hidden, yet obvious meaning behind his inquiry.

Aramei bows her head and says, "I do, Milord, but...." She looks up toward the top of the hill expecting to see Filipa come running toward her any moment now, but she can't decide if that's what she wants or not. Only one man has ever showed interest in her. Aramei is very beautiful, but her father had always been somewhat of a bully towards potential suitors when it came to his daughters. This man, Viktor, somehow gives Aramei the feeling he might not be as hard to scare away.

Viktor waits patiently for her to continue, his face beaming and somewhat dark.

"...I shouldn't be seen with you, Milord."

"Why not?" he asks, stepping up closer to her. She takes two steps back to retain the distance. "Is it the woman?"

Aramei looks up again, finally meeting his eyes. "The woman?" she says.

"Yes, the one who pulled you out of my sights just yesterday?"

Aramei smiles bashfully, twisting a lock of hair between her fingers. "Filipa is no woman. She is my sister."

Viktor coughs a small laugh and Aramei can't help but join him, realizing too late what she had said.

"Well, I just mean that—"

"She is a man?" Viktor teases her with a very serious face, but Aramei can easily detect the smile behind his fine green eyes.

~~~

In the following days, Aramei snuck out to meet Viktor and they walked in the forests together, swam in the lake hidden between the North and South Hills an hour away from the village and once he even took her on a hunt. Viktor was an expert bowman. The two shared a meal over an open fire in the late afternoon before Aramei had to slip away from his company and head back home. Filipa and their father had their suspicions—Filipa more unforgiving of Aramei's lies, but their father knew nothing about this stranger and Filipa felt it best not to tell him anything. Days became weeks and Aramei grew closer to Viktor, but he mistook Aramei's affections and her willingness to be out with him as something more than what it was.

Aramei had lived a sheltered life, having experienced little outside of her village and village life was quaint and uneventful most of the time. Aramei found a sort of freedom in Viktor, but she was slow to develop a real attraction that went beyond the one she had for him when he first approached her as she washed the laundry in the pond that day.

And Aramei had no experience with men. She had never been with a man in any sense and had no idea that all this time with Viktor she was setting up her own demise.

~~~

Present Day – In the cabin

I wake up lying next to Aramei in the center of the bed; Eva is sitting next to us, swabbing a cold, wet cloth across my forehead.

Lifting up slowly, I brace my weight against the mattress with my palms and try to pull my head together.

"Did I pass out?" My head is throbbing, my vision slightly blurred. I reach up and massage my temples with my fingertips, bridging the palm of my hand across my face.

"Not exactly," Eva says, dabbing my cheeks with the cloth once more. "You went under."

I open my eyes and look right at her. "Under what?"

"You were in Aramei's mind," Eva says softly so as not to wake Aramei, "living what she lived and knowing what she knows."

I lift farther away from Aramei and decide to get off the bed altogether. "How is that possible?" I say, pacing across the floor barefooted. Eva must've taken off my shoes. I stop and turn to face her, my gaze penetrating hers from the foot of the bed. "That felt completely real to me…it wasn't a dream, it was *real*, like I was *right there* watching her."

Eva nods once, smiling faintly.

"You have been connected to Aramei in this way since the day you were bonded to Isaac," she says, standing from the bed, too. She walks over to the table next to the balcony and places the wet cloth in a bowl of water. "Those who have been bonded by blood are often connected, but some connections are stronger than others." She walks over and stops in front of me, folding her hands together resting on her pelvis. "But now that you are a Black Beast, and female, your connection to Aramei is strengthened ten-fold."

I don't know what to say because I'm too stunned by this information to understand it just yet. So, I just let Eva continue.

"She is trying to tell you something," she says. "What did you see?"

"I-I…," I move away from Eva, letting her hands fall away from my shoulders and I approach the bed again. "I saw Viktor Vargas…and I think—." I gaze down at Aramei sleeping; a few strands of her silky hair move gently in time with her breath.

"You think what?" Eva says from behind.

I turn around to face her, but still all I really see is the scene with Viktor and Aramei still fading from my mind. "He was in love with her…."

6

I STAY WITH EVA and Aramei for several hours, but Aramei remains sleeping and I can't seem to get inside her head again. I even tried waking her at one point, taking both of my hands and shaking her body gently back and forth but it's like she's in a coma.

To think I could've been like this....

I'm anxious to get back inside her mind, but it looks like what I saw is all that I'll be seeing on this visit.

"Aramei will not able to hold the connection for very long at a time," Eva says while lighting a lantern on the other side of the room. The afternoon is quickly slipping away into the evening hours, and the cabin, shrouded by a thick forest, is becoming dark fast.

I sit at the table overlooking the downstairs floor, watching servants come and go, dust and mop and stand quietly until they are called for by Eva for any number of duties. One brings up a plate of fresh fruit and vegetables with Ranch dressing and some other weird-smelling sauce that I really have no interest in. I'd like a Black Angus burger or a melted ham and cheese sandwich, but I don't expect I'll be getting anything like that around here.

Before long, the area is bathed in orange light from the lanterns; the shifting shadows on the log walls slow and deliberate. Everyone here is so orderly, taking their time in every little thing they do as if to make sure they get it right the first time. They never speak. Never. When I think back on it, even when I saw Aramei in the cave so long ago, the servants didn't speak then, either. At least not to one another. Just thinking about it makes me anxious. I could never live like they live, so submissive and disciplined and seemingly without any sense of self-determination or freedom.

But even still, not anything nor anyone else can hold my thoughts more than Aramei, who still has not moved or whimpered or fluttered her eyes since I came out of her mind.

I can't believe I was even *in* her mind. Or rather, I do believe it. It's hard to push extraordinary things like this away anymore. I *am* a werewolf, after all, and if that doesn't help me believe that there are many strange things in this world that I didn't know before, then nothing will. But regardless of believing it, some things are and probably always will be hard to understand. This is definitely one of them.

As I begin to wonder when I'll be able to leave, I hear a vehicle pulling up to the front of the cabin. And before I think to head downstairs and see who it is, the front door opens and Trajan is walking inside.

Eva's demeanor shifts back to that solid, quiet manner as she walks over to stand against the wall.

Trajan's footsteps coming up the stairs make me edgy.

I take a deep breath and go to sit at the little table. When Trajan makes it onto the upstairs floor he doesn't say anything to me at first. He walks right over to Aramei, leans over and brushes his strong fingers through her hair and then walks over to the nearest lantern, turning the little knob to raise the fire.

"I don't think you…want to know what I saw," I say to Trajan, jumping right in rather than letting it linger.

Trajan stops in the center of the room and folds his hands together in front of him. He peers across at me, his deep blue eyes piercing into mine and that fixed, expressionless look on his face makes me all the more nervous. He wants to know everything, like he said before, no matter how much I think it will anger him.

I tear my gaze away from his and say cautiously, "Viktor was in love with her. It was a long time ago."

Trajan moves toward me and my muscles tense every inch he draws closer. His steps are calm and gradual until finally he makes it to the table where I sit and he stops directly in front of me. I feel the warmth seething off his body; his shadow looming over me like a mountain.

Carefully, I look up at him.

"She told you this?"

I hate it that I can't read him, that there are no distinguishable emotions on his face, or anything in the tone of his voice to indicate how I should react.

I shake my head once. "No," I say cautiously, "I saw it."

A flicker of curiosity blinks across his features. "You saw it how exactly?"

I let out a sharp breath and softly hit the palm of my hand on the table. "Do you mind not standing over me like that?" I say, fed up with being too intimidated to think straight. "Really, I…it's making me uncomfortable."

A tiny, almost unnoticeable snarl ruffles the side of one nostril and the corner of his lips. He's obviously irritated with me, but thankfully not intolerant. He moves back and takes the empty seat at the table with me.

I sneak a sideward glance over at Eva to my right and catch the slim smile she flashes me so fast that if I were to have blinked in that half a second I would've missed it.

"It was like I was there," I finally go on. "It was as real and vivid as I'm sitting here with you right now."

Trajan nods slowly, as if taking in my explanation with the utmost attention. "Interesting."

I wait for him to go on, but he doesn't.

Geez! I don't know how anyone can stand being in the same room with him. He's about as interesting as a block of wood.

I turn around, pulling my legs underneath the table and I look across at him. "How is that interesting?" I fold my hands together out in front of me on the table.

Trajan takes his time about answering, casually tending to his attire, smoothing an invisible wrinkle in his shirt, dusting an invisible something-or-another from the leg of his jeans.

Finally he says, "I can read her mind because she is connected to me, but I cannot peer as deeply into it as you apparently can. The things I see are indecipherable, flashes of thought about she and I, or things that have happened in front of her recently."

I'm surprised he hasn't said anything about Viktor being in love with her, or that he doesn't seem at all disturbed by the information. This tells me that he probably already knows and has for a long time.

"What did you see of her life?"

I pause, thinking back to hours ago that still feel like minutes ago. "It was when she first met Viktor, in her village."

"Go on," he urges me with the gentle nod of his head.

"He was kind to her," I say, "and she took to him easily. In a short time she was sneaking out of her village to see Viktor, but…." I have to think about this part because I want to be sure that I'm right. "…she didn't feel the same way about him as he did about her. It was more like she just enjoyed his company and he was something new, someone different from anyone she had ever met and he excited her.

But she didn't love him. Clearly, he fell in love with her though."

Trajan nods once more, appearing deep in thought. He brings one hand up and props his chin on the pad of his thumb, his index finger pressed against his cheek.

"*Did* Viktor love her?" I ask carefully, unsure about how rapid the waters are that I'm treading with this topic.

"He thought he did, but Adria, don't mistake love for obsession," he answers and I'm surprised he gave up the truth so easily. "Viktor and I were at war long before either of us knew of Aramei, but his so-called love for her would be what ultimately caused the greatest treachery our kind has ever known."

I swallow hard, but don't dare say a word, not because I fear him but because I want to know as much as he's willing to tell me and I don't want to interrupt.

"Viktor wanted my throne," he says. "His defiance and his wars and all of the rebellious tricks that he pulled were never treacherous. They were normal. He knew he could not defeat me in battle, one on one, and so he did anything he could do to make my reign more…difficult. But when Aramei came into our lives, his defiance and rebellion turned into madness."

Trajan stops and stares out ahead of him in some dark, distant memory that even troubles me though I don't know what it is.

"His hatred for me made him a rogue," he says still staring out ahead. "Hatred of that magnitude changes our disposition and we evolve into something far more irrepressible. Viktor was the first rogue in the history of our kind. And he did *unforgivable* things."

I've been holding my breath practically this whole time, only realizing it now as I let it out in a long, wheezing shudder.

I can't grasp that he's even telling me these things.

"What did he do that was worse than waging war against you?"

Trajan turns his head casually to face me. "You already know what he did."

I gaze across the room at Aramei and then back at him. "Bonding her to him is worse than defying you or trying to take your throne?" I find it totally believable, but at the same time, odd.

"To be at war with one another is a part of our life," he says looking away from me again. "It is our nature to obey and serve and challenge and conquer. Some of us have mated with the same females—Viktor and I both have offspring with Nataša and Sibyl, for instance—but to perform a Blood Bond with a *wife* is a treachery that can *never* be absolved."

I see Trajan's jaw is clenched and it slowly relaxes as he lets the memory course through him.

I, on the other hand, am a little disgusted with all of this talk of sharing mates and whatnot, so I know he had to notice the barely contained look of mortification that had been twisting my face and hardening my eyebrows. When I notice I'm still sort of looking at him that way, I let my expression soften.

"You said wife," I begin. "Were Nataša and Sibyl not your wives?"

"No," he answers without pause, "mates are simply that: mates. We share a bond of a different kind, one of equal need to have offspring, to keep our bloodline strong. But a wife...," his gaze falls on Aramei and he stands up from the table. "...the difference is undying love. And Viktor sealed his fate the night he defiled her with his blood and his hatred and his sedition."

His boots tap gently across the wooden floor as he approaches Aramei.

I remain seated.

"My son is here for you," he says nonchalantly, staring down at Aramei sleeping.

My head snaps around when the front door swings open downstairs and bangs into the wall. A few gasps and squeals can be heard from the servants startled by Isaac's entrance.

I rise to my feet and look out over the balcony to see Isaac storming his way through the room and past the servants who quickly move out of his way. He looks pissed. My heart is hammering against the walls of my chest and I become unfrozen just in time to meet him at the top of the stairs and try to calm him down.

"Isaac. Stop. It's fine," I say, pressing my hands against his heaving chest. For a moment I think he's going to push me aside and disregard my plea altogether, but he backs down only for me.

His eyes bore into Trajan's back, full of fury and wrath and intolerance, but I know as well as Isaac knows that Trajan is fully aware of his anger.

"Baby, I told you not to close your mind off to me," he says with worry and relief in his voice. He grabs my wrists and stares deeply into my eyes and then pulls me beside him, grasping his arm around my waist. He glares back at his father with even more anger than before.

"If I have nothing to worry about," he snaps at Trajan, a growl reverberating in his throat, "then why have her shut off her mind to me?"

"Isaac…," I try to stand around in front of him again, but he holds me still at the waist. He never takes his eyes off Trajan, who still has yet to even turn around.

Before Isaac has a chance to dig himself deeper into a hole with Trajan, I push Isaac's hand away and glare at him. "Isaac!" I roar and then let my voice lower a level when I see that I have his attention. "He didn't."

"What do you mean?" he says, looking upon me with confusion. "What…so you *willingly* closed yourself off to me?" He seems wounded by the very thought of it, that I would do something so dangerous.

I shake my head no and soften my expression. "I didn't do it, either."

As if to break the tension in the room once and for all, Eva steps away from her quiet, invisible spot against the wall and says, "It was Aramei, Milords." She bows her auburn head lower than usual as if asking forgiveness of Trajan for speaking out of turn.

All of us look right at her, even Trajan who turns fully at the waist. And when Eva isn't chastised for speaking, she continues as though Trajan's silence granted her permission.

"I believe it was Aramei's doing," she says. "It must take everything in her to retain the connection."

"But how would Aramei know to do something like that?" Isaac says beside me, his body still rigid, but easing slowly. "How is that possible?"

"She is right," Trajan says. He moves away from the bed and toward us, stopping several feet away. "Though it may only be speculation, Evangeline I believe is right."

It seems as if Trajan is covering for Eva, though for what reason, I can't possibly know.

Trajan nods toward Eva and says, "You are dismissed," and she bows first to Trajan and then to Isaac and me before heading downstairs to join the other servants.

Hoping to keep the room in order, I don't wait to go right back to convincing Isaac that his anger is out of place. I'm standing in a room with two Alpha males, but not just any two Alpha males and this is probably one of the most nerve-wracking feelings in the world. And just knowing that even I could Turn in the midst of a fight between the two of them and inadvertently get myself killed only makes me more determined to do everything in my power to maintain the composure in the room.

I take Isaac by the hand and say to him in a soft, determined voice, "Please come sit down with me." I look him right in the eyes and hold my gaze firmly to show him how important the request is to me.

He looks across at his father as he lets me guide him to the chair, never taking his eyes off him.

I don't know what happened in the two weeks that I was gone right after Isaac infected me, but I know that Isaac's relationship with his father changed. Maybe it was because Isaac became Alpha in my absence, that because he is a true Alpha now that their tolerance for one another changes due to dominance. Or, maybe something else happened that Isaac just isn't telling me. He and I have talked about my time away and he told me all about the ceremony and how it went peacefully, but I always did feel like he was holding out on me the day he gave me the details. I honestly don't think it went as smoothly as he claims, but how would I really know the definition of 'smooth' in such a circumstance? All that I do know is that whether it was something that happened then, or afterwards, Isaac is different when it comes to his father. He's defiant and frighteningly intolerant of Trajan anymore.

It scares me to death.

"Isaac," I say, enclosing his hands underneath mine upon the table and he looks right at me. "I'm glad I came here. I admit I wasn't as sure this morning and I was a little afraid, but after sitting with her and seeing the things that I saw, I can honestly tell you that not only am I glad I did it, but I'm looking forward to doing it again."

This time I'm telling him the truth.

Isaac's eyes narrow. "Did my father threaten you?" He moves his hands from underneath mine and holds mine instead. I feel his fingertips pressing firmly around my knuckles.

I shake my head firmly and sigh a deep exhausting sigh. "*No*…your father has been—" I stop myself because the word I had started to use was 'kind' and that might be too generous and only make Isaac even more suspicious. "He's been reasonable. He hasn't threatened me or even scared me for that matter."

"She is right," Trajan says and Isaac and I both look over at him simultaneously. "I would say that you have a rather… insubordinate wife."

I blink back the shock of Trajan's comment. Wife? So Trajan believes me to be Isaac's wife and not just his mate? My face suddenly feels hot and my stomach kind of feels like it's in my chest just below my collarbone, swirling around like a chaotic swarm of butterflies. I barely have the mind to notice that Isaac seems to be grinning, but I soon see that it's not because his father called me his wife.

"Insubordinate?" Isaac says, looking across at Trajan with a smirk. "I'm proud for that."

"And you should be," Trajan says with a single, solid nod of approval.

Isaac turns his eyes back toward me and his expression has done a one-eighty. He's not looking like he's ready to kill his father anymore, but instead he's looking at me like he's ready to throw me on the bed or something.

My face is boiling hot now.

I look away.

"You may leave," Trajan says, abruptly changing the mood in the room. He turns his back to us again and goes toward the bed. "Isaac," he says as he sits down on the edge of the bed and goes to remove his boots. "Bring her back in the morning. Aramei is trying to tell me something and I want to know what it is before this week is over."

Isaac stands from the table and takes me by the hand to stand with him. Surprisingly, he bows to Trajan and says, "Yes, Father," giving him the same respect he has always given him as if he had never been angry about before.

Trajan removes the second boot and turns at the waist to look across at us. And then as if it comes completely natural to me, I find myself bowing in the same manner that Isaac had. Trajan nods to me as if to accept it.

"I'll…see you tomorrow, I guess," I say smiling squeamishly and sort of fumbling over the words, sounding completely unlike any formal werewolf in the presence of the Sovereign.

I doubt I'll ever be able to do that, to say 'Milord' or use big, sophisticated words that will only make me sound like an American trying to talk with an English accent. I'll just stick with who I am and absorb a few essential tricks along the way that will at least make it *seem* like I know what I'm doing.

7

BY THE TIME WE make it back to Hallowell, it's pitch dark. I know I have to go home tonight and see Aunt Bev and Uncle Carl so they don't start worrying. Thankfully, Genna helped with erasing their minds of my two week disappearance before she disappeared herself not long ago. But I haven't been home in a week because I was sort of tied up, literally, in the basement of the Mayfair house. I did call a lot and talk to Beverlee and Uncle Carl, just to let them know I was okay, but I could tell in Beverlee's voice the last time I talked to her that she was depressed about me being gone so long.

But I have to give the credit to Harry for using his Praverian powers of controlling emotions, which has eased their minds about me staying away like this in the first place. They aren't completely approving of it—I refused to let Harry manipulate them fully because it isn't right just to suit my everyday needs—but they are more at ease about it at least.

I'm equally glad that it's still summer vacation and I don't have to find ways to dodge going to school for the same reason. I'll cross that bridge later.

This new life, this new existence of mine is hard to juggle when I have human family members that love me and who have no idea that once a month every bone in my body breaks and I tend to…eat things. It's just not something you talk about over dinner.

We pull into the drive and Isaac puts the Jeep in park.

"I'll be here to pick you up around six," he says turning at the waist and resting his left wrist on the steering wheel.

"Six? Like a.m.?" I feel my eyes widening.

Isaac grins softly and says in a you-got-yourself-into-this sort of way, "When my father says 'in the morning' he doesn't mean after your shower and breakfast."

Of course, I didn't get myself totally into this; I had no choice in the beginning, but I did make it easier on Trajan by practically admitting openly my desire to continue.

I smirk at him, crinkling one side of my nose. But really it is okay and despite having to get up so early, I do look forward to seeing Aramei again.

~~~

Just like Isaac said, he was here at six on the dot and I barely got my teeth brushed before I was hopping in his Jeep. I slept the whole way, at least as much as the bucket seat would allow. Twice I jerked awake when Isaac went over a bump in the road and my head popped gently against the window next to me. And when we got to the cabin, Trajan forced Isaac to stay outside where he waited impatiently for me, talking to Raul while I got absolutely nowhere with Aramei in three hours.

She was awake the whole time, but I couldn't get inside her head. She was just regular mindless Aramei. Eva tried coaxing her and I tried talking to her, but our efforts were wasted.

Trajan agreed to let me come back tomorrow and try again, rather than making me hang around all day and night. But this was more vital than just being relieved of severe boredom; Isaac, Nathan, Daisy and me have an important trip to take today to find someone Harry calls a 'Harvester' who will—or might (Harry said they are wicked and spiteful and never do anything for free) give us what we need to trap the Dark Praverian.

We're heading to The Cove to meet up with Harry now so he can give us the rest of the details. He can't go with us because they harvest, or rather 'reap' Praverian souls.

As if this couldn't get any weirder....

We pull into the parking lot by the Kennebec River, the same one where the fight broke out between the Vargas pack and ours last fall. It's vacant and looks like the City came and cleaned it up of all the trash and beer cans left over by the crowd that got busted not long ago. I feel nervous just being here, especially now that there are several NO LOITERING signs posted and we aren't supposed to be hanging around here. But if any cops come, at least we don't have to worry about getting tossed in jail for underage drinking or drug possession. They'll probably just slap us on the wrist and tell us not to come back.

Harry and Daisy are sitting on the hood of his old car with Nathan parked next to them, sitting inside his FJ Crusier. We pull in on the other side of Harry's car and get out.

"I don't like this one bit," Daisy says getting off the hood and crossing her arms stubbornly as she walks toward me. "Did you know about this, Nathan? Isaac?" She glares at both of them and then her big blue eyes fall on me. "You're not going to like this, Adria." She shakes her blond head slow and heavy and her curly ponytail swings side to side. A pair of little jangling gold earrings hangs from each earlobe.

"I told you," Harry says to Daisy, slipping his arm around her waist, "as long as they don't let it slip that I live here I don't have to worry about them finding me."

"You worry too much," Nathan says jumping onto Harry's hood. "They're human and they can't read minds, so how would he or she know Harry lives in Hallowell, or that you're his very *over*protective girlfriend?"

"Shove it, Nate," Daisy snaps and Nathan shakes his head, grinning.

She turns back to us and Harry.

"You're right," I say to Daisy, "I don't like it either even though I don't know very much about these people, but we have no other choice, I guess."

"No," Harry says, "you don't and if there was something else, I'd do it before taking this route."

"Isaac moves to Harry's car and sits on the hood with Nathan. I stand by Daisy, who looks distraught. She does have more reason to worry than I do since Harry is a Praverian and his life could be at stake. This Harvester, or whatever, isn't going to come looking for Isaac or for me.

"You say they're human." I look right at Harry, crossing my arms much like Daisy. "How can they hurt you then? Or rather, how can they reap you?" I sense Daisy tense up next to me after I said that telling word, reap.

Harry runs his hand through his messy brown hair and leans against his car, crossing his arms and his feet.

"It's an archaic sort of witchcraft," Harry says, "definitely not like any of that Wicca stuff you see nowadays or anything like that. That's all new. This craft is the mother of modern-day witchcraft and voodoo and that hocus-pocus mumbo-jumbo." He uncrosses his arms and starts to gesture as he explains. "A single bloodline has carried this craft down for generations—people who've thrived almost as long as *we* have, but they're thinning out. There's not too many left anymore."

"I say that's a good thing," Daisy scoffs.

"In a sense, it is, but believe it or not we need them," Harry says.

"Like in *this* situation," Isaac says from the hood of the car. He sits with his boots propped on the front bumper, his legs splayed and his hands folded, draped between his knees. "They're the only ones who know how to trap a Praverian gone Dark."

Harry nods to confirm Isaac's assumption.

"Well then," I say, "how do you know where to find one?"

"The phone book," Harry answers.

I roll my eyes and glance over at Isaac whose face remains standard. I guess I'm the only one who finds Harry's answer sarcastic.

Oh wait…no, by that smirk creeping up at the corner of Harry's mouth, he does too. Daisy snarls at him and cocks her head to one side, reproachfully.

"The phone book?" I say dryly, pursing my lips and with one brow raised.

"Yeah," Harry says with a mild shrug, "well a little research on the net and *then* the online White Pages, but that was about it. They come from an ancient Norse family and their surname has changed over time, but since we have to stay out of their way it's kind of our job to keep track of them."

"Okay, so who are we looking for?" Isaac says.

Harry turns at the waist to face him and reaches inside the back pocket of his jeans and pulls out a folded piece of paper. He holds it up and flicks it hard with the fingers on his other hand and a *snap* ripples through the air. Walking over to Isaac on the hood of the car, he hands it out to him.

"Minna Abrahamsen," Harry says and Isaac takes the paper. "Providence, Rhode Island."

"*Rhode Island*?" I say, exasperated. "That's a little far, don't you think?"

Isaac unfolds the paper and he and Nathan peer into its contents. Daisy just shakes her head more solemnly beside me.

"Well, it was either Rhode Island or Akron, Ohio," Harry says raising his hands, palms up. "Like I said, there's not many left."

I walk over to stand beside Isaac and look down into the paper, too. It's just an address. "So, when do we go?" I say, looking up at Harry again.

"I say we get this over with," Nathan speaks out and I've hardly seen him look so serious before. "It's been long enough. I want whoever it is found and dealt with."

Isaac slips the address in his back pocket. "I agree," he says, straightening his back. "Just knowing that there's been a traitor possibly living in the same house with us all this time makes me crazy. It's like I can't trust anybody anymore and it's causing a lot of tension around the house."

I slip in and stand between Isaac's legs, propping my arms on his thighs. I feel him lean over me from behind and chills race across my skin when he kisses my bare neck. After he leans back up and the chills subside I say, "Yeah even Zia and Sebastian are starting to take offense. And it's hard for me not to confide in Zia, y'know?"

Daisy sighs and looks sad all of a sudden. "And I hate to say it, but worse than those two, we're starting to make enemies of our own blood." She shakes her head glumly. "Camilla thinks I hate her and she's my favorite sister."

"And Xavier," Isaac says, "I think he's pissed at me. The other day he wanted me and Adria to go swimming with him and this new girl he's seeing, but I said no."

I turn at the waist to see him behind me. "You didn't tell me about that."

He looks at me apologetically.

"Well, it's odd for Xavier to invite anyone out with him and one of his girlfriends, anyway," Daisy adds.

Isaac says, "Exactly. I don't know, maybe I'm paranoid because of this whole traitor thing, but Xavier wanting anyone to tag along when he's just trying to get laid is reason for suspicion if anything is."

I've always known Xavier to be a man-slut, but I feel kind of bad for him, that his brother refused to hang out with him apparently the one time he asked. "Maybe he really likes this new girl," I say, "and he just wanted you to meet her."

Nathan and Daisy burst into laughter, while Isaac doesn't laugh as hard probably for my benefit, but still he can't keep that ginormous smile from spreading across his face.

Nathan jumps off the hood of the car and pats me on the shoulder. "You've got a lot to learn, doll."

My face warms under an obvious blush.

"I think it's safe to say that the only way we're going to know who it is, is after you talk to this Minna," Harry says and he is the only one of us not smiling.

His serious face brings the rest of us back to the matter at hand.

"We can sit here and talk about who's acting weird, or who it might be and why we think they might be the one, but it won't solve anything," Harry adds and I'm getting the feeling he's more worried about the traitor than he's ever really led us to believe.

Daisy stands beside him and leans up on her toes to kiss the corner of his mouth. "You're right, love," she says and then looks back at us. "I say we leave as soon as possible."

"Are you and Adria done with the babysitting job?" Nathan says to Isaac.

"For today, yes," Isaac answers after letting out a deep breath. "But it looks like that will be an everyday job for a little while."

Daisy shakes her head as if to pity me. "Sorry our father is already using you for his own needs. I thought he might at least wait a couple months."

"No, really I don't mind," I say to the surprise of everyone but Isaac. "I *want* to stay with Aramei."

Nathan and Daisy both look at me with equally disfigured expressions, but I don't feel like explaining myself right now. Actually, some deep part of me feels that it's best to keep this as much a secret as I can for now. I don't know why, but I've adopted this burden for myself and feel that I don't want to share it with anyone else.

"So when do leave for Providence?" I say, steering the topic before they start asking questions.

"I say we go back to the house, grab a few things and head out," Isaac suggests, sliding off the hood now, too. He takes me by the hand.

"Daisy," Harry says, "why don't you stay with me?"

"No," she refuses without question. "I want to see this Harvester for myself."

"That's why I don't want you to go," Harry says, taking her shoulders in both hands and leaning over to kiss her forehead. "These people may only be human but they have a way with getting under your skin. And Minna will probably sense it right away that you're more involved with one of us than you're letting on." He turns to Isaac now and looks between him and me and Nathan. "It's vital you all get the story straight and stick to it. They're wicked smart and if for a second she thinks you're lying to her she'll follow you here."

"I don't like this, Harry," Daisy says, pulling away from him.

"Harry's got a point," Isaac says. "Look at the way you're acting now—It's probably not a good idea."

"I agree," Nathan says, holding up his finger above his head.

Daisy growls under her breath and it shocks me a little. I've never once seen her lose it. I've never even see her lose her temper mildly. She's always been sweet, caring, fun Daisy Mayfair. But right now, I can feel the angry heat coming off her rigid body and the resistance boiling in her blood.

"You will stay behind," Isaac says sternly, stepping around me to get in front of Daisy. In this moment, he has let the Alpha come out so naturally that I can't decide whether to be anxious or turned on by it. "Go back to the house with Harry."

Daisy, although reeling about not being able to go, is always respectful. She bows her head without reluctance and moves her way past him toward Harry's car.

Once she closes herself up inside, Isaac turns back to Harry and says, "So what's the story we have to get straight?"

Nathan steps up next to Isaac.

Harry reaches up and scratches the side of his jaw where a little stubble is starting to grow. "Since Genevieve is already gone," he begins, "you can use her as the scapegoat." He notices the disapproving lines appearing around my eyes and says, "She won't care. She's long gone and if you try to make up some random name and pass it off as one of us, you'll run the risk of getting caught in a lie easier. Minna will ask questions: names, past lives, anything she can think of to trip you up. It's better to just go with what you all already know."

"About Genna?" I say, still not comfortable with this tactic, which is only making me feel kind of like a traitor myself.

Nathan doesn't look all that accepting of it, either.

"Yes," Harry says, getting a little aggravated with my doubt. "You can be honest about everything except me. And when it comes down to any questions about who her Charge is or was, that's the only part you have to lie about."

"We'll just say we don't know," Isaac says.

Harry nods. "Yeah. One lie is easier than a hundred of them."

"I never thought I'd be intimidated by a human," Nathan says, smirking. He glances over at me it seems as if to say 'no offense', but at the last second he retracts it. I guess I'm still so new to this werewolf life that I'm easily forgotten. He turns back to Harry. "At least she can't do anything to *us*." He backtracks a bit, suddenly unsure of his brash theory. "Right?"

Harry grins. "For the most part, yes," he says. "They're not really a threat to anyone or anything but our kind—her house is probably rigged to catch someone like me as soon as I enter the door—but the most you have to worry about is pissing her off and becoming her next hex target."

Nathan and Isaac both draw their chins inward, their faces riddled with distrust.

"Want to elaborate on that, man?" Isaac says.

Harry is grinning from ear to ear. "Just don't piss her off," he says just before Daisy leans out the passenger's side window and shouts, "Harry, come on! *Please*."

Just as Harry starts toward his car, he turns back and says, "Oh! And don't let her get to you about my kind. She'll say anything to make you believe it's in your best interest to tell her everything you know." And then he opens the car door and hops inside with Daisy who will probably look as bitter as she does now, for a while.

But she still manages to blow me a kiss as they speed off.

8

NATHAN FOLLOWS US BACK to their house and while I'm up in Isaac's room grabbing a few items of clothing to take, Zia comes running into the room, laughing hysterically. I jump when she squeals coming around the corner and slams the door behind her, pressing her back against it.

"What the hell?" I say, trying not to smile, but it's kind of hard not to.

Her body jerks against the door when a loud *bang* hits the other side.

"Help me hold it!" she says to me, laughing.

The door jerks open an inch every few seconds as whoever is on the other side continuously bangs against it.

"Adria!" Zia shouts and finally I run over to help her hold it shut.

"Open the door, Z!" I hear Sebastian growl from the other side.

He doesn't sound happy.

"What did you *do*?" I say, still trying to hold back my own laughter. My back jerks against the door and I'm wondering all of sudden why she didn't just reach up and lock it.

I go to turn around, still bracing one hand against the door and just as my fingers pinch the flat cone-shaped lock to twist it locked, one more bang hits the other side and the door swings open, sending me and Zia onto the floor.

Sebastian storms in. Completely bald.

While I'm trying to register what I'm seeing, frozen in my spot on the floor, Zia is trying to scramble away in the other direction toward the window. Sebastian rushes her and grabs her around one ankle. She can't stop laughing and it's really the only thing keeping me from thinking Sebastian is here to literally kill her. There's not an ounce of humor in his body or in his face, which has grown even more enraged over the past few seconds.

"I'm *sooory!*" Zia screeches, her eyes shooting tears from laughing so hard. "I swear I didn't mean it!"

Sebastian rolls her over and sits on top of her, straddling her waist, both of his hands pinning her to the floor by her wrists. "So, it was an *accident* that you shaved my head while I was asleep?" Sebastian roars down at her. The rumble in his voice shakes me a little.

Finally, I get up from the floor, but I move around to the side, keeping my distance. I'm still not sure if I need to jump in and help Zia, or if I should just leave her to whatever punishment he has in store.

Oh my God…I can't believe she shaved his hair off….

"No…it's just that…," Zia still can't stop laughing even though I also see there's obvious pain in her face maybe from how much pressure he's putting on her body. But she can take it; this, I'm sure of.

I'll start worrying when she stops smiling.

Her spiky white-blond hair bobs up and down, back and forth against the hardwood floor as she tries to break her way free from him.

"Adria! Help me!"

Sebastian barely turns his head to see me standing off to the side. His eyes are churning with anger and revenge, but they're not black and this tells me that he's not as enraged as he appears to be.

I put up my hands in a surrendering fashion. "Hey, don't look at *me*. I can't believe you shaved his hair off. Really."

"Oh seriously!" she shouts and Sebastian releases one of her wrists and holds her face in his hand, squeezing her soft, creamy cheeks beneath his fingers. "Look me in the eye, Dria, and tell me he's not fucking sexy with a shaved head!"

I look back and forth between them. A couple more times. Okay, so maybe she has a point. He *does* look hot.

"See!" she squeals with her cheeks still pressed between his fingers. "Even she thinks so! Now let me up!"

Sebastian's head spins around harshly to see me and at first I'm not sure why, but apparently he's waiting on me to confirm or deny that what she's saying is true.

"Yes," I say, "I admit it's a sexy look on you."

Isaac walks into the room and says, "Damn straight, Bas. If I swung that way, I'd do you."

Zia cackles with laughter. I think her voice is starting to become hoarse from laughing and yelling and crying so much.

Sebastian loosens his grip on her face and starts to get off her waist, but Zia reaches up and grabs him by the front of his green t-shirt and pulls him down to her. "Tell me you love it," she says with their lips not even an inch apart, but she doesn't give him a chance to answer. She pulls him into a hungry kiss instead, his heavily muscled arms tightening as he holds his weight up from the floor by the palms of his hands.

"Are you ready?" Isaac says, ignoring them altogether.

I think Isaac's disinterest in them using his bedroom floor as a make-out pad piques Zia's curiosity. She breaks the kiss and rolls her head to one side to see Isaac and me standing above her.

Sebastian pushes himself off her and helps her to her feet afterwards. He runs his hand over the top of his bald head.

"Where are you two going that's so important?" Zia says, still smiling hugely and out of breath. She reaches up and rubs his head, too, dragging the tips of her fingers down the center and then over the bridge of his nose.

Isaac grabs a black sling back from the floor of his closet and pushes a few things down inside and shoulders it.

"We'll be spending more time with Aramei for a while," Isaac says and never looks at me because he knows I'm not slow to catch on.

I shoulder my small bag, too.

Zia raises a finely groomed brow. "Oh? He's found a new slave to look after Aramei now?" She grins over at me, draping an arm around Sebastian's waist.

"Looks that way," Isaac says. But he never makes eye contact with her; instead, he rummages through the top drawer of his nightstand.

Zia's smile drops from her face and both of her hands drop to her sides. "What's with you two lately?" she says. "I wasn't going to say anything before but you've both been acting weird ever since...," she looks right at me, "...well, since you started growing hair in all the wrong places." She smirks playfully, hoping to get a reaction out of me.

She always does.

"You suck, Zia," I say, smiling across at her.

"But you love me," she says, striking an overly dramatic pose. She bats her eyes and pooches out her lips.

"Yeah, I do," I say, beaming.

"Okay, all joking aside," she says, "what's going on with you? And with Daisy, Harry and Nathan, for that matter."

I hear a *crunch* as Sebastian casually cracks his knuckles. "I'd like to know myself," he says and his deep brown eyes fall on Isaac as if he's the one of us who he expects will give him the answers. Maybe it's a guy thing.

Isaac leans away from the drawer and shuts it softly, afterwards slipping a pocketknife down into his front jeans pocket.

"It's crazy what my father expects of us," Isaac says so convincingly that even though I know he's making up this excuse as he goes, I'm totally believing the pace of his story. "Adria and Aramei both being bonded apparently has set off a shit-storm of expectations from my father."

I jump in, "She's been trying to communicate with me."

Zia's mouth forms the letter O. "No way! Like actual communication? Are you serious?"

I nod. "Yes," I say, "but I've not been able to get anything out of her, at least, not what Trajan wants, anyway." It's a huge lie but necessary just the same.

Zia crosses her arms and looks off toward the wall in thoughtful amazement. She shakes her head a few times. "That's pretty incredible," she says finally looking back at me. "Just that she's tried to communicate with anybody at all, really. Don't take it the wrong way, but I'm glad it's you and not me."

I scoff. "How else am I to take that?"

"C'mon," she says grinning, "I'm just sayin'."

I just smile at her hopelessly.

I can sense Isaac getting anxious. I take a few steps toward the bedroom door to show them that we really do need to go, but I pause before stepping out into the hall.

"I do feel sorry for her," Zia says about Aramei, seeming sort of lost in a sad memory, probably of the times she herself spent caring for her. "I would *never* want to live like that."

The ensuing silence gives us the opportunity to cut this conversation short.

"Well, we need to head out," Isaac says coming up behind me. He stands in front of Sebastian and a slim smile breaks his face. He shakes his head, laughing gently. "I can't believe she shaved your head, man." And then he steps out into the hall with my hand locked in his.

Isaac's final comment set the tone for more craziness and the next thing I know, Sebastian has Zia slung over his shoulder and is carrying her off to the end of the hall towards their room. Zia kicks and screams and laughs the whole way. By the time Isaac and me make it to the top of the stairs, their bedroom door slams shut and all I can hear is Zia's muffled laughter behind the door.

I shake my head, laughing under my breath as we descend the stairs.

Nathan comes out of the kitchen as we enter the den. He's also carrying a bag over his shoulder and he's changed his clothes. He stops at the den entrance wearing a tight black t-shirt that says OBEY across the front in bold red letters.

"Ready?" Nathan says with his mouth full. He swallows down whatever he was eating and takes a big gulp of water from the bottle in his other hand.

"As ever," Isaac says nodding toward the door. "Let's go."

I follow them out and just as I emerge onto the front porch, a familiar smiling face is staring up at me from the bottom of the steps.

"Adria!" It's annoying Cecilia from the skate park. I don't know how she found out where we were, or why she's here, but there couldn't be a worse time for someone like her to be showing up out of nowhere.

Isaac glances over at me nervously. Nathan looks at me with a curiously raised eye.

"What are you doing here?" I say to Cecilia as I come off the bottom step to meet her.

Her smile widens, displaying all of her teeth. She's wearing a skin-tight babydoll tee with a low-cut V-neck that scoops right down in-between her plump breasts. She only ever dresses like this when she's trying to gain the attention of a guy. It's how she landed her ex-boyfriend, Marc: her huge boobs, which makes me feel even worse for her. This girl has always been in serious need of a straightforward friend to guide her off the path of being the most gossiped about girl in Hallowell. I would consider taking on the role, but with Cecilia, there's a lot more to it. Like my sanity, for starters.

"Baby, we really need to hit the road," Isaac whispers at me harshly from behind.

Cecilia is all but glued to Nathan. I notice that she's slow to answer my question because she can't seem to stop gawking at him. And Nathan, well, he suddenly appears uncomfortable, avoiding direct eye contact with her, which I find sort of hilarious.

"Sorry," Cecilia says taking one step up, "I found out from your aunt where you were—," she turns all of her giddy attention on Nathan and only Nathan, "—Hi, I'm Cecilia, a good friend of Adria and Isaac's." She reaches out her hand and Nathan reluctantly shakes it but he looks as if he's doing something he's going to regret.

Isaac and I exchange looks, probably thinking along the same lines though we aren't inside each other's heads at the moment. Since when did we become good friends of hers?

I take a deep breath and let it out sharply. "Cecilia," I say, "I'm really sorry, but we were just heading out and we're kind of running late."

Cecilia's face lights up even more. "Oh? Mind if I go? Where are you going?"

"No offense," Isaac says, stepping up to move this along because he knows I can't force myself to brush Cecilia off and risk hurting her feelings, "but we really need to leave and we can't bring anyone else where we're going."

Cecilia's face falls.

Isaac comes down three steps so that he's standing level with her and he looks her right in the eyes, I know softening his own eyes because he doesn't want to hurt her feelings any more than I do. "Maybe if you come back tomorrow, we'll be around and you can hang out."

The front door opens behind us and Isaac and Nathan's youngest sister, Camilla, steps outside. She's holding one of her famous Barley Green and broccoli health smoothies, sipping on the end of a straw.

I shudder and grimace just watching the green gunk shoot up the clear straw and into her mouth.

"Hey!" Cecilia says, pointing at Camilla, "aren't you friends with Gracie Mathers?"

Camilla lets the straw bob away from her lips and she gazes down at Cecilia with a look of survey. She begins to smile slowly as she apparently realizes that she knows Cecilia, too. She points her finger. "Yeah, that's right," she says, "I met you at Gracie's party last month."

Isaac grabs my hand and starts to tug it. Nathan is already heading to Isaac's Jeep since we all decided to ride together.

"Cam?" Isaac says, looking up at his sister impatiently, "do you mind?" He covertly nods toward Cecilia and Camilla easily catches on.

Camilla gestures for her to follow. "Come on in," she says.

Isaac wastes no more time and pulls me away from the porch; I wave as I pass Cecilia up, but I don't think she notices—easily distracted, that girl.

"That chick has got a huge red flag emblazoned on her forehead," Nathan says from the backseat as Isaac and I jump inside.

I turn around in the seat, tossing my bag in the back next to Nathan and say, "Just don't be mean to her. She can't help it, really."

Nathan shakes his head and says with laughter in his voice, "What do you take me as? Xavier?"

"You know what I mean," I say gently. "I don't like being around her, but I feel totally bad that no one else likes to, either."

"Okay, so it's about four hours to Providence," Isaac says from the driver's seat, peering down into a paper map and ignoring our conversation.

"A map?" Nathan says. "Why don't we take my ride? I've got a brand spankin' new GPS system installed in there."

Isaac shakes his head subtly, still looking at the map. "No thanks." Isaac is a lot like Aunt Bev when it comes to technology.

I turn back to face the front and I begin to think about the strange turn of events, about Cecilia showing up out of nowhere like that and how it was such a convenient coincidence that she and Camilla have met before, too.

I turn to Isaac, pause for a second to rethink my words and then say, "...Never mind."

Isaac looks at me inquisitively, resting the large unfolded map against the steering wheel.

"Never mind what?" he says.

It didn't even dawn on me that I hadn't actually said anything; I was too lost in my thoughts.

"What?" Isaac urges me, still anxious about getting on the road and maybe a little tired of all the obstacles being thrown in our path.

Wait. Obstacles.

I snap back into the moment and say, "I'm just being paranoid."

Nathan pushes himself in-between the front seats, poking his head into our view. "Spit it out, gorgeous," he says with a serious, yet lopsided smile. "Paranoid or not—what's on your mind?"

I feel my eyes blink rapidly a few times as I gaze out the windshield and toward the house.

"I don't know," I say staring off at nothing really, "but it just seems weird that she would show up like that."

"Well, she *is* a weird girl," Nathan says.

Isaac raises both brows and nods once to indicate: Yeah, he's got a point.

"Like I said: paranoid." I shrug and leave it alone.

"I know what you're thinking," Isaac says, "and Cecilia could be a valid concern, but probably the least likely candidate." He glances toward the house too, where Cecilia is inside with his sister and then he looks back at me. "She's only ever at the skate park. She doesn't even go to the same school."

"True," I say, "but that doesn't mean it's not her."

"She has a point too, bro," Nathan says. "This could be one of those situations where the least likely candidate is the *most* likely."

"Fine," Isaac says, reluctantly agreeing, "we'll put her on the list of suspects, but I'm going with my gut on this one: I don't think it's her."

"Fair enough," I say. "I guess we officially have a list now."

"One person doesn't constitute an actual list," Nathan says.

"Well, then tell me," I say, crossing my arms and glancing between both of them, "I know you both have to have *someone* you're suspicious of. At least one person."

Nathan and Isaac look at each other briefly, but I can tell it's not because they share the same thought on this matter. It seems more like each of them is testing the other out to see who's going to speak up first, neither of them really wanting to admit they are suspicious of anyone.

"Well?" I urge them.

"I'm not saying this because I really and honestly believe it," Nathan begins and is no longer smiling. "I'm only going to add Sebastian to the list because he's the only one in the house who came in around the time you became involved with us here in Maine. I think he's a good guy and I swear I don't think he's the traitor, but if I had to pick someone, it'd be him only for that reason."

I give it a moment's thought and nod, accepting Nathan's theory.

We both look over at Isaac at the same time with the same interrogative expression on our faces.

Isaac lets his breath out heavily and gazes off toward the house again.

"Zia," he announces and his voice is distant.

My head draws back in a stunned motion.

"*Zia?*" I say. "Why would you think it could be her?"

He turns back to me and shrugs. "No reason in particular," he says. "Just a gut feeling."

~~~

Isaac choosing Zia as his pick for person of interest has more of an effect on me than I could've imagined. I never would've even considered Zia for a second. And even Isaac admitted that he has no real reason to pick her, but still, this whole situation has become a hundred times more uncomfortable to me because of it. I guess I had just assumed all along that the traitor would be someone I don't like, maybe someone that I despise—Rachel, for instance. Yeah, I hope it's Rachel because then I would have every justifiable reason in the world to wish bad things upon her, maybe even get my own revenge and kick her ass once and for all. But of course, if she is the Dark Praverian, that kind of tosses my ass-kicking plan out the window because there's no way I can fight one of them. Actually, if it's Rachel, I have more reason than ever to be terrified of her, especially since I'm the only one among us she seems to despise with every fiber of her being.

Okay, so maybe I would rather the traitor be someone else, after all.

9

WE MAKE IT TO Providence by mid-afternoon and drive for what feels like forever up and down Angell Street and Butler Avenue until we find the two-story house of Minna Abrahamsen.

"We'll park at that church we passed and walk back up," Isaac says driving past the house again and towards the intersection. "Don't want her to see my Maine license plate."

I hadn't even thought of that.

We park the Jeep and head back the way we came, Isaac and me hand-in-hand as we walk along the sidewalk. I grow more nervous the closer we get and Isaac's hand tightens around mine as though he senses the nervousness churning around in my stomach.

"Maybe she'll be hot," Nathan says on the other side of me.

I roll my eyes and smile looking over at him.

Isaac says, "Sure, bro, and since you're the only one of us who's single you can be the one to show her how hot you are for *her* so she'll give us what we need."

The house draws closer. I can see it out ahead perched on the corner with one big tree in the front casting a swath of shade across the grass and sidewalk concrete.

Nathan spats a laugh. "Yeah, if she's hot," he says, "otherwise hell no."

"No, you've been officially nominated," I say smiling hugely. "What, can you not…perform?"

Nathan's mouth falls open and Isaac laughs beside me under his breath.

"Babe," Nathan says, "that's not an area I have any problem with."

I laugh out loud. "Well, we're not trying to pimp you out or anything, but let's just hope you're her type and that this plan doesn't fall through."

"Yeah," Isaac says, pulling me closer, "let's hope because it's the only plan we've got."

When we make it to the house, we stop on the sidewalk and just stare at it for a moment until Isaac pulls me along and we ascend the short steps onto the porch. Nathan stays below on the walkway and as I look back to get a quick glimpse of him, I notice he's not Mr. Smiles anymore. He looks really tense. I would normally get a laugh out of Nathan's torture, but right now as Isaac knocks on the glass window on the front door, I can do anything but laugh.

I hear movement inside and this time decide to let my keen sense of hearing open up fully so I can listen further. I hear a television playing. It's TV Land and the first thing I hear when the intro commercial fades and the programming resumes is: *Shirrrl*! and a lot of old-timey sitcom laughter. A few seconds later: *Laverrrn*! Whatever it is, it's obnoxious. I hear footsteps padding down the carpeted stairs and heavy, raspy breathing followed by intense coughing that makes me wince and my stomach curl.

"She's definitely not hot," I whisper harshly to Isaac.

Nathan hears my comment and says, "Oh man, it sounds like there's an old hag in there. Shit, bro, I'm really not likin' this."

Isaac raises his fist to knock once more but then stops as a shadow moves across the octagonal window to our right, covered by a sheer burgundy-colored curtain.

There's a click as the door is unlocked from the inside and then the slinking sound of a chain being slid between two pieces of metal. And then another bolder click as the deadbolt is turned. And then the slithering sound of a slide-lock being pulled away from its tiny metal chamber.

This woman must get 'dangerous' visitors like us often.

Finally, the door cracks open and the stench of cigarette smoke funnels outside and practically suffocates me. I reach up quickly and pinch my nose with my fingertips. Having a superhuman sense of smell is definitely the worst of all the senses.

"What do you want?" a hoarse voice says with her face obscured by the darkness.

"We need your…expertise," Isaac says carefully and slips his hand around my hip.

The door slams shut, rattling the large piece of glass embedded in the wood and then the series of locks all quickly go in reverse. "Get off my porch!" she says through the door.

Odd thing is that she doesn't sound to be very afraid, but instead, annoyed by our presence.

Isaac pounds on the glass again. "Look, we came a long way and if you won't let us in to at least talk about why we're here, then we'll let ourselves in."

My eyes widen and I move away from Isaac and take two steps down the porch. "Are you *crazy*?" I whisper harshly.

Nathan hasn't budged from his spot on the walkway and I'm starting to consider joining him.

"I'm not helping any of you freaks!" she shouts. "I'm not the Witch of Wayland, you hear me? I'm sick of all you mutants pounding on my door for love spells and all the like! I *told* you, I don't *do* that backwoods modern-day, wannabe Wiccafuck stuff! You *hear* me?"

"Ma'am," Isaac says with a raised voice so she can actually hear him over herself, "we're not here for any love spells. This is something far more…well, for you, I'd say interesting."

I see the white curtain covering the glass on the door move as though she is pressing up against it now. Silence ensues for a few seconds while Nathan and I keep looking back at one another, wide eyed.

"Interesting as in how?" Minna says with her face closer to the glass.

"Praverian interesting," Isaac says in a softer voice than before.

The white curtain lifts away from the glass and there is a long silent moment before the locks start to make noise again.

The door opens slowly and much wider than before. Minna stands in the doorway in all of her leathery suntanned, smoked-four-packs-of-cigarettes-a-day glory, dressed in a dingy white nightgown and bath robe. A pair of worn-out pink house-shoes dress her feet; open-toed, which displays her gross, thick toenails painted hot pink but which can't distract from the other 'crustier' features.

I want to look behind me at Nathan, just to see the mortified look on his face that I know is there, but I can't turn away from this woman who I'm totally wary of.

Minna cocks her head to one side, propping her hand on the doorjamb just a little above her average height. Her gown lifts a couple of inches with her arm, revealing her thin, bony ankles streaked by varicose veins.

"Please come in," she says somberly and moves to the side, gesturing us in with her other hand palm up.

Strange how her attitude flip-flopped from crazy, screaming hag to calm, methodical woman.

Isaac waits for me to step back up behind him before we head inside. Nathan follows but still can't bring himself to say anything, probably hoping it might steer Minna's interest to one of us, but something tells me Nathan is going to have a very uncomfortable, prison-shower sort of day.

The house stinks of more than cigarettes; there's a strong waft of something like powdered sugar and cooking oil coming from the kitchen. And coffee; no doubt black is the only way she drinks it. I also smell something cheap and fruity, like some kind of potpourri, maybe. The walls, although covered by hideous tapestry wallpaper, are yellowish-brown from all of the smoke over the years she must've lived here.

Minna walks us past the kitchen and into the living room and all along the way I see tons of clutter strewn about everywhere. Magazines. Newspapers. Unopened boxes of crap obviously bought off TV for the 'low price of just $19.95!" and off to the side, in the far corner of the living room, there's a giant glass curio cabinet full of hundreds of little elephant figurines.

Actually, now that I'm paying more attention to detail as opposed to my need to get out of this place in one piece, I see that Minna *really* loves elephants. A giant elephant painting hovers over the back of her couch. Elephants sit on every available bit of furniture space there is in various different forms from glass to brass and porcelain and plastic. The blanket folded long-ways and draped over the back of the recliner has an elephant on it. I think if she could fit an actual elephant inside this house, she would no doubt have one for a pet.

"You've got to be kidding me," I hear Nathan mumble from behind.

Minna closes her robe with one hand and turns to us, "Have a seat."

I covertly glace over at Isaac and grasp his hand, but none of us sits down quickly. We don't want to actually sit *on* her furniture. There's no telling what we might catch. Lice. A smell that will never wash off. Elephant fever.

When Minna starts to walk toward us, all three of us decide to take a seat just in case she's intending to help us in some way. We sit on the very edge of the couch cushions, side by side, with our hands placed in our laps like some scared, unruly children about to be handed down the worst punishment ever.

"Make yourselves comfortable," she says, her voice crackling. "I'll get you all some coffee."

I want to say no thanks, but quite frankly I'm more inclined to accept her hospitality rather than risk offending her.

The second she slips around the corner and out of the room, Nathan comes alive.

"There's no fucking way, bro," he says, the words whistling through his teeth. "I can't even pretend be okay with *looking* at her, much less flirt with her."

I can't force myself to make fun of Nathan this time…not as much as normal anyway.

"Just go with the flow," Isaac whispers back at him on the other side of me. "It might not even come down to anything like that. Just calm down."

"I don't care what it comes down to," Nathan says, shaking his head, "like I said —"

"Here we are," Minna says coming back around the corner carrying a wooden tray. She places it on the coffee table in front of us, moving aside an elephant statue. Three mugs of black coffee sit around a plate of homemade fried donuts covered in powdered sugar.

Not one of us wants to go first, so we remain still and quiet with our hands between our knees and hope she doesn't notice.

Minna slinks her way into the recliner next to us in front of a window covered by another burgundy-colored curtain.

"Well," she says, gesturing towards the coffee and donuts, "Eat up. Go on. Or are you too good for my food?"

As if that was a challenge none of us wants to accept, all three of us reach for a mug, take a sip and then start to nibble the end of a messy, powdered donut. I only pretend to actually drink the coffee, of course, and Isaac and Nathan are likely pulling the same ruse.

"First things first," Minna says and then stops to hack a disgusting cough, her whole body rattling in the chair, "who sent you here?"

"A Praverian named Genevieve," Isaac answers and places the rest of his donut back on the plate.

Minna gives Isaac a suspicious sidelong glance, the wrinkles in her leathery-brown face deepening around her eyes. She purses her dry, cracked lips in contemplation.

"And where is she now?" Minna says.

"We don't know," Isaac says, retaining his confident composure and keeping his answers simple.

"Is that so?" she says, still suspicious. "You want me to believe that she just told you where to find me and then disappeared?" She whirls her bony hand in a circular motion above her.

Isaac nods. "Yes," he says. "Whether you believe it or not, that's exactly what happened."

Minna snarls and leans her back into the recliner, crossing her legs. "Well dear boy," she says with a sneer, "you're going to have to elaborate a little more or we can end this discussion here and now so that I can get back to my shows—you know, they don't make shows like they used to. No they don't." She shakes her head very matter-of-factly.

I glance over at Isaac, seeing in his eyes that he knows he's going to have to take it up a notch or risk her not helping us. But to her, his face remains standard, revealing no difference.

I've never known Nathan to be so utterly silent. I laugh inside just thinking about what's going on in his head right now.

"Genevieve came to our town," Isaac begins, "because of her Charge, but then she found out that there's a Dark Praverian among my family and thought we should know. So, she told us all about it and said that he or she is dangerous. So now we're here because apparently you're one of few who know how to trap it."

Minna reaches out and takes her own mug of coffee by the handle and brings it slowly to her lips. Her dark eyes never leave us as she takes a careful sip. They peer at us over the white rim of the mug; cold, distrusting eyes scanning over every inch of Isaac as if searching for something to use against him.

"I find that hard to believe," she says after pulling the mug away, leaving a bright hot pink lipstick stain in a half-moon on the edge. She sets it gently back on the glass-top coffee table. "Since when do Praverians care about the lives of anyone other than their Charges?"

When Isaac doesn't answer as quickly as he had been all along, I start to get nervous that he doesn't have one.

So I speak up instinctively. "Genna did seem more worried about her Charge," I say, "which is why she told us about the Dark Praverian. I think she was worried that since she didn't know who it was herself, that her Charge was in more danger, so she was using *us* to find it."

Minna narrows one eye and takes another casual sip of her coffee; a little swirl of steam rises above the rim and fades around her nostrils.

Suddenly, I feel my mind get heavier and Isaac nudges my leg with his.

I let him in.

"You shouldn't have said that," he says to me telepathically, but never taking his eyes off Minna. *"But it's okay, just let me do the rest of the talking."*

"What did I say?"

"She's going to think we know who Genna's Charge is," he says, *"And—"*

"And just who is this Praverian's Charge?" Minna says.

"We don't know," Isaac says. "She wouldn't tell us."

She pauses, both eyes narrowing now.

"Has anyone you know gone missing since this 'Genna' disappeared?" Minna's face has become much more confident now and this is making me immensely nervous. I know that one wrong word, one slip-up, might leave us and our entire story caught in her snare.

"Several people have moved out," Isaac says and Minna's confident expression melts into one of disappointment.

I breathe a quiet sigh of relief.

Isaac goes on: "But no one has actually disappeared. Why?"

Damn, Isaac's good. He knows exactly why she asked that particular question: If he would've said no one, she would know he was lying because a Praverian wouldn't leave without their Charge unless the Charge was also a Praverian, like Harry turned out to be (and according to Harry, that's rare). If he would've hesitated even a fraction, Minna would detect that he was only trying to figure out what name of what missing person to use, which would also indicate a lie.

Minna loses eye contact and says, "I'm just testing you."

"We have no reason to lie," Isaac says. "We just really need your help."

I notice Minna's gaze skirt Nathan, but for now she doesn't hold it on him. It felt awkward though, as if she's sizing him up, or maybe picturing him doing really nasty things to her.

I think I just made myself sick….

"Well…," Minna says with a new sort of confident look on her face, "you should really be careful trusting this Praverian, this Genevieve, as you call her. They aren't what they appear to be."

Harry warned us of this.

"Of course they're not," I say, going on the defense for Harry, "they seem to appear in many forms."

Minna's nose crinkles at my sarcasm and I feel Isaac and Nathan on both sides of me begin to shift almost invisibly on their cushions. Maybe I should just keep quiet, but as I've proven in the past, sometimes that's not such an easy thing for me to do.

Minna chews gently on the inside of her bottom lip making her cheek twist inward and then she says, "Maybe so, but if you befriend one you're sure to regret it later. They are double-crossing bastards, believe me." She smiles crookedly and takes one more sip of coffee. "And if you're a Charge, don't ever think for a second that they really have that pretty little head of yours in their best interests."

"What's that supposed to mean?" I say, though not believing her con for a second. And it felt like Isaac was about to say something to me in my mind for a moment, but then he stopped abruptly, maybe curious about Minna's answer, too.

"Their Charges are their most important duty, yes," she says with a deep smirk on her face, "but that duty could easily be that they need to make sure you die as much as they need to protect your life."

I roll my eyes obviously and shake my head. "*Really?*" I say with a distasteful shear in my voice, "and why would they do that?" Maybe a small part of me believes her. And maybe that was exactly her plan, whether what she's saying is true or not.

"Baby, please stop now...."

Minna's vindictive smile just gets wider and wider and then I realize I may have just made this easier for her.

"For someone who isn't friends with this Genevieve," Minna says, "you sure seem to take offense to me telling you the truth about her."

I swallow hard and my acerbic expression falls.

Well, at least if Minna is onto me like I'm starting to believe, she doesn't know anything about Harry. She can look for Genna all she wants, but she'll be sent on a wild goose chase if she relies on any information from us to find her.

We have no idea where Genna is.

"So, can you help us trap it, or not?" Isaac says, trying to shift Minna's focus before I say something I'll regret. He fits his fingers around the handle of his mug and brings it to his lips. I think he took a real drink, too. Wow, he's really playing his part, that's for sure.

"Maybe," Minna says and crosses her other leg. "Where did you say you came from?"

"We didn't say," Isaac answers, "but we're from Boston, if you'd like to know."

"About where at's in Boston?"

"Back Bay," Isaac answers just as quickly, as though all of these lies have been filed away neatly inside of his head ready for this special occasion.

I just wish he would've shared the details with Nathan and me on the ride here. Then again, it could be too that he really is making this stuff up along the way.

Minna leans over and takes a donut from the plate. She takes a big bite, leaving white powder dusting her sloppy pink lips. Her jaw works the food vigorously around in her mouth and all three of us start to look at anything but her because it's not pleasant to watch her eat. She swallows and then licks the tips of her fingers clean of powdered sugar, "It's not easy to trap one of those bastards," she says.

"With all due respect," Isaac says, "we didn't expect that it would be."

"They can appear as anyone," Minna adds. "They can be sitting next to you and you'd never know it."

I feel like I can elaborate a little more, having heard her very familiar description, but I stop myself from making that huge mistake. I can't let her know anything more about me. I've done enough damage. There's no telling what she might do if she knew for a fact that a Charge is sitting in her living room at this very moment.

"How do you know that *we* aren't one of them?" I say instead.

Minna grins impishly and says, "Well, the obvious answer would be that your delicious boy here," she points to Isaac without looking at him, "said the magic word at the

119

door." She nods towards Nathan now, but adds a curious little smile that disappears as soon as her eyes fall on me again. "However, the other two of you I know check out because you're sitting in a trap and haven't tried to kill me yet."

All of us look down at the floor and then up and all around us.

Minna stands up from the recliner and waltzes around to the other side of the coffee table. She looks down at us, watching Nathan more than Isaac or me, but trying to be covert about it.

"This whole house is a trap," she says and then her shriveled hand comes up to press against her chest as she begins to cough violently. Nathan's body impulsively leans away, out of the path of her cough and presses into my shoulder. His hand comes up, the side of it shielding his nose and mouth.

Minna shuts her eyes and lets her breathing calm before opening them again. She looks down at us and continues, "You think being what I am, I'd let just anyone come into my house?"

To all of our surprise, Minna takes a seat on the couch right next to Nathan. Even Isaac tenses up next to me, but nothing can compare to the rigidity of Nathan's body.

God, she smells like baby powder and Aspercreme and…there's something far more devastating underneath the skin. I try not to think about being able to smell it, any of it, because I know if I try too hard, it'll only get worse. But Minna has finally made her interest in Nathan more obvious now and she's all but nuzzling up next to him, biding her time and dragging out the inevitable.

Poor Nathan. I really do feel bad for him right now, all laughs at his expense aside, because no one deserves this.

Nathan seems to have stopped breathing. His big blue eyes are huge in the sockets, his shoulders fallen completely away from his neck as his back shoots straight up as if to summon some kind of wall between their bodies. Thankfully, she hasn't actually touched him yet.

"I will help you," she says in a scary, manipulative voice, "but you should know that I do nothing for free."

10

WE ALL KNEW THAT was coming, but Nathan had dreaded it a hundred times more. I can sense that Isaac and Nathan are communicating telepathically, so I open my mind to Isaac to listen in.

"*I'll owe you one,*" Isaac says.

"*You'll owe me more than* one*!*"

"*Just work your charm. I've seen you do it. Come on, bro, I'll buy you a steak later.*"

"*Just a steak?*"

"*Yes, an expensive one—Fine, two steaks then.*"

I jab my elbows into both of them at my sides and glare at them as if to say: Get on with it!

They straighten up and Nathan turns to Minna who's so disturbingly close that it even makes *me* shudder.

She gives Nathan 'the look', batting her wrinkly eyes and letting her tongue gently lick her top lip.

"*I think I just threw up in my mouth,*" I hear Isaac say in my mind.

"I know what you are," Minna says, disrupting the flow of our thoughts suddenly.

She gets up from the couch, surprising all of us, and I see a thick layer of relief suddenly wash over Nathan.

But he's certainly not out of the woods yet.

Minna walks away from the couch and to the center of the living room, crossing her arms and letting her long, bony fingers dangle over her biceps. The hot pink nail polish contrasts brightly against her white robe.

I don't know what just happened, but it's obvious that Minna is playing a different game than what any of us expected of her.

"You're lycanthrope," Minna says and we remain perfectly quiet and still. "Tell me, is Vargas still vying for the power of Sovereignty?"

"Always," Isaac says, retaining his professional demeanor.

Minna nods and paces back and forth over the same strip of shag carpet and then stops to cough again. This time she can barely stand on her own; her body heaved violently into a coughing fit where she stumbles her way to the nearby wall to hold herself up. To my complete surprise, Isaac and Nathan both instinctively jump to their feet to help her, but she fans them away with one hand, the other hand still pressed against the yellowed wall.

"G'on back to your seats," she says in a croaky voice. She wipes her mouth with the back of her hand and when she wipes her hand on her robe I glimpse a streak of blood left behind, seeping into the plush, dingy fabric.

"Oh no," I say under my breath, but I keep the rest of my thoughts to myself.

I have a feeling I know where this is heading.

Minna moves away from the wall and straightens herself up, gathering whatever composure she has left and looks back at us as if about to make a speech.

"My price is immortality," she announces and I think the three of us each share completely different feelings about the turn of events. I'm indifferent only because I've not had but two seconds to let it sink in that she actually wants what I'm totally against. Why would *anyone* want that? But then after a few more seconds I become sympathetic because it's obvious she's dying already—probably lung cancer. Isaac, on the other hand: I know he's completely *un*sympathetic and now will have to make a very difficult Alpha decision which I know he doesn't want to make. Nathan? Well, his heart and stomach just fell at the same time because he knows that out of the three of us here, he will be stuck with the job of bonding this woman to him. That's like giving a ninety-year-old woman her last dying wish and asking Nathan to have sex with her, except only worse, because a Blood Bond is usually only done between lovers: two people so devoted to one another that they would die for each other without thinking twice about it.

This isn't just repulsive. This isn't only asking Nathan to do something 'gross' that we can make fun of him about later. No, this is a serious matter that no one in their right mind would ever consider turning into a joke.

"And I won't accept anything else," Minna adds.

Nathan takes a deep breath and rolls his head back, his eyes shut heavily. He brings up both hands balled into fists and presses them against his temples and then shoots up from the couch. "Do you have any idea what you're asking?" His face is twisted by sadness and disappointment rather than anger.

"Of course I do," Minna says and presses her palm against her heaving chest. "I've been coughing up my lungs for nearly six months and I don't have much time left." She's struggling even more now to breathe as she speaks and I see her glance toward the side of her recliner where an oxygen tank is partially obscured by the chair arm.

Nathan begins to pace, the muscles in his arms hardening, crossed firmly over his ribs.

Isaac stands up, too. "You can't ask my brother to let you drink from him," he says stern but calmly. "If you know what we are then you know what emotional effects that will have on him."

I'm listening intently, engrossed in this tragic twist. My face feels stiff with anticipation, but my heart is hurting, too. It's as though being a werewolf now, I'm picking up even on Nathan's emotions, which are surely the most turbulent in the room.

"Yes," Minna answers hoarsely, "I know that a Blood Bond is only ever done out of love. I know that if he does this, not only might he become someone darker, but that he could become a rogue as a result. But that's not my problem."

Now I'm the one shooting up from the couch, my eyes wide and enraged. "*What*?" I say, dropping my hands to my sides. My head jerks swiftly over to see Isaac, my face full of question and shock and disbelief. "What does she mean by that? A *rogue*? You're not serious...." I turn to see Nathan now, but he can't look at me. He has stopped pacing and now only stands there staring off into nothingness.

"Oh dear," Minna says, "You must be a new one."

"Yes, I am!" I lash out. "But let's not get off topic. Someone needs to explain this. I'm serious."

Minna can't stand any longer. She makes her way back to her recliner, carefully sitting down with her shaky hands gripping the arms of the chair for balance. For a second it seems she intends to reach for the contraption hanging off the oxygen tank but then she decides against it. She takes three heavy, unsteady breaths and then looks back at me.

But Isaac is the one who answers:

"A Blood Bond is sacred," he says, "No one of our kind—except for rogues—has ever, nor *would* ever, share that bond with someone they had no intention in sharing

125

everything else with, too. If Nathan does this, they'll be linked forever or at least until one of them dies." He sighs and glances behind me at Nathan. "I won't ask him to do this. I refuse. We'll find another way." Isaac shoots an angry glare back at Minna and then he grabs my hand. "Let's go, Nathan. We're out of this shithole."

"No," Nathan says, stopping us both in our tracks. "We have to do this, little brother. All of us are at risk and it needs to be dealt with before someone gets killed."

Minna remains quiet, letting us come to the final conclusion all on our own which she already knows is going to go her way. I glimpse her from the corner of my eye, that sickly smug look on her face and it takes everything in me to keep from marching across the room and knocking it right off.

"But I'll only agree to it," Nathan says, turning fully at the waist to face Minna, "if you agree that you won't drink directly from me and this is the only time you'll *ever* drink of my blood."

That seems to have sparked an unexpected reaction. Minna's smug face collapses.

Nathan, clearly the one in control now unfolds his tanned, muscled arms and walks toward her. "Take it or leave it," he says. "She knows as well as I do that there won't be any other desperate werewolves lining up at her door to do it anytime soon, and time is something she doesn't have." His eyes never leave Minna, who is slinking more and more into her chair.

"Fine," Minna spats out the word, "I agree to your terms."

"Nathan," Isaac says, "as Alpha, I forbid you to do this."

Nathan turns to face Isaac and I feel my body stiffening as they stand toe to toe.

"I respect you as my leader and my brother," Nathan says, "but if you don't let me do this, you're risking Adria's life."

Isaac looks away from him.

"You know it, man," Nathan goes on. "The traitor is the reason for everything, for the attack in the car that almost killed her, for the Blood Bond, for *everything*. I don't know about you, but I think it's obvious that this Praverian has it out for Adria more than anyone."

"I know!" Isaac roars, startling me with both his voice and his admission. "I *know*...." His voice calms and his rigid body loosens, his shoulders falling. He looks away from Nathan and gazes down at the floor. "I've known this since Genna told us all about the traitor. I've known, but I didn't want to believe it."

"Then you know I have to do this," Nathan says stepping up to his brother and softening his voice. "I would do it for either of you."

"*I'll* do it then," Isaac says.

I stiffen.

"Oh hell no you won't," Nathan argues, narrowing his eyes. "You've already been bonded. That would cause worse emotional repercussions than it would if I did it."

"Don't I have a say in this?" I speak up. "Apparently it's all about me, right? Then I should have a say." I cross my arms.

Minna hacks and coughs into a tissue, but no one pays her any attention.

"Sure, doll," Nathan says with a playful grin, "you can say whatever you want. Get it all out. But it won't change anything."

I march right over to him and stand looking up at his tall height with my arms crossed angrily. "But what about that emotional stuff?" I say, gritting my teeth. I look over at Isaac once too, letting them both know I need answers no matter which of them I get them from. "You risking your life for mine sort of makes this my business, therefore I should have a say."

"Maybe it won't be so bad," Nathan says, "if I'm not letting her drink directly from me, that takes out the intimate factor at least."

Minna waves her hand in front of her. "As much as I'd love to drink from those delicious veins of his, I'll settle with a cup."

"Disgusting," I say snarling across at her.

Isaac finally jumps in, "...And since Nathan won't be sharing his blood with her but this once, that might lessen the emotional *trauma*," he glares at Minna with the emphasis of that word.

"You're *agreeing* to this?" I say, disappointed.

Isaac steps up to me, taking my hands. I can tell by how thoughtful and regretful his expression reads that he's about to give me one of those why-he-has-to-do-it speeches, but I shake my head and pull away from him.

"Don't...," I say, putting up my hand. "Isaac, do you have any idea how it feels to be the cause of so many people you love getting hurt?"

"Baby—"

"Stop!" I say, moving farther back away from him and crossing my arms. "Don't you understand? My shoulders are *full*. I can't carry anymore." I feel like I want to cry, and in a situation like this I normally would tear up, but I can't. I'm angrier than anything. And something wrenches at my insides and I quickly realize that I'm on the verge of shifting into my mediate form so I try to calm myself fast. Deep breaths. I shut my eyes and just breathe.

"Wow," Minna gloats from behind, "I don't need my TV shows to keep me entertained, I've got all the drama I need right here, live in my living room."

I storm over with black, swirling eyes and just before I reach out, intent on knocking the old hag from the chair, Isaac grabs me around my waist from behind and pulls me back.

Nathan steps in-between me and Minna.

I allow my body to calm and my eyes to shift back to their natural color and only then does Isaac release his hold on me.

"Fine," I rip the word out, "let's be done with this. I want this traitor caught so that maybe we can all get on with our lives." I glare down at Minna, but her face remains full of malice despite being in a room with three werewolves who despise her. I figure she doesn't have anything to lose anymore and all she has left are her treacherous ways so she might as well make the best use of them.

I turn away and walk to stand near the glass curio cabinet, absently staring in at all of the different elephant figurines. Vaguely, I can hear the television still playing somewhere else in the house, but I'm too infuriated for it or any other unsolicited noises to amplify the volume. There's another shelf next to me holding a mountain of books; everything covered in a thick layer of dust.

"How are we gonna' know," Isaac says, "If whatever you tell us to do to trap the Praverian is actually going to work?"

"Good question," Nathan adds. "If I bond you to me and this trap is a bust, I'll—"

"You'll *what*?" Minna says and I turn at the waist to see her because I detect a malicious grin in her voice. "You can't kill me; we all know that."

Unsettled by this information, I take a few steps back over to them so that I know I won't miss any of the conversation, including facial expressions.

"Maybe *he* can't," Isaac says, "but I *will* kill you."

"Why can't he?" I finally say, standing behind them with my arms crossed loosely.

"Just like I knew I couldn't hurt you all that time you were bonded to me," Isaac says, "they won't be able to hurt one another, either."

"Well, that's easily fixed," I say, stepping up farther so that Minna can see the threat in my face. "Just like Isaac said, if Nathan can't deal with you, then we will."

Minna stands up again, though very slowly. "You're a cocky little bitch, I have to say."

Minna makes a fraught choking sound as Nathan's hand grips firmly around her throat. I know it would've been Isaac standing there if Nathan hadn't of been closer to her than Isaac when she said what she said. Her thin, bony hands come up, gripping his wrist, clawing at it futilely.

"Pl...*please!*" she begs between breaths; her eyes are starting to roll into the back of her head. "I-I'm s-*orry!*" She coughs and chokes, tiny droplets of saliva spewing out.

Nathan releases her and she falls to the floor, but this time no one is running to help catch her.

Holding her sickly body up with one hand, she raises the other to her throat, rubbing the area where Nathan's hand had been. She looks up at us, never really losing that cold, malicious grin and she says, "It will work. I'm not going anywhere, even after the blood heals me. I've lived in this house for forty-years." She pushes herself to her feet and catches her breath. "And so soon you three forget what I am."

"An old witch," I say, smirking.

She smirks right back at me. "I'm a Harvester," she says, barely letting on that the title 'witch' actually offended her. "I live to trap and reap these bastards, these dangerous beings that you three so blindly trust." She walks toward the exit that leads back into the kitchen and stops in the doorway. "I'll get you a cup."

Nathan walks over to the coffee table and takes up his coffee mug. Minna stops before leaving the room completely and watches him curiously.

"Here," Nathan says. He pours his coffee into the flower pot of a nearby fake plant sitting on the floor. "This'll do just fine." And then without even pausing to think about it, a razor-sharp black fingernail juts out at the tip of his finger and he slashes the skin on the under-part of his lower-arm just above the wrist. Blood oozes out of the wound in a stream of thick, heavy crimson; a few droplets staining the carpet at his feet just before he positions the mug underneath his arm to catch it. I stare at his blood filling up the mug so quickly; my eyes slanted horrifically, my fingertips dancing on my parted lips.

Minna walks right past me and toward Nathan, leaving the smell of Aspercreme in her wake, but I don't budge, not even to move out of her way. I'm in a sort of grossed-out mild shock.

She goes to reach for the mug, but Nathan pulls back his hand. "The blood is out of my veins," he says, holding the bloody mug away from her reach, "I'd say that's the half-way mark. You give us what we need and you can have it."

I feel the heat of Isaac's body behind me now, pressing into my back. His heart is hurting for his brother and it's crushing me. Without taking my eyes off Nathan and Minna, I turn my body at an angle so that I can press myself deeper into Isaac's chest. He holds me so tight that I feel like I'm the only thing standing between him and Minna and his need to take revenge on her. But Isaac knows that what Nathan said was true, that he has to do this, and it's not just for me; it's for all of us.

"Follow me," Minna says with the curl of her finger. She glances over at me and Isaac to indicate that we can come, too.

That was never even a question. We would've followed with or without her permission.

Hesitantly, Nathan sets the mug, dripping with blood down the sides, onto the coffee table and then covers his forearm with the other hand to help stop the blood flow.

Minna walks us through to the large kitchen area and I see that this isn't a house really at all, but a genuine elephant museum. It's disturbing how many she has, littered everywhere as we pass into a dark hallway. Even all of the pictures lining both walls down the length of the hallway are of elephants. I don't recall seeing a single portrait of a human being anywhere in this house. Maybe she has no family. Or, maybe they all disowned her and so she took their pictures down and threw them out with the garbage.

We follow Minna into a utility room where an old rickety door stands embedded in the wall locked by a simple slide-lock. "Don't touch anything," she says turning to face us and sliding back the little metal lever. The door clicks open to reveal a set of stairs that descend down into darkness. Minna reaches over and flips a switch on the wall and a dim glowing light floods the basement floor.

I feel like I'm about to descend the steps right into Hell.

11

WE MAKE OUR WAY down twelve concrete steps and stand inside a vast basement, which is almost as cluttered as the upstairs floor. Strangely enough, there are no elephants down here, but what I do see before me is equally disturbing.

Like something right out of movie, every wall of this enormous space is chock full from floor to ceiling with shelves of old books and dusty jars and bottles and shiny miniature trinket chests which I'm afraid to know what's inside. Hanging from the ceiling are dozens of weird-looking necklaces that look to be made of bird skulls and animal vertebra and even a thin ropy twine with canine teeth dangling from it. Perched high on the wall over an old furnace is some kind of enormous headpiece made of bones and feathers and deer antlers. But what disturbs me more than anything is what's inside some of those jars. I peer farther across the room with my new keener sight to see some kind of pinkish liquid in each jar, containing various animal and human body parts: a baby bird with bulging eyes, a pig's foot, a human ear, a finger with a heavy gold ring still wrapped around its lower half—My skin is crawling all over and I just want to leave this place. Minna was bad enough by herself, but seeing all of this crazy, voodoo, serial killer stuff is over my tolerance threshold.

Minna catches her breath first and then motions for us to follow again where she leads us to the far corner of the room where there's a giant free-standing wall safe big enough for two people to stand in, sitting against the wall. Her house shoes shuffle across the concrete floor eerily, like a zombie wandering aimlessly across a desolate room. She stops in front of the safe, shielding from us the secret numbered keypad set in the reinforced steel door. We watch her from behind, keeping a five-foot distance. Then a loud *click* resounds as the safe is opened.

We inch our way closer now, curious but leery about what's inside.

"She probably keeps her family members in there," I say to Isaac telepathically.

He squeezes my hand, agreeing.

When the door opens with absolutely no sound, the glint of glass reflecting off the overhead light above us flits across my vision. More jars. Dozens of them. But there's something very different about what's inside than those scattered about the shelves of the basement walls.

"What *is* that?" I say, pushing myself forward to peer more closely.

The jars are regular Mason jars with golden and silver lids twisted tightly at the top to keep the strange bluish-gray smoke floating around inside from escaping. A few contain reddish smoke.

Minna stops me in my tracks, putting up her hand.

"Stay on the other side of the line," she demands in a distrusting, raspy voice.

I look down and the only 'line' I see is where there is a perfectly straight break running through the concrete floor. I step back once to put that line in front of my shoes.

"Don't even think about it," Minna says, snarling her already wrinkled nose at me. "The ones I reap will always belong to me."

"The ones you reap?" Isaac says, pushing his way closer now, too. "Are those…*Praverian souls*?"

"You keep them in *jars*?" Nathan says with an air of disbelief.

"Well, if I could drink them, I would," Minna says bending over and reaching down for something on the floor of the safe. "But all I can do is keep them."

I think of Harry and of Genna right about now and I imagine them being like *that*…in *there*…and I just grow even more intolerant of this crazed, disgusting woman.

Minna raises herself and turns to face us holding another jar. This one is huge, a giant pickle jar full of what looks like nothing but dirt.

"This safe is protected," Minna says, "so if you get any trite ideas, like breaking them all to set them free or something stupid like that, you'll get one nasty surprise." She lowers her eyes forebodingly and purses her lips.

Me, Isaac and Nathan glance briefly at one another.

Minna holds out the pickle jar and I, being closest, reach for it and take it into my hands. Her own hands are shaking, unable to hold the heavy weight of it any longer. I stand here holding the jar of dirt and just look at her like the lunatic she is, waiting for her to tell us what we're supposed to do with it.

She points to a small silver table near me against the wall that looks like an examination table from a veterinarian clinic. I think that's exactly what it is.

"Set it down over there," she says and shuffles toward it.

I walk over and place the jar there while Minna flips another light switch and a beam shines down on the table from above.

Nathan and Isaac step up next to me and Isaac starts doing all the talking.

"Just so you know, if you tell us there's a heart inside that jar and that it belongs to Davy Jones or something like that, I'll just go ahead and put you out of your misery now."

He's not joking. Not in the slightest bit. I think he's looking for any reason to 'put her out of her misery' after what she's done to his brother.

Minna doesn't answer. She just rolls her eyes, coughs a few times and goes to twist off the lid. "This is earth from Sorrento, Italy, my dear boy," she says, laying the lid on the table. She reaches over to a small shelf beside her and takes an old, faded purple Crown Royal bag into her hand and loosens the drawstring. "One of few sites in this world where the earth can be collected—not just any dirt will work."

"Want to elaborate?" Isaac says.

"Not really," she says, reaching her hand into the jar. "Information wasn't part of the deal and since you three are fraternizing with my enemy, I'll die without the blood upstairs before I tell you anything."

"Whatever," Nathan says, slashing his hand in the space in front of him, "just get on with it already."

Minna takes out several handfuls of the dirt and carefully places it inside the Crown Royal bag until it's nearly full. Then she twists the lid back on the pickle jar and pulls the string on the bag to close it tight.

She hands it out to Isaac, letting it drop in the palm of his hand.

"The earth has already been prepared," Minna says. "The trap needs to be placed outside in the air. Place a bit of it on the ground at four points: north, east, south and west in a space smaller than this basement room and keep all manmade objects out of the trap."

"Just put the dirt on the ground?" I say, thoroughly confused about how that makes any sense.

"Four points. North. East. South. West. Outside only. About this big." She walks around the basement, stopping at each point to show us that the 'trap' should be no bigger than about thirty feet equally across from each point. She stops to cough, this time spitting up a great deal of blood into her hand where she wipes it away on her robe.

I visibly shudder.

"All you have to do is get the Praverian to walk inside the trap," she says holding out her hands, palms up. "Oh, and you might want to time this whole thing with your weather because if it happens to rain, the earth will be washed away and then you're shit out of luck—worse if it happens to rain after you've already trapped it inside."

"What happens then?" Isaac says.

"The line will be broken and you'll set it free. Since its one gone Dark, it will probably kill you then because you've exposed it."

"Okay, wait," I say, pushing my way past Isaac and towards Minna in the center of the room. "Once we get it inside the trap, *then* what?"

A devilish smile breaks in Minna's leathery brown face, her eyes twinkling with the same malicious tenor. "That wasn't part of the deal, either."

Isaac moves past me like wind and grabs the front of Minna's robe, viciously pulling her body toward his. He leans down into her shrinking face, "*Make* it part of the deal, or the deal's off!"

One side of Minna's nose curls into a deep-set series of wrinkles, but the grin never fades from her mouth. When Isaac feels he has made his point clearly, he slowly releases her. Minna brings her hands up and pulls her robe closed again. Her hand is shaking more now, because regardless of her attitude, she is afraid of what Isaac will do to her.

"It's not part of the deal…," she says and Isaac starts to go for her again until he hears her next words, "…because I know you won't take me with you." Her eyes slant at Isaac as she sizes him up. "So back away from me."

Isaac doesn't move.

"My house is protected by a trap, as I've told you," she goes on, "but it's held together by me, not some spell or some special earth like you have there. By *me*. Because of what I am. That isn't something that can be taught and it can't be given away like dirt in a pickle jar. What you're stuck doing is a temporary fix and has nothing to do with my willingness to screw you over and send you packing. No, I would love to join you and help you trap it, but since we all know you're not going to tell me where you really live because you're protecting this 'Genna', then you're going to have to settle for the temporary fix."

I let out a miserable, defeated breath. "You're right," I say, "you're not coming with us, but it's not because we're protecting a Praverian. We told you that Genna disappeared. We don't know where she is and we don't care. All we care about is trapping the Dark one living among us." I glance briefly at Nathan and add, looking right at Minna again, "The reason you can't go is because of Nathan. It's bad enough he's bonding you're wretched old ass to him; there's no way in this life or the next we'll let you know where he lives, too."

"Good save, baby," Isaac says to me in my mind.

I know Nathan appreciates it just by looking at the faint smile on his face.

Nathan jumps in now, "So, what do we do with it if you're not there to reap it?"

Minna shakes her head gravely. "You'll have to figure that out on your own, I'm afraid."

Isaac's hands ball into fists at his sides, but he doesn't reach out for her this time because we all believe that she's actually telling the truth.

"Isaac," I say telepathically, careful not to look away from Minna, *"Harry will know something. Let's just leave it at this, go back and tell him what she told us and hopefully he'll know what to do from there. If anything, he can reap it himself—that's what they do anyway, they hunt each other."*

He nods subtly and turns to face Nathan at his right, apparently letting him in on our conversation. I notice Nathan nod his head, too, and then all three of us turn to face Minna again.

"Do you have a phone?" Isaac says to Minna, catching me off-guard.

She raises one brow and answers, "Not one of them fancy cellular phones you probably have, but yes, I have a phone."

"Write down your number," Isaac says, "and when we trap it, we'll call you to come reap it."

Minna's smile widens as she looks at us in a sidelong glance. "What are planning to do then," she says, "lure a large group of people you *think* might include the Praverian, far away from where you live and trap it there? That's a lot to risk just to keep me from knowing where you live."

"We'll be moving away from there," Isaac says, catching me off-guard yet again, "after we get rid of the Praverian, so I guess it won't matter then, will it?"

Minna, maybe tired of the games herself, or just in dire need of getting back upstairs and drinking down that blood, shakes her head and moves toward the stairs.

"You've exhausted your welcome," she says. "I'll give you my phone number in the kitchen and then you should be on your way."

It's the best suggestion I've heard all day.

By the time we make it back into the kitchen, Minna is so out of breath and wheezing heavily that I can't help but feel bad for her, despite what kind of woman she is. She braces her hands against the wall, letting it keep her balance as she makes her way toward the hall that leads back into the living room. She nearly falls twice, but we stay back and just watch her. She doesn't want or deserve our help, but there's a great sense of relief behind that fact.

"I'll be right back," she says as she slips around the corner and out of sight.

We wait here in the kitchen, surround again by clutter and elephants, but it's better than fingers and teeth. Each of us gazes all around us, grimacing at just about everything.

"I almost feel like I'm in an episode of Hoarders," Nathan says, titling his head back to look upward at the numerous decorative plates mounted along the top of the wall and covered in two inches of dust.

But then his head falls and his fingers come up unsteadily against his forehead, the tips of them barely touching the skin.

"Are you okay, Nate?" Isaac says, looking worried.

"No. Not at all."

Nathan lowers his body into a crouch and braces his elbows on his knees, thrusting his head in his hands.

"I think I'm gonna' be sick," Nathan adds, his voice hiding a desperate, painful ambience.

Me and Isaac rush over to him, but he waves us away with one hand. His head comes up, but his eyes are squinted shut tight as though a migraine is throttling his brain.

In seconds, Minna is coming back around the corner and entering the kitchen with us, but as a somewhat healthier person. Nathan remains crouched as Isaac and I turn to see her fully. She's still the same ugly, leathery woman that will never get laid again, but Nathan's blood is already working its magic through her. She stands in front of us without shaking hands or a wheezing, raspy chest. Even her smile appears healthier, as if her personality is getting a makeover, too. But that's just a façade; nothing can make her a better person.

It makes me sick thinking about Nathan's blood coursing through her body, but it is what it is.

Minna reaches out her hand to Isaac and produces a business card with a wrecker service imprinted on one side. We peer down into it confusedly until Isaac flips it over to see Minna Abrahamsen and a ten-digit number scribbled on the blank side.

Nathan rises to his feet behind us, but I don't look back at him, hoping to detract Minna's attention from him as much as possible. But I feel his emotional pain and his combined with Isaac's over the whole situation, makes my chest ache.

"It *will* kill you," Minna says in a voice as smooth as silk, as though her lungs had never been touched by cancer. "You remember that when you're staring it in the eyes. Do the smart thing and let me reap it."

Without another word, we leave the home of Minna Abrahamsen, Nathan walking out first so he can be as far away from her as quickly as possible. When we make it onto the sidewalk snaking along against the street, Minna says from the porch, "You taste as good as I knew you would."

Nathan picks up the pace; his arms as stiff as bricks down against his sides, and his hands clenched into massive fists.

12

I TURN AROUND IN the front seat of the Jeep to see Nathan sitting behind Isaac. I don't want to sound cliché and ask him how he's feeling, or if he's alright, but I feel so bad for him that I need to do or say *something*. I just don't know what it is.

A smile breaks in his face and although I know it's forced, I just smile back and accept it.

"Y'know," I say, "if you were still dating skinny little Hannah, she could take care of Minna easily."

I remember how jealous Hannah was when we were in Portland last month. So coy and quiet and meat-deprived, but at the end of the day I knew she was as dangerous as we come, especially when it came to Nathan.

"Yeah, well since she dumped me I'll have to settle with my brother." He pats the back of Isaac's seat, grinning hugely and trying to brighten the mood even if only for himself. Nathan never was one to show much anger or be open about any of his emotions except the playful, positive ones. I don't expect him to start now.

"And I will, bro," Isaac says, glancing up in the rearview mirror at him, "as soon as we deal with this, I'm on it."

~~~

It's dark when we make it back to Hallowell and the drive home was filled mostly with conversation about how we were going to go about trapping the Praverian. Each of us had our own ideas, but not one of us could agree that any of them were likely to work. And Nathan wasn't himself really, as to be expected, so his ideas weren't as thought through as they could've been. His mind drifted more than he could contribute to the discussion. Isaac and I tried hard to distract him with jokes and banter, but usually to no avail.

But Nathan is good at keeping a smile on his face, never letting the true depth of his pain dictate his natural personality which makes Nathan, Nathan. Of course, I know that sexy bad boy smile of his that never fails to melt any woman he crosses paths with is just a mask.

I just wonder how long he'll be able to wear it.

We pull into the drive at the Mayfair house and all is quiet. Only a couple of cars are parked out front and a few lights burn in the windows of the upstairs floor.

Since I became a werewolf and Isaac officially became Alpha, life around here has been calming down now that order has been established. Isaac, despite still being the same guy I fell in love with, has certainly taken on his role as Alpha when it comes to just about everybody else. It amazes me how he became the one dominant force among all of them without having to do anything except wear the title. He never had to prove himself to anyone or put anyone in their place. All he has to do is give an order and without question or argument (except from Nathan, but that's different) that order is fulfilled.

Even Rachel, who will always hate me and would rather see me strung up and quartered than see me with Isaac, treats me with as much respect as she's capable of giving. And as always, Isaac allows her a little more slack than he would someone else, given she came from a rogue bloodline and can't help it that she's an inherent bitch.

"I'm going to shower in scalding hot water for about an hour and then I'm going to bed," Nathan says after he closes the door on the Jeep.

Isaac walks over and embraces his brother firmly. They pat each other on the back hard and then pull away. I hide the fact that seeing them like that, so close and protective of one another, chokes me up. I think of my sister, Alex, but force her face out of my mind before it affects me too much.

"Thank you," Isaac says to Nathan, "for what you did."

"Oh shut up, man," Nathan jokes, though his smile is warm with appreciation.

"I'm serious, Nate," Isaac looks at him intently. "I can never repay you for that sacrifice."

"Dude, you don't have to," Nathan says, patting Isaac against his upper arm. "You're my little brother—over me at a leadership standpoint at the moment, but that'll change—," He grins wickedly, "but it's my job to protect you and your bullheaded girlfriend." He grins over at me and I playfully rumple my nose at him.

Always the charmer. Always the first one to step up. And never one to complain about it. Those are the types you feel the worst for when something unfortunate befalls them.

Nathan says goodnight and jogs up the porch, letting the front door shut softly behind him.

"This sucks," I say, crossing my arms loosely. "Are you really going to deal with it when this is over?" I don't doubt Isaac's promise one bit, but this is my way of showing him I need to talk about it.

Isaac nods still gazing toward the porch where Nathan last stood and looking lost in thought. Finally he turns back to me and smiles weakly, pulling me toward him with my elbows cupped in his hands. "Want to go swimming?"

"Right *now*?"

"Well yeah," he says, letting his smile brighten. "It's late and no one's around. I haven't been able to get you by yourself in a while, it seems."

My indecisive expression becomes more accepting as I smile back up at him. He's right about us not having time alone lately with the whole Aramei thing going on and now this situation with Minna and the traitor.

"Let's go," I say, taking him by the hand and leading him toward the porch.

"The pond's that way," he says, stopping me.

"But I need a bathing suit."

"No you don't," he says, trying not to grin too hugely. "Really, I'm not trying to get your clothes off, babe, it's just that it'll only be the two of us and you can swim in your panties."

Most of what he said is genuine; he really is just trying to be efficient, but this is Isaac and I don't believe for a second that he has no desire to get my clothes off. I tilt my head to one side and smirk at him. "So you *don't* want to just get me naked then?" I pretend to be offended and turn away with my arms still crossed.

"Nah, I'm good," he says, turning my game around on me.

My head jerks around and my mouth falls open with a spat of air. Isaac's impish grin widens and he takes off running towards the woods leading to the pond behind the house.

I scream out after him and then take off running, too, thankful that the path through the woods is wide and clear so I'm not having to weave my way through tree limbs and around fall-breaking rocks. And in under a minute, I make it to the bank of the pond where Isaac is waiting for me, standing on the end of an old, weathered wooden dock looking out over the dark water. I walk calmly up behind him and he turns at the waist to see me.

"It's warm enough," he says now bending over and brushing his hand through the water. He leans back up and takes off his boots, kicking them gently aside on the dock.

I come up closer and run my hands up his back and over his shoulders until he turns around to face me fully. I press my body into his, letting my fingertips dance on the sides of his neck as I take him into a ravenous kiss. He kisses me back with the same passion and then pulls away, looking down into my eyes.

I grin deviously and shove him off the dock and into the water.

When he hits the water a gush sprays on me soaking my jeans. I laugh hysterically, feeling my chest shrink as though terrified he's going to leap right out and catch me.

"If you weren't so beautiful," Isaac says as he bobs in the water, "it would be over for you, babe."

I kick off my shoes and peel off my wet jeans, setting them in a sloppy pile next to his boots and then sit down on the edge of the dock. I dip my toes in cautiously at first and then when I feel it really is warm enough, my legs slip into the water up to just below my knees. Isaac swims the few feet over to me and moves in-between my legs, resting his arms on my thighs. He leans his head over an inch and I feel his lips gently brush the skin just above my knee and tiny tremors burn inside my stomach.

His hands move up my thighs and rest on my hips. And then he just looks up at me thoughtfully.

"I know the best way to do this," he says and I'm not sure what he's talking about at first, so I just let him talk. "There's only one place outside I know of that everyone inside that house walks."

I nod slowly, understanding, and trying to think about what that one place could be before he tells me, while at the same time combing his wet hair away from his face with my fingers.

"The driveway," he says.

Chewing on my bottom lip in thought, I look up and across the water at the pitch dark woods that surrounds us.

"Yeah," I say, "we can set the trap in the driveway and just tell Harry where it's at so he doesn't stumble into it." I look back down into Isaac's eyes. "But what about the cars? Minna said there can be no manmade objects in the trap."

Isaac contemplates it for a moment and then says, "Maybe it's time for a new driveway."

"What?"

He nods to himself as if still coming up with all of the details as we speak. "Yeah, I can say that in addition to repairing the basement wall that we're having pavement laid in the driveway, too."

"That could work," I say, though I'm really not sure how well.

"So, are you actually going to pay to have the basement redone and the driveway paved?"

"The basement, yes—reinforced steel, like a friggin' bomb shelter to keep *someone* I know inside once a month," he says, squeezing my hips gently, "but not the driveway."

"Where do you get the money for all this stuff anyway," I say, running my fingers through his wet hair. "The only one around here that actually works is Nathan and I know his salary at Finch's isn't enough to pay for an FJ Cruiser."

"What?" Isaac says with a grin and I feel his fingers pinch my hips. "Are you with me for my money?"

I wrap my legs around his upper chest and squeeze really hard. Isaac fastens his hands firmly around my hips and pulls me off the dock and into the water. My body slides down against his until we're face to face, his hands holding me at the center of my back. I wrap my legs around his waist underneath the water.

Isaac kisses me once. "Being a six hundred year old Alpha has its perks," he says. "I guess you can call us a bunch of spoiled royal sons living off daddy's money."

"I wouldn't call you that." I press my lips softly to his once in return. "Your life is different and those human stereotypes really don't apply."

"I guess so," he says.

"You said 'sons'—what about your sisters?"

He pushes farther away from the dock, easily keeping us both afloat.

"We give them money," he says, "because we take care of the girls. Technically, they're not allowed to take care of themselves—well, financially anyway."

My eyebrows crumple with perplexity. "Seriously? That's kind of messed up."

Isaac nods and looks away from my eyes. We're drifting farther and farther away from the bank and my mound of clothes is getting smaller on the dock. I can just barely see a light shining through the trees off in the distance from inside the house.

"I agree with you," Isaac says, though he seems lost in thought. "But hopefully that will change soon. Hopefully a lot of things about our way of life will change." The last of his words seem to drift away into the warm night air.

"How so?" I don't like the feeling I'm getting from him. For a second I think of opening my mind and listening to his thoughts which are unreadable all over his face, but I decide against it. If it's something he wants me to know then I want him to tell me on his own time.

Isaac breaks free from those deep thoughts and smiles in at me. He kisses me on the nose. "Being a twenty-year old Alpha also has its perks."

I curl my fingers around the soaked fabric of his t-shirt and unpeel it from his body. He lifts his arms and slips it the rest of the way off, letting it fall into the water. Cradling the sides of his neck in my hands, I pull him towards me, instantly feeling the heat of his bare chest through my shirt. "We're alone out here, you know." His breath is warm and sweet on my lips and I shut my eyes softly, intoxicated by his closeness.

"But for how long?" I whisper against his mouth.

He teases my bottom lip with his tongue until I fold and kiss him hungrily, digging my fingers into his hair. The waist of his jeans is thick with water, scratching against my inner thighs. I wish he would just take them off.

He moans against my mouth, kissing me savagely. His fingers press aggressively into my back and my insides shudder.

And then *splash!*

I yelp, jerking around in Isaac's grasp to see behind us.

Two more bodies leap off the edge of the dock and barrel into the water afterwards.

The first head that emerges, bobbing at the top of the water is white-blond, short and still kind of spiky despite being soaked with pond water.

"Zia!" I yell out, turning around so that my back is pressed into Isaac's hard chest, "you scared the *crap* out of me!"

"That was the point!" she yells back as she begins to swim closer. "Yeah, so if you two were gettin' busy aquatic-style, please do us all a favor and stop!"

"Jesus, Zia," I laugh, "you are so frickin' sick!"

"I know," she says, "I can't help it."

When she's in retaliation distance, I thrust my hand on the surface of the water towards her, sending a gush of water in her face. Seconds later, we're in a splashing war and I can't tell if Isaac has joined in too, or if he's swimming backward and away from us. Our screams resonate across the pond, until suddenly I'm pulled under. Water is flooding my nose and my mouth as I didn't have enough warning to prevent it. I kick my legs free from Zia's hands and swim around her, emerging at her back.

"Oh, you bitch!" Zia screams just before her head goes under, forced down by both of my hands.

Knowing she'll get me back in worse ways than I can imagine, I swim away from her fast, looking for Isaac who is just a few feet to my right. I swim in behind him, hiding at his back for protection, all the while laughing hysterically.

"Zia," Camilla says from the water in her small voice, "maybe we should leave my brother and Adria alone."

"No way," Zia says. "Camilla, you need to grow a pair!" She swims toward me and I shriek as she gets closer, holding onto Isaac for dear life. My arms are tight around his neck and my legs straddle his waist. Isaac may not have wanted any part of this war, but he doesn't have much of a choice now because there's no way I'm letting go.

If Zia wants me she has to go through him.

The third person, whose identity I'm only now realizing, swims in behind Camilla and cackles with laughter. I think I'm more surprised that Zia is out here with the likes of Cecilia than I am about Cecilia still being here since we left her with Camilla earlier before we set out for Providence.

Cecilia bobs next to Camilla with her trademark crazy grin that always shows her full set of teeth. Her plain-Jane brown hair, short and spiky like Zia's, is plastered to her head making her look like a boy in the darkness. "I don't know why you didn't invite me over here sooner," Cecilia says to me. "I've never met cooler people—well, I did know this girl once who had a baby skunk for a pet—Oh! And I did meet this guy when I lived in New Hampshire whose life goal was to be a UFC fighter, and my God that was once serious piece of eye candy—." She stops abruptly and puts her hand vertically against her mouth as if to whisper and says, "He flipped me all kinds of ways one night," and my face sort of freezes right there. "But really—I love it over here!"

Same old Cecilia. Eccentric and easily entertained, but never lacking the ability to stump a person in just a few sentences.

I hear Isaac cough a small laugh and feel his hand slip between my thighs underneath the water. My body locks up and I tighten my legs around his waist from behind; my way of warning him that he better not go there right now. But something tells me by the way he's turning his chin to see me with such a devilish grin at the corners of his lips that I'm going to have to try harder than that.

"You better not," I warn him telepathically. I fail miserably at sounding serious and it probably isn't helping that I can't stop smiling, either. *"I swear it, Isaac. I won't give you any for a week."*

His grin just gets bigger. *"Really?"* he says and his hand easily wedges itself in-between my crushing thigh and his waist. *"A whole week you say?"* he taunts.

I gasp as his fingers move closer and I try to tighten my legs around him even more intensely.

"You better stop!" My face feels like it's on fire. *"You are so cruel!"*

"Girl, you have some 'splainin to do," Zia says, pulling me out of my little bubble with Isaac and his magic fingers.

"Huh—what do you mean?" I'm paranoid she knows what's going on with me and Isaac and my face just gets hotter.

"Why you didn't invite Cecilia sooner," she says and relief washes over me.

Zia is starting to calm down, now floating on the top of the water rather than forcing her way violently through it to get to me. Maybe she has given up because of my strategically placed Isaac wall.

I look over at Cecilia, wiping the dirty water from my eyes, which only makes them burn a little more because my hand is also wet. And my nostrils are burning. I think about Cecilia's earlier comment and want to reply with: "But I didn't invite you over here at all." I settle with:

"Well, it wasn't ever really my place to invite you."

Isaac says, "This is more your home than it is anyone's."

I look down, trying to conceal the blush in my face, but also the awkwardness. I hope Zia and Camilla don't take offense to his words.

"So true," Camilla says, beaming, her pretty oval face glistening in the moonlight from the water dripping over her plump cheeks. Her hair, naturally dark brown like Isaac's, looks black when it's wet.

I'm still trying to toil my way through Zia's unexpected acceptance of Cecilia. It wasn't that long ago she couldn't stand the girl. Something extraordinary must've happened while we were in Providence. I don't know, like maybe Cecilia revealed that she was related to Dax Riggs—Zia's man-crush underground singer from about a dozen different bands—or, maybe Cecilia offered Zia a friendship in the form of money with any number that has a lot of zeros behind it.

I can't think of anything else that might cause Zia's change of heart.

Isaac slips his fingers under the edge of my panties and I squeal. Thankfully, he's just messing with my head and isn't actually going to touch me where he shouldn't with others around. At least I hope like hell he doesn't plan to. Regardless, I don't think I can contain myself much longer.

"You didn't answer my question," Isaac says in my mind, slowly moving his fingers closer. *"Are you* sure *you'll hold out on me for an entire week?"* I want to kiss that confident grin off his lips, but I can't move any part of my body now but my eyes.

Finally, Isaac moves his hand away, pulls me around in front of him, my legs still straddling his waist, and crushes his mouth against mine.

"Ahhh!" Zia yells out. "Come *on*! I'm not into porn!"

Isaac breaks the kiss and says without taking his eyes off mine, "I guess I'll just have to wait a week."

He won this battle a long time ago and knows it.

I lean in and gently tug on his bottom lip with my teeth and then kiss it softly.

I don't have to say a word.

We leave Zia, Camilla and Cecilia in the pond and can't seem to get to his room fast enough.

13

ISAAC HAS ME AT Aramei's cabin before the sun comes up the next morning. On this day, there are fewer guards outside; at least those in plain sight anyway. Raul is one of them, standing outside at the front of the cabin with a sword sheathed at his hip. I think he's Trajan's number one guard because he's the only one I've seen consistently since the first time I laid eyes on Aramei months ago.

"Another day of volunteer work," Raul says as we approach the front porch.

The early morning sky is borderline dark. A faint blue hue bathes the forest in just enough soft light that I can see everything clearly but it makes me feel like I should still be in bed.

"Unfortunately," Isaac answers in a sullen tone. He pats Raul's shoulder with one hand.

I leave them to their usual conversations, kissing Isaac once on the lips and slipping inside the cabin. It looks exactly the same as it does every day except that just like the guards, there are fewer servants working on the bottom floor than normal. Eva, Aramei's chief caregiver, stands on the top floor overlooking the bottom and she smiles down at me.

As I make my way up the stairs, I realize how relieved I am to be with Aramei again. The more that I see her, the more I sometimes feel like I never want to leave and although I find that strange and maybe even unhealthy, I don't care to seek the answers why. Aramei is special to me. I think maybe she always has been since the moment I met her. Being connected to her like this has only enhanced my feelings for her and every day it drives this insatiable need to help her and maybe to protect her.

I don't know, but I truly feel like our connection means more than helping Trajan to know what's going on inside her mind. I feel like I'm here for Aramei and not Trajan and that he really has nothing to do with it. And the more I think about this the more I feel like I want to lie to him, keep him out of my time with her entirely. Because after all, I think if Aramei were trying to communicate with him, it would *be* him she has called out to. She would have said his name and not mine.

"Good to see you, Milady." Eva bows and I put up my hand and shake my head.

"You're really gonna have to stop doing that," I say. It seems I have to remind her of this every time I come here, but she is a slave to habit.

She nods her apology, her soft hands folded together in front of her laying against the black sheer fabric of her gown.

"She's awake," I say walking over to Aramei sitting on the edge of her immaculate bed. I lean over her and comb my fingers through her light-colored hair, brushing it back behind her ears and I look across at Eva. "Has she seemed any different since yesterday?"

"Yes," Eva says walking up to join us, "she has appeared more anxious than usual. Just an hour ago she could only stare off at the window overlooking the driveway. I could be wrong, but it seems as though she could sense that you were on your way."

I smile at Eva, glad to hear this news and then I kneel in front of Aramei so that I can be more at level with her eyes. The lantern on the bedside table casts a soft orange-yellow glow on one side of her face, accentuating her long, thick eyelashes and her angelic, unblemished white skin. Her legs are bare and I reach up and gently pull the ends of her sheer white gown down from being pushed near her thighs, and smooth the fabric over her knees. Her restful hands lay in her lap, sinking slowly in-between her legs in the slope of the thin material. As always, she smells wonderful, like vanilla and jasmine oils that have been rubbed into her skin.

I peer deeply into Aramei's placid green eyes, searching for some sign of conscious life.

"How does she eat?" I say to Eva, but not looking away from Aramei. I don't want to miss anything, having learned that she comes and goes so sporadically that the blink-of-an-eye saying fully applies to her.

"She doesn't."

I do look over this time. "*Never*?" I say, unable to grasp the absurdity of it. "I know she's immortal, but I guess…," I look back at Aramei and rise to my feet, "…I don't know, I guess I just assumed that she at least ate, even if you had to feed her."

I cross my arms and turn to face Eva fully. "Then again, it makes perfect sense, too."

Eva nods. "She will not die of starvation," she says. "Trajan's blood provides her body with all of the nutrients that it needs. She hasn't eaten in over one hundred fifty years."

Astounded, I can't do anything but shake my head over and over, staring downward toward the floor.

I lift my eyes to Eva and say, "Would you mind bringing me some fruit?"

Eva looks at me curiously. "Of course," she says and heads for the stairs.

"Thanks."

Eva disappears from the top floor and I turn back to Aramei who still has yet to move. It always makes me anxious to see her sitting like this for long periods of time seemingly without twitching a muscle. It's like my own body starts to feel stiff and unhealthy just looking at her. I think about blood clots and poor circulation and all kinds of conditions caused by an inactive body. I know Aramei will never die or even be affected by any of those things, but it doesn't keep me from feeling uncomfortable by it just the same.

I stand beside her, brushing the silkiness of her hair between my fingers and then I take a chance and position one hand underneath her arm, trying to coax her statuesque body into a stand. But she doesn't move, so I move around and in front of her again and bend over, taking one of her legs into the cradle of my hands. Back and forth I move her leg, bending it at the knee as if I'm performing her physical therapy. But she still doesn't budge, or show any signs of comprehension.

Eva comes back upstairs with a small glass bowl of strawberries. She walks over to me and holds the bowl out to me. I take one strawberry off the top and carefully dig my fingernails into the juicy top to pinch away the leafy green stem.

"You mean to try feeding her?" Eva says curiously.

"I'm going to try," I say, though I don't feel any confidence that it'll produce any results. I kneel in front of Aramei once more and squeeze the fruit so that a little of its juice comes to the surface. I place it to her lips and move it across her bottom lip slowly, wetting the sensitive skin there with the sweet juice.

After a few more times of doing this, and I admit, taking a tiny bite for myself, Aramei's pale green eyes shift so subtly that for a moment I do think I was only seeing things. I try with the strawberry again, but Aramei never changes, so I pop it in my mouth and sigh as I swallow it down.

"Kind of dumb," I say looking over at Eva standing at the foot of the bed. "I thought maybe something her body used to be accustomed to before she lost her mind, might help her to wake up a little."

"That is not at all dumb," Eva says with a smile in her voice.

I go to my feet, already feeling defeated and thinking this day is going to turn out like yesterday, but then I sense movement behind me. Before I turn around I check Eva's face and sure enough she's staring behind me at Aramei as though my luck has finally changed. I turn around to see Aramei looking up at me. Her almond-shaped eyes blink twice and a shiver runs through my back. Without turning away from her, I reach around behind me for the bowl of strawberries in Eva's hands and fumble another one into my fingers. I kneel in front of Aramei again, pinching the stem off at the same time. Her head and eyes actually follow me, but I feel like the strawberry has nothing to do with her attention. I want to turn and look at Eva so that she can see the shock and relief in my expression, but I'm afraid to take my eyes off Aramei for one second. I bring the strawberry up to her lips and just before it touches them, Aramei stuns me and Eva both, "Release me from his prison," she says and I can't breathe.

And then the life in her face grows cold once more.

When the stun of her bizarre words allows me to move my head, I turn brashly to look up at Eva, searching her face for answers, but I can see that she won't have them.

Back and forth I look at each of them, finally letting my desperate gaze fall upon Eva who is the only one of the two I can get anything at all from. My lips are slightly parted, eyes slanted and focused.

"What *was* that?" I finally say. "*His* prison?" I don't think I've ever been so perplexed.

Eva's face softens. "Delusions," she says. "A Blood Bond, as you know causes the mind to experience things that are not real. Milady Aramei has been speaking these strange things for two hundred years."

Something Trajan said to me the day he came for me courses through my mind: *"...trapped in a world of her own, some strange world inside her mind that I've never been able to comprehend...,"* and I grow more perplexed than ever. But what Eva says about this makes perfect sense. And the only thing I've seen inside her head are the memories of her past and there is nothing strange about them.

"Can you leave me alone with her?" I say gently.

"Yes," Eva says and bows. She places the bowl of strawberries on the table next to the balcony and leaves us without another word.

I crawl into the bed and nuzzle next to Aramei facing her and I brush the softness of her cheek with the backs of my fingers. Her eyes are open and before long I realize that she's staring at me. She knows that I'm here. And I know now that the key to opening her mind is that we have to be alone together. But why? Is what she has to tell me a secret? Is she afraid even of Eva who has watched over her for so long? It could be anything, but no matter what it is I'm determined to unravel it.

"I'm here," I whisper to her, our faces mere inches from one another. "I need to see what you see...please let in."

Aramei's hand comes up and slowly her fingers rest on my lips. I don't freeze up this time, but I do remain quiet and still.

"Close your eyes," she says so softly that it could lull me to sleep if I let it.

I close my eyes, feeling the smoothness of her fingertips on the edges of my lips.

And then the whirlwind of Time and Space takes me up again, hurling me through the ages and into the life of a young woman in Serbia.

Balkan Mountains – Eastern Serbia – Winter 1761

The wolves are bolder in the winter. They patrol the thickly snow-covered mountains like kings, scavenging the brave wildlife that dares to tread out in the open hunting for a scarce meal. But the wolves have also been hunted by humans for generations for fear they are the beasts eating their cattle. In some cases, this is true, but the real truth is that the locals fear that believing in the Black Beasts will *make* them real, so they blame it on a creature less frightening as if this will satisfy their hearts. The people of this small village and all of the villages that scatter the mountains go out early in the morning, trudge through the heavy snow wearing the furs of the wolves they killed the winter before and they hunt them down, year after year. But the cattle are never spared, no matter how many gray wolves are eradicated. And the horses and the sheep; they are being killed, too. Savagely. Sometimes there is nothing left, not even the bones, but most of the locals refuse to bring back the Old Myths, the stories their ancestors told of the Black Beasts that stand on two legs and are taller than any man.

Secretly, each of them believes the Old Myths. All of them grow up from children knowing that there are things in the vast Balkan Mountains far worse than anything man has ever known. They have feared the beasts for a thousand years, but superstition keeps them from admitting it openly.

On this frigid winter day, Aramei wakes to the sound of her sister's scream piercing the outside air. Aramei jerks up and shakes the stun from her mind, rushing out of her tiny makeshift bedroom and out the front door of her cottage. Still in her nightgown and with bare feet, she stands in front of the rickety wooden door with the snow up to her ankles. In seconds, her feet are stinging from the cold. She rushes back inside and thrusts her feet down into her father's boots and then yanks her father's thick coat from the back of his chair, letting it swallow her small form.

Filipa screams out again and Aramei bursts back through the doorway and runs out into the snow, the oversized boots loose on her tiny feet.

"Father!" Filipa shrieks from somewhere behind the house. "Father! It's Vela! The wolves got Vela!"

As Aramei comes around the corner of the house she spots a trail of dark red staining the bright white snow and coming from the stables. Her steps pick up, as much as the big boots and the weight of the snow swallowing her feet inside of them will allow.

"Where's Vela?" Aramei shouts as she enters the barn.

Filipa sits crouched over the dead horse, a pool of thick warm blood pools on the ground where the horse's lower half used to be. Steam rises from the blood and entrails in the bitter cold, making the sight that much more haunting.

"Oh, no, Vela...," Aramei runs over, nearly tripping in the boots and she falls to her knees beside Filipa and the horse's corpse. "Oh, girl," she says, stroking the horse's stiff snout; its eyes are glazed over, the tongue lolled out of its mouth. But Aramei can only be saddened by the sight and never sickened or afraid. She doesn't even notice that her father's coat is covered in the horse's blood.

"Look at her!" Filipa rips out the words angrily, pointing to the back end of the horse. "There's nothing *left*! What kind of wolf could do *that*?" Tears are streaming from Filipa's eyes, but they are tears of anger.

Aramei, still gazing down into the horse's black, lifeless eyes says, "Viktor told me about the black wolves deeper in the mountains. They are bigger than the gray wolves that father hunts every winter. I think only they could have done this."

"Black wolves?" Filipa says, rising to her feet and gazing down at her sister. "Don't you dare mention this to Father. You mean the Black Beasts! Who is this Viktor? Why have you been sneaking off with him this many months?" Filipa is growing angry, but more-so worried for Aramei. She crosses her arms over her chest and glares down at her disapprovingly.

Aramei stands and faces Filipa, her bloody hands resting helplessly at her sides. She had told Filipa that Viktor went back to his homeland last fall and this was true as far as she knew, but it didn't stop Viktor from visiting Aramei at least once a month.

The last time he had come to her village was just days ago. He came to warn her about the 'black wolves'.

"Please don't tell Father," Aramei says in a soft, pleading voice. "I will tell you everything if you give me your word you will keep it to yourself."

Filipa's green eyes widen with disbelief. Aramei has never kept secrets from her sister until this stranger, Viktor, came along and Aramei knows that it will be hard to finally tell Filipa the truth.

Just then, their father comes stumbling into the barn, still dressed in his long-pants and thick socks that he always sleeps in to keep warm. Aramei and Filipa move away from the corpse and stand side by side, huddled together to share their body heat. Their father looks at the horse first and then makes note of his coat and boots which Aramei is wearing. He shakes his heavily-bearded head at her, but doesn't say anything about it.

He moves toward the horse, examining the amount of blood and damage.

"Must've been an entire pack," he says and then his dark eyes wander around the rest of the barn to see that their cow and three goats have been left untouched. "Did you see it?"

"No, Father," Filipa says.

He looks to Aramei and she shakes her head.

"Get inside," he demands, pointing towards the cottage, "And Aramei, please make use of your own clothing."

"Yes, Father."

The sisters scurry out of the barn and back inside their warm cottage where a fireplace burns heavily in the front room. After putting her father's coat and boots back where she took them, he comes in after her, dresses for the weather and heads out with six other men from the village, equipped with rifles and axes, to hunt the wolves.

Filipa watches her father from the window until his dark form contrasted against the snow disappears over the top of the hill leading deeper into the valley. She wastes no time and storms over to Aramei, grabbing her vigorously by the elbow.

"Who is Viktor to you?" she lashes out. "Have you given yourself to him?"

"No!" Aramei says, offended by her sister's accusations. But then her face softens as she can't hold an angry emotion for more than a few seconds at most. She reaches out takes Filipa's hands. "He is just a man," she says. "He has been wonderful company and has taught me things that I would never have learned here."

Filipa moves back slowly so that Aramei's hands fall away and she looks upon her warily. "Men do not befriend young women just to teach them things unless it is how to properly lie on your back when he needs to pleasure himself." She sneers and then says, "What kind of things did he teach you?"

Aramei ignores Filipa's cruel ridicule altogether. "I know how to live in the wild if I ever need to," she says. "He taught me to trap small game and to hunt with a bow. What woman in this village do you know who has ever held a bow, much less become good at using one?" She points toward the wall to indicate the village women as a whole and adds, "Sweet bread. And laundry. And planting. And of course, child-bearing—as you so eloquently described it. That's the most any woman from here will ever know, Filipa."

Filipa snarls. "Why would you need to know how to use a bow?" she snaps. "And why would you ever need to know how to live in the wild? Do you plan to run away with this stranger and live in the wild with him?"

"Oh, Filipa. Sissa. I'm not a child anymore." Aramei walks toward the window and peers out. "You have cared for me all of my life, even before Mother died, you were always there for me." She turns around at the waist to see Filipa. "But you can't be my mother forever."

Filipa inhales a deep, aggravated breath and combs her hair away from her shoulders. But she avoids this particular subject and moves quickly onto the next.

"Tell me what this man told you," she says in a calm, stern voice. "What is this about the black wolves in the mountains?"

Aramei's petite shoulders rise and fall as she stands peering out at the vast blanket of white covering the landscape. She turns fully around to face Filipa, "Maybe the black wolves that Viktor spoke of and the Black Beasts of legend are one in the same; I do not know, but Viktor has told me that they are growing in numbers. And that they are different from the gray wolves we see on the mountains."

Filipa tilts her head to one side, looking upon Aramei curiously. "Yes," she says, "different as in more savage, but not because they are these...beasts. You would do better not to believe such things, too."

Aramei snaps around, her arms still crossed with her delicate fingers peeking over the bend of the elbows. "Why, Filipa?" she says. Her voice is laced with discontent, which stuns Filipa momentarily. "Because *they* fear them?" She makes a slashing motion with her hand out in front of her. "When are you going to start thinking for yourself?"

Aramei turns her back on her sister, partially fed up with the prospect of being just like everybody else, but also it was hard for her to be so firm towards Filipa, to speak her mind for once.

"Are you saying you believe what this man tells you?" Filipa has lowered her tone and seems to be attempting to be more understanding towards Aramei. She moves behind her, placing her hands gently on her shoulders.

Aramei turns to face her. "Viktor did not tell me anything of the Black Beasts, Filipa...I believe in them on my own. I always have, since I was a little girl and I...."

Aramei looks away from Filipa's engaged eyes, seeming afraid or ashamed for whatever she was about to say.

"What is it, Aramei? Tell me."

Aramei raises her soft green eyes to Filipa once more, "…I do not believe that Mother died of the fever."

Filipa's chin draws back in a suspicious motion. "What are you saying?"

Aramei walks away, leaving Filipa standing by the window. She paces the room once and then stops, staring down at the clay vase their mother had made two years before she died. She remembers the vision of her face, staring up at her from the bed the day she told Aramei a dark secret. She remembers how her mother clutched Aramei's dress tight in her hands as she leaned over her sweating body amid the soaked bed covers. Her skin was pale gray and sickly, her green eyes tired and fringed in red, inflamed by the infection coursing through her body.

"I was attacked by a beast," her mother said, her voice straining and raspy and desperate; sweat glistened on her face like hot wax. *"You must kill me, my dear child! You must —."*

Aramei wipes away a tear with the tip of her finger.

"Sissa," Filipa says in her most loving voice. "*Please*…."

"I believe Mother was killed by one of them," Aramei says. "I was only ten then and thought that the fever was only poisoning her mind, that it was making her say things." She turns around. "But I believe in my heart that she was telling the truth."

Filipa stands there, stunned by Aramei's admission. For a long moment she can't seem to say anything, but Aramei soon realizes that Filipa doesn't believe her. Or, also afraid of the superstitions, she doesn't *want* to believe her.

"I want you to stay away from this man," Filipa says with a bit more care than before. "I beg of you. He is turning you into someone I do not know."

Aramei, not wanting to create a divide between her and her sister, nods once to acknowledge Filipa.

But soon after, it would be Viktor himself who would cause Aramei to stay away from him.

14

JUST DAYS AFTER THE savage death of Vela, Aramei, bundled in her heaviest winter clothes and boots, sets out alone to meet Viktor in the forest. Last night he came to her window and asked that she meet him at sunrise past the eastern border of the valley that merges with the woods.

He told her to come alone.

She had spent many days with him alone and had grown to enjoy his company and the many things he was so willing to teach her. She hopes that on this day he will teach her more, maybe of hunting the black wolves that Viktor spoke of, those that keep killing the village's livestock, the ones that killed her horse and left nothing but half of the carcass behind.

Aramei tucks her knife down into the front of her coat where it's hidden well behind the thick fabric. Although she trusts Viktor and has no reason not to, she has always at least carried her knife along. It gives her a sense of security even if she's fully aware that he could easily overpower her if he wanted to.

She ignores the fact that she has any reason to carry a knife around him at all, makes herself believe it's just precautionary when truly her heart knows something her mind isn't telling her.

She slips out before Filipa wakes up, but that was always an easy thing to do because Filipa had always been a heavy sleeper and never likes to get out of bed early if she can help it.

Thirty minutes of walking in the frigid winter air, Aramei sees Viktor's figure approaching her in the distance. She raises her gloved hand to wave at him and her smile brightens. She pulls her woven hat tighter around the edges of her face, trying to warm her ears.

"You came," Viktor says, but he's not smiling back. Nothing about his face suggests that their meeting will be like any of the others and instinctively Aramei's hand disappears underneath her coat. She looks all around her without moving her head, wondering what's caused him to appear so alarmed.

He moves to stand in front of her, the thickly-packed snow crunching under his leather boots.

"You must leave these mountains," he says with a forceful urgency. "You cannot stay here."

Aramei shakes her head, perplexed by not only his demeanor, but now his words as well.

She takes one step backwards, her eyes darting all around every which way.

"Why, Viktor? Why do you say these things?"

He steps toward her, closing that one-foot she just created, but she doesn't move. "Because I must," he says. "Come with me. You will be safe under my protection."

"No...," she shakes her head once more, taking yet another step back, her face hardened by doubt. "I cannot just leave my family, I—"

"Milady, you have to." He reaches out and takes a hold of her shoulders and she freezes with fear. "Please trust in me."

Aramei jerks her body back, forcing his hands away from her and she takes two steps to the left.

"You expect me to leave my father and my sister to go somewhere with you because it's not safe for me here?" she says, her small voice rising with every syllable. "Yet you won't tell me why. And worse, you would want me to leave my family *behind*?"

She's put off by the very thought of it, were it not for that she might've actually listened to him.

Viktor lets out a deep, heavy breath and brings his bare hands up in front of him, balling them into fists. But then he seems to think better of what appeared to Aramei as some kind of impending outburst, and he lets his fingers unfold from his palms. The soft lines around his mouth are deepened only briefly, accentuated by the scruff of his facial hair. He has grown a long, dark goatee since the summer and he wears it braided now; a heavy weave of hair that winds down to the top of his chest. His handsome green eyes stare at her under dark brown eyebrows and a matching frame of hair that falls around his face and drapes his broad shoulders.

"A war draws closer to this valley every day," he says, softening his hardened eyes, but not his voice. "I do not care about any soul in these villages except for yours and I mean to save it."

"But it is my soul to save," she says, her eyebrows hardening. "What war, Viktor? The Turks? Russia? Who could be invading *now*?"

Viktor reaches out a hand, but pulls away when he sees that she quietly detracts from it.

"This is a war of a different kind," he says. "Between my people and those who were once my kin."

Aramei senses that there is something hidden in his words, but it's too vague to give her any reason to probe further. She buries her hands inside the sleeves of her long coat, each hand shoved in the opposite sleeve, and tightens her arms over her chest to shut out the freezing air.

"Aramei, *listen* to me," his voice grows intolerant and it only makes her more leery of him. "If you stay here you will die. I can help you...you have to leave with me."

"Not without my family!" she shouts; a wisp of visible breath spats from her lips like a puff of smoke. "Why do I feel like you are lying to me? Why can you not understand that my family is more important to me than my own life?" Her hands break free from her sleeves and she motions them out in front of her, her once gentle face now misshapen by confusion and disappointment. "And if you cared for me at all...Viktor, you would not ask me to leave them."

Viktor's face falls underneath his winter scruff, the tense look in his eyes vanquished by something deeper. He takes a deep breath and suddenly kneels in front of her in the snow; one knee is bent upward, the other lying pressed against the ground. He reaches out his arms to her in a desperate, pleading display, "I beg of you to come with me...because...I have fallen in love with you, Aramei of the Valley, and because of who I am, your family will never approve of our joining."

Aramei's eyes grow wide. Her breath is caught in her chest and she feels like she's lost control of her thoughts suddenly. Absently, she shakes her head over and over as if to deny his admission on her ears.

"Love?" she says, unbelieving. "No...Viktor, I never meant...I never meant to lead you to love me. Forgive me, please, for it was not my intention. I take full blame. Forgive me." Her backward steps become more numerous and her fears more profuse. She had never even remotely contemplated love with Viktor. She never visualized the two of them sharing more than company and friendship. Aramei had only ever wanted to become something more than a wife of the valley, she wanted to see the world and her dreams had only ever been occupied by travel and experience, but she rarely had time to dream of love.

Her idea of love was freedom.

"I'm sorry," she says again and goes to leave, barely turning her back to him because there's still this strange feeling scratching away at the back of her mind, warning her that she isn't safe, that even though he has professed his love for her, that it is not without danger.

Viktor, unable to retain his dominant emotions, reaches out quickly and grabs her by the back of her coat. She gasps and her heart solidifies like metal inside her chest; for a moment it refuses to beat. Her green eyes are wide with fear as she looks up into his angry face horribly warped by rejection.

Aramei looks down quickly at his hand as it makes its way to her wrist, his strong fingers clutched around her tiny bone with enough force to cause her pain. She tries to jerk her hand away, but his grip is like iron and she can't move it.

"You're hurting me!" she cries out. "Let go!"

Viktor thrusts her body forward and their chests slam against one another. She can feel the heat of his breath all over her face, making it feel like a layer of sweat has formed over the surface of her skin. "You *refuse* me?" he spats with venom in his voice. Her heart slams against her ribcage, the blood shooting through her veins like scalding hot water. Her lungs would be heaving rapidly if she could pull her chest away from his, but the weight of him restricts them, as if she were pinned to the ground with a large rock on her chest.

"I said let go!" She screams out, and half a second later her free hand comes up against his face, her fingernails digging into the skin under his eyes and along his cheekbones, but it doesn't seem to faze him.

A deep growl reverberates through his body and he stares down into her tear-streaked face as a man she has never met, one that had never been kind to her. One she had mistakenly grown to revere. This is a man with a darker soul, one who she never would've befriended if she knew the true depths of his real self. She struggles in his grasp like a butterfly whose wings are trapped between his powerful fingers. Tears barrel from her eyes and her heart beats so fast now that she briefly pictures it exploding. Is that what he wants? Would Viktor rather see her dead than to see her run away from him?

The thought intensifies her fears just when she thought she couldn't be more afraid.

In a split second, Aramei, without having any sense of plan, instinctively thrusts her free hand into her coat and fumbles for the hilt of her knife. Once she has it, her hand comes out of the confines of the thick fabric and the glint of the silver blade is distinct enough that it catches Viktor off-guard. And in only a half a second more when he pulls away from her, Aramei plunges the blade right into his chest. She screams out as the pain of realization devours her, as she sees what she has done, what she knew she had to do.

Viktor clutches his hands over the wound and the bloody knife tumbles into the snow.

Aramei stumbles backward and falls, but she can't stop looking at him, peering deeply into his eyes as if frighteningly mesmerized by them in their final moments of life. She tries to look away but it's as if Death himself is forcing her to look, punishing her by refusing her any reprieve.

Viktor falls to his knees and looks down at his hands in shock and disbelief. Blood pours out of the wound and oozes in-between his fingers; a pool of red soaks up in the snow as his body begins to lean forward. "Why?!" Aramei screams out at him. "Why would you make me do this?" She nearly chokes on her own tears.

Viktor's face begins to emit heat, his skin becoming inflamed and red. The veins in his neck appear on the surface, hard and bulging and moving like worms underneath the surface of the skin. But under his eyes and around his cheeks and temples, tiny veins appear that are black. Aramei's breath catches, sucking in the frigid air, burning her throat and her lungs. Her bloody gloved-hand comes up over her mouth and nose, her wide eyes peering over the edge of her index finger. She knows this is her chance to run away, that she's wounded him enough that she can go back to the safety of her family, but the sight before her shatters her will and grounds her boots to the snow. Viktor's eyes have become solid black pools. He struggles to breathe; his throat seizing rapidly at the air almost as if the air is poison and he's choking on it. His bloodied hand still presses abrasively against his chest.

And suddenly, as if his whole body has turned to stone, every muscle ceases to move and his expression locks in a horrific, painful display. He falls face forward into the snow and doesn't move again.

Aramei's hands now press firmly against her stomach, her fingers grasp at one another in a restless, chaotic motion. Her eyes have remained unblinking the past many seconds and are starting to burn. Finally gaining some sense of dire awareness, her flight-response kicks in again. She rips away running through the snow-covered forest, tripping many times over hidden debris in the forest bed before finding her way to the edge of the valley. She has run for so long and so hard that when she makes it out of the cover of the trees, she falls to her hands and knees, gasping for air and dry-heaving violently before finally able to expel the food in her stomach.

Aramei lies on her side against the snow, covered only by the inadequate warmth of her coat. Her hands and feet are cold to the bones, but she can't go any farther. The weight of what she experienced combined with her body's unwillingness to push further; Aramei is doomed to lie in the snow until someone finds her, or until death claims her.

15

Present Day – In the Cabin

MY MIND IS HURLED from Aramei's chaotically, the colors and shapes of the scene zipping past me so fast and unexpected that I come out of it on my hands and knees, puking my guts up. My back arches as I heave violently onto the floor, a pool of vomit in front of me, which only makes me sick again as the revolting stench rises into my nostrils.

"Adria!" Eva says running up the stairs.

I'm trying to catch my breath and I move inches away from the vomit and roll over onto my back on the floor by the bed. My vision is doubling, tripling, until finally it pulls together into focus. Eva kneels down beside me; I feel her knees pressed gently against my side, her hand smoothing back the sweating hair from my forehead. "You're done for the day," she says with resolution in her voice.

I still can't meet her eyes. I stare up at the tall ceiling, letting the patterns and swirls in the wooden rafters dance in front of my eyes, but I don't actually see any of it. All I see are the memories of the vision I just came out of.

"You need to lie down and rest," Eva says, trying to help me up, but I motion for her to move away.

"No," I say shaking my head against the floor. "I have to see more. I need to go back under."

"Adria, I—"

"If Aramei's able," I interrupt, finally meeting Eva's eyes, "I'm going back in."

Reluctantly, Eva nods and gives in to me, but there's no absence of disquiet in her face.

Eva pushes herself back into a stand and wrings out the cloth that always sits on the table next to Aramei's bed and she goes to clean my face. I let her. I lay still on my back as the cool cloth moves across my forehead first to wipe away the sweat, and then around my mouth. I shut my eyes and take in the comfort of the cloth, feeling my suffocated pores opening up to the coolness of it. After lying here for a moment longer, I pull myself up and lay next to Aramei again. I comb her hair with my fingers and stare down into her angelic, sleeping face. I never say a word. I can't. I can never possibly describe to anyone how much I feel for her, because no one would understand. Not even Isaac. But my journeys into her past, although few, have brought me closer to her than even her own sister had been. Because I *feel* her emotions, because I am right there with her, experiencing everything that she sees and hears and tastes and smells and touches. It's as if *we* are sisters, but share so much more with each other than anyone can possibly know.

And I've become addicted to her, to traveling into her past and living her life through her eyes. And I truly want to help her. I know better than anyone her pain and life. I could've been her. I keep saying that to myself over and over: *I could've been her.*

But she never had a choice. She never even had a chance. Not like I did. Infecting her very likely would not have turned out the same as me. I don't doubt for a second that Aramei would've died and that's why Trajan never risked it.

Aramei knows that I'm right there with her in these visions. She wants me here and she needs me to help her, though I still have yet to understand what for.

I have to know. And soon. Because her emotions are killing me.

Eva leaves us again without me having to ask her to go. I barely hear her when she quietly makes her exit after cleaning the floor where I had my little accident. I keep my eyes on Aramei the whole time, unable to tear my gaze away. And now I stroke her face again with my fingers and whisper softly near her mouth, "I know you can show me more."

I can feel her steady breaths on my lips. Her eyes don't flutter and she doesn't move any muscle in her face to indicate that she can hear me, but I give her time. I lay with her for nearly an hour before she shows signs of being 'coherent' again.

And when I feel her breath quicken, I'm only given seconds before I'm thrust into her world again…and again.

~~~

Much later, I open my eyes to see Trajan standing over me, but I can't make out where I am at first. I realize that I'm naked, sitting upright in a deep bathtub with Eva sitting beside me on the edge of the porcelain. Panicking, I lurch forward to cover my nakedness with my arms, pulling my bare knees briskly toward me and pressing them against my chest. A great gush of water rolls over the top of the tub and onto the floor.

"No," Eva says gently, putting out her hand as if to calm me, "you are safe." She smiles down at me. "Forgive me, but I couldn't get you to wake up, so I thought getting you into the water might help."

With my arms pressed tightly across my breasts, I jerk all around every which way to find my clothes or a towel, *anything* to cover myself with. I see that this tub is an old-timey standalone claw-foot situated away from any walls. Away from anything I could put around my body.

"What are you doing in here?" I snap at Trajan, my eyes full of resentment glaring across at him. At the same time I'm thinking: What am *I* doing in here? Because Eva's explanation really hasn't sunk in yet.

Trajan is unfazed by me. He stands over me with his hands folded together behind him. No emotions in his face. Just the same domineering look he always has when he expects information from me. I know he could care less that I'm naked and that I'm clearly pissed off that he's invading my privacy, but it doesn't stop me from being openly irate about it.

"Do you *mind*?!" I shriek.

"Tell me what you saw," he says simply, completely ignoring my anger.

"Look," I growl at him, "I draw the line right here! You force me to help you, threaten me and threaten Isaac—you have no boundaries! The least you could do is show a little respect! I don't care *who* you are!"

Trajan moves so fast towards me that I don't have time to blink. My naked body is pushed down against the side of the tub and I thrash about, splashing the water out all around me as I gasp to fill my lungs with air again. A thunderous *boom* resonates through my head as the back of my skull is rammed against the porcelain and a thousand black and yellow spots flutter around in my vision. I feel Trajan's powerful hand around my throat, his thick fingers squeezing my muscles with just enough force to terrify me into total submission.

I've gone too far. And I knew that I had before the last word even escaped my lips.

I despise him, but at the same time I can't help but respect him because of what he is. He's not human and for me ever to think that I could treat someone with his power, someone of his *kind* with the same defiant nature as a human, I admit I'm one stupid girl for it.

Trajan only releases his grip when he feels my body give in to him. My hands slowly slide away from his wrist where his own hand is around my throat. I stop thrashing and gasping and my silence leaves only the sound of water trickling onto the floor. His fingers slide away from my neck and he slowly raises his body, but his dark, piercing eyes never leave mine. I see Eva from the corner of my eye as she stands against the wall; indifferent on the outside, but I see in her face, total dismay.

Finally, I look away from Trajan and down at the water rippling beneath me with all of my subtle movements.

"I'm sorry," I say and raise my eyes to him again. "Not because I'm afraid of you, but because I'm not." Curiosity sparks in his eyes, almost unnoticeable, but I catch it.

I go on, "But it doesn't mean I don't respect you...and...," I look across at Eva and finish, "...I'm not like Viktor Vargas. I can hate you without losing my dignity."

It seems that my willingness to accept his authority, even with defiance in my words, is all I needed to gain his respect. He gives me a single nod of sanction and says, "I will be waiting for you in the main room. Do not keep me waiting." And he turns and leaves me alone with Eva in the downstairs bathroom.

Silence fills the room for a moment and we just look at each other. Maybe she's trying to figure out what to say the same as I am, but then she smiles and walks over to me with a thick black bathrobe.

"You cannot go under for that long again," she says, holding the robe open for me and I rise from the water and step out, slipping into the fabric. "It's very dangerous, you must understand. You risk never coming back out."

I tighten the rope around my waist and look at her.

"How do you know this?"

She's hesitant at first, glancing downward at the floor. "We shouldn't keep Milord waiting."

Eva points to my clothing on the pedestal sink and then slips out of the room, ignoring my question.

I get dressed slowly, but not to intentionally keep Trajan waiting. I can't help it that every movement I make is dictated by deep thoughts. My head is overloaded with a lot of everything, so much that I can't focus on one thought alone long enough to actually remember it a second later when the next one comes around. I bring up my hands, my fingers spread in a claw-grip and I clutch my head on both sides, my eyes squinting as if trying to force down all of these thoughts into a place where they can be controlled. I move my hands from my head and brace my palms against the wooden wall and just lean forward. My head drops and I stare down at the floor.

After I feel I've kept Trajan waiting long enough, I take in a deep breath and leave the spacious bathroom.

He and Eva are waiting for me; Trajan is sitting comfortably on the couch with Eva standing against the wall nearby in all of her gentleness and servitude. And her secrets, which I will not ignore forever. All of the servants have already been told to leave. I know Aramei is sleeping soundly upstairs; I can hear her soft breathing and only wish that I could be there with her, instead of down here staring into the face of my undoing.

And just like the last time, I tell Trajan everything that I saw and experienced. I hold back nothing. I learn during our conversation what I already suspected: Viktor had been trying to get Aramei out of the area because the war between his army and Trajan's was spreading fast and soon to engulf all of Serbia. Viktor's rebellion had just started months before to infect locals, to bring more to his side so that he could eventually overthrow Trajan and claim his throne. Because Viktor knew he could never defeat Trajan on his own, nor could he defeat him with such a small army. Viktor's actions were limitless and within a couple short months, there were so many rogue werewolves under his command that the humans who had not yet been infected were terrified to leave their homes. Rumors of the Old Myths being true had started to spread as fast as Viktor's growing numbers. Villages days from the carnage heard of the rumors of the Black Beasts who were spreading through the countryside.

But I also learned something I never expected.

Nataša, after Viktor went rogue was made Trajan's Right Hand in place of Viktor. But Nataša had always been crafty and vindictive. She had been spying on Viktor and all of the time that he spent with Aramei, she had been watching from the shadows. Viktor never detected her presence because his infatuation with Aramei blinded his senses, but every encounter that Viktor had with Aramei was being watched with vengeful eyes.

To become involved with a human the way that Viktor was with Aramei was not only against their laws; it was against their nature and Nataša was the most unforgiving of all. She had always hated humans and because Viktor had become infatuated with a human, Nataša would be the one to set in motion the plan to bring about Aramei's death.

I leave the cabin with more information than I ever thought I'd have. And I start to see now more than ever how the pieces of so many mysteries are quickly coming together.

~~~

"Why do you serve him?" I say to Raul sitting in the driver's seat of a black SUV. Isaac had to go to Augusta and deal with another challenge made by a werewolf who apparently wants control of the Maine territory. I, knowing the nature and the importance of these types of challenges, understand that Isaac had to leave and deal with it.

I was still under with Aramei when Isaac left.

Now, Raul has been appointed my chauffer and is taking me back to Hallowell. It could've been worse; I'm happy I didn't get stuck on a long drive with Trajan as my company. I like Raul and Isaac trusts him, and so do I. I'm pretty sure Isaac had words with Raul before he left about watching over me.

"He is the Sovereign," Raul answers, glancing over at me. His enormous, muscled arms look awkward out ahead of what appears to be a tiny steering wheel; his giant hands grip the wheel on each side. I'm surprised he can fit in the seat.

"He is a bastard," I say.

If this were any guard other than Raul, I likely would not have said that out loud.

"I know," Raul says and it stuns me.

I turn my head to look at him.

"To be Vukašin doesn't mean for a goddamned second that anybody has to like you." He laughs a deep, rumbling laugh. "Someone like him has more enemies than friends."

"I can't imagine him having *any* friends," I say, looking out the windshield now.

It's late in the afternoon and the sun will be setting soon.

"Nah," Raul says, "he doesn't, but that's best being in his position. There are no such things as friends in his case."

"Well, serves him right."

"Other than their fear of him," Raul says, "he associates with no one by his own choice. If I were the Sovereign, I would befriend no one just the same. Too risky."

"Oh, so you'd shun me?" I cross my arms and scrunch up my nose looking over at him, trying to lessen the bleakness of the conversation.

I've had enough of bleak.

A giant grin etches across Raul's big face and he wriggles his bushy brows at me. "Oh, no ma'am! You'd be my *only* friend." Then a sneaky look appears and he adds, "I'd let you be anything to me that you wanted."

Even Raul knows that I'd never give him the time of day, but I'd also never dream of not going along with his innocent teasing, either. I love me some Big Raul.

"Yeah, yeah," I say, "you couldn't afford me."

Raul throws his head back against the seat and laughs.

"Baby, after one night with me, I wouldn't be able to get *rid* of you!"

I laugh right along with him, never uncomfortable with his sexual comments. The truth is that I don't think I ever could be. He's totally harmless.

The sun has set by the time Raul drops me off outside at the Mayfair house.

"You be careful on the drive back, Raul," I say standing outside at the driver's side window.

He draws his square-shaped chin in a circular motion, looking out at me with an awkward, thoughtful expression. "Well, thanks for your concern." I realize that Raul may have never really experienced a genuine human gesture of concern like that before. I can see all over his face that he's contemplating it and his smile seems to deepen.

"Thanks for the ride," I say, pat him on the shoulder and head toward the front porch.

Raul drives away and in no time I hear the big tires on the SUV braking over the little pebbles at the very end of the driveway.

I step up onto the first concrete step but then halt in my tracks.

Something's not right…

All of my senses have suddenly gone into overdrive. The tiny hairs on my arms rise and the back of my neck all the way down my spine prickles with alarm. My eyes shift black out of nowhere and it completely shocks me because I've only ever known it to happen in times of rage or lust, not when I have no idea what's going on, or which emotions to act upon. I take a deep breath, close my eyes and calm myself, letting the blackness fade. And then I open up my ears to the sounds inside the house. There are voices in the den that are muffled by grave whispers, a flurry of words that I can't make out because they are all talking at the same time: "…to kill her," I hear one voice say. "Where is Isaac?" and then another, "…maybe she's a spy." And the last one I hear says, "Hope she's still in the cabin," which causes me to burst inside the house to find out what's going on.

I walk quickly into the den and all of the whispers cease in an instant; more than a dozen pairs of eyes are looking across the vast room at me.

"What's going on?" I say; my eyes jerk around in every direction searching for some sign.

Isaac's sister, Camilla, and Zia both walk toward me. Zia's smoky gray eyes peer at me solemnly. She steps up in front of me and whispers, "Rachel caught someone snooping around the woods behind the house." She glances toward the hallway which leads into the kitchen. "They've got her in the basement and they've been more or less beating the shit out of her for information for the past hour."

"Really?" I say, my eyebrows knotted. I look toward the kitchen briefly and then back to Zia because I sense she's not exactly telling me everything.

Then Zia leans in even closer to my ear and says, "I think she could be that Praverian you guys have been looking for."

I gasp and my face freezes in all of its stunned glory. As Zia's face gradually moves away from mine, all that I can move are my eyes to follow her. I feel like I'm trapped inside my own body and have lost my ability to control any part of it.

Oh my God, she said it. She said Praverian. At least I know now that she's not the traitor, but how did she know?

I look down at my shoes and then out at all of the eyes peering back at us, Camilla standing just a few feet behind Zia. Not one of these faces can look at me fully. It's as if every time I make eye contact, their glances stray away from mine.

I grab Zia by the elbow and pull her into the dimly lit hallway.

"How did you know about the Praverian?" I whisper harshly through my teeth. I can't help but continuously glance down the hallway in both directions to see if anyone might be in earshot.

I still haven't let go of her elbow.

"Girl, you can't hide stuff from me," Zia says, grinning. "Don't you know that by now?"

"Tell me how you know," I say and I'm not smiling. I don't give in to her natural humor. Not yet. My eyes are wide and focused as I stare intently at her.

Finally, Zia pulls her elbow gently from my hand.

"Chill the hell out, Adria," she says. "Look, I don't like being left in the dark and I knew that for you to keep secrets from me that it must've been something really serious. So, I did what any nosey girl would do and I listened in on a conversation between you and Isaac—." She grins deeply and adds, "I guess you thought I was still in Augusta with Sebastian that night, but we came home early."

I'm not liking where this might be going. I rip through my mind, trying to figure out what night she's talking about and what Isaac and me might've said.

"Well, what did you hear?" I say, still showing trepidation about her knowing anything at all and she's starting to take offense to it.

The grin disappears from her face and she looks at me confused and maybe even a little snubbed. "Just something about a Praverian being a traitor—I don't know why you never let me in on it and I won't lie and say it doesn't bug the shit out of me, but come on, I know now. What's with the paranoia?"

The 'paranoia' is anyone else other than those who already know being aware of what Harry is. It's too risky, even for one more person to be let in on the secret. We have gone to great lengths to protect Harry's secret because if the Dark Praverian gets wind of what he is, he's as good as dead.

We can't afford even those closest to us knowing. All it takes is one person, one slipup and this whole plan will fall apart.

I grab Zia's arms and pull her toward me, "Zia, have you told anyone else about what you heard? Sebastian? Anyone at all?" My voice is harsh and desperate, almost on the verge of being more than a whisper.

Zia's eyes fall under hard wrinkles, stunned by my reaction.

"No," she says and I'm not sure I believe she never told Sebastian at least. "This was just a few nights ago and me and Sebastian don't do a lot of heart-to-heart talking…if you know what I mean." That playful grin creeps up on her face again and I know exactly what she means. So, maybe she's telling the truth after all because she and Sebastian have always been more 'hands on' than conversational.

"Good," I say, only a fraction relieved. My hands slide away from her biceps. "You can't tell anyone, okay? And because I was ordered by Isaac not to talk about it, I can't tell you more than you already know."

That is a total lie. Isaac never ordered me to do anything, but using him as my excuse is the only way I'm going to get out of having to tell her anything else. Because she knows that even me being Isaac's girlfriend, I can't go against his orders since he's Alpha. I just hope she buys it. I'm so unbelievably relieved that Zia isn't the traitor; she was one of few that if it had turned out to be her, it would've seriously broken my heart, but still, I can't confide in her about it. Until we know who the traitor is and after we trap it, only the five of us need to know the details. I hate keeping things from her and I just hope she believes that.

Zia sighs and says, "Alright, alright. I won't say anything." She smiles and adds, "But you owe me, girl. Uh huh, I might have you cleaning my room for a month or something." She wrinkles her nose and looks up in thought. "Or, I could make you cook me breakfast or give me a pedicure—Yep! I'm totally going to call in a pedicure."

"Fine. Whatever," I say, having no time to joke around with her right now. "I'm going downstairs."

Zia grabs me and her smiling face shifts gravelly. "Why don't you just let Rachel handle this?"

I jerk my arm away from her and suddenly feel like she may have been trying to distract me all along. Something in her eyes puts me on edge and I get the strangest feeling that she doesn't want me going into the basement.

16

GENNA. OH NO....

I tear my way past Zia, accidently shoving her against the wall and I throw open the basement door, taking two steps at a time as I fly down them. I leap off the last step and stand before six girls who I recognize instantly as Rachel's underlings. One girl, known mostly for her bright red hair and millions of freckles, puts up her hands to stop me. She's the same girl who helped Rachel set me up to walk in on Rachel in bed with Isaac months ago.

"You can't go back there."

"Move out of my way," I demand, "or I'll move you myself."

The other five girls step in closer and I wait before making any sudden movements. I gaze off toward the back of the basement near the area where the wall has already started being repaired. A band of light stretches across the dark floor and spreads out in a cone-shaped pattern. It leads just around the rock wall where mold is starting to grow within the moisture. A figure is moving back and forth across the light, blinking it out every few seconds. I hear Rachel's venomous voice and the sound of heavy breathing and the familiar chains embedded in the wall as they clink and scrape across the floor. And then a loud *whap* resonates through the air, followed by the crunching sound that only a crushed bone can make.

"Get out of my way!" I shout and start to move through the six girls.

The red-head grabs me by the back of the hair and my body instinctively whirls around at her. My eyes shift black and I glare at her with all of the warning my body can muster. I don't have to say anything and all six of them back away to let me pass.

I round the corner to find Rachel standing there in front of a body huddled on the floor against the rock wall. I can smell the blood from her wounds rising up into my nostrils and my pores and taste buds immediately open up to it.

"Oh, this should be interesting," Rachel says with a wicked, hateful gleam in her eyes.

"Who gave you permission to torture people?" I say.

I'm trying to get a glimpse of the girl who I'm starting to believe isn't Genna, but Rachel is making it a point to stand directly in front of her, obscuring my view.

"*Permission*?" she says with disbelief as though the very thought of it is absurd. "Isaac's not here. I do what the fuck I want."

"Dria?" I hear a voice say weakly.

The air is suddenly sucked from the room. I can hear my heart beating so loud and so fast, but I can't feel it. My lungs feel solid and without breath, yet my chest heaves rapidly behind a rattling ribcage. I feel nauseous. Before I have a chance to move to stop her, Rachel throws out her leg and buries it in my sister's neck, causing Alex's head to slam violently against the wall and her battered body slumps over onto the floor.

Blinded by a hot white light of rage filling my head, my black claws protrude in the same split second it takes me to dive across the length of the room toward Rachel. I scream out in rage, my voice exploding in my ears just as my claws spear Rachel's shoulders and chest. We crash into the wall and rotted wood from the beams holding up the ceiling splinters and falls around us as the foundation shakes and trembles.

I wail on her, raining down on her face blow after bloody blow, my body latched to the wall, holding hers in place beneath me. I don't have time to stop and contemplate how I'm able to defy gravity and sit with my knees pressed vertically against the stone wall. I just keep pounding her face with my fists, letting the fury take control of me.

The pain of one rib cracking just below my breast throws me off course, thrusting me back into the reality of what will happen if I don't calm down. But this sidetracks me just enough to give Rachel the upper-hand. In seconds, I feel my body whirling across the room with my legs out in front of me. My back collides with a wooden beam and my body crashes right through it, tearing the beam completely apart. I crash down in a pile of old wooden crates and bicycle tires and vintage glass bottles. Shards of thick glass prick and stab the backs of my arms and the palms of my hands.

Rachel is on top of me before I can get up. My body stings and burns as her razor-sharp claws slash away at my skin. Blood from gashes on my face drains into the corners of my mouth. "You don't belong here!" Rachel shrieks between blows, each sending a hard ringing through my ears and bouncing around inside my skull. "You. Weak. Stupid. *Bitch*!" she yells out and this time I manage to push her off me.

Her body skids across the floor and I leap up so fast that it's as though she had never hit me, and I lunge at her. Both of us roll across the basement floor in a mass of claws and blood. I can hardly see anything but her raven hair crowding my face and the whites of her eyes looking down at me. I grab her by the back of her hair and swing my body around on top of her, pinning her to the floor.

Just as my skull starts to split and the rest of my ribs start to break as the Change begins to take hold, I feel a set of hands slip underneath my arms from behind and pull me off of Rachel.

It's Harry. And now more than ever I appreciate his power to calm my emotions, to help me tame my beast and keep it inside. I feel his unnaturally warm hands on my face as he presses his palms down on me and a tingling sensation engulfs my body. *"Calm,"* I hear his voice say in my mind. And I know that he's doing this as covertly as possible so that no one else in the room will know.

I have to play along.

Within seconds, between Harry's power and my own desperate efforts, I'm already calm enough that I know I'm not going to Turn. But I pretend for a few moments longer to be struggling with it.

"You can tame it," Harry says out loud, pretending to be simply my friend who is trying to help. I keep my eyes closed as I lay across the floor with my head in his lap. He carefully strokes my face with his fingertips. "You can do this, Adria. Don't wolf-out on me, especially not in my lap, alright? These are my favorite jeans."

I let my breathing steady and then slowly open my eyes. Harry's looking down at me with a crooked smile.

"Where's she at?" I say, rising up quickly from the confines of his lap.

Rachel is sitting against the wall across the room, her friends surrounding her. The red-haired girl, squatting in front of her, reaches out to help her up, but Rachel smacks her hands away. "I don't need your help," she barks. The girls slowly back away from her and Rachel reaches up and wipes a gush of blood from her mouth. She glares across the room at me, but I don't care about her right now.

I look over to my right and see my sister gazing at me through a heavily bruised and bleeding face; her long, dark hair is falling down all around her face in bloody strands clumped together and wild.

I run over to her and fall to my knees at her feet.

"Alex," I say desperately, reaching up to touch her face, but I hold my fingers just inches from her cheek.

I can't believe that she's here…and right now I have to put aside my distrust. I know that she's not like me and that she could be a danger to me, but my human heart won't let me be anything to her other than her sister, even if only for this initial moment. Tears stream down her face. I'm smiling and frowning and am wholly confused all at the same time.

"I'm sorry, Dria," she says weakly and I cup her beaten face fully in my hands. "I'm so sorry for everything…,"

A tempest of emotions and questions whirl around inside of me. "What are you doing here?" is the only thing I can pull together to ask.

"She was spying," Rachel retorts somewhere behind me. "I caught her hanging around the woods behind the house." She adds after a few seconds, "And she's a Vargas bitch, so that's all we need to know."

I jerk my head around, "*You*, Rachel, are a Vargas bitch! Do I need to chain *you* to this wall and beat you like you beat my sister?!" Hatred swirls heatedly in my eyes and I know she can see it from across the darkness of the room.

Rachel's expression stiffens. She had no idea that I knew the truth about her, that she had also been Turned by the Vargas family and had been betrayed by them. After a long and tense eight seconds with her eyes boring into mine, Rachel gets up from the floor and walks toward the basement stairs. She stops before she rounds the corner, "But *I'm* not a spy," she says glancing at Alex next to me, "and not even Isaac will allow her the freedoms that I have."

"If you go anywhere near her again," I say with the purest threat in my voice, "I'll kill you myself. Even if my sister can't be trusted, she's mine to deal with—is that understood?"

Every set of eyes in the room falls on Rachel: Harry, the six girls who follow Rachel like the Queen Bee, even Zia, Camilla and Daisy who I am only now realizing are here, too. The silence in the space is so thick that the sound of cars driving down the main road in the far distance is well-defined.

"Yes," Rachel forces the word through her teeth, "it is understood."

I am the Alpha female. I have been since I was Turned, but only right now in this eye-opening moment when Rachel submits to me, do I see it.

And it is very…sobering.

Rachel and her minions disappear up the stairs, leaving me with my sister and my friends.

"Make us all leave," Harry says telepathically.

Without even glancing at him, or questioning his reasons, I look up at everyone, "I'm sorry, but I need to be alone with her. Please."

Daisy, already knowing that this is probably Harry's doing, nods and gestures for Camilla. They leave together.

"If you need me," Zia says, "just yell." She looks at Alex once and then at me again with that distrustful look in her charcoal-painted eyes.

"She's chained to the wall," I say to Zia, "She won't be able to hurt me. I'll be fine."

Hesitant, Zia finally leaves too, and Harry pretends to follow her up, but I have a feeling that he hasn't really gone anywhere at all, but only made everyone believe that he had.

"I'm right here," he says in my mind, confirming it.

I turn back to Alex. "What happened?" I want to ask if she's alright. I want to run upstairs and grab a First-Aid kit and some peroxide, but I know she's fine and that in no time her wounds will heal.

"I've...been trying to warn you," she says and I'm completely suspicious of her. "I've been trying for months."

"Warn me about what?" I sit down in front of her and move away some strands of hair adhered to the side of her face by dirt and blood.

"You won't believe me, Dria," she looks away, defeated, letting her head fall to one side near her shoulder. "And I can't blame you if you don't."

"I can't say that I will," I whisper, "but I want to hear what you have to say. I'll at least listen to you."

She raises her head again and tries to sit up straighter, positioning her back against the wall, the sound of the chains bound around her wrists clanking against the floor.

I won't remove them. I'm not stupid.

Her blue eyes meet mine and all that I see in them is pain and shame and desperation. I want to hold her and tell her everything will be alright, but I know I can't do that, either. For a moment she glances around the room as if to make sure we are alone and then she looks back at me.

"Someone in your pack," she begins, "someone in this house, is a fledgling of Viktor Vargas."

I don't say anything, but I just look in at her intrusively, my eyes creasing with perplexity.

She goes on, "I don't know...it's really strange...."

"No," I urge her, "just tell me whatever it is, no matter how strange it might seem."

She nods a few times, comforted by my assurance.

"This girl met with Viktor several times while I lived with them," she says, still showing signs of pain, "and Viktor...well, I get the feeling he's afraid of her—that's one reason why it's strange."

I nod but remain quiet, hoping I won't have to continuously coax her to go on. I just need her to tell me everything she knows, whether she's telling the truth, or not.

Her breath is unsteady, but slowly it's becoming smoother.

"I don't know everything...I-I don't know much of anything about her or what she and Viktor are involved in, but...Well, it took a few visits for me to realize that she wants you dead. *You*, Dria...and I don't care that we're bound by enemy blood, you're my sister and that blood connection is stronger."

Not believing this, I rise to my feet and step away from her, completely out of her reach. Continuously, I shake my head. I'm not going to let her manipulate me with her deadliest weapon: sisterly love.

"Dria, I don't care if you keep me down here forever," she says, her voice hardened and trembling with grief, "but I'm telling you the truth. I'm not here to—"

"Just stop," I say, putting up my hand. "I don't even want to talk about us, alright? Just tell me what you know about this girl. Who is she, Alex? What does she look like?"

The truth is that I do want to talk about us, but I can't let her know that. And it's not the important topic right now as much as I want it to be.

Alex glances down at her bound hands, coiling her fingers around one another, maybe out of nervousness, maybe because she wants me to believe her and I'm not letting her in like she had hoped. She looks back up at me, "She's not anyone I've seen here. She's tall and strange-looking with bright white-looking eyes and long, white hair. Dria, she's not human."

"Don't say anything," Harry says, *"just let her talk, but don't elaborate about my kind."*

"Okay," I say, though I had no intention in bringing up to Alex that this girl is a Praverian, and is probably the one we're after.

"But you said she was Viktor's fledgling?"

"Yes," Alex nods. "I overheard them talking once—no, actually it was a fight. Viktor said something about giving her a gift—the power of a Black Beast—and that she owed him." Alex laughs a little under her breath, shaking her head. "Oh, she didn't like that much. They went at it, like fists and claws at it, y'know? Last thing I heard her say was that if anything, Viktor was who owed *her* and that if he ever said anything about her to anyone that she'd kill Aramei."

Something Eva said once suddenly flashes through my mind and I start to piece this puzzle together. I glance toward the wall, plunged deeply into the memory and then I turn back to my sister, my eyes full of realization. "It was you," I say, gently pointing towards her, "You were the one that went to Trajan to warn him about someone dangerous living in this house."

Alex nods. "Yeah, I went to him and he almost killed me."

"She's telling the truth," Harry says in my mind. *"I haven't sensed an ounce of dishonesty in her yet."*

Alex goes on:

"I was doing it to protect you," she says. "I really didn't care about Aramei, but I knew if I tried to come to you or to

Isaac, that no one would believe me. So, I went to Trajan to tell him that Aramei was in danger and that the threat was living inside this house. It didn't really turn out like I planned. He was going to kill me there in the cabin, but changed his mind and decided to use me instead."

"Use you how and how did you know for sure the girl lives in this house?"

I squat down in front of her again, but stay out of her reach.

"She said a lot of things that made it obvious," Alex answers, looking into my eyes. Already her wounds are healing and I see that she's getting her strength back. "She talked about how she hated sleeping here, pretending to be everyone's friend when all she wanted was to watch you suffer."

I turn away from her and look to my left where I assume Harry is standing judging by that odd sensation I feel on that side.

"And the way Trajan planned to use me was that he told me to go back to Viktor and try to get more information about this girl. He wanted me to go back to the cabin and tell him, but I never went. I know he would've killed me after I gave him the information." Alex drops her head; her chin lies near the top of her chest.

After a tense minute, she raises her head to see me again and she just looks across at me like the human sister I grew up with. Those eyes, they look exactly the way they did the night I sat with her under the giant oak tree in Georgia when she was explaining to me why she was going to move out of our house and in with Liz and Brandon. She wanted me to understand that she was only doing it because it had to be done, but she didn't want to see me get hurt by her leaving. I try to look away from her eyes because I'm afraid I'm going to cave and let her manipulate me with lies. But I can't look away. I can't because I know in my heart that this time she really is telling the truth.

"I know I messed up," she says, her voice trembling again, "I don't know what was wrong with me. I blame it on the bloodline, because a part of me felt like it wasn't really me saying those things to you, but the bloodline. It was like my body was possessed by something evil and I couldn't control it."

Tears are choking the back of my throat and my eyes are starting to burn. But I don't say anything. Not yet. I couldn't get any words out even if I tried.

Alex reaches her hands out to me, pleadingly; her dirty, bloody face contorted by anguish. "You have to believe me, Dria...I had no control over my own mind! It wasn't until after a few full moons, after I started to adapt, that I started to feel my human emotions again." Tears streak their way through the dirt on her face, leaving discolored lines down her cheeks. "Finally, I came to my senses and left the Vargas pack in Massachusetts and ran back here."

She drops her voice and stares out ahead of her. "I've been in Hallowell since April. I've been sleeping in the barn at Uncle Carl's house."

Stunned by this information, my tears stop falling. Now I'm just in shock. Alex has been at the house for the past *four months*? Oh my God...And how could I not have known? Aunt Bev and Uncle Carl might've been in danger all this time and I never knew a thing.

"Harry?" I say, *"Please tell me you still think she's telling the truth."*

I hear Harry sigh and then he says, *"Yeah, I still think she's telling the truth...wouldn't trust her just yet though, not until we know more about what's going on—"*

"I know," I interrupt him out loud.

Alex looks up at me faintly curious.

"You knew all along I was in the barn?"

"No," I say before I can think about it. "I was…just thinking out loud."

As much as I want to run over to her, I refrain and try to keep my composure.

"Dria, look at me," Alex says.

Hesitantly I do, but I'm afraid of what she might say. I feel like at any moment my heart is going to break into a million pieces all over again. I stare into my sister's face and wait for her. Her eyes soften and a small, warm smile of affection appears at her lips.

"I'm really proud to be your sister," she says. "You've turned out better than I could ever be."

I choke back more tears and straighten my back.

"You know I can't let you out of those chains," I say, changing the subject before I break down in front of her. "At least not right now." I let my face harden a little to show her that I still haven't surrendered to her and that I won't be easily fooled. "I do love you. I'll always love you. But I don't trust you and I don't think I ever will again."

Alex nods gently. "Fair enough," she says. "But I'm going to prove it to you. You'll see. I don't care what it takes, or what I have to do, but I want my sister back."

I gaze across the room at her, at how the swath of orange light from the light bulb above lays partially over one half of her body, the rest hidden in the dark shadows of the basement. The moonlight filters in through the wall opening where new rocks and steel beams have been set up in front of it to form a new reinforced frame. I glance one more time at the chains bonding her wrists, wondering if they are strong enough to hold her when the same kind of chains on the other side of the room weren't even enough to hold me.

But more than anything I wonder about Alex and the things she said to me. And I feel it in my heart…I know that my sister has finally come home.

17

"SHE *SPECIFICALLY* SAID THAT this girl wanted to see *you* suffer?" Isaac says for the second time as if he hopes to have heard me wrong the first.

He paces near the window in his bedroom, having just returned from Augusta and another triumphant challenge.

"That's what she said," I answer, sitting on the edge of his dresser.

Harry stands off to the side by the bedroom door.

"But we already knew this," I say. "Isaac, this isn't new."

Isaac starts to pace heavier. His magnetic blue eyes are focused on anything that happens to be in his line of sight, but I doubt he actually sees any of it. He appears anxious; his hands are balled gently at his sides. Back and forth he walks, bringing up one arm across his stomach and resting the other elbow in his hand. Then he stops and shoots a look at Harry. "Do you think she could be the traitor?"

I look to and from them both with my legs dangling over the side of the dresser, my hands propped against the wood finish. And I'm trying to hide my own anxiousness; all I really want to do right now is see Alex.

"I don't know," Harry says. "She *could* be, but not any more or less than anyone else. She seemed sincere and truthful, but in the grand scheme of things, if she *is* the traitor, her ability to be believable is better than any of ours." He arches a brow and grins, "Well, except maybe for mine."

Isaac looks quickly back at me, "And you say Zia actually said 'Praverian' to you?" He doesn't let me answer, but lets out a deep breath and throws his hands in the air. "Great. We rule one out and just gain another," he says perturbed. "Another possible suspect, not to mention another headache that we don't need right now. Even if Alex isn't the traitor, we can't *deal* with her right now...," he looks over at me, softening his words and his eyes. "Baby, I don't mean to be an ass—it's your sister and I get that—but you have to agree with me on this. This is the worst possible time for her to be showing back up in your life."

I sigh and look down. "I know," I say dejected, and then I meet his eyes again. "You're right. But Isaac, we can't send her away, either. So what are we going to do?"

His index finger points up in the air. "Bondage," he says and I look at him blankly.

"Follow me," he adds and walks right out the door.

~~~

An hour later, Nathan comes back to the house with two sets of custom-made iron shackles, apparently infused with real silver. They used them on Rachel when she first joined their pack.

"I don't want to know why Xavier had these," Nathan says, handing a black duffle bag to Isaac with the shackles hidden inside. "I almost asked him, but...," he holds up his hand as if to make an announcement, but then his expression changes and he sort of grits his teeth and shudders. "...I dunno, bro, you might want to wash those before you touch them."

Nathan, Harry and I follow Isaac down into the basement where Alex still sits against the wall in a pool of filth.

Zia, Sebastian, Camilla and Daisy have been guarding over her on my orders, for both our safety and Alex's.

"She won't talk to us," Zia says.

"I told her not to," I say.

Isaac goes straight over to Alex, bypassing our conversations, and falls into a squatting position in front of her.

Zia is looking at me, offended more than ever now.

"Zia, I'm sorry, but right now we need to talk to her and figure out some things—"

"Whatever," Zia says, affronted, "I get it. I understand that I have no rank in this family, but I thought that by now I would've at least earned everyone's trust."

I've never seen Zia like this before. Never. She is truly hurt and it rips me apart, but I can't fix it as much as I want to.

"Zia—"

She puts up her hand and walks past me. "I'll be in my room," she says and rounds the corner; Sebastian looks across at me as if to say he's sorry, and then he leaves with her.

"Damnit," I say, dropping my hands hard at my sides.

"Don't worry about her right now," Daisy says stepping up and touching my hand softly. She brushes a tendril of my hair between her fingers. "I'll go talk to Zia." She pauses, looks over at Alex and then she smiles warmly back at me. "I'm really glad that your sister is here, Adria."

"So am I," Camilla says. "Her aura reads in funny colors to me, but I believe she really loves you."

Not even Harry's so-so assurances could make me feel as good as Camilla did just now. Somehow, coming from her, someone who embodies peace and the ability to read other's energies, she seems more convincing.

Daisy and Camilla leave together and as I watch them ascend the steps, I hope that Daisy can fix this stuff between me and Zia.

"I'm going to put these shackles on your wrists and ankles," Isaac says holding the shackles in his hands. "The silver in them will make you weak, maybe sick after a while, but it's necessary—unless you would rather stay down here." He's speaking to her in a calm, comforting voice. Maybe it's more for me than for her, but either way, I'm relieved.

Alex sneers at Isaac and grits her teeth. I swear she might've been about to spit in his face. I move closer to them and crouch down beside Isaac.

"It's to be expected," he says to me without looking away from Alex. "Rachel was the same way for a while."

"A *while*?" I say mockingly. "Yeah, I don't think that 'while' has ended yet."

I turn to Alex. "I thought you said you'd do anything to prove yourself?"

"For *you*, Dria," she says and her dirty hair falls over her eyes. "But not for *them*. And I already see how far their *hospitality* goes." She juts out her chin, letting the hair fall away to expose her bruised and bloodied face in the full light streaming from the bulb above.

"To cooperate with them is cooperating with me," I say. "Please, Alex...you can't be like this—"

"Defiance is and always will be her nature," Isaac says, but then he puts his attention solely on Alex. "The one who beat you down here; she doesn't represent our 'hospitality'. Truth be told, you and Rachel are a lot alike."

Alex laughs and says with dark sarcasm, "We're *nothing* alike. I wouldn't need six girls to help catch her like she did me. I would catch her alone and I would beat the shit out of her alone."

To hear my sister talk this way is a shock to my system even after everything she's already done. She had always been so loving and kind when she was human, except when she got angry and punched Jeff or our step-brother, Trent. Intolerance and violence I guess has always been inside of her and the Vargas bloodline has just brought it out in brazen, hostile ways. I shut my eyes and sigh softly just thinking about it. But she's back and my heart tells me that she'd never hurt me. Not again. She may be a cruel, angry bitch the rest of her life, but as long as she stays devoted to me, I guess if I look at it in a positive light, this could actually be a good thing.

I reach over and take one set of shackles from Isaac's hands.

"This will just be until we figure something out," I say. "You'll be able to hang around the house with me—I'll take you first thing to the bathroom and help get you cleaned up."

Alex's eyes soften and she nods.

Isaac sets the second pair of shackles on the floor next to my feet and moves back to stand with Harry and Nathan who have been extra quiet this whole time.

"But you have to promise me one thing," I say.

"Anything," she says, but then smiles and adds, "Unless you want me to do any maid-type stuff. I'm no one's maid, alright?"

My face breaks into a smile. "Now that's the Alex I remember." And then I get serious, "Promise me you won't leave again."

She smiles back at me and underneath all of the dirt and blood and fading bruises, that smile looks just like my sister's smile. The one when we were both human and when we were inseparable.

"I promise," she says.

Alex reaches out her hands toward me, wrists-up, and I look to Isaac for help with taking the old ones off, which are connected to the stone wall. Isaac holds out his hand to Nathan and Nathan puts the key in his palm.

"And Alex," I say just before Isaac goes to unlock the shackles, "this is Isaac. And I love him. And he treats me just how you always wanted a guy to treat me. So please…at least cooperate with him, if no one else."

Alex narrows her eyes up at him, but this time it's more out of scrutiny than defiance.

"And you're the new Alpha now, I hear," she says to him, looking him over. She appears more like my overprotective big sister than an inferior werewolf staring up at the Alpha. "Well, I'll warn you now….if you ever hurt my sister, I'll make your life a living hell."

Nathan and Harry are whispering something behind me, but I don't listen in.

I swallow hard and glance over at Isaac to see a slim smile sneak up on his face.

"I'll definitely keep that in mind," he says gently, obviously tolerating her for my sake, "and I won't hurt her. I give you my word."

Alex ruffles her nose. "We'll see."

I suppress my laughter, but can't completely suppress my smile. I can already see that they're going to butt heads, but something tells me that—if all goes well and she really isn't here with heartless intentions—she and Isaac will more or less share an understanding.

Once Alex gives in, Isaac leans over to unlock the shackles around her wrists and I move in afterwards and put the new ones on, clamping the clasp down and locking the iron-silver pin in place. Alex unfolds her legs out from

208

underneath her and we do the same with the shackles around her ankles.

"I'll make sure everyone in the house knows to keep to themselves," Nathan nominates himself and starts toward the steps. "Primarily Rachel—Damn, bro, we're gonna have our hands full with these two." He shakes his head, laughing gently.

Alex, carefully rising to her feet, snarls at Nathan and says, "As long as she keeps her distance, there won't be any problems."

"That's what I'm worried about," Nathan says smiling. "Rachel conveniently forgets her boundaries sometimes." I wonder if the thought of Alex and Rachel in a 'girl fight' is somehow turning Nathan on right now. Judging by that look in his eyes, it probably is.

"Good," Alex says with a sly grin, "I can't wait."

I have to admit, I'm grinning inside because Rachel deserves every bit she dishes out. But this is Alex and right now I'm feeling like the little sister all over again and enjoying every bit of it.

"Please just be good," I say, encouraging peace instead of Rachel 'getting hers', which I really would rather see.

But I quietly take a step back inside myself to remind me that I still don't know if she can even be trusted. It wasn't long at all and I had already fully committed to her without realizing. I can't do this; let her manipulate me if that's what she's here for. I have to find that balance that'll allow me to be kind to her and be a sister to her without handing over too much of my trust.

I loop my hand around Alex's elbow and walk with her toward the basement stairs. Nathan zips up them first so that he can go lay down the law in advance.

Aside from the dirt-stained short cotton varsity shorts, I briefly notice that Alex is bare-footed and I reminisce about the beat up flip-flops she used to wear. I look over at her and smile stupidly.

"*What*?" she says.

"Nothing, I was just thinking."

"About what?" Her eyebrows crinkle.

I shake my head, beaming. "You look terrible."

"Well, thanks," Alex scoffs, reaches up with her knuckle and frogs me hard on the arm.

"Ahhh!" I yell, trying to hold in my laughter.

She smirks over at me.

Harry finally speaks up, "I'm Harry," he says stepping in front of Alex and it seems a little unnatural. His face breaks into a wide, dopey smile. "I'm the only human around here, so uh, can you please not eat me or anything like that because that would seriously ruin my day."

Alex's eyes roll over to look at me beside her as if to ask me if he's for real, then she looks back at him. "Okay....well, for the record, *Harry*, you're probably the only one around here I'm going to like *because* you're human."

Harry blushes and buries his hands deep inside his pockets and falls back behind us as we head up the stairs.

"Are you coming?" I say, looking back at him.

"I'll be up in a minute," he says. "Going to check out the new construction on this wall—hey, tell Daisy to come down."

"Alright!" I shout from the top of the stairs and Isaac opens the door, letting the light from the kitchen flood into the stairwell.

As I walk with my sister through the kitchen and the den, it's obvious that everyone knows about Alex because everyone is watching as we pass by them. Rachel and the girls who helped her catch Alex are lounging around on various pieces of furniture in the den with grins and sneers. But Alex keeps her cool; just a solid, expressionless glance and I know that all of the girls see the dangerous retaliation in her eyes. The only one that doesn't stop grinning is, of course, Rachel.

We shuffle up the stairs; Isaac behind us and Alex in front. The chains around her ankles knock against the steps and then drag ominously across the hardwoods on the upstairs floor. I can't wait to get down the hall so I can get Alex away from all of the eyes staring at her as if she's a sadistic serial-killer walking Death Row.

"I really don't want to leave you alone with her," Isaac says telepathically and I open up my mind to him fully.

"But you have to," I say. *"Harry will be around, maybe even inside the bathroom without me knowing it—I'll be fine."*

"Oh, so now you think I'm some creepy peeper," Harry says and it makes my head snap around because I thought he was still in the basement. Of course, I don't see him anywhere.

"You're going to have to stop doing that, Harry!"

We make it to the bathroom door and stop just outside of it; Alex looks at me curiously.

"Ah, I see," Alex says, "talking about me in a way that I can't hear."

I look at her sadly, hoping she'll understand.

Alex shrugs. "It's alright. I guess it just depresses me a little because I no longer have anyone to communicate with telepathically."

This comes as a mild shock to both Isaac and me.

"What happened to Ashe?" I say.

Isaac is just as curious.

Alex's gaze strays toward the floor. She looks both dispirited and indignant. "He became Alpha of his own pack and went to Nova Scotia."

"Why didn't you go with him?" Isaac asks, more interested in the information on his enemy than her love-life.

Alex narrows her eyes at him, but doesn't answer.

"Can we go in now?" she says, looking at me.

I know my sister and that reaction was definitely an embarrassed one only masked by an outer layer of animosity.

Isaac looks at me briefly before I slip inside the bathroom with Alex.

I run the bath water for her and leave her in there alone long enough to go across the hall to Isaac's room and grab her something of mine to wear. She's already sitting in the tub when I come back. Her tiny shorts, underclothes and white t-shirt are ripped in half and lying on the floor.

"I was going to unlock you so that you could undress." I set the clean clothes on the counter.

Alex shrugs and leans back against the deep tub, resting her arms over her chest awkwardly since the chains confine them to about one foot apart. She stares up at the ceiling for the longest time as the water gushes from the faucet into the tub. Eventually, I'm the one turning the water off because it's getting so close to the top that if she makes any heavy movements it will run over the sides and soak the floor. I twist the knob lastly on the cold and it squeaks off, leaving a constant *drip, drip, drip.*

It's kind of weird being in here while my sister takes a bath; not like I've never seen her naked before, but we've never hung around and watched one another bathe. At first, I had been looking only at her face and how filthy the water is becoming so fast, but I can't help but notice and blatantly gawk at the number and size of scars she has all over her body.

"Alex…what happened to you?"

She doesn't even look down, or directly at me for that matter, but she knows what I'm referring to. She sighs and stares at the ceiling for a moment longer.

"Fights. Turning. Same thing that happens to you."

I shake my head slow and solemnly.

"No," I say, "I don't have scars like that. And the first fight I've been in with someone non-human was the one you saw today with Rachel." I move closer and sit on the edge of the tub, looking down at her, heartbroken and knowing. "How did you really get those scars?"

I notice the center of her throat move as if she's swallowing down the truth and her eyes can't seem to stay on mine.

"I wanted to get away from Mom," she says going back a little further than I expected, "and I planned to run away once before my fourteenth birthday, but I didn't want to leave you behind." She stops abruptly and locks her eyes on mine. "Dria, I'm not blaming you for anything so don't look at me like that."

Maybe I was starting to feel like she was blaming this on me. I straighten my face and let her continue.

"For a little while, I thought Ashe was the best thing that ever happened to me. He was so protective and I felt like I was on a pedestal. He worshipped me. But I started to see what was really going on not the first or fifth time he attacked me, but…," her nostrils flare all of a sudden and her eyes turn black. I start to move away from the tub, but just before I do, her naked body calms and she closes her eyes, taking in a deep breath. When she opens then again, her eyes look natural.

Alex looks dead at me. "I always worried you'd be the one who turned out like Mom," she says. "I guess I was wrong about a lot of things."

"You're here now," I say. "And maybe I'm giving myself too much credit in thinking I can read you because you're my sister, but I get the feeling you were the one that left Ashe."

She nods reluctantly and looks away from me again, plunged into thought. "Yeah," she says, "I looked in the mirror one day and saw Rhonda Bradley. That was the day I left."

I smile down at her.

"Then you're not like Mom at all. You're Alexandra, my sister and my best friend."

She smiles carefully at me and a few tears stream down her face.

"Here, let me help you wash up," I say, standing up and moving to the end of the tub where her head is. I take up the nearest bottle of shampoo—pricey salon stuff, so it's probably Zia's—and squeeze a little into my hand.

Alex leans up to let me get all of her hair and I work the shampoo into a lather.

"I punched him in the face last month," I say.

"Who?"

"Jeff. He beat her up again and I rushed to Georgia to see her in the hospital."

Alex never turns around. She just listens as I scrub her hair with my fingertips. This kind of news is nothing out of the ordinary so she understandably finds no reason to be shocked by it.

"He showed up with apologies and the same old shit, huh?"

"Yeah," I say, "and flowers, too—I don't ever want to see her again, Alex."

This, however, does provoke extra interest in her. She turns her head to the side enough so that she can see me.

I look down at her soapy hair and can't bring myself to face her. What I said about our mother made me feel like a horrible person, so I can only imagine what she's thinking about me right now. But what I said is the truth. The last time I saw my mother as she was laid up in that hospital bed and was more excited to see the man who beat her than to see her own daughter, was the day I knew that I never wanted to see her again.

"You're right to feel that way," she says and casually turns her head away again.

The air is rife with silence, except for the steady dripping of water. For a moment, I even stop scrubbing her hair because the quiet in the room has caught me off-guard.

"Dria…I really am sorry for everything. I feel like I haven't slept in four months. Not peacefully anyway. I was supposed to protect you like I tried to do when we were kids, but when it came down it, I was weak and I'll never forgive myself for how I turned out."

My fingers stop moving in her hair and I say behind her, "You didn't try. Alex, you *did* take care of me when we were kids. And you can't blame yourself for how you turned out. It was forced on you."

I take the cup on the nearby counter and fill it with water to start rinsing the shampoo from her hair.

"So you punched him, huh?' she says with a smile in her voice. "Did you bloody his face? I hope you drew blood."

I laugh gently behind her and pour more water over her hair, tilting her head back a little to keep from getting soap in her eyes.

"I'm glad you're here, I really am," I say.

"Me too."

I move away from the tub and walk to the window overlooking the tree-enveloped backyard of the house below.

Daisy waves up at me. I nod subtly, glad she's where I secretly told Harry I needed her to be just in case Alex decided to try sneaking out the window.

Then I walk over to the bathroom door.

"I'll let you finish without me," I say, placing my hand on the doorknob. "Clothes and towel are over there—yell at me when you're done and I'll unlock you so you can get dressed."

Alex glances over at the casual lounge pants and random Sailor Moon t-shirt Camilla gave me, sitting on the counter.

"Are those *my* pants?" she says, leaning up to peer over and get a better view.

"Uh, yeah I think they are, actually."

We smile at one another for one more moment and I shut the bathroom door softly behind me.

18

IT TAKES ALL OF the time Alex spent alone in the bathroom, and then some, for Isaac and me to decide that neither of us knows where Alex is going to sleep. Or, who's going to babysit her while I'm babysitting Aramei. I can't take her with me. Trajan will have her head on a pike.

I never anticipated that these sorts of petty things would be harder to figure out than more obvious things like whether to send her away or keep her chained in the basement. I thought that Isaac's solution with the new shackles was the worst of it.

"I can stay with her," I say.

Isaac and I are downstairs in the hideously yellow kitchen while he makes a sandwich. I spin around on the bar chair to see him as he moves over to the cabinet beside the fridge.

"No way in hell I'm leaving you alone with her like that," he says as he rummages through the cabinet. "She could cut your throat in your sleep."

"What if we make her a pallet on your bedroom floor?" I say, slouching my shoulders as a defeated breath drains right out of me.

He leans up with an unopened bottle of mustard clutched in his hand and looks at me like I've just said something dumb. He walks over to his foot-long sandwich on the counter and sets the mustard down.

I crinkle my nose up at it. I hate mustard.

"I know," I say with a long, deep sigh, "but I really don't want to put her back in the basement like a prisoner. Maybe if it didn't stink down there and mold wasn't growing on the walls, it'd be okay."

Isaac pops the lid on the mustard and squeezes a sloppy line down the length of his sandwich with the mayonnaise and about a hundred random other things he put on it before. Then he puts the mustard away in the fridge.

"Want half?" he says, folding the top bun over onto the mound of meat and condiments.

"You know I don't like mustard."

His shoulders fall and he looks down at the sandwich briefly. "Sorry, babe. I forgot."

"I'm not hungry, anyway," I say, gazing off toward the kitchen entrance where on the other side of the wall, Alex sits in the den with shackles on her ankles and wrists. "I can't eat with what's going on." My voice is distant.

Camilla runs into the kitchen, staring across at us with wide almond-shaped eyes. She turns her head to gesture toward the den and her long, silky ponytail swishes around when she looks back at us, restlessly. "You might want to get in there," she says, pressing her hands on the doorjamb.

My heart sinks and I jump off the barstool faster than Isaac can get around the counter. Camilla moves to the side so that we can push out ahead of her, but then just before we get to the den entrance, Isaac moves me behind him and we stop. "Just wait," he says.

Slowly we come around the corner to peer into the den, but we stay out of sight without putting any effort into actually hiding.

"Go ahead," Alex says looking up at Rachel from the couch, "show everybody how you can win a fight with a girl in chains—you've already proven how you can win a fight after six other bitches hold me down first."

Rachel snarls and her head sways gently around in a grinning, snide motion.

Alex reaches into a bowl of Chex Mix I had given her, sitting on the edge of the coffee table. She looks absolutely unafraid of Rachel, even makes it a point not to look directly at her much as if to show just how worried she is that Rachel is standing there. Zero worried. I'm a different story. My palms are sweating.

"Isaac—"

He reaches back and gently touches my wrist, "I won't let it go too far," he whispers, still keeping his eyes on Rachel and Alex.

"Well it's not right that Adria's sister is chained up," Camilla says softly behind me and I feel her body pressing into my back as she tries to see between us.

I hear Rachel say, "You think you can just come here and be accepted because you're Adria's sister—wrong—It took me *months* to gain their trust."

"Yeah," Alex laughs and pops a pretzel in her mouth, "I hear you wore these same chains." She stops chewing and brings the chains on her wrist up to her nose and sniffs. She pulls away with a mild disgusted expression. "Definitely smells like a skank wore them at *some* point."

She reaches impassively into the Chex Mix again and pops another piece in her mouth.

I just wince and grab Camilla's hand without knowing it's her hand at first.

Rachel's smirking face becomes much more heated; both sides of her nostrils flare up as she presses her lips together tightly.

I catch a confident smile in Alex's eyes and then I hear *crunch, crunch* as she happily chews. A few seconds pass and when Rachel hasn't decided on what to say, Alex swallows and looks up at her, cocking her head to one side. "Do you like watching me eat?" She bats her eyes.

Rachel slams her palms down on the coffee table, leaning over and glaring at Alex, eye-level. "You have no idea who you're screwing with," she growls.

Alex leans toward her, boldly, "Neither. Do. You."

They're practically face-to-face, their noses only a few inches apart. When it looks like a draw, they both pull away at the same time, neither of them letting the other believe they are the slightest bit intimidated. Rachel stands up straight again and crosses her arms. Two of her six friends step up behind her as if to have her back, but she throws up her hand in a harsh gesture, telling them to back off.

They step away with their figurative tails between their legs.

"So, rumor is you were infected by a Vargas bastard, too," Alex says injecting a tiny bit of mock laughter. She continues to eat, appearing more interested in her food than in Rachel.

"Yeah," Rachel says and her hip pops to one side. "So what if I was?" She gets a chance to inject laughter now and a devious grin tugs one corner of her lips. "Don't think for a second that means we're related in any way."

Alex stops chewing and finally looks up at her with that oh-hell-no look on her face. "Yeah, you don't have to worry about that. Trust me. I'd slit my wrists before I considered a blood relation to you."

"I can help you with that," Rachel says, sneering.

I'm really getting tired of this back and forth, but Isaac insists I stay put and maybe he's onto something. Camilla is pressed so closely behind us now I feel her breath on my shoulder. I glance back once at her and she sort of smile-grimaces and whispers, "Sorry," before pulling away just a little. Really, she wasn't bothering me, but that's just Camilla.

Out of the corner of my eye, I catch a glimpse of Nathan and Daisy standing in the hallway on the opposite side of the den. Daisy looks as worried as I know I do, but Nathan looks thoroughly excited.

I just roll my eyes.

"So who was it?" Rachel says, suddenly showing a tiny bit of curiosity without letting down her wall of hatred. "That infected *you*?"

Alex crunches away a few last bites, brushes her hands together to wipe away any leftover crumbs and then she leans her back casually into the couch. She goes to cross her legs, but forgets the chain around her ankles and tries again more strategically.

Nathan's grin is getting bigger and bigger. Daisy notices and she elbows him in the ribs.

Alex looks up at Rachel, purses her lips and says, "Why do you care?"

Rachel sneers. "I don't care, you stupid rogue *freak*. It was just a question."

Alex jumps to her feet and the coffee table is sent flying across the room as she shoves it away to clear the barrier between her and Rachel.

Camilla yelps behind me and grabs onto my bicep, practically digging her fingernails into my skin. But I barely notice; I push past Isaac and step into the full light of the den with Isaac at my side.

Alex and Rachel stand toe-to-toe, black claws at the ready down by their sides, eyes like black, endless pools of rage.

Nathan is like a little boy in the bathroom with a Sports Illustrated magazine.

"Isaac, do some—"

"I thought this pack knew all about what went on in the Vargas family?" Alex growls, the tiny black veins rising to the surface of her skin all around her eyes and cheeks.

Rachel moves in so close that they could kiss if they didn't hate each other so much. "I only care about what goes on with them when they threaten us *here*." She looks Alex over quickly, her dark eyes flashing for a brief, detestable moment. "Like why you're here and why I caught you sneaking around. I don't waste any energy on your kind outside of our pack!"

"Wow," Alex says, sneering, "he must've really screwed you over, huh?"

Oh great…that tone of hers was a taunt if I've never heard one.

Rachel's entire face flares up; her lips twist open, revealing her teeth and a series of raging lines deepen around her mouth and nose. "*He*?" she rips the word out. "What makes you think it was a guy?"

Alex laughs a little and her smirk grows.

"It's obvious. Whoever infected you only wanted you long enough to get his rocks off. Maybe you were infertile. Or, maybe he just got tired of the missionary position—"

Rachel jumps on Alex and pins her to the couch; her claws tight around Alex's throat.

Alex is unaffected. She's smiling up at Rachel's angry face. Smiling!

Oh no…this can't happen.

Isaac, me, Nathan and Daisy all rush the rest of the way into the den to surround them. Isaac starts to reach for Rachel to pull her off Alex, but stops abruptly.

"It was Ashe," Alex says and Rachel freezes on top of her, stunned.

"*Ashe*?" Rachel looks like she just got hit in the back of the head with a rock.

"Mind getting off of me?" Alex says sarcastically. "I'm not into girls."

Rachel does move off her, but not because Alex asked her to; it's as if she's trying to get her head together.

It's already obvious to all of us that Ashe was who sired Rachel, too, before she even admits it aloud.

And Alex is the first to bring it out in the open.

"Yeah," she says, pretending to dust herself off once Rachel has moved away, "he mentioned you a few times. Said you were one crazy bitch." She looks her over. "I see he was right," she adds casually.

Rachel finally pulls her stupefied thoughts together and looks downward at Alex, but she doesn't say anything. Something different is taking place between them and I'm not sure I'm believing what I'm seeing.

Alex goes on, "But really, Ashe has no room to talk about someone else being crazy. He should be in a nut house…without nuts."

"He did the same to you?" Rachel says.

Nathan throws his hands up in the air, his dreams crushed, and Daisy laughs under her breath as he leaves back down the hallway.

Isaac looks back at me, takes me by the hand and we quietly move back toward the hall leading into the kitchen.

"What just happened?" Camilla says still standing at the den entrance where we left her.

"I'm going to eat my sandwich," Isaac says. He leans over and pecks me on the lips. "I think Rachel just solved our babysitting problems, babe."

I nod absently, still not quite believing how things just happened. "I think you're right…."

Isaac slips back down the hall and into the kitchen.

"…You're frickin' serious?" I hear Rachel say as I listen in on the middle of a conversation. "Well, I totally believe it. The second that Lyla girl joined the pack, I was last week's news. Stupid blond whore." Rachel's nostril's flare again.

"*Lyla*?" Alex laughs. "Well, I guess you can say she got what was coming in the cycle of paybacks because when Ashe sired me, *she* was last week's news."

Rachel smiles first before bursting into laughter.

I don't think I've ever seen Rachel actually smile. At least not in the happy, spirited sense.

It's kind of freaking me out.

Camilla and I look at one another simultaneously, both a little baffled.

"Come on," Rachel says with the nod of her head, "I'll show you my room."

As Alex walks in short, confined steps with Rachel toward the staircase, she looks back at me and winks before heading upstairs.

A smile breaks in my face and I just shake my head. Alex always was as slick as oil, but in this situation, I couldn't be more impressed. Not only did she refrain from all-out war with Rachel right there in the den, but she just became Rachel's new best friend all in a matter of a few minutes.

~~~

After thinking on it for a while, I decide to head upstairs to talk to Zia. I stand outside her bedroom door and knock a few times, knowing she's inside because I hear her talking plain as day. It's when her voice stops abruptly and then rises even higher that I realize she knows full well that I'm out here, but she's not ready to talk to me. My shoulders fall over in a slump and I start to walk back down the hall when I hear her door click open.

Sebastian steps out and closes the door behind him.

"She hates me, doesn't she?"

"Nah," he says, shaking his shaved head. "She'll get over it."

I sigh and lean my back against the wall. The red-haired girl who apparently *used* to be Rachel's number one sidekick shuffles past, smiling at me. Positions in Rachel's little clique are shifting fast with Alex here; already Rachel's 'old' friends are looking for sides to change loyalties to. I smile back faintly as she slips down the stairs, hoping not to give her any hopes. I really want no part of that.

"I want to tell Zia everything," I say to Sebastian as he leans against the opposite wall, crossing his arms, "but I can't. Like *really* can't. I have no control over it. I wish she understood."

"Between you and me," Sebastian says quietly, looking back once toward Zia's door, "Zia is dealing with a lot of rejection lately."

"Rejection?"

"Yeah," he says, "even her brothers have pretty much blown her off and she never sees them anymore. They're too busy doing their own things, y'know?"

Zia's brothers, Damien and Dwarf, are rarely ever at the Mayfair house anymore. I haven't seen much of them since Seth's going-away ceremony the day Nataša was here and I fainted in front of her. And even before then, it was like they had moved out of here and only stopped by on occasion. New girlfriends are to blame. But I admit that I kind of miss

Damien's dark natured playful attitude and Dwarf's big mouth.

"I wish she would talk to me."

"Just give her time to cool off," Sebastian says. "It's really not about you, so don't put too much into it."

He looks towards the door once more and moves over closer to me and whispers, "What is this thing you guys are looking for anyway?"

I pause, suddenly untrusting of him, or just being paranoid again.

"A Praverian," I say. "Like Genna who had been following me. And Malachi, the one I met when we were all in Portland last month."

Sebastian nods, but doesn't say anything.

"Why do you ask?"

He shrugs. "Just looking for something to tell Zia when I go back in there." He smiles and runs the palm of his hand across his bald head. "I hope it grows back soon."

"Seriously?" I say, looking surprised. I'm glad the topic has shifted. "It's a good look for you, like I said before."

Sebastian crinkles his nose a bit. "It makes me feel naked—Well, I better get back in there with the…," he holds up his fingers in quotations, "…*info*, before Zia has my head."

"Ah, so she sent you out here?"

The right side of his mouth lifts into a confirmation, "Yeah." Then he leans in and adds quietly, "So if you could help me out with a little more than what she already knows, that'd kick ass." He leans away, grinning.

"Hmmm…," I purse my lips and mull it over for a moment, "well, you can tell her that I wouldn't tell you jack because I'd tell Zia before I ever told you."

His grin gets bigger. "Very smart," he says, nodding.

And then he disappears back inside Zia's room.

I want to go see my sister, but I think I'm going to give her and Rachel time to hang out and get to know each other. It's important for both of them, I think. They technically are the outcasts here, if I think about it. Both of them of the Vargas bloodline. Both of them pretty much rogue, but strong enough not to give into rogue behavior completely. Now I actually feel bad for Rachel, realizing that she's been the way she is because she can't help it. But she's never done anything to lose the Mayfair's trust; in fact, she attacked and beat Alex because she thought Alex was a threat to us.

As much as I want to catch up with Alex and do all of the things two long lost siblings might naturally do after being reunited, I know that Alex fitting in is important right now. But more than that, I'm still not sure she can be trusted and I'm not going to jump into anything with her too soon. I need to feel her out. We need to trap the traitor. There are several things that need to happen before I can commit my heart fully to my sister again.

And Aramei is one of them.

19

Balkan Mountains – Eastern Serbia – Winter 1761

FIRES HAVE BEEN BURNING on the horizon for six days; plumes of smoke spiraling into the heavily overcast sky. And at night, the fires are more frightening as the flames lick the black sky all over the mountainside and throughout the vast valley and beyond. A war is spreading. It's drawing closer to Aramei's village and everyday life here has all but come to a halt. The people have boarded up their homes and stables. Families sit huddled around a low, inadequate fire for fear of too much smoke rising from their chimneys and drawing attention. "Maybe it'll pass us up and head west," a man said during the village meeting earlier this morning.

But none of the villagers believes that. Aramei doesn't believe it. She knows more than anyone about what is coming and although she doesn't truly understand the extreme of it, she still knows more than they do. She's afraid to tell anyone about Viktor. She committed murder and if they knew, she would be ripped from her family and hanged. But this hasn't stopped her from doing everything in her power to convince the people of her village to prepare. It was because of her they decided to board up early rather than later. She had told her father how afraid the fires on the horizon had made her and begged him to call a meeting in the village.

"I have a terrible feeling about the fires, Father," she said on that day. "Nightmares attack my sleep every night. You must warn the people! *Please*, Father!"

And he did because he felt it, too.

While most of the villagers in the beginning let themselves believe this strange unknown war that had nothing to do with the Turks would pass them by, Aramei's father knew it might not. And so after a two hour debate, it became unanimous that the village must protect itself.

Aramei and Filipa have been sleeping huddled together on a bed in Filipa's room since that night.

"Filipa," Aramei whispers lying next to her, "I have to tell you something."

Filipa rises to sit upright on the bed. "What is it?"

Aramei lifts from the bed, too, and pulls her thick robe tight around her to keep in the warmth. She gazes toward the window where she can see a single fire, far off in the distance, dancing victoriously against the sky. But at the last minute, Aramei decides against confiding in her sister. It never goes the way she hopes it will and if Filipa knew anything about Viktor's murder, she would be in as much trouble as Aramei. Guilty by association.

She lets out her breath and lies against the cot, staring up at the low wooden ceiling.

"I'm just afraid," she says; her voice distant.

"So am I, sissa. So am I."

They lie together, curled against one another's body as the night falls into an eerie, silent darkness. A howling unlike any they have ever heard before carries on the bitter winter air. But both of them are too afraid to speak of it, neither of them willing to admit they heard it because it truly sounds more monstrous than natural.

They tremble and shake against each other.

Silently, Aramei cries into her pillow. But she doesn't cry because she's afraid. She cries because she killed a man.

Finally, after hours of lying awake, the sisters fall asleep, but Aramei's sleep remains tumultuous throughout the night, her dreams rife with horrifying images of Viktor's face. She wakes with a start, sweat soaking her cotton gown and pillow. She presses her hand against her breast and waits for her heartbeat to settle. But soon she realizes that it wasn't a nightmare that had woken her. The low mooing of the cow in the barn sounds frightened and the sheep are…silent. Aramei looks over at Filipa lying next to her. Filipa is out cold, sleeping on her back with her mouth hung open. Carefully, Aramei crawls out of the bed and slips her feet down inside her boots. She takes Filipa's heavy fur coat hanging on the back of the door and wraps herself inside of it, pushing the hood over her head.

Her father is passed out on the chair in the front room; a low fire burns behind the hearth in the fireplace, but it needs more wood; it'll burn out soon. As Aramei goes toward the front door, she stops when she stands in front of it, placing her outstretched hand upon the wood. Slowly she pushes it open after sliding the lock away with her other hand and the wind licks at the flames in the fireplace as it escapes into the room.

Her father stirs, but doesn't wake up and Aramei slips outside into the cold night and makes her way to the barn. The snow crunches underfoot as she draws closer and it and the cow are the only sounds that she can hear.

The barn door is open.

Like the house, the back portion of the barn had been boarded up leaving only one way in and out, but the barn door swings unevenly as if it had been knocked off one hinge. It makes absolutely no sound as it swings back and forth in the mild wind.

Aramei spots one sheep moving across the land about fifty feet from the barn and she expects that the rest of them have also gotten out. She hurries her steps through the thick snow and enters the barn. Something doesn't feel right. The cow is agitated, constantly bumping her hind against the wood guard across her enclosure. The three goats also appear more agitated than usual, but they aren't putting up as much of a fight to get out. Aramei approaches the cow and reaches her hands over the top rail, patting it on the hind. "It's okay, girl. It's okay." The cow moos and smells god awful, especially with its back end facing her.

As Aramei looks away from the cow, she catches movement in the back of the barn from the corner of her eye. Peering further into the bluish-black darkness, puffs of breath coil up from behind Vela's old stable and disappear into the air. Aramei's breath catches and her hand springs to her chest, but she calms down once she realizes that it's probably one of the sheep. And she approaches it, taking small, cautionary steps as though something in the back of her mind is warning her to stay away.

She pushes open the stable door and her entire body locks up in fear when she sees the giant beast lying bloodied on the barn floor surrounded by hay and the remains of one sheep.

She stumbles backward and falls over a wooden tool crate, cutting her forearm on something she can't bear to investigate. Her heart hammers inside her chest. Her breath comes out in rapid, heaving puffs of hot air swirling amid the frigid cold through her gently parted lips. Her arm stings from the cut, but she's too afraid and mesmerized to look away from the black beast-like creature staring back at her with dark predatory eyes.

"Father...," she tries to shout out, but it comes out raspy and weak and dry. *"Filipa...."*

The beast, three times the size of her and twice her height, groans and growls as it tries to adjust its position. This is when Aramei notices the hilts of three swords protruding from its chest that should've been obvious before if she weren't so mesmerized by its massive head. The beast moans in pain; blood has soaked up so much within its black fur that it looks drenched and heavy and sticky. Six-inch razor-sharp claws jut out from each of its ten massive fingers.

If Filipa were here, Aramei would already have been dragged right out of the barn with Filipa's screams piercing the air for miles. Filipa was the sensible one, but Aramei, she had always been the curious one.

The beast's left eye catches Aramei and for a split second the lid blinks over it. It raises its head carefully, revealing the other eye, which is also bleeding profusely as a great gash has been cut across the corner and along the bone toward the bottom of its pointy, hairy ear. It grunts suddenly and Aramei jumps in reaction to the frightening sound.

Its head falls back to one side as though it can't bear to hold it up any longer.

Aramei takes a deep, concentrated breath, pushing down her fear and moves forward toward it, taking small, cautious steps. Her small fingers are clutched around the opening of Filipa's long-coat and her soft, pale face peeks out from underneath the furry hood; wisps of her light hair blow gently across the bridge of her nose when a little breeze makes its way inside the shelter of the barn.

She stops about eight feet from the beast and crouches low to the hay-covered floor. And all the seconds that it takes her to go into a full crouch, Aramei's curious, childlike eyes scan over every massive inch of this strange creature, every frightening feature from its tall animal, yet human-like hind legs to the enormity of its snout where a set of razor-sharp teeth are visible.

"You're one of them, aren't you?" she whispers as softly as the wind coming through the roof. "You're one of the Black Beasts that live in the mountains."

The beast's glistening dark eyes move over her as it tries to adjust its head to better see her. Aramei can sense right away that it's aware she had spoken to it. Its colossal chest moves slow and unsteadily as it struggles for breaths.

Aramei moves closer.

Her perilous actions are part curiosity, part vulnerability, but most of all determination. Maybe now, once and for all, she will know that what her mother said happened to her was true.

Her hand emerges slowly from the sleeve of her coat as she reaches out to touch the beast's foot. She pauses inches from it, waiting, searching its eyes for any sign that might cause her to stop, but sees none. And then she rests her fingers gently within the beast's black fur. Her whole body shakes uncontrollably beneath the coat; the blood pumps through her veins so fast and so hard that she can feel it in the tips of her fingers and hear it walloping in her ears.

The beast's black eyes roll over to search her; hot, visible breath emits from its nostrils sometimes followed by small shuddering noises that no longer seem to be any cause for alarm and so Aramei ignores it. A wounded creature of any kind can makes noises like that and she can tell the difference between those of warning and those of pain.

She strokes the beast's foot, splitting her fingers through its long, coarse fur.

"I will help you," she says gently, "but you will probably die." She moves closer, now crouched at level with its knees and she knows she can't go back now. She is fully in its reach. All the beast would have to do is reach out its massive arms and grab her. But she remains calm and continues to talk to it, showing it her most prominent quality: compassion.

Aramei reaches out her hand now to touch its arm and when she sees that it hasn't rejected her, she runs her hand through the fur around its elbow and then downward over the solid muscles and to its hand. She never takes her eyes off its eyes and it follows hers intently. Briefly, she looks over at the sheep's head lying severed from the missing body, but she doesn't lose focus on the beast. Her hand now moves to one of the sword hilts.

"How can you still be alive?" she gasps quietly, carefully running her fingers along the intricate design that had been expertly carved into the silver. She sees that none of the swords have hit its heart, if in fact, its heart is in the same general spot as hers.

Her breath comes out in a long shudder, both from the cold and from the moment.

"I have to get the salve," she says, carefully rising to her feet.

She looks down at the beast, which has not once taken its gaze off her, and she shakes her head sadly. She knows in her heart that there's no possible way that this creature is going to live through the night. But she wants to help it die peacefully if she can.

She leaves the beast lying in the barn and comes back minutes later after rummaging quietly through the house for medicinal salve, clean rags for bandages and a sewing needle and twine and a small jug of clean water. The beast is lying in the same unmoving position as it was when she left. She goes to her knees fully this time, kneeling next to its body. And she stops and places her hand on its giant heaving chest, feeling the intense heat coming off its body in waves. Its heartbeat is unexpectedly measured and calm, but when it does beat it beats with the force of a fist thrusting from the inside, trying to force its way through the chest cavity.

Aramei touches the first hilt and sees that she's going to need to stand upright in order to pull it from its chest.

"I'm going to pull them out," she says with care and caution in her voice and then she rises into a stand. Wrapping both hands around the first hilt, she sucks in a breath and holds it there, shutting her eyes momentarily as if to prepare her body for what she's about to do. She purses her lips and opens her eyes, meeting the beast's gaze once more just to be certain and then she pulls. A long, agonizing growl rumbles through its body as the blade slides from its flesh. Aramei places the sword on the hay next to her and holds both hands over the open wound; blood pours from the opening, running thickly through all of her fingers. And as much as it is excruciatingly painful, the beast never loses focus; it never takes its eyes from her.

When Aramei feels it's okay to continue, she removes the last two swords. By the time she's done, she's already had to remove her coat and her gown is covered in blood. She cleans its wounds first with the water, washing away the dirt and clearing a path through the fur to expose the beast's thick, dark skin underneath. She continuously talks to it as she sews the wounds, hoping to ease its mind, wondering all the while if it can understand anything that she's saying. And always afraid it might turn on her kindness and kill her, but her need to help this creature is stronger than her need to flee from it.

"I think my mother was hurt by one of your kind," she says as she carefully slides the needle through its thick skin. "But she wasn't killed by it. She died in bed, staring up at me.

She wasn't killed like Vela, or the sheep." Her eyes move over to the sheep's head several feet away to indicate it. "And you haven't hurt me yet." She's still trying to convince herself of her own safety as much as she is trying to comfort the creature.

As she tends to its wounds, the beast begins to show signs of calming. Clearly, it's still in great pain, but its body doesn't struggle against its breath as much and something in its eyes appears to Aramei, accepting and even grateful. The eyes can reveal everything about one's soul and Aramei can see that she's in little danger in the company of this beast, if any danger at all.

She stays with it just until dawn, talking to it and telling it everything about her life. But she finds herself curious as to how or why she could feel so comfortable and safe with this creature. Why did it feel so natural to tell it all of the things she told it? And the entire time, it listened intently to her soft, melodious voice. It understood her. She could feel this and she knew this because she saw it in its eyes.

For the next three days, Aramei insisted that she take on Filipa's chores, which involved cleaning out the stables and feeding the livestock.

"Let me do it, sissa," she said to Filipa on the first day. "I want to do for you as you have done for me. You can do the cooking this week if you'd like."

Filipa always preferred the house chores as opposed to the barn and outside chores, so it was easy to keep Filipa out of the barn. Her father rarely went into the barn except to get the horse for travel, but now that there was no horse, it was easy to keep him out as well. He was too busy with the other men in the village as they scoured the valley by day, looking for signs that the war was coming closer and setting traps for the wolves. Aramei worked double-time, spending hours out of the next few days inside the barn tending to the beast. And to her astonishment, instead of dying, the beast quickly began to heal.

On the seventh night, Aramei sneaks into the barn late like she has every other night before to find the beast crouched on the ground, its great, muscled arms propped on the floor to hold up its weight. The sight is frightening, almost enough to send Aramei scrambling for the exit, but when it locks eyes with her, her legs solidify and prevent her from moving any farther. A low, grumbling moan rumbles through its body, but it sounds more affectionate than threatening and so instead of running away, she goes toward it slowly. When she is in its arms reach, she stops. Even crouched low to the ground its height is level with her standing; its head and chest so massive that three of her could fit in its shadow.

The beast reaches out a giant, clawed hand.

Aramei stiffens instinctively, but soon her muscles relax and her heartbeat slows. She knows it doesn't want to hurt her. She gazes deeply into its eyes, seeing a dark and vicious soul, but also a longing and caring heart somehow she feels is shrouded by violence and power.

She steps into the curve of its hand and it gently pulls her body against its massive, warm chest, cradling her frame.

A soft breath releases from her parted lips and her eyelashes fall as she wilts into the comfort of his powerful, yet gentle embrace.

Never in her life has she felt safer.

The beast nuzzles his great snout against her head and another low moan grumbles through his chest. It feels almost like a purr vibrating against her small body.

Aramei opens her eyes to his hand caressing her face and she leans into it, taking in the comfort of his touch as if drinking in a vial of warm euphoria.

Carefully, the beast pulls her away from him and he stands fully on his tall hind-like legs, towering over her. The cow and the goats work themselves into a frenzy.

But Aramei can't be afraid of him. She tries. She knows that to be afraid is natural and likely and expected. A small part of her *wants* to be frightened so that she can prove to herself that she isn't so unlike her sister, or any other mindful human for that matter. But no matter how hard she tries, she cannot evoke fear among the flurry of elated emotions that she is feeling right now as he towers over her.

The beast looks into her glistening, teary eyes one last time and then turns and pads away into the darkness.

20

Present Day – In the Cabin

TRAJAN STARES OFF TOWARD the wall, his gaze penetrating it so deeply that the whole of the room has fallen completely silent. My words have become the focus of his memory and the more that I describe to him in such vivid detail, the further back in time he goes himself to revisit his life with Aramei.

Eva lowers her eyes away from him after having stared intensely at him for so long, mesmerized by his reaction to my retelling of Aramei's story. I gently turn my head to see her and she looks sad.

Trajan's calm, distant voice brings us both back to him.

"I could not let her see me for what I was," he says, looking at neither of us. And then he appears uncomfortable, as though talking any further about his feelings is completely irrelevant and then he looks right at me.

"When I left Aramei in the barn that night, I had no intentions of ever seeing her again. She was human and it was forbidden. I was Alpha and the last one of my kind that could defy the laws that my father before me erected and that I had enforced for generations. Two of my sons were put to death because they were found to be infatuated with human women."

"You killed them?" I say, horrified, but not fully showing the extent of my disgust. I sit next to Trajan at the small table overlooking the downstairs floor. Always he's too close for comfort.

He doesn't look at me when he answers:

"No. That was Nataša's doing. But I do not condemn her actions; she had only been carrying out the sentences that I set forth at the beginning of my reign. Because they were my sons did not exclude them from the consequences of breaking the laws."

I hate him. He's such an unimaginable, hypocritical bastard that I feel polluted by his presence. But I also respect him and this part of me I doubt I'll ever understand. Because I know it's not the human part.

He looks across at Aramei who, as always, lies asleep on the bed. "But I *did* go back to see Aramei. After six months and after I shifted the war into the west to protect her, I left Golubac Fortress every other night to see her." He pauses and says, "From afar, of course."

"You loved her even that early." I say absently, remembering how quickly Isaac and I fell in love and I can't help but think about just how extraordinarily similar our stories are. Like Aramei, I had an overprotective older sister and a long lost mother. Like Aramei I was thrust into this dark, supernatural world against my will. Like Aramei, I saw Isaac for what he truly was, also in a barn, bloodied and beaten and frightening. And like Aramei, I was also bonded by the blood of a werewolf.

It's truly uncanny how much our stories are alike; so much so that I feel unnerved by it. But thankfully, the similarities stop there. Yeah, I'm grateful for that....

Trajan nods in response to my comment, still gazing at Aramei from across the room. "I loved her in seven nights time—," he looks solidly at me, sending a shiver through my spine, "but love is a weakness, as you can see."

Not sure if he was referring to me or to him with that statement, but I have something more pressing to ask.

"Can I ask you a...difficult question?" It wasn't the word I was looking for, difficult.

The slow turning of his dark blue eyes is the only movement his body makes. When he doesn't say no, I go on.

"Did you know about Aramei's mother?" I say in a steady voice. "I mean, is her mother's death the reason you never sired Aramei? Because you knew the transformation would likely kill her because it killed her mother?"

"Yes," he says and gestures Eva over with the wave of two fingers. "Those nights she spent with me in the barn, as you know, she told me everything about her life, including the details of her mother's death. The strength to live through the transformation, as you are also fully aware, runs in families. She would not have survived it—Prepare a bath for Aramei."

Eva bows low at the waist and heads down the stairs.

Trajan turns back to me.

"Has she told you nothing?" he says and for a moment I'm confused about whether he's speaking of Aramei or Eva.

"Not yet," I say. "All I've seen is what I've told you. She hasn't spoken directly to me. I...don't think she can...."

That was a lie, although a small one. Aramei has spoken directly to me, but she's never said anything that would indicate she is capable of actual mindful conversation. But I can't tell him this. I'm still not sure why I feel so protective of her when it comes to Trajan, but until I find out I'm sticking with the story.

Trajan slaps his hand on the tabletop, causing the table to wobble on its tall metal base. I jump on the chair, startled. I'm afraid to look at him, but my eyes turn against me and look anyway. His face is solid, though I can just barely see his strong jaws clenching with impatience. His eyes are filled with everything but anything nice; not that that's new, but I prefer it when he isn't clearly angry.

He stands up and folds his hands together in front of him. I stay at the table where I feel safer and I watch as he paces across the brightly lit room. The mid-afternoon sun beams in through all of the cabin windows. It's a perfectly beautiful day with not a cloud in the endless blue sky, helping the sun's rays to filter down through the trees surrounding the cabin. All of the windows were ordered open and so the breeze pushing through them is cool on my face and bare shoulders.

"Your sister came to me," Trajan says, pulling me harshly back into the moment and that cool breeze suddenly feels sucked from the room.

"Oh?" I say and I know I must be obvious, but I play it off the best I can.

He looks at me with those dangerous eyes, scanning my face, maybe searching for something to use against me.

"Have you found the Praverian gone Dark?"

My body stiffens and I stop breathing.

"How did you know about that?" I finally say.

"I have my sources."

Of course he does. He's the Sovereign. He knows just about everything.

"They have their hands in everything, you know," he says matter-of-factly, as if he's known this for six hundred years and is bored with it. "Praverians are everywhere. They have an agenda. They always have."

I nod. "Yeah, to protect their Charges."

He looks right at me, his hands now folded and resting on his backside, but I catch a glimpse of something cryptic in his face and then he says, "Yes, I suppose you're right," and a faint smile appears in his eyes.

This alone stuns me.

I just want him to elaborate. Or, maybe I don't. My stomach feels like there's a burning hot stone in the bottom of it, the way you feel when you're about to find out something you know has the potential to crush you.

"What is their purpose, then?" I ask and regret it before I get out the last syllable. I swallow hard, feeling the knot wedge itself dead center in my throat.

"To protect their Charges, of course," he answers simply and Eva comes back up the stairs.

I know there's much more to his half-way mocking answer than that.

Eva bows and says, "It is ready, Milord."

Trajan pauses as if he's going to say something else to me, but then walks over to the bed and lifts Aramei carefully into his arms. I stand up to properly bow as he leaves and I remain here as he disappears down the stairs with Aramei cradled against his chest.

"Adria," Eva says in a cautious whisper.

I pull my gaze away from the stairs and look across at her as she stands with her fingers interlaced.

"Yeah?"

She glances once toward the stairs, too, and then says, "You cannot continue to go under. It is too dangerous."

I move toward her.

"Eva," I say in a low voice much like she had, "You need to give me some credit. I know there's something else going on here." I step right up to her and take her hands into mine. "I know you're afraid to tell me because you're afraid that he'll find out...but you *need* to tell me everything you know." I'm trying to assure her with my body language and the pleading, desperate look in my eyes that I would never do anything to risk her well-being or her life.

Eva's pale green eyes glance away from me and her hands feel unsteady within my own. Gently, I tighten my fingers around them and force her gaze again. "*Please*, Eva…I give you my word that I won't even tell Isaac anything that you tell me." It's difficult to promise something like this, but to protect her life I will not go against my word.

Her hands slip from mine and she crosses her arms horizontally over her chest; one hand goes up to cradle her pouty mouth. Her long, red hair lays neatly against her back, which only makes her look softer. She turns at an angle and peers off toward the window and without looking at me she says, "The things you see now of her past are harmless, but when you start to see other…things and…places; by then it might be too late."

I move quickly around in front of her. "Too late for what, Eva…?"

She can hardly keep her eyes on mine. I feel like there's a conflict going on inside of her whether to continue, to lie, or to tell me anything at all. She's frightened and it's only making me want to know that much more.

I thrust her elbows into my hands and shake her.

"*Tell* me!" My voice is a strident whisper.

Silence.

"…I can't."

Her answer shocks and infuriates me at the same time, rendering me motionless.

"Just remember my warning," she says and walks away from me, "when things start to appear…different…you should think twice before going under again."

I leave on this day wanting nothing more than to take Aramei with me and hide her somewhere in the mountains myself. Away from Trajan. Away from Eva, who is so thoroughly terrified of and loyal to Trajan that I know as kind and caring as she is towards me, she would sell me out to him in a heartbeat.

But I *will* go back tomorrow and I *will* go under and no matter what I see, I've decided not to tell the truth at all anymore except to Isaac, who I am spilling everything I already know to right now.

"Evangeline is his most loyal," Isaac says, softly brushing his fingertips across my arms. I lie between his legs on the bed with my back against his chest. "She's been around since I was a child."

I feel his lips press into my hair from behind. We sit upright on his bed, his back against the headboard.

"She's petrified of him," I say. "And who can blame her?"

"I know," Isaac says softly.

"But what about what she said?" I add, becoming more rigid with worry the more I think about it all. "About being in Aramei's mind and it being dangerous."

Isaac leans around me further and kisses my jawline. "We'll figure it all out soon, but babe, maybe she's right. Maybe you shouldn't go anymore."

"No...," I say, staring at the bedroom door, lost in thought, "...I have to find out what she's trying to tell me."

Isaac knows that this will not be an argument and that my heart and mind are set on helping Aramei. He says nothing in response, but wraps his arms around me from behind.

"Isaac?"

"Yeah, babe?" He moves a hand up and brushes a lock of hair behind my ear.

"I don't think Alex is safe here." I turn my head slightly, though I can't see his face. I only feel his breath on the side of my neck. "Trajan mentioned her, but didn't really didn't go into it and it worries me."

I lean up and away from his chest and turn around halfway to face him. "Do you think he knows she's here?"

Isaac traces the tip of his index finger down the bridge of my nose and then rests it upon my lips. "He probably does," he answers and I tense up instantly. "But if he wanted her dead, she would already be."

He watches my lips and I feel them react under the hungry gaze of his eyes. My heart hammers down into my stomach as he studies them before gently parting them with his own. "Don't worry about Alex," he says between kisses, "Don't worry about anything. Not right now." He teases me, nipping my bottom lip before slipping his warm tongue into my mouth. He lifts my body around on his lap to face him; my bare knees burrow into the pillows behind his back.

The kiss breaks, but his mouth is still so close to mine that I can taste the mintiness of his breath. "Did you lock the door?"

"Yes," I whisper into his lips and feel my eyelids close softly when he crushes his mouth over mine again. Isaac peels off my shirt and cradles his arm around my naked back, flipping me over to sit on top of me. He grabs both of my wrists in one hand and pins them above my head. I look up into his ravenous eyes and know that I better not squirm. If I do, he'll pin me tighter and my wrists will hurt.

But I do squirm because that's exactly what I want him to do.

My eyelids are heavy, tingling and numb, and I can hardly keep them open. His free hand slides down the soft curvature of my hip leaving chill bumps in its wake. And then he moves his head down the length of my body with it. He kisses my ribs, one by one, painfully working his way to my bellybutton and my body wilts under the magic of his mouth.

"Be still," he demands softly as he lets go of my hands and sinks further below my stomach.

And I do exactly what he tells me to do because I don't want him to stop. The heat of his hand slipping under the fabric of my shorts sends fire through my legs.

I shudder out a moan before he even touches me.

~~~

BAM! BAM! BAM! I jolt awake and practically fall right out of Isaac's bed with the sheet wrapped around my body. It takes me a second to realize that the banging is coming from the other side of the door. Isaac lifts up in the bed, an intolerant expression lies on his face.

"What?" he shouts at the door.

"It's me, bro," Nathan says from the hallway. "Get up. Put your Spiderman boxers on and let's hit the pond!"

I look over at Isaac, eyes as wide as plates. Then I glance at the bedside clock. It's ten o'clock at night. "Is he serious?" I hiss and look back at the door. "Are you serious, Nate?!"

Isaac jumps out of the bed and slips his boxers on, which I might add are *not* Spiderman.

"Let's go," he says with the jerk of his head. "Get dressed."

A spat of air bursts from the back of my throat and my eyebrows draw together in confusion.

"I'll explain it on the way."

"But what about swimming trunks?" I say while at the same time practically tripping into my shorts.

All I want to do is go back to sleep.

"We're not going swimming."

He grabs my hand and walks me briskly out the bedroom door; I'm clumsily trying to cover my boobs with my free hand because I didn't really have time to put on the bra before my t-shirt. And we zip down the stairs and out into the night air.

"We did something while you were with Aramei this morning," Isaac says as we dash across the front yard and toward the path through the trees.

I'm easily keeping up, but still the human part of me is paranoid I'm going to trip in the darkness and fall on my face if I don't watch my footing.

"What exactly did you do?" I look over at him in a wary sidelong glance.

All kinds of things rush through my mind, but nothing I can immediately fit into this puzzle thrust on me out of nowhere.

Just as we reach the opening through the woods near the pond, Isaac stops abruptly and jerks my body by the hand to stop with him. This is getting more confusing by the second. I hear voices coming from the path behind us and Isaac just stands there, staring into the trees as if waiting for whoever it is to move into view.

Nathan emerges from my right with Harry at his side.

"What the hell is going on?" I say.

"Just wait," Isaac says, lowering my hand with his fingers on my wrist. He never takes his eyes off the path.

"Here they come," Harry says and he looks extremely nervous. His eyebrows are knotted and his jaw continuously moves around as if he's gritting his teeth.

Nathan is sporting a spiteful grin and I'm not sure what to make of that.

I hear Cecilia's voice and crinkle my nose absently at the sound of it. She's going on and on about...no one ever knows. As the voices get closer I gather there are more than just a few and the large swath of shadow falling out ahead of them tells me there is a rather large group walking down the length of the path. Daisy, Zia, Sebastian, Cecilia, Camilla and even Shannon, Phoebe, Elizabeth and Xavier; Isaac's other siblings that I rarely ever see.

And everybody else, too.

My head snaps around to Isaac, "You set the trap!" I whisper harshly.

He nods.

Oh my God...Oh my God...

I can't breathe all of a sudden.

"We had to wait until we could get Cecilia here since she's a suspect," Harry whispers behind me and the group is coming up fast.

"Yeah," Nathan laughs, "and that really wasn't hard to do. Just dangle a few biceps in her face and she's on it like flies on shit."

I grasp Isaac's hand tight and my adrenaline is suddenly burning like acid through my veins. Nathan's grinning face had at first made me feel a sort of excitement, but now that the reality of what is about to happen sinks in, I find myself completely and utterly panicked.

21

THE GROUP FINALLY EMERGES from the canopy of trees and they all step into the light of the moon in the grass-covered opening together. Most are in bathing suits. A single pole light glows and hums close to the dock with a power line stretching from the top and through the trees, giving the house its electricity.

The first face I see even though she's packed near the center with Rachel at her side is my sister. My blood races furiously through every loft of my body. I feel sick to my stomach and find that already my hand is pressed over my belly. Sweat beads in my hairline and an annoying rogue vein constantly twitches near my left eye leaving an intense itching sensation that I can't even bring my hand up to scratch, I'm so fixated on the scene.

Harry steps in-between Isaac and me.

"There's just one thing we didn't have time to work out yet," Harry says in my mind and I know Isaac and Nathan hear it too because they both look in at us between them after Harry's comment.

"Unfortunately," Nathan says, *"it's a major thing, but we have to do this now. Bas and Zia were talking about going to Boston again and taking Camilla with them."*

"Wait!" I say, *"You've been planning this trap all this time without me?"* Surely they hear the bitterness in my tone.

"Baby, it wasn't intentional," Isaac says without looking at me. *"The best time for us to plan has been in the mornings while you're with Aramei. Most in the house are still asleep."*

"Okay, so what part did you not figure out?" I say, still bitter. I might be for a while, actually.

Before any of them can answer, Cecilia speaks up from the crowd:

"Where's the beer?" She's standing at the front with Camilla and Zia on each side of her and she's dressed in a skin-tight pair of shorts that barely cover her butt cheeks; her face cheeks are all rosed-up with pink blush.

"Beer's on its way," Nathan says doing a weird little dance that embarrasses me.

"Dude, you suck," I say telepathically, but find myself laughing, too.

He winks at me because he doesn't care.

I just shake my head.

Beer? I'm not even going to ask. I'm sure it was just to get a certain few out here to 'participate'.

"We'll party after," Isaac announces, "but first I've called you all here because I have some announcements to make."

A chorus of voices moves briefly on the air as everyone whispers to the person next to them what they think these announcements might be.

"Hopefully it's about letting me out of these stupid shackles," I hear my sister say.

"Isaac's going to name his Right Hand," Camilla says.

"But that's really not an announcement." Zia says. "We already know Nathan is second in command here."

"Yes," Daisy says, "but Nathan will be leaving for Serbia sometime so Isaac will have to name someone new."

Daisy is actively participating with the 'suspects', but she obviously knows more about what's going on than I do. I catch her eye briefly; that knowing, be-ready-to-react look is hidden in her creamy-white face. Not to mention, she looks extremely nervous, like she's about to walk across a mine field, which is the space between them and us.

I catch myself looking around the ground for signs of little mounds of dirt. But they weren't stupid about it and made the trap obvious in any way.

Isaac's fingers slide away from mine as he steps forward.

"First," he says, folding his hands in front level with his waist line, "I need to get something out of the way." He holds out one hand palm up. "Alexandra? Will you step to the front please?"

Oh great! He's starting with my sister. I'm all for getting the hardest out of the way first, but I would've liked a little advanced warning. I shut my eyes and breathe in an unsteady breath.

Alex pushes her way through the crowd, taking awkward steps through the grass and into the empty space between us and them; the shackles restricting the length of her strides.

I swallow six lumps in my throat.

She stops and looks across at us, waiting with one raised eyebrow; her hands are fixed closely together near her pelvis because of the shackles on her wrists.

When Isaac doesn't say anything, I gradually step up next to him and look to him at my side. I'm about to nudge him with my elbow when I hear his voice in my head:

"It's not her...."

"What? She already walked through it?" I start to crane my neck, looking every which way for evidence of trap lines,

but Isaac grabs my wrist. *"Don't do that,"* he says harshly. *"You'll make it obvious."*

"Oh...." I blink away my folly and try to look natural, but I can tell by how stiff my face is right now that I look anything but natural.

Isaac clears his throat.

"As you all know," he begins, "Alexandra is Adria's sister. Yes, she is of the Vargas bloodline and she did...," he glances at Alex briefly and I can tell he's still seriously distrusting of her despite not being the Dark Praverian, "...she did cause a lot of problems for Adria months ago—nearly killed her, in fact—," there was poison in that statement. I look to and from both of them nervously as he goes on, "but like Rachel, Alexandra is to be given a chance to prove herself and she'll not be treated as a traitor by anyone in this pack."

Some faces are staring back at us awkwardly and I realize that I'm sort of doing the same thing. This announcement has pretty much already been established when Alex first got here. It was never made into a ceremony like this, but...Isaac better come up with something else, fast.

"I thought it was her...," he says absently, still not looking at me.

"Well, it's not," I say, *"so you better speed this up or move onto something else before* you *make it obvious."*

Xavier steps out of the crowd now and stands beside Alex, his short blond hair naturally a little messy in the front, which apparently helps with his sex appeal. He has dark blue eyes that always appear hooded, and a facial bone structure that could land him any six-figure modeling contract if he didn't think male models were such pussies.

"She can stay in my room," he says with a deep, dimpled grin.

That familiar grin always reminds me that he's Daisy's twin.

"Ummm, *no*?" Rachel says, also stepping out of the crowd, "She's staying with *me*." She snarls at Xavier, but Xavier smiles back at her with charm and confidence.

"Maybe you should ask *her*," he says.

"What is happening?" I say quietly, trying to keep a straight face as I watch.

Nathan laughs behind me and says under his breath, "You're witnessing what Xavier is famous for?"

"Being a man-slut?" I say, mortified.

I'm glaring at my sister now with warning, but she's not even looking at me.

She snarls at Xavier. "Who the hell do you think you are, anyway?" A look of unbelieving disgust warps her face.

"I'm the guy you're going to sleep with before this week is over."

Nathan and Isaac both can hardly contain their laughter. I'm still trying to make myself believe I'm actually standing here listening to this. *Seriously*? Did he really just say that?

Alex crosses her arms—always awkwardly because of the chains—and steps right up to Xavier with a heavily wrinkled nose. "Wow. You really have me seriously fu—."

"Alex?" I say, waving a hand at her to calm down, but I only have her attention for about two seconds before she's back in Xavier's sexy grinning face.

"You keep telling yourself that, okay?" she retorts, popping out one hip.

"Oh, I will," he says confidently and then he leans towards her slowly and touches his lips along the side of her jaw. Alex doesn't move, but for a second a flicker of confusion flits across her eyes.

I think Cecilia's eyeballs are about to drop out of her head.

Alex just stands there looking at Xavier as he pulls away and walks casually back to the front of the crowd.

"Oh man...," Nathan whispers, "he's got her."

My head snaps around and beams of anger shoot from my eyes at him. "I wouldn't be so sure about that," I snap. "Alex isn't easy like the girls Xavier's used to."

"Nathan," Isaac says also with laughter in his voice, "I think you should've said *Alex* has *Xavier*."

Nathan brings his hand up and rubs his chin in thought. "Y'know, I think you're right, bro. Adria's sister looks like she wants to pop his eyes out with a fork—no one's ever refused him like that before. She didn't even giggle."

"Can we get *on* with this?" I say as the resentment starts to boil closer to the surface. I won't have someone like Xavier using my sister for sex and tossing her aside like trash. And it really gets under my skin that Isaac and Nathan seem to be getting a kick out of this.

But that problem is for later....

I have been so dumbfounded by the exchange between Alex and Xavier that it takes me a few minutes to realize that two more—Xavier and Rachel—have just been marked off the list.

"It's not Rachel...," I say aloud, but in a quiet whisper more to myself. I can't believe it. I wanted it to be her, at least, up until she and Alex latched onto each other's company. "It's not her...."

I raise my chin slowly to see the other faces in the crowd. There are several, but it's already been narrowed down to mostly people I care for, but can live with being the one. Alex and Zia were the two I feared the most and now that they have been ruled out I feel like I can breathe a little easier.

Alex takes it upon herself to walk back to stand with the crowd, assuming Isaac is finished making her the center of attention.

But then something strange catches my eye in a sort of morbid slow-motion, the kind that as you watch you start to see something traumatic being set in motion and you have no time to react to it. Zia smiles a chilling smile across the space between us and she slowly curls her fingers around the chain dangling between Alex's wrists. In all of a few seconds, Alex's body is hurled into the air above Zia's white-blond head and bashed against the ground face-first. Several people scatter outward, tripping over one another as they scramble for safe distance. Isaac's sister, Phoebe, suddenly drops to her knees before she can get out of Zia's path and she reaches up, clawing at her throat as if being choked to death.

Isaac, me and Nathan start to run forward towards them, but our feet come out from under us and we soar backwards through the air as if snatched in mid-run by the backs of our shirts. I land hard on my butt, feeling my left wrist twist painfully underneath my leg.

"You can't!" Harry screams at us and then I'm being dragged across the dirt and grass by my other wrist. "She'll kill you!"

I don't know how Harry did it, but it's obvious now he was the one who stopped the three of us from running toward Zia to help the others.

"Stay out of the trap!" he yells. "She can't hurt you outside of it!"

Nathan and Isaac are already on their feet again, looking to and from Zia and Harry, wondering what to do and starting to feel like they could care less about Harry's demand and go for Zia anyway. They remain still; Isaac in so much shock he doesn't run to help me up like he normally would and I'm in so much shock I can't get up by myself. I sit on the ground with my back arched forward, my hands holding up my weight.

Phoebe's curly raven-black hair is twisted around her face. Her dark eyes are bulging from their sockets as she gasps for air and claws at her throat as if trying to pry away invisible hands she thinks are choking her. Her black claws protrude from her fingertips, but she can't do anything. She can't transform and she can't move.

Zia drags Alex across the ground on her stomach to the edge of the trap line, knowing that it's there but she can't cross it.

Xavier bursts through the crowd that has gathered away from the trap and runs toward Zia, eyes swirling black. With my keen senses, I can hear his ribs breaking with every thrust of his feet. He's starting to shift form, but the second he crosses the trap line and into Zia's realm, it's like he runs head-on into a brick wall. His body slams into the invisible barrier that Zia created and then he's sent flying through the air. His back hits the light pole near the pond with so much force that it snaps in half and crashes into the water; sparks spew and sizzle and pop until the light blinks out completely, leaving the landscape bathed in an eerie blue smoking haze.

Phoebe falls forward, gasping for air. I watch helplessly as the veins in her face come to the surface and implode underneath the skin creating pools of blood around her eyes.

"You're killing her!" Isaac roars.

He starts to move forward again, but Nathan grabs him by the arm and stops him.

I see Daisy standing near the crowd with Camilla clutched to her side, their faces streaked with tears. Daisy's probably the strongest one here, but she knows not to shift. I know Harry has drilled this moment into her head over and over again so that when the time came she would know to do nothing. It would be suicide.

To the amazement of everyone, Zia's true identity begins to unravel before us. Her short hair grows longer and starkly whiter—I never imagined it could be whiter than it was. The tips of her silky strands seem to shimmer in the darkness, moving unnaturally around her shoulders as though alive. Her eyes glow the brightest pearl-white I have ever seen.

Sebastian is still on the ground, like me, staring at Zia in such shock that he looks frozen in horror.

Zia cracks her neck and cocks her head to one side, looking down at Phoebe's struggling body.

"A sister for a sister, Isaac?" she says venomously and a terrifying grin spreads across her perfect white face. She reaches out her free hand in front of her and crushes it into a fist. Phoebe's neck caves in on itself and her body stops moving in a gruesome instant. She slumps over onto the ground, dead.

An eerie silence falls over us all.

I can't look at Isaac because I literally can't move, but I can feel him, the wrath coming to the surface in a sort of delayed reaction caused by shock. I feel the beast inside as well as inside of Nathan, on the very fringes of control.

Isaac wants revenge for his sister's death, but he sucks it down into the pit of his stomach and holds himself back.

He steps forward and I finally jump to my feet, but he thrusts his hand backward at me and I stay put. It feels like my heart is about to burst. I feel it in my kneecaps and in my toes.

Harry steps past me to stand with Isaac and Nathan grabs me and holds me still, probably just in case. He's right to do it. All three of them know that I could make a run for it at any second, trying to get to Alex.

I can't bear to watch her die like I just watched just Phoebe die.

"Who are you?" Isaac says carefully, but something in his tone leads me to believe that he has an idea now of exactly who she is now.

Zia smiles bitterly and yanks on Alex's chain, causing her to flip over onto her back, her arms suspended above her head.

I can't understand how, but the entire area about thirty feet outward in four directions around Zia seems vaguely brighter than everything else. It's as if the trap barrier is keeping not only Zia inside of it, but also the strange light that emits from her body, which is similar to the color of her eyes. But it's faint, just barely noticeable.

"Is it not obvious by now?" Zia says cocking her head to the other side and looking upon Isaac with mock fascination. "Think back a couple of years. Surely you haven't already forgotten about Avril. Or—," she gazes coldly at me and my heart reacts to it by skipping a few beats, "...has Adria helped convince you that it wasn't your fault that Avril died? That's what a good girlfriend does, right? She pats you on the back when you're feeling guilty and tells you all the reasons why you shouldn't."

"Avril was your sister," Isaac says.

Zia smiles in answer and jerks Alex's chain again just to keep her from getting comfortable. "My sister *and* my Charge."

I feel the hope of the situation completely draining out of me. I think back on the story Isaac told me of his ex-girlfriend, Avril, who died after he sired her. And then something Genna Bishop told Isaac once: *"They go Dark for endless reasons—pick anything that might make you want to betray your own kind and it could be a reason."* I see now that I have been the source of Zia's revenge since the night I met Isaac on that dark street after leaving the skate park. She knew I had caught his eye and she wanted to take from him what he took from her.

A flash of the attack by Sibyl in the car, the one that technically killed me, crosses my mind, too. It was her. It was Zia who was with Sibyl and Viktor that night, the unknown werewolf that Isaac never could identify.

"But how could she say the word Praverian?" I think to myself, dumbfounded. *"She said it! I know I heard her say it. Twice!"*

"The answer is simple, Adria: illusion," Zia says and I see that I have been so traumatized by this that I let my mind wall down without knowing it. "I didn't really say it. You just thought I did." She points her index finger upward, "Oh, and I was the one that wrecked the car with you in it. I was the beastly face staring in at you from the shattered windshield."

"You've been plotting with Viktor all this time...," I say, my voice trying to agree with the disbelief in my mind.

Zia chirps a small laugh, but somehow it still manages to sound spiteful. "I wouldn't say plotting—I have Viktor by the short n' curlies. He sired me in exchange for protecting his mindless little human bitch, Aramei. Being what I am, I can only hold illusions for so long." She rolls her eyes as though that is an unfortunate inconvenience.

Harry speaks up, "And so you became what they are so you wouldn't have to maintain an illusion."

Zia's grin just gets bigger with Harry's voice. It's like he's the cherry on top of this massive retributive treat.

"I should've known you were one of us," she says. "Your attraction to me in the beginning—we're always more attracted to our own kind. I guess I dodged a bullet with you."

Tears are burning my eyes and when I catch Alex's tortured gaze near Zia's feet, those tears burst to the surface.

I can't lose my sister again.

I throw my body forward to try and run, but Nathan's arm is tight around my waist. I wail. "Please! Just let Alex go! Please, Zia!" I can hardly see straight the tears are clouding my vision.

"I don't think so," Zia snaps. "I don't play that an-eye-for-an-eye bullshit, Adria." She glares back at Isaac in a sidelong glance. "You take one eye from me and I take two. Consider it interest."

"NO!" I slam my body against Nathan's, over and over again trying to break free from his relentless grip, but I can't move.

When my ribs start to break and my skull begins to expand, I'm suddenly rendered immobile and powerless. I can't shift, just like Phoebe couldn't and I don't understand why until I look over and see Harry's glowing red eyes staring back at me. How is it possible that he can control a full shift in such a way?

He turns back to Zia and Alex, but it's Zia who speaks:

"You know you can't drink my Soul." There's a grim warning in her voice, dancing around maliciously on her grinning lips.

Isaac moves toward me and looks up at Nathan, "Get her out of here."

"What? Wait….No I'm not leaving!" I thrash around in Nathan's hands.

"I can't hold her off much longer," Harry says and suddenly I realize he's talking about me. He's starting to show signs of distress; his eyes open and shut from exhaustion as he does everything in his power to continue holding back my transformation.

"PLEASE JUST LET HER GO!" I finally break free from Nathan's grasp, but just fall right into Isaac's who seems to have been waiting for it.

As Isaac holds my thrashing, screaming body back, I see Alex on the ground looking at me. Our eyes lock and then in one solid motion, she breaks the chain between the shackles in half and then just as quickly reaches down and pulls apart the ones binding her ankles. Almost a half a second too late, Alex rolls out of the way just as Zia realizes what is happening and she makes it across the trap barrier. Zia's hand barely brushes through the strands of Alex's hair, but misses the handful she had been going for to keep Alex inside the trap with her.

Now Zia is inside of it all alone.

22

"ALEX!" I SCREAM OUT her name as Isaac lets go of me and I run towards her. We crash into each other's arms. But the moment is quickly changed when the ground begins to shake and rumble beneath our feet.

Alex drags me back with her to stand with Nathan and Isaac, who like Harry, can look at no one but Zia.

Zia falls to her knees and raises her fists in the air and when they come back down against the earth, the ground ripples outward around her in all directions but crashes into the barrier and stops.

"How is she *doing* that?!" I shriek.

Isaac and Nathan fall into each other, almost knocked completely from their feet.

"Harry *do* something!" Isaac shouts, grabbing onto my arm and pulling me and Alex towards him.

Daisy and everybody else are all doing the same to stay on their feet as the ground shakes; some have fled into the woods.

"I can't!" Harry yells back. "I told you I can't reap her!"

"Why *not*?" I scream, gripping Isaac and Alex both each in one hand. "That's what you do! You drink each other's Souls!"

Harry, tired of letting Zia do all the damage, stumbles closer to her and makes one violent slapping motion through the air with his hand and Zia falls backward as if his hand had actually made contact with her face. She skids a few feet across the dirt.

But so does Harry. He falls beside us as if the trap was also helping keep his power from doing much damage inside as it is keeping Zia from doing damage to the outside.

Harry jumps to his feet and looks back at us, "Not one gone Dark," he says, out of breath, "If I drink her Soul I drink in her darkness, too!"

So, this was what he meant earlier when he said there was one thing they hadn't quite worked out yet.

Great. Just great!

From the corner of my eye—and I do a double-take— an old figure with leathery-brown skin and deep-set wrinkles around her eyes emerges from the path on the other side of Zia. Harry and Zia both stop cold and the ground stops shaking in an instant.

Minna Abrahamsen.

And then in the snap of two fingers, Harry is gone.

My head darts all around every which way and Daisy runs out of the crowd to the place he last stood. She runs over and grabs me by the shoulders, "Where did he go? Adria!"

"I-I don't know!" I look across the space at Minna, fearing the absolute worst.

"Not him!" I say, pushing Alex and Isaac away from me and running towards Minna. "What did you do?!"

I stop just short of Zia's barrier. My chest heaves with breath, my eyes are wide and panicked.

"Good to see you, too," Minna smiles crookedly, "And I appreciate the confidence you have in my abilities, but I didn't do nuthin' to the skinny one." She shrugs her old, decrepit shoulders. "He saw me and did what they all do and got the hell outta Dodge."

She dismisses me and shuffles right up to the edge of Zia's trap; a purse hangs from her right shoulder.

"Well hello there," Minna says, wriggling her bony fingers at Zia.

Isaac and I share the same look of utter shock—how did she know where to find us? Nathan can't seem to move his muscles anymore and he looks like he's just come down with a stomach bug.

"Get away from me," Zia warns with her teeth clenched. She backs away from Minna, but keeps her pearl-colored eyes on her.

Minna chokes out a laugh and crosses her arms over her chest. She cranes her neck; the rope-like muscles in her throat stretch bizarrely. She begins to walk the length of the invisible barrier as if inspecting it. "I guess it did work, after all."

Isaac and I look right at each other and he's probably thinking the same thing: What? Was she not sure it even would?

Zia backs up farther until she can't anymore and her sadistic, grinning face has fallen victim to trepidation. When Minna reaches down inside the purse she carries and pulls out a jar, Zia presses hard against the back of the barrier like a frenzied cat trying to scratch its way out of a box. "I WILL KILL ALL OF YOU!" Zia roars and with it the wind seems to blow, shaking the leaves of the nearest trees. Her pearl-colored eyes are swirling with white-hot light, the shimmering tips of her hair dance madly in the breeze behind her.

Isaac and Nathan both push Alex and me safely behind them. We hold our arms around each other so tight that I can feel Alex's ribs grating against mine. The cold silver of one shackle still locked around her wrist sends painful shivers up my spine.

Minna begins to chant strange words into the night; her eyes roll back in her head.

"Don't let her do this to me, Adria," Zia yells out to me. Fear has dominated all of her features. "You were my best friend. And I lost my sister just as you did! You should know how I *feel*!" She screams out the last sentence hoarsely. "Stop her, Adria! Don't let her do this!"

My *best friend*? I shake my head at her, my eyes wide and unbelieving and scared of what will happen to her just the same. I feel the wind drying out my front teeth as I inhale small, rapid breaths through my parted lips. "No, Zia...," I can't stop shaking my head and the more I think about everything she's done, the more rapid my head begins to move side to side. "No...you tried to kill me. You tried to kill Alex and you—." I look a few feet away from Zia at Phoebe's dead body lying on the ground, her eyes still open peering at me, lifeless and cold and empty.

I look back up at Zia, not having to say the words I had started to say about Phoebe.

When Zia sees that nothing she can say will save her, her fake pleading face becomes something more hateful. Her white hair begins to move in a frenzy above her, like snakes on the head of Medusa, and she brings her arms back behind her, fists clenched. She opens her mouth and an ear-shattering scream is forced from her lungs, sending all of us scrambling farther backward with our fists pressed against our ears. All except for Minna, who remains standing close to the trap, chanting her strange chant. The trap barrier absorbing the movement of the intense sound starts to become visible. It begins to fade in and out like a dull fluorescent light constantly licked by a short in its wires.

Zia falls to the ground, gripping her head in her tightly-clenched fists. "Cras es Noster!" she says to Minna, pushing the foreign words through her teeth. "You'll never harvest us all!"

My eyes grow wider as Zia's form becomes wispy and transparent. Three, five, six duplicates of her appear and disappear like wind blowing through intricate swaths of smoke, each one of her ghostly faces screaming out into the infinite night.

I feel my fingers pressing and shaking against both sides of my face; tears barrel from my eyes.

And with a great and loud whooshing sound, Zia's smoke-like body is sucked into the jar in Minna's hand and all sounds cease to exist except the small clinking of the lid being placed back on the jar and tightened.

The barrier blinks out indefinitely and all that is left inside the trap is the stirred dirt falling down softly against the ground and around Phoebe's body.

No one can speak. Or move. Or do anything for several long, silent moments.

Isaac breaks the quiet.

"How did you know?"

Minna carefully slides the jar swirling with reddish smoke, down into the bottom of her flowery purse. For a brief second, even amid all that has happened and is still happening, I think about how tacky that purse is.

She tucks the purse back under her arm and pats the side of it once. "Young people amaze me," she says. "Why don't you ask that delicious man-cake standing behind you?"

Everybody looks at Nathan, who still looks sick and depressed. When he realizes everyone is staring at him he shakes off the stun of the moment and holds up his hands, palms up, "What?" The creases between his eyebrows deepen.

Minna rolls her eyes and whips out a cigarette, placing it between her cracked, leathery lips and it dangles there precariously until she lights it with a Bic. Inhaling deeply, Minna closes her eyes and savors the moment as if that cigarette is the most pleasurable thing she's ever experienced. She drops her head and opens her eyes as she exhales; smoke filters up and around her lips and creeps into her eyes.

"Ahhh," she breathes with a smile. "Knowing that I can smoke forever and it'll never kill me makes each one taste better than the last—I smoke three packs a day now!" She says this triumphantly.

"You look like you smoked *four* packs a day *before* the Blood Bond," I say, snarling.

I find myself constantly looking to the spot where Zia last stood and back and forth to Minna's purse where she is now and it makes me sad.

Zia….

"Well, you're welcome," Minna says, pursing her lips haughtily. "I save your asses from that Praverian scum and this is the thanks I get." She takes another toke of her cigarette, leaving bright pink imprints around the filter.

"Just get to it, alright?" Isaac says. "Tell me how you knew where to find us."

Minna smirks. "The Bond, of course—how is it that I know more about it than you do?" She clicks her tongue.

"I closed my mind off to you," Nathan says and he looks truly appalled. "Believe me, I know how a Blood Bond works. It was bad enough I had to bond you to me. Y'think I'd leave the link open?"

"Of course not," Minna says with smoke billowing between her lips and slipping into the night air, "but when you're asleep and dreaming, you seem to have no control over your mind wall."

Nathan breathes in deeply and his eyes shut softly with regret.

"You have a lot of dreams about a pretty black-haired girl," Minna teases and I see the muscles in Nathan's arms harden and his nostrils flare. "You know, I could pretend to be her for you if you'd like." Her rough lips lift into a carnal grin.

Isaac's arm swings out horizontally to stop Nathan in his livid steps forward.

"You're going to leave our friend alone," he says in a low, stern voice. "Harry isn't like Zia, the one you reaped here. You're going to get in your car, or whatever it was that brought you here, and go back to Providence to your miserable existence. And if any of us ever see your face again, you will be killed."

Minna twirls her hand around with the cigarette between her fingers. "You can threaten me all you want," she says, "but it will never change what I am and what I do. Maybe I won't be the one to harvest that Soul, the one you call Harry, but one of us will. In due time."

Daisy lunges on Minna, knocking the cigarette from her fingertips and they crash to the ground; her purse with the jar inside falls a couple feet from her hand. Before Minna can get a word out, Daisy starts to transform sitting on top of her. I stumble backward into someone, I have no idea who. Her transformation is so fast. She doesn't go through the waves of pain or the seemingly endless, torturous minutes it takes us all to shift. In a matter of seconds she is fully transformed, rising many feet above Minna's splayed body and she leans over her, blade-like teeth dripping with saliva. Isaac, Nathan and all of their siblings left standing outside jump on Daisy together, all of them in their mediate forms with swirling black eyes and long, black fingernails and graying skin. But they look like birds attacking a bear. Elizabeth is tossed past me, soaring inches from my head. Xavier is thrown to the ground and just misses being crushed by Daisy's beastly foot.

Isaac and Nathan struggle to hold onto her and I just watch in horror.

Amid the carnage, Minna rolls over onto her hands and knees, grabs desperately for her purse and scrambles as far away as she can.

I keep my eyes on her, just in case she tries to run, but she seems too traumatized to let her mind tell her legs what to do.

What looked like a mound of bodies starts to shrink toward the ground as they finally get Daisy controlled. Isaac and Nathan pull her giant arms behind her back and it takes all of their strength combined. Daisy starts to calm; her enormous body is pinned against the ground, each breath forced from her nostrils stirs the dirt around her snout. Gradually, her skin and hair begins to change; the golden-blond replacing the wiry black fur, the black-grey flesh turning creamy-white again.

She lies naked against the earth with Isaac now holding both of her wrists still.

"I'll take her inside," Xavier insists, waving Isaac away from her. Xavier, looking concerned and furious, bends down and takes his twin sister into his arms. And as he goes to leave with her he points at Minna and says to Isaac, "Kill that crazy old bitch, or *I* will!" And he and Daisy slip into the trees down the dark path leading back to the house.

Nathan runs over and picks up Phoebe's body.

He and Isaac stare down at Phoebe ceremonially. Isaac reaches out his hand and brushes the blood from the corner of her mouth.

I literally choke on my tears, bursting into an uncontrollable sobbing fit. I bury my face in Alex's chest and she holds my shuddering body tight against hers.

"So what now...," I hear Isaac say and I lift my head from Alex, "...you take Zia back in a jar—I can't believe I just said that in a literal sense—," he looks back at us momentarily, "—and hide her away in your serial-killer basement safe? I'm sorry, but something about that just doesn't give me much peace of mind."

Nathan disappears with Phoebe through the trees following the same path that Xavier just took.

Minna sucks on her cigarette and flicks the long ashes on the ground. "They're perfectly secure," she says. "The ones you saw have been there for a very long time—I told you, the safe is protected." She moves closer to Isaac a few steps. The fully smoked cigarette falls to the ground at her feet and she crushes it with the toe of her granny-boot. She just looks at him for a moment, studying his face. "You people are so blind," she says pursing her mouth sourly. "But one day you'll know—if you were smart, you'd leave people like me alone and turn your misguided disgust towards the ones you call friend."

I step away from Alex and stand next to Isaac. "Nothing you can say is going to turn us on Harry. He said you'd try that. It won't work."

Minna smiles a chilling smile and I hate her even more for it actually having an effect on me. I swallow down the doubt that her manipulative words have brought to the surface. "You got what you wanted, now leave." I glare at her with all the revulsion I can squeeze out of my face.

Minna smiles and readjusts the purse strap on her shoulder. She looks behind us at the small crowd of people still watching and listening and probably still trying to understand everything that happened. Then she turns her gaze back on Isaac and me. "You know...I will need werewolf blood sometime," she says and Isaac tenses up next to me.

I take a hold of his contracting hand.

"You won't be getting it from anyone here," Isaac growls. "Not even my brother."

The corner of Minna's wrinkly lipstick-stained mouth lifts into a subtle, shrewd grin. But she doesn't respond. She turns and walks away, disappearing into the cover of the trees in the opposite direction of the house.

I can only wonder what that grin meant, what kinds of tricks and scams her wicked mind is conjuring up.

Alex runs up behind me. "Okay—." She pauses in mid-sentence and holds up a finger. "What the hell was that?"

My shoulders finally relax as I let my breath out. I didn't know I had been holding most of it in the entire time.

"I'll explain it inside," I say.

Feeling an intense pang of grief, I realize that it's coming from Isaac and I turn to him, grasping his hand. "Baby, what is it?"

He can't look me in the eyes, but stares down at the ground instead. I curl both of my hands around the curvature of his jaw, gently forcing his absent gaze and even though he's now looking me right in the eyes, I sense that he doesn't really see me.

"Phoebe's dead," he says, seemingly more to himself, his own callous guilt. "I can't believe she was Avril's sister. Phoebe is dead because of me."

His eyes and his full attention lock on me now and the pain is straining his face. I lean in and kiss his lips tenderly.

"Don't do that. Please," I say.

Isaac kisses me back softly and then he smiles faintly under his grief. "But you're safe now and this is over."

I smile back, running the tip of my finger along the side of his neck.

"I think I'm going to let you spend some time with Alex."

I look at Alex on my right. She's waiting impatiently with crossed arms and a raised brow. I look down at her wrists and wonder.

"You broke out of them."

Alex grins hugely and raises both hands in front of her; the chain links left dangling.

"Yeah, I could've broken out of these babies a long time ago."

"Well, why didn't you?"

"Because then I never would've gained your trust, Dria." She cocks her head to the side.

Isaac reaches in his jeans pocket and pulls out the key to the shackles. "Let me take what's left of them off."

Alex holds out her wrists and Isaac removes them, afterwards, kneeling down to remove the ones from her ankles. She moves her wrists and legs around as if readjusting to the comfort of being free again.

"Much better," she says.

I smile warmly at her. This is real. My sister is home, where she's supposed to be.

"I'll see you upstairs later," Isaac says and kisses me goodbye. I start to stop him because I don't want to leave him alone, especially not after what happened, but he says in my mind: *"No...I want you to be with your sister. Do that for me."*

I nod and reluctantly let him go.

Once he's gone, the others from the small crowd leave, too. Sebastian walks out last and I run over to stop him.

"Sebastian—"

He puts up his hand and doesn't turn around to look at me. "Not right now. Just...," his hand bobs a couple of times,

"...just not right now," and he makes his way down the dark path and out of sight.

I feel so much sorrow for him and I can't imagine what he must be thinking right now, how he's going to deal with knowing the girl he loved wasn't who she pretended to be and obviously didn't really love him back. She used him. And I hate her for it. I try to shake the depressing, angry thoughts from my head and turn back to see my sister. But a small, childlike form sitting on the ground where the crowd just stood catches my eye.

"*Cecilia*?"

Seeing that it really is her and she looks to be in a state of shock, I run over to her and lean over, taking her hands and helping her to her feet. "Oh my God...Cecilia, are you *alright*?" I brush my hands across her face as if pushing hair away from her eyes even though her hair is too short for such a thing.

Alex steps up behind me.

"Is she...," Alex squints at her as though looking at her really close might answer her own question, "...*human*?"

My eyes widen warningly at Alex.

Cecilia suddenly snaps out of her mind and looks at Alex as if the h-word used in such a way is finally what's going to set her completely over the edge.

"You people are fucking crazy," she says holding up a finger. She steps away from me. "It's a crazy-house. And my mom is forcing *me* to see a shrink?" Her hands come up in surrender and she draws her chin back. "I don't think so. I'm outta here!" She pushes her way past us and hurries toward the path.

"Maybe I *do* need a shrink!" she yells out as she continues to walk away from us. "That's it! I'm getting on that Thorazine stuff. Yep! I might even get my very own straitjacket! I hope Hollister makes strait-jackets!" And her shouting voice fades as she disappears.

"I'll have Harry fix her right up," I say nervously to Alex.

She nods as if to say, "good idea—whatever that means" and we head into the house.

23

FOR ONLY THE SECOND time since I stepped foot inside the Mayfair house, I'm inside Rachel's bedroom. The first time was months ago when she set me up to witness her molesting Isaac when he was going through his before-full-moon stage. Of course, something like that is the only reason I could believe when he told me he didn't remember kissing her and that he wasn't in his right mind. If any regular guy ever said something like that I'd know he was a lying, disgusting pig.

But valid excuses never really have completely wiped that scene from my mind. And it's why I kind of refused to sit on Rachel's bed moments ago when I first walked in. I cringed when she offered for me to sit down. And then I felt the need to clean out my ears because I wasn't sure if I heard her kindness right.

She's a totally different Rachel, practically overnight. Okay, not totally. She's still a difficult bitch with no qualms about speaking her mind, but she now treats me a lot like Zia treated me.

I miss Zia. I really do. But this is something I'm going to have to get over.

"Where are they going?" Alex says about Isaac and his brothers and sisters.

Rachel moves to the window to look out over the driveway. Alex and I walk over to stand beside her.

"To bury Phoebe."

"What, like to *literally* bury her?" Alex says and it's the same thing I was going to ask with the same amount of confusion.

Isaac walks out of the house and into the light filtering down from all around the house, carrying Phoebe wrapped in a long, thin black cloth. Nathan, Xavier, Daisy, Shannon, Elizabeth and Camilla follow closely behind. They vanish into the woods single file.

"Well, they'll bury her afterwards, but...I've only seen it once before."

I turn around at the waist to see Rachel at my side, "Seen it?" I stumble over my words because I can't decide what to verify first. I settle with what came first. "Wait...they're going to bury her body here, *in the woods*? After *what*?" I just can't wrap my mind around either possibility.

"They'll cremate her first," Rachel says somberly, "and then bury what's left of her bones."

My neck springs back and I feel my eyes blink a dozen times. "You're serious?"

"Yeah, I think she's serious, Dria."

I look over at Alex and then back out the window.

"It's the Law," Rachel says plopping down amid her evil, memory-searing mattress. "Try reporting every death that a family like this suffers to the police. Way too much exposure, girl. It doesn't take a frickin' genius to figure that out," she scoffs.

I turn my back to the window and lean against it, looking across at Rachel to let her finish and ignoring her mock comment. That's just the way she is and how she'll always be. Funny how I'm already comfortable with it.

"We don't attend this burial because the one who died is a direct sibling," she says. "Now if it was Isaac who bit the dust, being Alpha, everyone in the pack would attend."

I flinch at her words.

Alex sits on the end of Rachel's bed and kicks off her Chuck Taylor's.

"You say you've only seen it once before." I walk forward a few steps with my arms crossed. "Who was it?"

"Zia's sister, Avril. Back before Zia joined the pack."

A thin silence falls across the room; all I can hear is the sound of my breath.

"I always thought there was something weird about that girl," Rachel adds, stirring the quiet with her less than sympathetic comments. "She snuck away a lot. I used to watch her like a paranoid meth-junkie." She laughs all of a sudden. "Now that I know what she was, it totally explains why one day, out of the blue, I trusted her more than I trusted anyone here. I just stopped watching her altogether—she must've messed with my head because she knew I was onto her."

"I imagine she messed with a lot of heads around here," Alex says.

I filled her in a little on the Praverians shortly before we came up with Rachel to her room.

"Yeah…," I say absently, looking toward the door and thinking about Sebastian. "She hurt a lot of people." I try to swallow down the ache I feel for him.

Just then, I see Sebastian walk past the bedroom door carrying a duffle bag. My hands drop to my sides and I run out into the hall.

"Sebastian?" I come up behind him and lay my hand on his shoulder. "Where are you going?"

He turns around and I quietly fold inside seeing the depth of the pain in his eyes.

Rachel and Alex stop in the doorway behind me.

"I'm going home."

I shake my head in a soft, jerking motion. "Home? But this is your home…."

Sebastian's robust shoulders slump over and he tries softening his expression for my sake. "Look, I'm sorry, but…this just isn't for me." His eyes scan the hallway, lastly falling on the door of the bedroom that he and Zia used to share.

He looks at me again. "I'm not cut out for this. I miss bitchy, shallow cheerleaders and watching football. Hell, I might even try *out* for football—I can run down a whole team now, after all." He smiles faintly at me and I smile back, trying to hold the tears inside. I reach up and pat him on his shaved head.

But I let my smile fade. "Don't let her do this to you. You can so easily find another girlfriend." It was a lame thing to say, but it just came out.

Sebastian laughs a little under his breath, also realizing how lame it was, but he lets it slide. "It's not about that; what Zia did was—shit, I can't even categorize it—but she was really the only reason why I was here. No offense to anyone, but I've been missing home ever since this started for me. I just want to go back to my old life, y'know? I want to go to college."

"But…Sebastian," I hesitate because I have to say this with the right amount of compassion. "…You can never go back to your old life, not being what you are."

"Yeah," Rachel speaks up from behind; "what if you hurt someone?" She moves out into the hall now, too. There's something hidden in her voice and then I realize what it is when she says, "I tried that once. I went home. I almost killed my mom." She's holding back her true feelings on the matter, making herself sound faintly amused by it when really I think she wants to either hit a wall, or break down and cry. "I had to find another pack after that—no way in hell I was going back to Ashe and his rabid family."

I notice Alex and Rachel share a look of agreement.

"I appreciate the concern," Sebastian says, shouldering the heavy duffle bag, "but I just can't stay here." He looks only at me again. "Tell Isaac I said thanks and if you see Harry again, let him know I'm alright and not to come looking for me."

I didn't even see until now that Sebastian has lost more than his girlfriend; he has also lost his best friend. Harry, the guy he grew up with, was never even human. It's not like he really has Harry left to go back to, either. Harry's life has changed in unimaginable ways.

My attempts to keep Sebastian here have been thwarted. I know that nothing I can do or say is going to change his mind.

Rachel steps in front of me and props her hands on her hips. "I say you stay," she demands.

Alex and I pass each other a look, both with a raised brow.

Sebastian smiles, shaking his head. "Thanks, but…I've gotta go."

He raises two fingers and waves at us as he moves down the hall.

"Don't even think about it," Rachel hisses pointing at Alex with a warning look on her face. "That hot piece of ass is totally mine."

Alex and I barely hold in our laughter and we slip back inside Rachel's room behind her. I shut the door.

"*What?*" Rachel says all cock-eyed.

She plops back down on her bed, crossing her bare feet at the ankles below. Her toenails are painted red and she wears a gold ring on each pinky toe.

We can't wipe the smiles off our faces. "Oh, nothing," we say melodiously at the same time.

An hour passes in which we spend talking about more human things and I sort of feel a little bit human again. It almost feels like the time Alex and I hung out with her friend, Liz, one night when Brandon was out of town. We gossiped and laughed and did all the normal things teenage girls do. But things are different now. We're not so much teenagers anymore. And our gossip consists of stuff about how certain girls in the house are still delusional about being with the Alpha—yeah, ummm, he's taken, thank-you-very-much.

There's a rhythmic knock on the door and since I'm closest to it, I look to Rachel first since it's her room.

"What?!" she shouts.

"Are you naked?!" Xavier says on the other side.

Rachel rolls her eyes.

Xavier lets himself in, peeking his blond head around the door. "Not like I haven't seen it before," he says grinning and steps the rest of the way inside.

Alex recoils from his presence with aversion and intolerance. I'm proud of her for that. I just want to slap that grin off his face. He is gorgeous; I'll give him that, but he's way too much of a slutty douche bag to be talking to *my* sister. I sneer at him, but he doesn't even notice me. He walks right over next to Alex and sits down on Rachel's vanity chair, leaning his back against the wall and splaying his legs out into the floor.

"Shouldn't you be in mourning?" Rachel says with a sneer and goes back to inspecting her fingernails.

Xavier, for a brief second, looks crestfallen, but he quickly wipes away how he's really feeling and smiles. "So," he says, folding his hands casually on his lap, "when are you going to go out with me?"

Alex's head snaps around. "Umm. Never?"

Xavier smiles a crooked smile. "How about tomorrow night?"

Alex's mouth falls open and cavernous creases take shape in her forehead around her eyebrows. I'm as revolted as she is.

"How about *never*?" she says.

Xavier glances over at Rachel and nods his head toward Alex. "Tell her I'm not so bad—not what she thinks I am, anyway."

Rachel puts up her hands. "Don't drag me into this."

"No, I'm sure you're exactly what I think you are," Alex interjects. "An uncompassionate sex junkie who uses people and is full of himself."

Go Alex!

Xavier blinks back the stun. Strangely enough, he looks totally taken aback by her opinion of him.

"A sex junkie, maybe. Full of myself—it's just my way of hiding my insecurities," he says, "but baby, I've never used anyone in my life."

What kind of tactics is he using? Sounds like he's playing the misunderstood bad-boy card openly. But Alex won't fall for it.

I hope not. Surely not....

Alex rolls her eyes and starts inspecting her long fingernails, too, but it's an obvious distraction so she doesn't have to look at him.

"I haven't! Tell her, Rach!" His whole face is one big smile and the more I look at him the more I see how much he and Daisy really do look alike.

Rachel sighs and drops her hands on the bed. "Xavier is a jackass, yes," she says and Xavier just keeps smiling, "but he's telling the truth as far as I know; he's up front, I'll give him that."

"I don't care, really," Alex says. She reaches over to Rachel's nightstand and takes up a bottle of electric blue nail polish and twists off the top. "You have no chance in hell with me."

Xavier's mouth lifts into a sly, sexy grin.

"You're up front, alright," I say to him. "Telling a girl she'll be in your bed by the end of the week is not only up front, but extraordinarily pathetic."

Xavier makes a face. "Pathetic?" He shakes his head, still smiling. "That's a low blow, girl."

"It's the truth."

Xavier laughs.

"So what do you say?" He turns back to Alex. "How about something simple, cliché and old fashioned like dinner and a movie?" He leans forward and props his elbows on his knees, letting his hands hang freely between them. "You'd be the first. I promise."

Alex laughs. "Yeah, ummm, something tells me with you I wouldn't be the first anything."

Xavier's chin draws back in a stunned motion. "I'm serious. I've never taken a girl to dinner and a movie. Ever."

There's so much eye-rolling going on in here right now I think we might all severely damage our eyesight. Alex gets up from the foot of the bed and marches over to the door, placing her hand on the knob. She smirks across the room at Xavier and says, "No. Now if you don't mind, we were getting ready to compare our boob sizes and massage each other's backs after such a stressful event and you shouldn't be in here when we take off our clothes." She opens the door and gestures toward the hallway with an artful smile.

Xavier's face just sort of freezes until a grin warms it back to life. He gets up from the vanity chair. "Oh, you are so cruel."

Alex smirks and waits patiently for him to walk out.

"You have *no* idea," she says as he passes her.

"So tomorrow night then?" he says right outside the door.

Alex shuts the door in his face.

Rachel and I look right at each other and then burst into a fit of laughter.

"You know you just made it worse for yourself," Rachel says filing her thumb nail down with a hot pink nail file. She rocks her crossed feet side to side on the end of the bed.

Alex goes back to her spot next to Rachel's feet and plops down. "Whatever. The guy's delusional."

~~~

I spend about an hour more with my sister in Rachel's room, which apparently is now also Alex's room, too. At first I wanted her to myself so that we could catch up and be together like we always were when we were growing up, but I found myself enjoying Rachel's company and didn't mind so much that she was with us. She and Alex are so much alike, especially considering Ashe, and it just makes me happy to see Alex fitting in so fast. But I never felt left out in that time I spent with them. So strange how things turn out. My worst enemy became my sister's best friend and one of *my* best friends became my worst enemy.

I don't think I'll ever forget Zia and the girl she was before I knew the real her. And despite everything that she did, I can't help but feel sorry for her. Maybe I could've turned out like her if I thought my sister's death was caused by someone. Zia became Dark because of a traumatic event in her life and while that is never a justifiable excuse to kill someone, deep down I know too that we are all capable of it.

I had set out to find Isaac, but in passing Zia's bedroom door on the way to his, I just have to stop. I push the door the rest of the way open with the palm of my hand and step inside. Everything looks the same. The strategically placed pyramid of empty soda cans by her bedside clock, the sloppy stack of CD's and the pile of paperback books piled against the wall and the black and red mosaic lamp beside her bed. The room had always smelled strongly of incense and tonight is no different.

I fold one arm across my stomach and rest my forehead in the other hand and just sigh deeply, feeling my stomach harden as I try to force down the tears.

And then I walk out, slamming the door behind me.

Isaac is lying across his bed when I go inside, his hands propped behind his head against the headboard and his feet crossed below.

I don't say anything when I sit down next to him. I feel like asking him if he's okay when I know he's not is just stupid. And without looking at me, he reaches out one arm and pulls me toward him. I lay my head on his stomach and he brushes his fingers through my hair as he stares off at the wall, his free hand still propped behind his head.

"Remember when we first met on that gravel road?" he says.

"Of course I do." It's one of the top five things I'll never forget for as long as I live.

"Shortly before that," he says, "when we were watching out for you in the parking lot at the skate park, Zia said something to me that always struck me as strange, but I never really understood it until now."

"What did she say?"

He continues to comb his fingers through my hair.

"She said, 'you'll just kill her, too', because I said we should follow you to make sure you got home safely."

I lean my head back a little to see him. "Come on, baby, don't do that blaming yourself stuff."

"I'm not," he says, finally looking down at me, "I know I couldn't have known what or who she was; it's just that now that I know, all kinds of things she said and did over time makes complete sense."

"Well, you did put her on the list," I say, "right before we left for Providence. You had a feeling all along."

He nods absently and stares out in front of him again; the motion of his fingers on my scalp is causing my eyes to tingle.

"I want this all to be over with," he says. "I'm tired of…well, I'm tired of everything."

"But it *is* over. Zia's gone. Everybody's safe."

"No…it's far from over," he says though he appears lost in some deep, dark reflection. "This thing with Aramei and my father—I fear this situation is far worse than the one with Zia ever was."

I lift my head from his stomach and hold up my weight over his lap with my elbow pressed into the mattress. "What makes you say that?"

He doesn't speak for a moment and he still rarely looks back at me. And then just like his reason for putting Zia on

The List, he says quietly, "Just another gut feeling," and slowly I lay my head back on his stomach without saying another word.

Because the truth is that I feel it, too. And I no longer believe in coincidence.

24

THE CRACKLING AND POPPING of flames licking the hay-covered roof wake Aramei from her sleep. In a split second, the haze from her semi-conscious mind pulls away, allowing her to see that this is not a dream. The tiny cottage is engulfed in flames. Aramei flies out of bed, tossing her worn cotton blanket onto the floor on her way across the smoke-filled room. She bursts through the bedroom door and out into the short hallway to see the flames spreading fast in the front room, crawling and licking their way up along the walls and consuming the four wooden beams holding the roof overhead.

She chokes on the smoke filling her lungs and pushes her way toward Filipa's room with one hand covering her mouth and nose, though it does little good to shield her face from the thick, suffocating smoke. A loud *pop* resonates through the space and just as Aramei passes the threshold and makes it into Filipa's room one of the beams holding the roof comes crashing down, collapsing the entire back section of the cottage.

There is no other way out now except through the window in Filipa's bedroom.

"Filipa!" Aramei screams through the smoke, her lungs burning. "Filipa! It's on fire!"

She pushes Filipa out of the bed and Filipa lands on the floor with a thud. But Aramei, realizing there is no time for Filipa's usual five-long-minute way of waking up no matter the dire situation, grabs her by her long, brown hair and drags her across the bedroom floor toward the open window where smoke billows out thickly.

Filipa screams out in pain as she's dragged, but things are happening too quickly for her to protest. Aramei pulls her sister from the floor when they make it to the window, allowing her to stand on her own. "Hurry!" she shouts over the roar of the flames getting closer every second.

Filipa doesn't hesitate and still dressed in her nightgown, she climbs quickly over the windowsill and falls onto the ground below.

Aramei crawls out next and drops to her feet next to Filipa who now takes the lead and grabs a hold of Aramei's arm and drags her farther away from the collapsing cottage.

"Father!" Aramei screams. "We have to save Father!"

"He's dead!" Filipa says, pulling her along, "The house is gone!"

They run out into the village square to find that they aren't the only ones out in their night clothes and bare feet, nor is their cottage the only one on fire. The entire village has gone up in flames. The villagers are running through the dirt-covered street screaming, crying and calling out to lost loved ones.

Aramei and Filipa run away from the flames of a nearby cottage and toward the people.

"My son!" one woman cries her face blackened by soot. "Where is my son?"

Just as Aramei goes to grab the woman and pull her away with her and Filipa, her son comes bursting through the front door of their burning cottage carrying a makeshift bag of their belongings he had saved from the fire. He rushes over and takes his mother's arm, dragging her away with him. "They're here! The Black Beasts!" he shouts to Filipa. "Get your sister out of here! Now!"

Aramei looks at Filipa with panic in her eyes. Filipa, equally panicked, grabs Aramei by the arm again and they take off running towards the forest. Only seconds in and they find themselves barricaded by a mass of black fur and gnashing teeth. They stop so abruptly that Aramei crashes into Filipa's back and they both fall over. Filipa scrambles for Aramei's arm, or hand, or whatever body part she can grasp onto. She can't take her eyes off the beasts standing before them so tall and terrifying that her entire body trembles uncontrollably.

Aramei stands up first and brings Filipa with her, pushing her behind her as they begin to step backward toward the trees. Aramei's face drips with sweat where streaks of black from the soot on the air trail down her face, making her look all the more primal in the faces of these beasts; those that look the same as the one she mended in the barn just six months ago. But these beasts are not like that one and Aramei knows it.

Filipa tries to take off running back into the burning village, but when Aramei won't move to follow, Filipa stops. Tears stream from her face. "What are you *doing*, sissa? We have to run!"

The biggest beast in the front rears up and comes crashing back down swiping its massive claws at the air toward them. Aramei and Filipa stumble backward into the brush and Filipa falls. The beast roars, blood dripping thickly from its teeth, but another beast comes in behind it and thrusts out its hairy arm, knocking it through the trees.

Aramei, staying on her feet, shouts at Filipa, "Run! Go, Filipa, *now*!"

"Not without you!" Filipa shouts, pulling herself back to her feet.

"I said, GO!" Aramei's voice is strident, but she never takes her eyes off the beasts blocking her path.

Reluctantly, Filipa takes off running through the woods, leaving Aramei behind. Aramei's eyes dart all around her, searching for anything she might be able to use to defend herself, but the cold, hard reality is that there's not much in the way of a weapon when all one is surrounded by are trees and brush.

She can hear the screams of the villagers piercing through the darkness in every direction, and the howls and the echo of structures collapsing under the weight and intensity of the fires. In her peripheral vision, Aramei catches a glimpse of dozens of these beasts darting through the darkness, some running on all fours while others hammer their way into the village on two legs, slashing down figures as they try to flee.

The beast standing tall in front of her is the only thing keeping the other seven at bay. They want her. Their gnashing teeth and guttural, demonic growls send terror through every loft of her body.

The beast pulls back its giant arms and cranes its neck, letting out the most menacing howl of them all and the other seven cower away, slipping into the trees and out of sight.

It's just Aramei and the one beast now as it stares down at her small, frail form. Aramei's body shakes and trembles. Her knees knock together beneath her thin, soot-stained gown. "Please...," she says, putting up her hands and slowly backing away. "Please just...spare my sister...." Tears choke her; she can hardly breathe anymore.

The beast then begins to change. His tall height shrinks as his hind-like legs become more human-like. His great snout sinks backward into the skull. He raises his arms above his head and wails into the night. The bones breaking and growing throughout his body are audible even to Aramei's human ears as they set themselves back in place, his ribs growing outward first and then falling inward into a cage. All the while the rubbery, hard skin fades from black to a more human-like complexion. His wiry black fur disappears into the follicles of his flesh.

Aramei had fallen to the ground at some point, but she can't recall when. She sits with her arms propped beside her, staring up at the man who was also a beast. Her eyes are wide and terrified; her mouth hangs open, her lips trembling.

"*Viktor*?" she forces the word from her lips as if it's the hardest word she's ever had to say and it literally leaves her breathless.

Viktor stands before her, naked and unashamed. His face holds no emotion, but the depths of his eyes are tainted by madness. Aramei tries to crawl away on her backside and hands, but Viktor walks over and kneels beside her, rendering her immobile. Her bottom lip trembles and she can't speak.

He reaches out and cups the back of her neck with the palm of his hand and pulls her rigid body closer.

The trembling of her lip spreads down into her shoulders and quickly down into her feet. No part of her body is without movement. Viktor cocks his head to one side, studying her.

"H-How do you live?" she finally gets the words out.

But he doesn't answer.

Viktor raises one hand and a long, black nail emerges eerily from the very tip and then he slices open his forearm with one swift pass of it. Blood drops become one heavy stream in just seconds, but he shows no signs of discomfort.

The nature of his smile chills Aramei to her very bones. Her eyes dart to and from his and the blood draining heavily from his arm.

In one blurry movement, Viktor grabs Aramei by the neck and pulls her toward the blood, forcing her mouth over the wound. "Drink it," he demands, pressing his hands into the skin around her neck.

She chokes and gags, trying to refuse it, but in the end she knows she can't. She swallows down every vile drop of it that doesn't manage to drain from the corners of her mouth. She nearly throws up, but the blood is too strong and she can do nothing to keep it from coursing through her body. She can feel the heat of it in her limbs and in her toes as if she's drinking down potent ale. It begins to tingle and itch in her veins and fill her mind with euphoric visions.

Eventually, she is completely intoxicated by it and she struggles against Viktor no more.

He pulls his arm away and lays her half-limp body against the ground. Her face and throat and chest are drenched in blood. But she feels like she can lay here forever and dream, to become lost in the blissful moment that his blood has so deceptively created in her mind.

The dark sky is layered by a thick orange glow with cinders and flames rising up in every direction. The village is an inferno where Black Beasts run through the streets, cutting people down with their massive claws, infecting them one by one. Aramei hears all of this as she lies on the ground next to Viktor's bare knees. She feels it when her sister is killed, *feels* it in her own heart the very moment that it happens, but she can't react to it. All she can do is lie there and stare into Viktor's piercing green eyes.

And then all sound is sucked from her ears when the blade is pushed into her stomach. Her breath catches sharply and her frail, helpless eyes widen up at him.

Viktor is no longer smiling. He looks upon her with pain and remorse and wickedness. Aramei chokes on the blood rising into her throat; her own blood this time and not Viktor's. She gasps for air and reaches up her bloodied hand to touch his unshaven face. Streaks of red are left in the wake of her fingers as they fall weakly away seconds afterwards because she's too weak to hold them up.

"You will never die," he says, the warmth of his lips hovering just inches from hers. He inhales her scent and cradles her head in his hand again to bring her lips even closer and he brushes them against his own. "As long as I live, you shall also live in my shadow." He kisses her softly. "You will never die and you will never be his." The chilling smile vaguely returns in his eyes, just enough for Aramei to see it.

Viktor twists the knife in her stomach, gritting his teeth and flaring his nostrils. Aramei whimpers and tenses with the excruciating wave of pain burrowing through her body. Her eyes are completely glazed over by thick tears. Droplets of blood trickle from her nostrils.

He slides the blade out and holds it up in her view and licks her blood clean from the blade. She sees that it is the same knife, her *own* knife, which she used to stab him with last winter.

His naked form blurs in and out of her vision as he walks away from her body. The howls of the Black Beasts and the cries of the people sound muffled all around her until it all eventually fades. The dark sky is filled with a billion stars as she gazes up at it. And for a time that seems quiet and utterly still, Aramei finds her peace. The life drains out of her quickly until finally the stars blink out of her vision.

~~~

There's a rustling nearby, or perhaps it's the shuffling of feet against the earth, but Aramei opens her eyes weakly to the sound of it. Everything is silent and still and surreal. She can see through the slit her eyelids have made that it is barely dark; the horizon is layered by a faint pinkish glow, indicating early morning just before dawn. The stench of the fires that have mostly burned themselves out through the night lingers heavily on the air, choking the back of her throat and stinging her eyes. She coughs; her chest rattles her body awake and she rolls over onto her side, her soft skin painted by dirt and blood as it lies pressed into the cool earth. Her vision triples and doubles before it comes together to create a single vague image.

Tall black leather boots walk towards her. She's too disoriented to try making out the rest of the figure. Her arm lays stretched out in front of her and she can see the figure coming closer through the hollow of her curled fingers. She feels like her body should be tensing up, fearing that it's Viktor, but she's still too weak even for instinct and so all she can do is lie there. She swallows down the last of her tears and shuts her eyes softly for a moment until the shadow of the figure, now standing tall over her, covers her body in a sort of calming darkness.

He kneels beside her and she looks up at him; hair so long and dark falling about his rugged, unshaven face adorned with the darkest blue eyes. A scar fouls his chin and one above his left eye, but they distract nothing from the intensity of those eyes. He reaches out a hand, one stained by dirt and blood and where a ring encrusted with onyx stones and a crest sits on his finger. He lifts her into his arms.

"Now I will repay your kindness and take care of you," he says. She can feel his heart beating against the side of her face as she lies against his chest.

Aramei doesn't speak, but she finds that she feels completely safe in his arms and there is a great sense of familiarity in them, too. Only one other time has she ever felt this way and slowly she begins to make the connection. She had seen Viktor as a beast. She saw him transform before her very eyes into a man. And as she lies in this man's dominant, yet gentle grasp, she knows he was the one in the barn all those nights.

She begins to cry softly into the fabric of his shirt and he cradles the back of her head firmer in one hand. The smell of his long leather coat and the natural scent of his skin soaks up in her lungs and she just cries harder, letting the fear and sorrow and relief and confusion out all at once. And he holds her there for a long time, letting her cry, until she senses when his chest hardens that someone else is nearby. Her chest shudders to a halt and she feels his arms tighten around her small form.

"Forgive me, Milord," a woman's voice says, "but I did not know that *you* loved her."

A low, almost inaudible growl moves through his chest.

"I was only upholding the law," the woman says, fear of retribution lacing her every word. "I thought it was Viktor that I was punishing."

"Did you bring your pack here?" the man says and the intensity of his deep voice reverberates through Aramei's body.

"It was my intention, Milord," the woman admits, "but Viktor found out that my plan was to destroy this village and to...end her."

Aramei's body hardens with the woman's dark words.

"But Viktor arrived first and claimed what he thought was his. My pack arrived minutes later but were confused by Viktor's actions. They did not understand why he himself would order the village of the human he loved, destroyed. It caught them off-guard and they were attacked. Amid the battle and the fires and the infections, Viktor took her away from it all."

Aramei feels the warmth of the man's breath emitting from his nostrils as he tilts his head to look down at her.

"Milord?" the woman says carefully.

"Yes, Lord Nataša?" The man slowly raises his head once again.

Nataša hesitates and her silence indicates something grave.

"Speak."

"The woman...Milord, taste her blood."

Aramei's eyes break apart again and she gazes up into the man's face. He looks to and from her and Nataša; a sort of distressing alarm shifts the calm in his features as if he already knows now what Nataša speaks of. His strong hands begin to shake, his fingers trembling angrily into the muscles of her thighs and her back.

"I am remorseful, Milord," Nataša says, lowering her head into a shameful bow. "What will you have me do? Shall I kill him...once and for all? Do you want me to end this?—"

"*No...*," he growls. "Viktor must not be touched. Anyone who ends his life will forfeit their own life. Go. Now. Make it known that Viktor shall be protected no matter the cost or the circumstance."

"Yes, Milord."

Present Day – In the Cabin

I wake up this time drenched in sweat and tears. I don't even know where I am. I can smell the fresh cut wood the cabin had been built with, but I don't recognize this place. I don't recognize until many seconds later that I am in Eva's lap. I shake my senses back into my head and lift away from her.

Trajan is standing in the room and as I allow my eyes to scan all around me, I see finally that we're downstairs. Servants walk back and forth, cleaning the furniture and pulling back the curtains on the windows to let in the morning light.

"Has she still told you nothing?" Trajan jumps right in and instantly I sense the growing impatience in his voice.

"No, Milord," I say and realize I addressed him properly only because I had just experienced a real-life interaction between he and Nataša. I'm still feeling the effects of the vision.

I rise up from the couch fully. "I'm sorry," I lie, "but still it's just stuff about her past." I don't want him to know anything and so I'm not sorry that I don't have any 'worthy' information to give him, but I admit to myself that even I'm growing more impatient with these visions. I want to experience them, yes. I don't want to miss anything she is showing me, but at the same time, I'm desperate now more than ever to know what this is all about, what Aramei has brought me here for.

Because I know in my heart that it's for something much more than reliving her past.

Trajan's eyes shift black momentarily, but he calms himself and the dark, majestic blue returns. From the corner of my eye, I see that all of the servants had stopped moving in that moment and only now that he is composed again, do they find it in their ability to breathe again.

Trajan looks dead at me and I swallow hard.

"You may return to my son," he says, standing tall over me, "but tonight you will come back here where you will remain until I have what I need."

My breath catches and tears start to angrily burn their way to the surface. I hold them back.

"But…I can't stay here like this," I argue, my body trembling. "*Please—*"

"Those are my orders. I cannot risk you not being here when she might be able to speak to you."

I ball my fists against my thighs and my nails dig into the skin of my palms.

"I had hoped to have the answers before the week was over. I must leave for Serbia in the morning and you will remain here with her until I return." He walks over closer and looks down at me. "Do not think that I am unappreciative of your assistance. Once you give me what I need, you will be rewarded."

"But I don't *want* a reward!" I cry, standing up from the couch. Eva flinches next to me and grabs my hand. "Tell me, *Milord*…," I force his title spitefully through my teeth, "did you know that your daughter, Phoebe, was killed yesterday? Do you even care about *her*?"

Trajan's face remains standard.

"Yes, I have been informed but no, I do not care."

His answer stuns me into total shock and denial. I feel like I've just been slapped across the face with the back of his hand. I dig my fingers into Eva's palm and grind my teeth aggressively behind my tightly-closed lips. The only thing keeping me from lashing out at him unlike ever before has nothing to do with fear and everything to do with my body's inability to move. I'm frozen in this spot; my feet are encased in the floor beneath me. I can't move and I can't speak.

Eva slips an arm around the back of my waist and holds me gently beside her.

Trajan leaves out the front door.

I collapse into Eva's arms, tears streaming down my face; angry, vengeful tears. Eva guides me to sit back down on the couch and I do without argument.

"You must understand," she says softly, "he is not who he once was, Adria. The many years of his existence and this relationship between him and Aramei, over time has altered his mind. It has taken him to a darker place."

I stare out in front of me, sniffling back the tears; my hands are pressed together in a steeple in-between my thighs.

"It's not an excuse," I say.

She touches a lock of my hair. "No…I suppose it isn't, but he did once love all of his children. Perhaps not equally because their kind tend to love the Alpha's in line, more than the others, but yes…there was a time when Milord would kill anyone for harming one of his own."

I turn my head to look at her beside me. "How can he be so cruel and heartless?" I bite my bottom lip, forcing the new tears back that burn my sinuses. She had already told me how, but I just can't accept that.

Eva suddenly retracts her hand from my hair and places both of them within her lap. She appears quietly nervous. And without having to say a word, all the servants in the cabin stop what they're doing in the same moment and shuffle out the front door. It's as if she had commanded them somehow, but that can't be. I come to understand even more now how much of a trained collective they all are, how they know what is being asked of them simply by a gesture or the language of Eva's body. To be a servant is to be as vigilant.

When the last girl is out and the door is closed, Eva looks over at me and says, "For the sake of your kind, he must be dethroned."

And for the second time in less than five full minutes, I'm stunned into an unmoving shell.

25

SHE PEERS IN AT me, her eyes soft but heavy with what feels to me like the weight of the world. She has done nothing less than seal her own fate by speaking those ten crippling words and although it would never be me who admitted to hearing them, she never would've said something so damning if she didn't already believe that she would be dead soon.

I turn away from her eyes because I feel like the longer I look into them the guiltier I will become.

"It has been a long time coming," she says. "Those who are loyal to him will always be loyal—Lord Nataša." She glances at the door indicating those outside, "But there are many who only pretend to be and would follow suit when the time came."

"*Shit*, Eva!" I hiss through my teeth, "Why are you *saying* this?" My eyes dart back and forth between her and the windows; I worry that anyone could be listening.

"Because it must be said. Because he has been destroying the lineage for the last two hundred and fifty years, since the morning he plucked Aramei from the aftermath. Since he forbade Nataša her duty as his Right Hand and the upholder of his own laws, to destroy Viktor Vargas and his rogue bloodline. Because in choosing love over duty, in taking something from a madman such as Viktor, Trajan's reign became only to have power over *her* and nothing else. Everything he has done since that day has been for *her* and not the sake of his own race. He has been blinded by his love for her; his need to protect her…Adria, he became a rogue of a different kind. And a rogue with Sovereignty is a death sentence to all."

I let out the breath I had been holding in unknowingly and then I spring up from the couch.

"I don't know why you're telling me this," I lash out, raising my hands up in surrender as I pace the floor. I stop suddenly and throw my gaze harshly upon her. "You really need to get out more." I laugh a hopeless, disturbing laugh and start to pace again. "If you knew the crap that I've already been through with this family—what I went through just *last night* in losing one of my best friends and watching her kill Isaac's sister—." I kick the coffee table and stop to stare coldly at her, my teeth clenched so tightly that the skin around my lips crumples into a series of hard lines. "WHY ME?! Why couldn't you…," I'm searching my head for someone who could actually fit the bill and my hand darts out to point at the front door. "Why not Raul, huh? Why not any one of Trajan's oh-so-loyal guards who have obviously been pinned under his goddamned boot heel for a couple hundred years? WHY PUT THIS ON *ME*?!"

Eva doesn't flinch as I roar at her.

"Because you're the only one I can speak to," she says composed. "I am no longer even allowed to converse with Isaac."

I shake my head helplessly and sigh heavily.

"He is the epitome of madness, Adria. You think that Viktor is dangerous, but Viktor is predictable. Milord is beyond anything you can imagine."

"Why do you stay here?" I say, exasperated. I think I'm just trying to find something else to talk about, but I know I can't get any of this out of my head.

I run over and thrust my feet down into my shoes, bending over and slipping my finger into the heel so I can get them on. I almost fall over.

"You know what—I'll be back tonight like Trajan told me to be." I stomp over and stare down at her. "And when I come back, I'm ordering you not to speak a word of this anymore to me, or to anyone else. I swear-to-God. You got that?"

Eva stands and bows to me with every bit of respect. "Yes, Milady."

This time I don't feel any need to tell her not to call me that. I just don't care. I also don't care that I was ever able to act like the Alpha's 'wife' and that it didn't feel odd but felt completely natural.

I rush out the front door and jump into Raul's SUV and he takes me back home.

~~~

I spend the rest of the day in a haze and I start to feel like how Sebastian felt just before he left for home. I don't blame him one bit because I see more and more as I'm confronted with unbelievable truths and obstacles that this isn't an easy life to live. My life before, the lonely one I felt stuck in with Jeff and my mom, it was frickin' Disneyland compared to this.

After lying in Isaac's bed for several hours while he's out with Nathan, I finally lift up from the pillow and look across the room at myself in the mirror. I get up and walk over to stand in front of it and I see that I look exactly the same as I always have, yet I look completely different. Maybe it's the eyes. The differences are all on the inside and can only be seen through the eyes. I peer even closer, propping my hands against the dresser and leaning in, practically pressing my face into the glass and I look deeply into my own eyes. I don't know what I'm looking for, but I know that something's there, staring back at me and I just can't find it. I let out a deep breath and lower my head, letting it hang freely between my shoulders.

The bedroom door clicks open.

"I need to make amends," Alex says coming inside.

I turn around and lean against the dresser, looking at her questioningly.

"With Aunt Beverlee and Uncle Carl," she says.

It takes a second to notice I'm actually smiling. I let my hands drop to my sides and I walk over to put on my shoes. "I think that's a great idea," I say, stepping down into them and not even bothering to bend over to tie them properly. "We'll go right now." Her suggestion couldn't have come at a more appropriate time; I need to breathe some human home-life air for a few hours.

Alex looks surprised and then shrugs. "Awesome. Who's going to take us?"

"We'll take Isaac's Jeep." I reach into the nightstand drawer and pluck out the spare set of keys.

Alex raises a brow. "You haven't even gotten your license yet, have you?" She's grinning like a trouble-maker.

I shrug and slip my purse over one shoulder. "No, I'm too busy turning into a werewolf and watching people die and all that *freaking awesome* stuff, to worry about crap like driver's licenses and graduation." Of course, I'm being totally sarcastic.

Alex smiles. "Well, you've gotta admit one thing."

"Yeah, what's that?" I stop in front of her, dangling the keys in my hand.

"You'd never go back to that old way of life even if you could."

I hate to admit it, especially after my little inner tantrum at the mirror, but she's right.

"Let's go," I say walking past her and stepping into the hall.

We pull into the driveway of Uncle Carl and Aunt Bev's house and Alex looks halfway nervous sitting in the passenger's seat. And I'm always a little nervous nowadays when I visit or talk to them over the phone because I feel so guilty for everything. Not so much anymore what happened to Uncle Carl—though I'll always feel somewhat guilty for that—but because of what I am and how I can't tell them anything. I have to lie to them constantly about why I'm gone so much and it's really hard because I know Aunt Bev feels abandoned. Uncle Carl probably feels the same way, but he's not as easy to read as Beverlee. I told Alex yesterday all about what happened to Uncle Carl last winter and she was taken aback by it. And then the anger followed because it was someone from the Vargas pack that caused the car wreck that put Uncle Carl in the hospital.

I put the Jeep in park and we sit here for a moment.

"What if they still don't want me in the house?"

"They're too forgiving for that."

Alex sighs and gazes at the wrap-around porch.

"I think it'll make them feel better knowing that you're alright and this time, sincere about your apologies."

She is definitely a far cry from when she came here the last time to 'make amends'. She still has that cocky Vargas attitude, but it doesn't feel uncomfortable to be around her.

I open the front door of the house and wait with Alex as Beverlee meets us. She's smiling hugely at me until Alex steps up from behind and into view.

"Alexandra?"

Alex smiles weakly and raises her hand to wave awkwardly. "Hi Aunt Beverlee." And then she puts up both hands and says, "I swear I'm not here to cause trouble."

Beverlee casts a skeptic glance at Alex and then at me, before pushing the door open the rest of the way and replacing skepticism with happiness.

"Come in," she says.

We spend the rest of the day with them and I couldn't be more pleased with how things turned out. Alex was on her very best behavior and she even got up numerous times while we were all talking in the den to get Uncle Carl a fresh glass of tea and to top off his cheese dip and bowl of Tostitos. She *really* shocked me when she started a load of Aunt Bev's laundry. I laughed under my breath, thinking about how she's laying it all on a bit thick. But it was genuine and that's all that mattered.

And to make the day even better, I got a call from Harry. He wouldn't say where he's hiding out at because he doesn't want to risk Minna finding out where he is, but at least I know he's safe. Of course Daisy is with him.

By six o'clock, Alex and I migrate upstairs to her old room where she just scans it for a brief moment instead of diving into everything like I thought she would.

"What's wrong?" I say, standing at the foot of her bed that hasn't been slept in in months. The bedspread is still plastered tightly over the mattress.

"It's just…well none of this is me anymore," she says looking around. "I try to picture myself coming back here and finishing out school, but I just can't imagine it anymore, y'know?" Her gaze falls on me.

I nod, but it takes me a moment to answer because I'm thinking about what she said except replacing her feelings with my own.

"Yeah, actually I do know." I walk over and sit on the chair that is always overlooking the window. "I intend to graduate, though I'm not sure why it matters anymore. Not like I'm going to get to go off to college or anything." I pause because I realize that I'm not making a good case. "It's just that nothing normal feels necessary anymore." I nod at my own words, finally finding something that actually holds true and hoping that I can make some sense of it. "Alex, I feel weird when I go the grocery store. Seriously. Or, when I pumped the gas in the Jeep on our way over here. I don't know why or how I'm supposed to feel about it."

Alex sits on the end of her bed and leans over, resting her elbows on her legs.

"I don't trust myself here, Dria." She looks away from me. "I don't trust myself around humans at all. I know I can never go back to this."

I swallow down my agreement.

"Can I come in?" Beverlee says from the doorway and Alex and I turn our heads around swiftly.

I wonder how much she heard and already I'm rewinding the things we said back through my mind looking for any incriminating keywords. But aside from those, pretty much our entire conversation was not something I wanted Beverlee to hear.

Aunt Bev walks in, smiling warmly and just seeing her face like that makes me feel worse.

"I can't force either one of you to stay here," she says. "Adria, you'll be eighteen next month—but I'm really concerned."

I start to speak, but Beverlee stops me.

"Let me finish," she says kindly, "I need to say a few things."

Alex and I just look at her, giving her the go ahead.

"You both always have a place here; I hope you'll never forget that. But whatever you decide to do or wherever you choose to live, I don't think I can sleep at night—." She lets out a sharp breath. "I don't sleep *now*, but I'd like to again someday. I just worry you're getting wrapped up in a dangerous lifestyle and that's the last thing I want for you."

Wow, there's absolutely nothing I can say to that. Dangerous doesn't even begin to cover it. But I know that Beverlee is referring to things like drugs and alcohol and abuse.

I stand up from the chair.

"Aunt Bev," I say, "I can promise you that neither one of us are into drugs or anything even remotely close to that. No one that we hang out with is, either. Isaac and his family are wonderful and he wants the best for me as much as you do." I feel guilty telling Beverlee this at all because the last thing I want is for her to feel that I'm choosing another family over her. She has been nothing but great to me and no one could ever replace her in my heart.

I make a decision in this moment, though I think it's one that I made after I returned from Athens Regional not long ago and I step right up to Aunt Bev, cupping her elbows in my hands.

"You're not like a mother to me," I say and her face becomes faintly confused. "You *are* my mother."

It felt so right to say it.

Beverlee's eyes coat with moisture and in seconds tears stream down her cheeks. She grabs me and pulls me toward her, wrapping her arms tightly around me. Her chest rattles with happy sobs.

"That means a lot to me," she says, pulling away.

"Well, I'm serious and I want you to know that when I decide I need to move away from here, that it's just your very grateful not-so-teenage daughter moving on with her life."

"Yeah," Alex says from the bed, "all mom's go through it and you won't be an exception—so just suck it up and be happy that your daughters are grown up and making you miserable with their absence...Well, that is until you realize you can turn our rooms into some kind of mom-only zone."

Beverlee laughs through her tears and my smile just gets bigger.

"Thanks," Beverlee says. She wipes her finger under her eyes.

~~~

It almost felt like closure, going to see Aunt Bev and Uncle Carl because I do feel so much better. And I know they feel that way, too, especially seeing Alex again.

Before we left, I assured Beverlee that I would finish school and she and Uncle Carl talked with me for a little while about taking out loans so that I can go to college, but I'm not about to let them go in debt for me and neither is Alex. I ended that conversation with a blatant thank-you-but-no. Alex was bit more open about her intentions and she told them that she might graduate, but that anything beyond that just isn't for her.

It was a much-needed visit, but aside from how well everything went and how good I left feeling about it, the entire thing also somehow feels like a means to an end, like I had to do it because I might not get another chance.

I don't know why it feels that way, but deep down it worries me. It's like I know that fate has something much bigger in store for my life, and it has little to do with my so-called fate that Harry said I'm supposed to fulfill. I don't know how in the world he could ever believe that I could be the cause of a war. A *war*! It even sounds ridiculous rolling off my tongue. It's not possible. And even if it was and I was perfectly capable of pulling something like that off, why would I do it?

No one in their right mind would ever consider it. And I'm perfectly in my right mind.

Isaac laughs when he finds out that I stole his Jeep.

"Baby, everything I own belongs to you."

He kisses me hard, lifting me from the floor with his arms tightly around my back.

"And that reminds me," he says as I slide back down the front of his body and my feet touch the floor again, "you should stop saying 'Isaac's bed' and 'Isaac's room' and 'Isaac's house'. It bugs me."

I blush. I think he'll make me blush even fifty years from now.

"Okay, so I hate to break the news," I say, half-smiling because I don't like what I'm about to tell him, but I also don't want to ruin the moment, "but looks like I'm not going to be sleeping in *our* bed for a while."

His playful smile evaporates in two seconds.

"Your father wants me to stay everyday with Aramei until he gets back from Serbia."

His right hand lifts level with his chest and his knuckles jut out as he balls it into a half-fist; his lips press together in a hard, angry line and his breath explodes from his nostrils.

He starts to hit the wall, but retracts his hand and calms himself.

"It's almost over," I say, cupping his face in my hands. "I'm so close to finding out what Aramei is trying to tell me. I can *feel* it, Isaac."

His jaw works abrasively beneath my hands. I hold my gaze on him, taking in all of his anger and impatience and worry and finally his surrender.

"Did he say for how long?"

I shake my head. "But how long is he usually away? You know he won't leave her alone for *too* long."

Isaac's eyes drift from mine as if he's thinking really hard about it. And then he nods slowly. "You're right," he says, finally looking at me again; my fingertips still touching his face. "But after this, I'm putting a stop to it. You can't keep doing this...."

I soften my eyes and smile faintly up at him. "I know," I say and peck him on the lips once. "I admit that a part of me loves Aramei and that I feel this burning need to help her in whatever way I can, but I love you more and I don't want my obsession with her to overshadow my obsession with you."

That lightened the mood; Isaac's mouth lifts into a grin. "You're obsessed with me?"

I smile and draw back my chin, wrinkling my eyebrows. "Baby, if I wasn't so rational, I'd totally stalk you."

He growls under his breath and pulls me to his chest again.

26

ON THE DRIVE TO the cabin, I fill Isaac in on mine and Alex's time with Aunt Bev and Uncle Carl.

"You can still go to college, you know?"

I look at him in the driver's seat and kind of laugh. "Isaac, I'm a werewolf. It's just...I don't know, I...," I'm getting frustrated because I'm still having a hard time pinpointing this issue, why everything humans do just feels unnecessary anymore.

"Your life doesn't have to be so different than you always imagined it," he says.

I just listen because I feel like maybe he's about to solve this issue for me.

"It's like...I don't know—take your uncle for example. He can't walk anymore. He knows his life has changed dramatically and for a long time it might feel like nothing will ever be the same. But nothing around him has changed. The only thing that's changed is *him* and how *he* can interact with it all." He pats my thigh. "Babe, before you can get past this you have to accept that you're different and stop trying to understand why."

Maybe that's it. It kind of feels like it might be, but I'll have to think about this more later.

"But still, college is just not feasible."

"Why?" he says looking back out at the road.

"Because it costs like a trillion dollars—besides, what would I go for? Zoology?"

He breathes out a laugh through his nose.

"You can go for whatever you want," he says, "and it doesn't have to be for something animal-related." I catch him rolling his eyes and I can't help but smile to myself.

"Well, it still costs too much and I'm not about to let my aunt and uncle refinance their house or start donating plasma just so I can go to school."

"You can go to New York," he says, glancing over.

He seems serious, but I just roll my eyes and stare out ahead at the road.

We pull up to the front of the cabin.

"Nate's not doing so well." We sit in the Jeep with the engine running. "This whole Blood Bond thing with Minna is really starting to mess with his head."

My face falls.

"I'm going to the racetrack with him tonight. Hopefully it'll help take his mind off things."

He leans across the seat and kisses me. "I love you."

I whisper it back onto his lips and kiss him, too, before stepping out and waving him goodbye.

As he drives away, I watch him go until I can't see the Jeep anymore and I feel this strange flutter of emotion in the pit of my stomach.

Aramei is sitting upright on the end of the bed when I make it upstairs.

"She's only been awake for a few minutes," Eva says, greeting me. She walks over to meet me halfway and stops directly in front of me, interlacing her fingers down below her belly and lowering her head into a small bow.

I just walk past her. I don't want to risk her trying to apologize for yesterday because then it's just like going right back into the subject all over again and I want to avoid that at all costs.

I walk over and sit next to Aramei. Her eyes are peering toward the candle burning on the bedside. The whole space is becoming darker as the night falls, leaving a dancing shadow on the wall from the tiny candle flame. The walls are bathed in a dark orange glow and everything feels eerie, maybe because it's always early in the morning when I'm here and venturing into Aramei's mind.

"I think she knew you were coming."

I nod, agreeing with her.

"Would you like for me to bring you anything?"

"No," I say, putting up my hand, "but thank you."

"Then I will leave you to her."

I can sense that Eva bows before she leaves.

I stand up again once Eva is gone and I lean over into Aramei's view as her gaze lies softly out ahead. I take her hands into mine and gently coax her body up and to my surprise, she stands.

We are the same height. I look into her seemingly desolate green eyes and a flicker of acknowledgment moves through her irises. I cradle her hands more firmly and kiss her softly on the forehead.

"Aramei…I'm here."

The room begins to shrink into a vortex as though something is sucking it all into one tiny point. But we don't move; not even my hair blows though it feels like it should be whipping about my face and wrapping around the back of my head threatening to take me into the point as well. My breath catches sharply and I shut my eyes before the motion of the room being stretched into oblivion makes me sick to my stomach. I feel Aramei's hands tighten around my own and this small gesture of understanding motivates me.

And before I have a chance to catch my breath again, my eyes are forced open and my body is thrust into a strange series of events unlike any of my past visits into Aramei's mind. It takes me a moment to wrap my head around what is happening and why it's happening so fast; why I'm not standing immobile in a room somewhere in 1762, picking up where we left off last.

Time is skipping. I see that now. Aramei's life is moving through the ages in gaps rather than a seamless, perfect sequence.

And it takes my breath away.

Golubac Fortress – Serbia – Summer 1777

Lord General Vukašin Prvovenčani takes Aramei as his wife in a traditional Black Beast ceremony. The two of them, werewolf and human, know love like no other. Aramei, despite being surrounded by death and danger and darkness, can never imagine herself anywhere else. She is Trajan's life and he is hers.

But others find their union blasphemous and have been plotting against the Sovereign since the day it was made public that he had taken a human girl as is mate. Vengeful eyes watch Aramei from everywhere.

She will never be safe.

Golubac Fortress – Serbia – Spring 1780

Viktor's rogue army has grown to immeasurable proportions. Every town along the Danube has been inundated by the infection. And the danger is soon to infiltrate the fortress where Aramei is kept safe.

"He *cannot* be destroyed!" Trajan roars among the meeting with the Elders and his Right Hand, Nataša. Nataša is the only one here who knows the truth about Aramei's Blood Bond to Viktor.

"It is not a proposal," Trajan goes on, standing tall and dictatorially at the head of the enormous U-shaped table. "I want him *alive*."

The Elder, Kruag, places his rugged hands upon the stone table; the sleeves of his dark robe drapes just above his scarred knuckles.

"Why do you protect Viktor? Why must he be left alive?"

Trajan's iron hand comes down upon the stone table, splitting it in half. Pieces of rock crumble at his feet, leaving a two-foot gap between the halves of the table. All of the Elders straighten their backs and raise their chins a few inches—but never higher than Trajan's—to show absolute respect.

"If Viktor dies," Trajan says in a searing, growling whisper, "you *all* die."

Golubac Fortress – Serbia – Summer 1780

The fortress is overrun. Trajan suspects that someone from the inside has let them in; that troops were ordered away from key gates just before dawn.

The plotting against Trajan and his blasphemy has finally begun to unfold.

"Stay with her!" Trajan orders Nataša. "Once you get her outside the forest, make sure no one finds you! GO! NOW!"

Nataša grabs Aramei.

"Milord!" Aramei cries, reaching out for him in Nataša's grasp. Tears barrel from her eyes. "My love! Please! You cannot stay behind! Please, come with me!" She screams so stridently that her voice becomes hoarse.

Trajan rushes over to her, ripping her from Nataša's hands. Pain and desperation is seared into his features. His dark, rugged facial hair streaked with blood from the Black Beast he killed just moments ago, the one that tried to get into the room at Aramei. He kisses her passionately, savagely, holding her head in both of his enormous hands. "I will find you! I will come for you!"

And Nataša rips Aramei from Trajan's arms and carries her down the top tower and into the bowels of the fortress by means of secret passages.

Bulgaria - Western Stara Planina – Winter 1782

The conspirators have all finally been captured. Six weeks after the attack on the fortress and the battle was won, Trajan ordered the seizure of any and all who were behind the plot to dethrone him and kill Aramei. If they only knew that simply to kill Viktor, which they wanted in the beginning, would have also achieved their great plot against Trajan and Aramei as well.

Now they sit in prison; nine different prisons spread throughout Serbia, Bulgaria, Romania and even as far south as Greece. Nine of the conspirators were Elders; each of them had served under Trajan's father.

"Execute them all," Trajan orders Nataša as she stands before his throne. "It is your commission to carry this out."

"Yes, Milord." She bows very low and holds it there for several symbolic seconds. Her belly is pregnant with her and Trajan's second child.

"And see to it that their heads are sent back here."

Bulgaria - Western Stara Planina – Fall 1792

It has been thirty years since the day Viktor bonded Aramei to his blood. But she hasn't aged a day. Trajan's blood has kept her alive and youthful and strong for so long. The empire of the Black Beasts is more powerful than it has ever been with Trajan at its head. But it is also more tumultuous and uncertain than ever in its history. Trajan rules with an iron fist. He takes no prisoners anymore, and passes execution without a trial no matter the severity of their crimes.

Fear is what makes this empire impenetrable. Fear is what gives birth to conspirators. But Trajan is becoming delusional in his reign. Blinded by his life with Aramei, Trajan is beginning to misjudge everything else around him.

All that he sees is her.

She is everything to him.

"Why can I not bare your children?"

Aramei sits in Trajan's lap upon his throne, cradled against his chest.

"You will one day, my love."

"But it has been so long, Milord." She lifts her head and takes his bearded chin into her fingers and brushes her soft lips against his rugged ones. "It is all that I want: to give you a child. If I can conceive, I can feel whole."

Trajan's head moves slowly to look down into her eyes. He moves her fingers from his face with the side of his hand.

"You do not feel whole?"

Aramei lowers her eyes, understanding the true nature of his question.

He lifts her chin in his fingers, gently forcing her gaze. "Never be ashamed to speak your mind to me, Aramei. You are the only soul in this world who can defy me and not die for it—now tell me; do you not feel whole?"

Her eyes flutter gracefully underneath her lashes, giving her that natural coy, childlike appearance she is known for.

"No woman is ever whole without bearing a child," she says softly. "It is nothing more than what nature asks of me."

Trajan can't look at her now. I see it in his eyes, the reason for that impenetrable, brooding stare into nothingness. He can't bring himself to tell her that because of the Blood Bond, she is barren. The only life her body can sustain is her own and not even blood as powerful as the Sovereign's is strong enough to allow her body to carry another life inside of it.

He almost smiles, but only allows her to see it in his eyes as he looks back down at her eager face.

"You will bear my child one day," he says, kissing her forehead. "It is only but a matter of time. Just be patient."

Aramei smiles and it lights up her face.

"Then you will never deny me?" she says, part thoughtful, part seductively playful. "You give your word that whenever I am ready and feel that I can conceive that you will come home from any war you're fighting, to be with me?"

Trajan's lips smile now as he gazes upon her. He traces his finger along the length of her jaw and says, "I give you my word."

Serbian Carpathians – Central Serbia – Summer 1810

Forty-eight years have passed. Many wars have been fought and Trajan's offspring with his mates have died fighting them. And as promised, even when Trajan was amid these wars, he came home to Aramei the moment he received word that she needed him. Aramei never really knew where Trajan was most of the time. In these years, he had begun to enslave human girls to care for Aramei in his stead. But this decision did not mean that his love for her began to falter. Trajan knew that in order to protect Aramei, he would have to take many matters of war and strife into his own hands. This was the only reason he ultimately chose to leave her in the care of others.

Viktor Vargas was fulfilling his life's goal to make Trajan's life a living hell. Viktor was becoming brazen and rash, sending his rogues ahead of him right into open war when he knew they were clearly outnumbered.

Viktor *wanted* death so that he could finally get the ultimate revenge on Trajan.

Trajan couldn't let this happen. His orders to protect Viktor had become futile because Viktor *sought* death. He couldn't take his own life, however, because his bond to Aramei forbade him to. To kill himself would be to kill her and no two souls bonded by blood can will themselves to harm the other. Not even a rogue.

Everything he did, every choice that Trajan made was for Aramei.

"And what is your name?" Trajan says to the beautiful red-haired girl on the floor beneath his throne. Her arms are stretched out on the floor above her head; her back arched over, touching her forehead to the stone.

She lifts her face.

"I am Evangeline, Milord. I am your servant."

Trajan inhales deeply of the air and looks down at Evangeline warily. "You are not human."

"No, Milord."

Trajan contemplates the moment. About a dozen eyes are watching them. Aramei sits quietly in her throne next to his—angelic white next to authoritarian darkness.

"I like her, my love," Aramei says. "She has a kind face."

Trajan looks over. "A kind face does not mean treachery cannot live beneath it." He lifts his leather-covered wrist from the arm of the stone chair and waves two fingers in a whimsical circle.

"Yes, but I want her."

Trajan, who could never deny any of Aramei's wishes, looks back at Evangeline.

"Very well," he says, nodding. "You will be my love's chief servant."

Nataša's narrow eyes widen with disbelief as she gazes across the room at him. She steps forward wearing her battle armor with a sword of pure silver attached to her hip. She grips the hilt of the sword and bows.

"Make I speak freely?"

Trajan nods.

Nataša glances at Evangeline next to her.

"Why trust this one so easily simply because Milady bids it so?"

Evangeline raises her pale-colored arm and her hand slips from underneath the long sleeve of her black dress. For a moment, Nataša's chin rears back and she goes to put up her hand to knock her away, but then she stops. She appears confused.

Evangeline places her hand on Nataša's shoulder.

"I will never harm her," she says with words as soft as powder. "I am here to serve and protect her. Nothing more."

Nataša nods reluctantly, as if her mind is fighting with the muscles in her neck. She steps away from Eva and bows to Trajan once more before moving back to stand in her position near the tall, stone pillar.

Serbian Carpathians – Central Serbia – Summer 1812

Fifty years into the Blood Bond and today, Trajan's world will be turned on its head.

Eva bursts through the double-doors of the throne room. "She is on the ledge, Milord! She walks along the ledge of the wall!" Her voice is vociferous, tearing through the vast room and echoing off every stone wall.

Trajan jumps from his throne, his long leather coat falling about his tall form.

"Come, Milord!"

Eva grabs the fabric of her sheer black gown to keep it from dragging the floor behind her and she rips away in the direction she came without looking back.

When Trajan makes it outside the walls of the castle, he sees Aramei's soft light-colored hair blowing briskly in the high breeze. The wall she walks along was made on the edge of the mountain, which overlooks the river below nearly one thousand feet.

Stunned by what he's seeing, Trajan hesitates before dashing across the stones and grabbing her just before she tumbles over the edge.

"Aramei, my love! What were you *doing*?" Trajan's face is misshapen by terror. He holds her out in front of him by her petit shoulders, shaking her as if she were an unruly child. But then he gathers her close, practically crushing her weight against his; her head cradled in the palm of his hand. "Are you unhappy? Will you never feel whole?" He squeezes her.

He pulls away and looks upon her, searching her face for answers.

She just looks at him, cocking her head to one side curiously. "Milord, why do you say these things?" She smiles as if she believes he's just being dramatic. Then her gaze strays beyond him and she looks bewildered.

"How did I get out here?"

Trajan's eyes lock with Eva's. He looks every bit terrified.

~~~

It was the beginning of Trajan's madness and the end of Aramei's life.

From that year on, Aramei only grew worse. The drinking of Trajan's blood in order to sustain her consumed them. Over time, it became every day, sometimes twice a day, but no matter how much or how often she drank, it would never make her better for long and nothing could reverse the consequences of her bond. Within six years, she did not know herself anymore, not even briefly. The only thing the blood would do was keep her body alive, but her mind was too far gone to bring it back. And the only thing that her mind seemed to remember as though that one small part of her life had been somehow trapped in the depths of her subconscious was her need to bear him a child. She could call him by his name in their native tongue, but it had only been to call him to her when she felt her body could conceive.

Throughout the remaining two hundred years of Aramei's immortal life, Trajan never allowed himself to believe that when she spoke his name it was only for this purpose and that she had forgotten him.

He knew it to be true, but he would die before he ever admitted it to himself.

~~~

Time and Space is pushing me through it again. But this time it's different. I see everything of the rest of Aramei's life all the way up to the day I saw her myself for the first time in the cave, but it all flashes by so quickly. I'm falling fast and hard into some unknown place because I know that it's not back in the cabin. I try to scream out a name, *any* name, but when my mouth opens I have no voice. It feels like my limbs are detached from my body, that I'm just a particle of dust being hurled through the ether. Everything is so loud, yet at the same time, I hear nothing. I see faces and their lips moving, but like my own, nothing comes from them.

And then my body is plunged into infinite darkness.

Is this Hell? Have I died and gone to Hell?

The air echoes all around me violently as if I'm falling through a black hole. I try to see upward into the heavens, to find the top of the tunnel, but I'm too far inside of it.

And then a sort of peace and calm overcomes me.

I shut my eyes and let my head fall back to feel the wind on my face. I'm ready to accept death because it's so lulling, so beautiful.

Everything stops.

I open my eyes carefully, expecting to see...I don't know.

And as my eyes creep open the rest of the way and my surroundings becomes clearer, I see that I am in no place I have ever imagined before.

27

Somewhere Unknown – Present Day?

I LOOK DOWN AT my hands, confused by how I can even see them; I've never been able to actually see myself in Aramei's mind before. My hands are filthy and bruised and fouled by tiny cuts. I'm clad in a tattered green dress which covers my arms to my wrists and my legs to my ankles and I see that my feet are bare. My hair is loose and falls messily about my face, which hurts tremendously just under my eye. I reach up to touch the bone and wince.

There is small window out ahead; just a hole in the rock with no glass or shutters or anything that might make it look modern or familiar.

Slowly, I walk towards the window and the torch blazing high on the stone wall reveals more of the space. Everything is made of stone: the walls, the floor, the twisting, spiraling steps that descend down into cold darkness behind me and even the scaling roof that towers above.

There's something foul on the air. I can only describe it as the smell of death because I've never smelled something so horrible and death first comes to mind.

I stop at the window and cautiously lean forward to peer outside, afraid of what I might see. My breath hitches in my lungs when I see the charred landscape which stretches farther than I can see in every direction. I must be more than one thousand feet over the land. I can see a giant river snaking through the black hills far off in the distance, and down below, nestled amid the rolling black hills I spot tiny dots of orange firelight as though burning inside small cottages.

This isn't right. Nothing about this place feels like a part of *anyone's* past. It doesn't seem to me like any real place that ever could have existed. It doesn't appear real, yet it feels absolutely real as I stand here as a part of it.

I walk backwards away from the view with my hands pressed against my chest, my head shaking side to side as if continuously telling myself "No" over and over again. No, this is a dream; this can't be real....

Suddenly I hear a violent scream echo through the stone stairwell. My body jerks around and my ears pop, amplifying the scream even more. The voice screams out again; blood-curdling and desperate. I'm afraid at first and can't move, but then I begin to walk towards it. It's coming from the floor above me. I stop at the foot of the stairs and gaze up, but can see nothing around the wall as the stairs spiral around and upward into the sky. I wonder how much higher this tower can reach.

The screams just get louder as I ascend the steps, funneling down into my ears and causing my heart to beat violently inside my chest. Though the air is cold and my feet are frozen to the bone, sweat beads off my forehead relentlessly, drenching my hair. A shadow moves along the wall and I freeze in my steps until I see that the shadow follows suit and realize that it's my own. Another blazing torch is mounted on the wall and the heat burning off it only offers my body more discomfort. When I make it to the next floor, I see an enormous wooden door set in the wall straight ahead. There are no more stairs leading upward so I know this is the highest point in the tower.

I feel my heart thrashing against my ribs, trying to burst out as I approach the giant door. A fiery torch burns on each side of it.

A voice resonates from inside and becomes louder as the door is pushed open and a tall, brooding figure steps out before me.

I freeze in my spot in the wide open. There's no where I can run except down, but it's already too late. I wouldn't have time to make it to the stairs before I'm seen.

The man walks toward me and my heart falls right down into my knees. All of the saliva evaporates from my mouth instantly. When he is within ten feet of me, I feel like I should be certain that I'm about to die, but instead I'm not even sure that he sees me.

He stops within three feet and looks around curiously as though he senses something odd, like when someone feels there are eyes watching them, hidden in the shadows.

I can't breathe.

And then he looks directly at me, but I sense that he's seeing *through* me instead. His black hair is buzzed short and a long, braided goatee dangles from his chin. He is dressed in strange leather-like attire: long, split coat like Trajan always wore, black leather pants and tall boots with silver buckles around the shins. Black silk shirt with a crisscrossing tie that holds each side together. His eyes are fiery red and orange, just like a flame. His cheekbones are strong and high making his eyes appear tightened and almond-shaped.

He sniffs the air around my head and a forked tongue snakes out of his mouth. I yelp, thrusting my hand over my mouth, but he doesn't hear me.

And then he walks right through me, taking the breath right out of my lungs. I don't move for what seems like forever, until finally I gather my composure and make my way to the door. Placing my palm against the wood, I take a deep breath before pushing it open.

Aramei is looking directly at me as she dangles by her wrists from shackles mounted high enough on the wall that her feet barely touch the floor.

"Adria...."

My stomach wrenches so violently that it crushes my insides into a ball. My mouth is hung open, my eyes wide and terrified and confused.

I dash across the giant circular stone room to get to her.

She has been beaten and tortured; her face is heavily bruised, her thin white gown is covered in blood and blackness like soot from a fireplace. I reach out intent on touching her, just to see first if she's even real, but my hands stop just inches from her waist. Her arms are stretched high above her head. Her long hair is wild like strips of dry straw and soiled with filth and muck.

"Aramei...I-I...."

I can't even begin to understand the meaning of conversation or inquiry. I feel like I need to wake up. Any second now I should wake up. But my heart tells me this isn't a dream. I'm really here and she is really there, speaking to me.

She's actually speaking to me....

"I've waited for so long," she says. Her tears are choking her into submission, streaming from her eyes in a display of suffering and absolute relief. "I've waited for you for two hundred years."

I can't hold my own tears back; they stream down my face.

"You know me?" I say, choking the words through my sobbing. "How can…What is this place?"

So many questions. I can't decide which is more important and then a fragment of my rational mind sears into my awareness. I look up at her shackles again and immediately know that I need to help her down.

"Where's the key?" I say desperately, my head jerking around in every direction looking for any sign of it.

"No, Adria…listen to me…."

I stop and look up at her.

"There's nothing you can do for me here," she says.

Two tiny droplets of blood fall in slow-motion from the end of her chin. For a moment, I'm mesmerized by how they fall, so poetically and quiet.

"You can't stay here long," she says pleadingly, snapping me back into her voice. "Adria, you have to leave this place."

"But…I-I don't understand. I don't understand any of this." I feel like I might die with the weight of all these questions and the uncertainties crushing my chest and my brain.

"You know what you have to do," she says softly and I just stand here, staring up at her.

"I'm getting you down."

"No!" she shouts, thrashing her hands above her making the chains resonate an ominous racket through the room.

The severity of her voice stops me cold.

"You *have* to free me," she says so desperately. "I don't want to be trapped… to feel the pain anymore."

And before I have a chance to protest, the door bursts open and the strange man from before storms back inside. I push myself against the nearest wall, pressing my fingertips into the grooves of the stone, clutching it with so much force that it hurts.

He still doesn't see me, but he stops once again like he did outside the room, because he senses that something is amiss.

Aramei screams out to me, "You can't stay here! Hurry!" and the man grins a wicked grin and slithers his way towards her.

In the moment she cries out at him and a set of giant black porous wings emerge from his back, I am sucked from this strange place and find myself dangling from the balcony in the cabin by Eva's hand.

The realization of my predicament snaps me into the moment and I panic. "Oh my God! Eva! Don't let me fall!" I grip her wrist, struggling to stay in her grasp until finally she pulls me back over the railing and we both land hard on the wooden floor.

The whimpers and quiet screams and whispers of the awed servants on the bottom floor are all that I can hear for a long moment. My back is pressed against the wood, my arms and legs splayed awkwardly as I stare up at the rafters in the ceiling. My shirt is drenched in sweat. My heart is so tired that it can't even beat fast anymore, but it thumps in a slow, awkward sequence.

I roll over onto my side and push my body up on one hand.

Eva is sitting on the floor with her fabric-covered legs curled in behind her. I look at her, studying the tired and slightly panicked expression alive in her face. She's breathing hard and she's making no effort to stand. I decide that I can't yet, either.

I look up toward the bed at Aramei, but all that I can see of her are her bare feet.

"Eva?"

"Yes…I am here."

I didn't realize that the way I called out her name did sound as though I couldn't see her.

My head falls back in her direction and I look right at her. But she spares me trying to find the way to ask the questions that I desperately need answers to.

"I am a Praverian," she says, "and Aramei is my Charge."

My head is shaking back and forth in small jerking motions, my eyes as wide as I can stretch them.

I point towards her, "You…why did you say it? Eva…you said it out loud…."

She finally stands and walks over to me, reaching out her hand. I stagger to my feet because my legs are incredibly weak. I can't stop looking at her, mesmerized by her admission and her death wish.

"I am tired," she says breathlessly. "I just want to rest and now that you are here to do what you were fated to do, I can finally…sleep."

"What are you saying?" My head is still shaking side to side, my mouth hung open in awe.

She smiles weakly. "Adria, I have lived *so* many lives, died *so* many deaths and protected so many Charges, that I can't do it anymore. Aramei, I knew, would be the last. She had to be or else I might go Dark myself, just as your friend did."

Harry's form solidifies with us in the room and I gasp at the sight of him.

Because I know why he's here.

I throw my hand out towards him. "No! You wait! Not yet!" I know I can't stop him from drinking her Soul, but he has to give me time to understand what just happened and to find out where Aramei is trapped.

For the first time since I've known Harry, even after we all found out what he was, I look across at him and he doesn't seem like the Harry I know. Right now as he watches us calmly with his hands folded together down in front of him, he is all Praverian and has put away any evidence of his human self.

It scares me.

"*Please*, Harry," I beg, tears forming in my eyes again, "…just…wait."

Eva takes my hands into hers and smiles at me as if to say that everything will be alright.

"How am I supposed to help Aramei? H-How…What was that place? Eva, I know you know everything."

Her hands come up and cup my cheeks.

"It's…," she stops herself and softens her smile even more, but I get the immediate feeling that she's backtracking her answer to cover up the truth. "The minds of the insane are intricate and vivid and strange, but they are not real."

"That was real, Eva. Don't you tell me it wasn't real."

"But it wasn't," she says and either she's telling the honest truth, or she's a really good liar.

She tucks a lock of hair behind my ear.

"Every time you went under inside Aramei's mind, you risked being consumed by it, by the madness that she sees. I feared for you because you were so determined, so addicted, that I knew you might go too far and end up like her, lost in her mind where anything she believes is real can become real." She lets her hands fall away from my face. "Aramei is a tortured soul and only you can set her free because only you can get close enough to her to help her. Only you understand…."

My eyes keep glancing to Harry at my side so that I can make sure he's still waiting and not making any moves forward.

"But what about you?" I say. "*You* understand—more than I do—." I laugh miserably and then sniffle the tears away. "You're here with her more than anyone."

"But I cannot help her, Adria. What has to be done I cannot do because I, being what I am, am incapable."

She wants me to Turn Aramei. *Why*?

I make sure my mind is shut off tightly to Eva and Harry. I can't let them fish around inside my head while I'm thinking these thoughts.

I look across at Aramei lying amid her covers, but her eyes are wide open as she lays sprawled on her back. Nothing about her position is graceful or angelic as she always appears. She looks…dead. But I know that she's not because I see the rising of her chest vaguely. And then I picture the way she looked at me in that strange place, the way her tormented and anguished and broken soul bore into my heart. I can still hear the sound of her pleading voice, the way her desperate words seared into my ears.

And I know that I have no choice. I have to do it. I have to help her.

I shut my eyes softly for a brief moment of understanding and then step away from Eva.

"I do hope you can find your peace," I say to her and I mean it from the bottom of my heart.

Harry moves toward her and the two of them share a silent moment, peering into one another's eyes longingly as if they are lovers. A dark reddish light begins to emit from Harry's body, the same color as his Praverian eyes, and it becomes a thin smoke surrounding them. Eva closes her eyes and collapses into Harry's arms, her arms dangling lifelessly around him. His lips part just inches over hers and a quiet sucking sound carries on the air as he begins to drink her Soul. A light purple smoke dances from her mouth and enters his. I watch as Eva's eyes open again and they are the most beautiful amethyst I have ever seen. Her long red hair takes on a life of its own, just as Zia's did that night in the trap; the very tip of every strand is luminescent in the darkness of the room. Harry drinks down all of her and with every dramatic passing second, I see visibly how his own body becomes stronger.

Not until every last wisp of amethyst smoke has been drained from Eva's body and into Harry's, does he stop and lay her against the floor.

She is gone. There is no life left in her, or a soul left to carry on into another life.

And it makes me sad.

Tears stream down my cheeks again, but my body makes no sound. I can't sob or wail or gasp for breath anymore because much like Eva, I am *so* tired. I am confused and traumatized and tired….

I sit down on the end of Aramei's bed and just stare at the floor.

"You've been coming here with me all this time, haven't you?"

"Yes," Harry says and already he seems to be himself a little more, the Harry I know and love. I feel a sort of comfort in him. "Sorry I never told you, but I thought you'd be mad."

"I would've been," I admit.

I still don't look at him.

"But I'm not now and I know you were just looking after me."

He moves to sit down next to me, but I stop him by finally making eye contact.

"Harry, did you know about any of this?"

I don't know why, but this feels like the single most important question I've ever asked him.

"I've only known of your destiny and that every bit of it had to do with Aramei."

"If I infect her, Harry, she'll die."

He shakes his head. "No...," he says kneeling down in front of me on the floor. "She is different, powerful. She's special. She can live through it."

"But *why* is she special?" More and more I'm questioning my trust in Harry and although it hurts, I know I have to be sure of my feelings. "Why is it so important that she be Turned? Is that what causes the war?"

Something isn't making sense. Actually, a lot isn't making sense. What Harry expects me to do and the things Aramei said to me don't add up. I stand up and walk away from Harry, moving around to the side of the bed. I look down at Aramei and contemplate everything she said to me.

Suddenly I turn to face him.

"If I do this, I want to be alone with her."

Harry stands up and nods, accepting my request.

"I'll go outside and wait for you."

And without another word, Harry leaves down the stairs and heads outside.

I sit down quietly on the edge of the bed, staring down at Aramei's comatose state. Her eyes are eerily wide and unblinking, glazed over by a layer of natural moisture. Her pupils are so dilated that her eyes look black and enormous. Her lips, which have always appeared soft and full, are dry and cracked and beginning to shrivel.

I reach out my hand to touch her face and a tear falls from her eye. I gasp quietly at the sight of it and my own tears begin to shudder through my chest.

Finally, I just let it all out.

I bury my face in my hands and wail, letting the sobs rock me for a long time until I can't cry anymore.

"I will free you, Aramei…from yourself."

ISAAC

28

I HATED LEAVING ADRIA in the cabin like that, but I knew it was something that she wanted. I really could give two-shits less about my father's orders—he has nothing to do with this and soon I know I'm going to have to face him and make things right. Right in the way I've dreamed since I sired Adria and was initiated as Alpha into this totalitarian empire. Things are going to change soon and I'm going to be the one to change them.

But this issue with Aramei has to be dealt with first.

"Isaac?" Alexandra says in the doorway of my room.

I look up from my book to see her standing there, wringing her hands nervously, which in itself is odd. Rachel is standing behind her.

"Yeah?" I set the book down on the comforter beside me and sit up, swinging my legs over the side of the bed.

Alexandra swallows and I notice her eyes moving back and forth from me and the window.

"What is it?" I urge her.

I don't like the feeling I'm getting from either of them.

"Ashe is on his way here," Alexandra says.

I shoot straight up from the bed.

"What the hell do you mean?" I point downward at the floor. "Here? As in *here*? He contacted you?"

Alexandra nods furiously.

Rachel steps around to her side, a hard, angry line set in her face. "Yes, *here*, Isaac but that's not all."

"Oh? You mean it gets worse than having three Vargas rogues on my property?" I'm being a complete smartass because as always, Rachel deserves it.

"I resent that," Alexandra says with a sneer.

"Well, get used to it because it comes with the territory—now on with how this gets worse."

"Nathan," I say telepathically to wherever he is in the house, *"get everybody ready now—we're going to have company."*

"Viktor is with him," Rachel announces.

I do a mental double-take and my eyes have stopped blinking altogether.

Alexandra nods solemnly at me, confirming Rachel's announcement. "It's my fault," she says. "They're coming for me."

"Not your fault," I say as I rush past her and dash into the hall. "Stay inside the house! Both of you!" I shout back at them as I take the stairs three and four at a time.

"Vargas?" Nathan says as he rushes up to meet me in the den.

Everybody in the house is scrambling from room to room, my sisters and Xavier all charge into the den with Nathan and me. We're all telepathically connected being siblings, so they've already heard what's going on.

Xavier steps up, combing his fingers through his freshly washed hair as though he just got out of the shower. "That didn't take long, did it?" he says, shaking his head. "His girl bails and already he's regretting his douchiness and coming to Romeo her back into his bed."

"Looks that way," I say, "but I'm more bothered by Viktor being with him."

"Yeah," Nathan adds, "I have to admit that not even I take Ashe to be the type to bring the ol' man along—it's not their style...over a girl, at least."

"No, it's not," I say. "Where's Daisy?" I ask, realizing she's the only one of my living sisters who's not here.

"Still hiding out with Harry," Camilla says. "That Harvester thing really has Harry worried."

"And she's closed her mind off to me," I say after getting no telepathic response from her.

I shove my way past everyone and head straight for the front door, pushing it open fully and stepping out onto the porch; everyone follows close behind. I descend the steps and stand my ground in the wide open of the front yard; my pack is close behind, casting a large pool of shadow across the driveway. We wait for several long, tense minutes; only the sound of summer insects buzzing in the still of the night. The quarter moon is high in the star-filled sky.

And then an out-of-place band of shadow moves up from the end of the driveway as Viktor, Ashe and two others I don't know, emerge from the darkness.

Ashe, looking as pathetic as ever stands beside his father, Viktor, with his head cocked confidently to one side. His short black hair is messy on top, like he'd been in a fight recently.

Viktor Vargas is the only one among them who has my attention.

He stands tall at the head of their small group, his burly arms crossed, an impious grin that I know is telling of so much more, is a permanent fixture on his face.

What is he really doing here?

I know that his part in this has nothing to do with Alexandra. She's a small, insignificant fish to Viktor Vargas and wouldn't waste his time with the likes of her.

He gazes across the yard at me and our eyes lock in an intense moment where two Alphas quietly come to an understanding: we are one in the same as Alphas and if there is a Challenge made here tonight, it will be between him and me.

Bring it the fuck on.

Viktor smiles chillingly. "I've been seeing and hearing some very interesting things as of late," he says. His head leans in on one side, his chin barely turning at an angle so that he appears inquisitive and the one holding all the cards.

"About what exactly?" I say, and although he's already succeeded in worrying me, I'm not about to let him know it.

Viktor grins. Probably because he already knows he's succeeded.

"First thing first," he says, unfolding his arms.

"Yeah, bring my fledgling girl out here," Ashe says, "before I go in myself and get her."

Viktor puts his arm out horizontally at his side and pushes Ashe back. "I did not come here for your little girlfriend," he says, "and if you interrupt me again, I'll see to it that you never produce an offspring."

As Ashe swallows his pride and steps off, Alexandra and Rachel exit the house and stand boldly together at the top of the porch. I grit my teeth behind tightly closed lips, but think better of reprimanding them for disobeying my order to stay inside. I realize before it's too late that letting Viktor and Ashe know that I don't have those two properly 'trained' yet, will put a serious hurt on my reputation as Alpha.

"I'm really surprised by your stupidity," Alexandra says to Ashe.

"His desperation is what I like to see though," Rachel chimes in.

I don't have to look at either of them to see the smirks and taunts on their faces. But I'm about to explode over their interruption.

Viktor looks dead at me, quietly questioning my leadership abilities.

I throw a warning glance back at Alexandra and Rachel and thankfully they see it.

But then Xavier opens *his* mouth, "Why don't you go back to the shithole you crawled out of?—you're not taking Alexandra anywhere."

I whirl around to face everyone behind me, including Xavier who instantly sees the anger in my churning black eyes. "ENOUGH!" My voice rumbles through my body, piercing the night air. My eyes remain black, claws at the ready where my stiff, partially curled fingers are challenging everyone from down at my sides.

I turn around to see Viktor and say, "Why are you here?" and the question rolls right out of me amid an infernal echo.

Viktor steps up closer and I do the same, leaving our groups several feet behind us. The light from the light pole nearby shines down and around us, making us even more-so the center of attention. Viktor's smile never fades, but in it he carries something other than violence or retribution. No, Viktor's face carries mystery and humor and relief. He's not here to Challenge me or even to fight, he's here for something much worse....

"First," he says, putting up his index finger, "I have to thank you for taking care of that little white-haired Praverian bitch—talk about a thorn in my side."

I say nothing. I just want him to get on with it.

"But what I really came here for?" Viktor smiles balefully. "That mate of yours and her rather 'unhealthy' relationship with Aramei."

My chin rolls stiffly to one side and I glare in at him in a sidelong glance.

He goes on:

"I haven't been able to see much into Aramei's mind in so long and then one day, out of the blue," he twirls both of his hands at the wrists and opens his palms out in front of him, "I start seeing shit you could never imagine."

He's momentarily lost in some memory that appears to amuse to him in a sick sort of way.

I keep quiet for now, letting him delight in his strange musings and self-importance, while giving me time to figure out how I'm to respond to any of this. I don't want to risk telling him anything about Adria or Aramei that he doesn't already know.

He folds his hands together behind his back and smiles upon me.

"Oh!" He laughs suddenly and his grin deepens. "I guess I don't need to explain to you how it is that I'm still alive?"

"No," I say simply, pretending not to be fazed by his mockery, but I'll always be hurt by the fact that my father chose to protect him all these years and risked his children's lives by doing so. "I've known for a long time. But that's not why you're here, so stop it with the performance and get to the point."

I take another step closer to him and he casually stands his ground.

"Fine," he says, rolling his green eyes in a chafed fashion. "You're going to lose the Dawson sister one way or another, and this time, I have nothing to do with it."

I step right up into his face as we are the same height.

"Why are you saying this?" I glare heatedly into his eyes.

"Because it's true," Viktor responds, never losing his slim smile. "There are only two ways that this will end, Isaac, and I don't see you saving her from either of them."

"TELL ME!" I roar and Viktor still doesn't flinch.

I sense both groups becoming rigid and quietly riled by the rising of my voice, but they retain their distance for now.

"Tell me, Viktor…," I say in an almost failed attempt at a calmer voice, "…what are you saying to me?"

And then in a strange shift, Viktor's grinning face suddenly falls and he looks confused and traumatized and then blissful and then confused again, all in a matter of seconds.

He steps away from me, stumbling backward with his wide eyes fastened to the ground. He holds his hands out in front of him and stares at them as if he's never seen his own hands before. His face, riddled with shock, becomes more unreadable as it shifts from one expression to another in rapid, conflicting phases.

He falls to his knees.

His hands come up above his head for a moment and when he arches his back over and buries his face near his knees, I finally snap out of how confused I am by his sudden, awkward show. I hadn't even noticed that I stepped away from him by a few feet, as if my subconscious was putting necessary space between me and an unpredictable madman about to prove unpredictability.

Viktor raises his head and straightens his back again, craning his neck as if to look up at the stars and then a crazy laughter resounds through the air.

All of us, my group and Viktor's, are looking down at him, equally stunned, and at each other equally confused.

"Father?" Ashe says. For a second, he goes to reach out for Viktor, maybe to help him up, but decides against it and backs away another step, instead. "Get up!" he hisses through his teeth. "What are you *doing*?"

Ashe's eyes keep bouncing back and forth between Viktor and me.

Viktor laughs again, this time with tears running down his face. But these aren't tears of sadness—Viktor is incapable of an emotion so human—but are of an eerie sort of exhilaration that I just can't place.

"Oh, by the Sovereign!" he sings, craning his neck back even farther, his big hands now attached to the sides of his head. A ripple of sadistic, delighted laughter thunders from his throat. "I can't believe it!" He laughs yet again and I'm growing more worried and fearful with every one of them.

Viktor suddenly lowers his head and looks right at me, grinning a victorious grin. His green eyes are hooded broodingly beneath his eyelids.

I reach out and grab him by the throat, bringing him to his feet again. I grind my jaw and feel a livid tremor move through my lips, unsheathing them from my teeth. My razor-sharp claws puncture the flesh around his throat and blood oozes slowly down my fingertips and my hand.

"WHAT. HAS. HAPPENED?!"

Viktor does nothing to get out of my grasp. His eyes peer in at me intently.

"You'll know soon enough." He smiles.

I shove him to the ground and he laughs the whole way. He doesn't even attempt to get to up once he hits it. Ashe and the two others who came along with them finally advance, but then so does Nathan and Xavier and, to my surprise, Sebastian, who I thought had left us to go back to his human family. He appears out of nowhere it seems and jumps on one of Ashe's sidekicks, pummeling him with his fists. Nathan takes the other, while Xavier crashes to the ground on top of Ashe, his bloodied fists raining down blows on Ashe's already scarred and angry face.

But the fight is over quick and all of the Vargas filth is pinned to the ground, except for Viktor who still hasn't moved from his spot. He's still smiling and I know something of unimaginable weight has happened and that it has to do with Aramei.

And Adria....

I lean over fiercely into Viktor's face. "Viktor, tell me! What has happened. Tell me!"

But he just laughs and leaves me with nothing.

"Take them all to the basement!" I command. "And make sure they can't move." I look right at Nathan with a cold, hard stare; my nostrils flaring. "Even if you have to take off their legs."

He nods and they drag Ashe and the others around the back of the house toward the new reinforced basement door.

I take Viktor myself, but he goes willingly. It worries me more that he doesn't fight back, that he suddenly, after hundreds of years, seems so different that I don't see the old Viktor in him much anymore. I want to beat the information out of him, *kill* it out of him, but somehow I know he's not going talk. He wants me to know, more than anything, but he isn't going to be the one who tells me.

Almost two hours pass and nothing.

I've already left Viktor in the basement chained to the wall with his son and the others. There's no way they're getting out of there: reinforced steel all the way around and chains made of silver and iron.

Viktor could probably get out if he really wanted to bad enough.

The rest of us have migrated upstairs and are all standing around on the sharpest of pins and needles.

"I still can't get her on the phone," I say. I grip my phone tight in my fist and move to smash it against the wall out of anger, but don't in case Adria does try to call me back. And her mind…it doesn't feel closed off to me intentionally. It feels…odd…like she's unable to communicate with me.

I'm going out of my mind!

Daisy bursts through the front door, shaking everyone from the furniture.

"Where's Harry?" she shouts, coming around the corner, her curly blond hair whipping about her frantic face.

"We thought you've been with him?" Nathan says standing beside me.

"No!" she screams. "I haven't seen him since this afternoon. But about thirty minutes ago, I got a telepathic message from him, telling me to meet him here and that it's deathly urgent—Where is he?!"

Before I have a chance to answer, the room goes quiet as Daisy's head snaps around to face the door.

She runs back out and we follow fast behind her.

I gently push her aside and head down the porch steps as I stare off at the figure coming around from behind Harry's car parked at the farthest end of the driveway.

Harry is carrying Adria in his arms towards us.

I run after them and stop just as Harry stops. We look at each other, Harry and I, for a powerful moment and then I glance down at Adria, whose eyes are open, but she seems oblivious to me.

"Isaac…," Harry says carefully.

"Harry…,"

He hesitates and adjusts Adria within his arms. I keep wanting to reach out and take her from him, but I can't yet and I don't know why.

Harry takes a deep breath.

"Aramei's dead, Isaac," he says and my heart stops. "Adria killed her."

29

ALL OF THE VOICES around me have been blocked from my ears…or, maybe they just aren't saying anything anymore. I hear nothing. Not the breeze combing through the trees, or the traffic in the distance, or Ashe's chains rattling violently as he tries to break free, or even Viktor's sadistic laughter that makes him sound all the more like the lunatic he is.

I feel sluggish movement behind me, but I can't comprehend what's causing it. It takes several long, ominous seconds before all of the sound and movement rushes back into my consciousness and I'm jolted awake as if I'd been punched in the face.

That sluggish movement from before was everyone clambering from the house, but my head was translating it all in slow-motion. I see two figures take off towards the woods.

Finally, I notice Harry still standing in front of me holding Adria in his arms.

I snatch her away from him.

"My God…oh my fucking God…."

This isn't happening. Not like this. I have been plotting all this time against my father so that I could abolish his dictatorship once and for all…but not like this!

Adria is coherent, but traumatized. She moves her body around in my arms so that she's upright now, straddling her legs tight around my waist. She sobs into my neck, her tears wet against my burning skin, her body trembling against mine. I hold her tight, wrapping my arms firmly around her back, crushing her; the back of her head cradled within the palm of my own trembling hand.

"I-I had to d-do it!" she wails, the words sputtering from her lips. "That's what she wanted, Isaac! She was suffering! She's been suffering inside her own mind for over two hundred years! I *had* to help her!" Her body quakes, racking against mine violently.

"I know, baby," I say softly, trying to calm her down. "I know…Adria, please don't be like this. You did the right thing—."

"I KILLED HER!" she roars, pulling her head away from my neck. "ISAAC, I SNAPPED HER NECK! I *MURDERED* A PERSON!"

I know she's not angry at me. It's obvious just by the extreme pain in her eyes that she's still trying to believe what she's done, trying to convince herself that she *had* to do it.

I shake my head. "No, baby, listen to me…Aramei hasn't been a person for a long time. You didn't kill *anyone*; you killed her pain. Nothing more." My voice sounds breathless in my own ears.

"You have to get her out of here, Isaac," Nathan says in a grave voice behind me. "Bro, you know what this means. She can't stay here. None of us can."

I break away from Adria's pain quickly because I know I have to.

"Harry! Get her out of here!" I go to pass Adria back to him, but she latches onto me. "TAKE HER! HARRY!"

"No! I'm staying here!"

Adria's feet touch the ground and she grabs me around the waist. I thrust her face in my hands, her tears streaming under my thumbs. "You have to go with Harry! My father will kill you! And I can't fight him if you're here—I'll be too worried about you!" Sobs rack my chest.

I truly feel like this is the last time I will ever see her again. Either my father will find and kill her, or he's going to kill me when I face him. Either way, I will never see her again....

"NO!" Adria's eyes turn black and the sheer hostility in her voice causes me to freeze. "You're not going to die because of me! LISTEN TO ME!" She grabs my face, her claws grazing the skin on my cheeks and causing a trickle of blood to trail down my neck. "This won't be a debate. I don't care that you're Alpha. I don't care that Trajan will kill me. I'm not backing down from this, Isaac. Not for you or for anyone else. If you fight him, I fight him *with* you!"

Xavier runs up behind us with Rachel and Alex. I don't turn to look at him even though I know he's seeking my attention. Right now it's just me and Adria and...I-I don't know what to do...

"AHHH!" I scream into the night, balling my clawed hands into vicious fists out in front of me. Anger and indecision and fear of what my father will do to Adria overwhelms every inch of me.

I sense that everyone backs away except for Adria. Their footsteps shuffle densely in my ears and every other sound around me is stifled, leaving only the sound of my blood pumping violently through my veins, pounding in my ears, and my own scream bounces around inside my skull. Adria, unafraid, walks up to me and says softly, "I love you so much, Isaac. I do. We're in everything together; don't you understand?" She brings her arms up to her chest, folding her hands underneath her chin and she presses her body against mine, her head lying on my heart. "In everything together," she goes on, her voice breaking, "we live and fight and die together."

Her words sting me. Reluctantly, I wrap my arms around her and bury my lips in her hair.

"Bro," Nathan says carefully, "come on man, we have to do something." I feel his hand on my shoulder from behind.

"Dria," Alexandra says stepping up.

Adria pulls away from me slowly to see her sister.

"I just got you back," Alexandra says. "If you get yourself killed over a guy, I'm going to be so frickin' pissed."

Adria chokes out a tear-filled laugh, unable to resist her sister's charms. And for the first time since Alexandra has been here, I find myself glad that she is. Without letting Adria see, I nod my heartfelt thanks to her sister and her eyes smile back at me.

"Nathan's right, bro," Xavier says. "I don't know what you plan to do, but the one thing I think we can all agree on is that we can't stay here."

I nod to myself a few times, thinking and agreeing.

Harry stands off to the side with Daisy. I don't like him anymore. This is his fault.

"We have to get away from the town," I announce. "Not only to protect the humans in it from all-out war, but we need someplace where we can stay until I come up with a plan."

Nathan and Xavier nod and continue to listen fixedly.

Adria's head jerks up like she just thought of something. "Isaac, what about the cave? The one your father kept Aramei in when you took me to see her the first time?"

Alexandra wraps her arms around Adria from the side and they both stand there together, waiting for me.

"Yes," I say, "that's actually the perfect place. Our father would never think to look there."

"And he never uses the same place twice," Nathan adds.

"Awesome," Xavier says, "Then I say we get the hell out of here before he finds out."

"Wait?" Alexandra says. "You mean Trajan doesn't know yet?"

I shake my head. "If he knew, *we* would know."

"Isaac?" Harry says and I whirl around at him.

"You stay back," I growl, pointing my finger at him. "In fact, I think it's better that you leave, Harry."

Harry blinks a few times, stunned. Daisy steps up beside him, thrusting his hand into hers and a hard line appears on her mouth as she looks at me.

"Daisy," I say, intolerant of her inevitable resistance, "Harry knew this was going to happen. He's known all along." My voice begins to rise and I point at him again, though my eyes haven't left my sister's. "Harry helped her do this and he could've easily stopped it!"

Adria moves out of Alexandra's arms and steps in front of me, placing the palms of her hands against my chest. "Baby, no, please listen to me."

Daisy's trying to hold down her beast; her teeth are grinding harshly behind her lips, her breathing is becoming more rapid and unsteady.

Adria's rapt voice brings me back to her.

"He didn't know what I was going to do, Isaac. He didn't know."

I look to and from Adria and Harry, searching for an explanation.

Harry shakes his head. "She's telling you the truth," he says. "She was supposed to *infect* Aramei…not *kill* her."

I blink back, stunned as much as Harry was before.

"*What?*" Nathan says. "How is it you couldn't *see* that!?"

Harry breathes in deeply and his gaze strays toward the trees before falling right back on me.

"It doesn't always happen the way it's supposed to," he clarifies. "And I'll face the consequences of my failure, later. But not from you or anyone else."

Adria and Daisy's heads whip around to Harry at the same time.

"Harry, what's that supposed to mean?" Daisy says.

He walks up and takes her shoulders into his hands, looking upon her with calming eyes. "That's not important; right now the only thing any of us needs to be doing is getting as far away from here as possible." Then he looks back at me, seeking my approval. "That is if you don't care I come along for the ride."

I'm still thoroughly pissed at Harry, because after all, he knew Adria was going to do *something* to Aramei and whether it was killing her or infecting her, the result as far as my father is concerned would likely have turned out the same way. I don't know. We'll never know. But right now, Adria needs all of the protection she can get.

I don't answer Harry directly because I can't. A verbal response just feels too forgiving at the moment, but when I don't force him away, he's fully aware of my decision.

Daisy breathes a quiet sigh of relief and laces her arm around his.

"What about Eva?" I say, looking to both Adria and Harry.

Adria lowers her eyes, indicating another unfortunate outcome and I'm not sure how many more of these I can take.

"She was a Praverian," Adria finally says.

It seemed that Harry was about to be the one to tell me this, but Adria took over for him.

"I drank her Soul," Harry says. "She revealed herself to me. I think much like Aramei, Evangeline was tired and just wanted to be at peace and so I drank her Soul."

He doesn't seem remorseful because of her death, but I get the distinct feeling that he is relating to how Eva felt.

I wonder just how old Harry really is himself.

"No one ever goes inside the cabin except the servants," Adria adds. "Your father might never know about Aramei until he gets back here."

Adria chokes out another sobbing fit and Alexandra hugs her tighter. Adria may be strong and she may be able to come to terms with what she's done sooner than some, but she's still devastated over it. She cries into Alexandra's shirt for several long seconds until she forces herself to suck it up.

I let her have her moment with her sister; there will be more, after all.

I look out at everyone else, my sisters and brothers, Rachel and even Sebastian who has been standing beside her the entire time (yes, I find it interesting, too, but this isn't the time) and I say, "I guess the real question here is, whose side are you all on?"

Nathan pats me on the back. "It's not even a question, bro."

Xavier steps up and smirks. "I go where you go."

"Me too," Daisy says.

I glance at Sebastian and Rachel.

Sebastian points his finger in the air. "This is and will always be my family, so I'm in."

Rachel grins wickedly from the side. "I go where the eye candy goes," she says, and although that's not much of a loyal response, like always I have to set aside her Vargas lineage.

The few others left who have always lived in the house with us, but were refugees and related to no one, step up to declare their loyalty to me.

"Let's get on the road," Alexandra says, holding Adria's hand. "The only one here I'm worried about is my baby sister."

More Vargas sensibility, but entirely forgivable.

Xavier's mouth lifts into a grin as he looks across at Alexandra. "I totally defended your honor with that bitch-ass ex-boyfriend of yours today, not to mention, when I rushed into the depths of Hell to try and break you free from that crazy white-haired chick—I still don't have your appreciation?"

Alexandra rolls her eyes and her head falls back. "The depths of Hell? Really?" She shakes her head. "Dramatic, aren't we?"

"What about Viktor and Ashe?" Nathan says to me.

I have been thinking about what to do with them all along.

I look toward the basement where on the other side of it they are still chained to the wall.

"Adria," I say and she looks up from Alexandra's chest, "you have five minutes to grab whatever's most important to you and get in the Jeep."

Everyone else knows the demand also applies to them and so they all take off together into the house. Alexandra seems reluctant to leave Adria, but finally she heads inside, too. Nathan stays with me.

Adria walks up to me and just stands there, looking at me. Then she wraps her arms around me and lays the side of her face against my chest.

I kiss the top of her head and say, "What are you doing? Five minutes, okay?" I want to just hold her forever, but we need to get on the road.

She looks up into my eyes. "You *are* what's most important to me." And she pushes up on her toes and kisses me gently on the lips.

~~~

Viktor is smiling hugely when Nathan and I stand before him in the basement. Ashe doesn't look happy at all and the other two just kind of sit there.

"You think you can defeat your *great father*?" Viktor says dramatically. He sits on the floor against the rock wall with his knees drawn up, his hands bonded by chains behind his back. I know one as old and as powerful as Viktor could set himself free from these shackles—not much can hold an Elder and they weren't made for Elders—but he hasn't even tried.

"How does it feel, being unbound to her?" I say. A small hint of mockery lies in the question, but I also genuinely want to know.

A flicker of pain moves across his eyes, but he retains the sadistic and humorous aspect of the situation, flawlessly. He smiles wide and says, "It feels *wonderful*."

I know that the biggest part of him is telling the truth, that he *is* happy to be free of her after two hundred fifty years, but there is that small part that not even he can hide entirely, in which he is devastated by Aramei's death and her connection to him severed. A Blood Bond of that measure, one that has endured for so long, isn't something any werewolf can just forget. It will take time and discipline and determination, but none of these things are things that Viktor Vargas has. He is his own worst enemy. He always has been. And I think that what's happened will only push him further over the edge of insanity and that sooner than later, he will be his own downfall.

"You can't leave us down here," Ashe growls, jerking his hands and legs, trying to get to me.

"I can and I will."

"You know this war isn't between us," he says. "We could give a shit less about you, or about your tyrant father — let us go!"

I shake my head almost unnoticeably, but I don't mock him or give in to the argument he wants.

But what Ashe said is entirely true. This war, generations of conflict between the Vargas family and ours, has always been about Viktor and my father. Viktor could've killed me that night I rushed in to save Adria from him. He could've killed me and bonded Adria to him as forcefully as he did Aramei. But he didn't because it was never about me or Adria or wanting her as his mate. I know this now.

It has always been about my father and Viktor's hatred of him. And Viktor took it out on anyone that had ever meant something to my father.

But Viktor is far from innocent in all of this. His treachery and his lies and the pain he has caused so many runs too deep. He passed any point of forgiveness a long time ago, though I know too that Viktor would die before asking anyone to forgive him for anything. He isn't a broken soul that needs mending or absolution, nor does he want it.

I nod to Nathan, indicating to him that it's time to go and he follows me toward the stairs.

"WAIT!" Ashe calls out. "You can't be serious! I just came here for Alex! I just wanted her back!" I hear his chains pulling and loosening and pulling, over and over.

"Bro, I don't mean to question your decisions, but shouldn't we take them with us?"

I shut the basement door after Nathan steps out into the hall near the kitchen and then I slide all of the new locks recently installed in place. The door is made of solid steel.

"It would be more of a headache than anything to take them with us," I say, sliding the last lock over. "And Viktor hates our father so much that I know he would never betray us to him. He's really on no one's side."

Nathan nods thinking on it a moment and then agrees.

"And when Viktor wants out," I say, "he'll get out."

30

WE MAKE IT INTO the depths of Sugarloaf Mountain by early morning. The sun hasn't even broken through fully in the sky. We park our line of vehicles along one secluded makeshift road and get out to travel the rest of the way on foot through the treacherous terrain. Humans rarely tread here. It's why my father chose this spot to hide Aramei, where he kept her hidden for nearly a year before moving her to the cabin. The cave is deep in the mountain, away from the skiers in the winter and more than three hours off the nearest hiking trail.

We shift into our mediate forms and glide along the tree-filled terrain with the quickness and dangerous grace of cheetahs gliding over a flat landscape.

Adria is beside me the whole way and I'm so awed by her agility and the elegant nature of her movements. It's as if she's been a Black Beast even longer than I have. So powerful and adaptive and...so incredibly hot that I....

Focus. I have to stay focused.

The entrance to the cave finally materializes and the sixteen of us enter the area two by two and stop. Harry was able to keep up somehow; another Praverian ability I suppose, but I don't care enough about that right now to ask.

We edge ourselves through the slim entrance in a single-file line and follow the cold path as it snakes in one direction and descends deeper into the earth. I hear water dripping from several far off spots in the rock and the echoing of their whispers from behind me. Adria grabs my hand and squeezes it.

"Are you okay, babe?" I whisper quietly.

She presses her thumb tighter against my hand.

"Yeah, I'll be fine."

I know this must be hard for her, coming here, to see the place again where she saw Aramei the very first time. I know it's hard and it quietly breaks my heart.

Several minutes later and we emerge from the pathway and into the enormous area that had once been my father's 'meeting room'. The only real evidence that anyone had ever been here before are the torches mounted on the rock, which Nathan lights as we pass, the enormous stone table situated in the center of the room and the skeleton of the man my father killed when Adria and I were here. It sits slumped against the rock wall, still wearing the modern clothes he had been killed in; they fit ridiculously over his skinny bones. The skull's jaw is lopsided and hanging wide open. Its neck hangs haphazardly to one side and I can see the bones where my father's hand had been just before he snapped them.

"Gross!" Rachel says when she sees it. She jumps closer to Sebastian and I notice him slip his arm around her waist. "That is just nasty!"

Adria stares at the skeleton, no doubt recalling the very second that the man died.

"Will someone get rid of that, please?" I say.

Adria puts her hand on my arm, but keeps her eyes on the skeleton. "It's okay…just leave it."

I nod.

And then I make my way to the stone table and find myself standing at the head, just like my father would. I glance down at my hands and notice how the tips of my fingers rest lightly on the edge, also just as my father's would.

I shake out of the moment to look up at everyone standing around the table, waiting for me to sit down first…and more and more I feel as if I'm walking in my father's footsteps, destined to commit the same crimes against our kind. Adria is next to me. I hesitate and then sit, taking Adria into the throne of my lap.

Everyone else follows suit.

"Isaac," I hear Adria's voice in my head, "you're nothing like him. You never will be. You're better than him."

I look up from my hands and at her sitting on my lap and there's nothing but love and understanding and trust in her eyes.

I thank her quietly for her words of encouragement.

And then I look out at everyone.

"I know how my father will go after his vengeance," I say. "His only priority will be Adria. He'll want her dead by his own hands. But the rest of you—" I look to each of them individually, "—anyone who sides with me and rebels against him will be hunted down by his army and also killed. It won't stop with Adria and you all have to know that."

"Like we said before," Sebastian speaks up, "we're with you in this all the way."

Everyone else agrees by nodding and the occasional verbal response.

"But we can't fight my father and those he brings with him by ourselves," I state. "We're going to have to spread out quickly and recruit the Alpha's who would be loyal to me."

"Yeah," Nathan says, "the Alphas are the only ones we have to convince. Gain the loyalty of the Alpha and his entire pack will follow devotedly."

"Does anyone here have a link to another Alpha?" I say.

One of the refugees, a guy named Ben who we picked up from Kentucky six years ago, raises his hand. "I was close to the Kentucky Alpha once."

"Was? Once?" Nathan says warily.

Ben nods solidly. "Yes, I ummm, well he's my brother. We fight a lot—I kinda slept with his mate—but he doesn't want anyone killing me but him."

Nathan raises a brow. "Well, okay then…."

"Alright," I say to Ben. "See if you can communicate with him. Don't reveal our location." I point at Harry. "Harry, can you listen in on his link to see if the Alpha is on our side, or just wanting us to believe that he is?"

Harry nods. "Yes, I can do that. Not one hundred percent fool-proof, but if he doesn't know someone like me is testing him, he'll be easier to figure out."

"Good," I say and two more refugees admit to also being directly linked to Alphas; one in Rhode Island and the other in Maryland.

After thirty minutes of discussion, Harry breaks away with all of them to listen in on their telepathic conversations, while Nathan, Sebastian, Xavier and I stay gathered at the table.

"I'm going to New Jersey to find Treven and Isis," I say and this gets Adria's attention.

"It'll be fine," I say, placing my fingers underneath her chin. "I trust Treven more than just about any other Alpha that I know and his pack is huge—sixty at least."

Adria's eyes narrow. "I shouldn't have opened my mouth about this cave."

"Why?"

"Because it's the perfect hideaway to leave me while you go out and do all of the dangerous stuff."

"My father will kill you," I say, hoping she won't fight me on this. "I just want you to be safe."

"I know," she says, looking away, but then she turns back to me again. "But I'm not going to hide like a coward and when the time comes and you need to understand that, Isaac. I won't...."

"I know, baby," I say and swallow down the argument. "I know."

When the time comes, I'll do whatever I have to do to keep her hidden away and I don't care if she hates me for it later. I won't let my father kill her.

"I thought you said you'd never close your mind to me?" she says softly into my ear.

I blink back into the present, but I say nothing in response. I did close my mind off to her for that brief moment, but right now she can't know what I'm really planning.

Ben and the others come back into the meeting room, Harry and Daisy with them.

All of them appear eager and somewhat excited.

"They're onboard!" Ben says. "The second I mentioned an uprising against the Sovereign, my brother's voice changed. They're *already* on their way to Maine."

"And bringing the West Virginia and Pennsylvania packs with them," Harry adds.

"Mississippi is onboard, too," Mari, another refugee speaks up.

"And Rhode Island," the other refugee says, "but their pack is pretty small."

"Doesn't matter," Nathan says, "a few is better than none."

I nod, agreeing.

"Most, if not all of them, should be in Maine by the morning," Harry announces.

"How can they get here so fast?" Adria says.

"They have their ways," Xavier speaks up from the other end of the table.

"Yeah, like an airplane?" Alexandra mocks.

"You're just making it worse on yourself," Xavier says to her grinning a lopsided grin. He pulls his legs up and props his feet upon the table, crossing them at the ankles below.

"Yeah?" Alexandra says, "How's that exactly?"

"Playing hard to get," Xavier says. He interlaces his fingers and rests the back of his head in his locked hands.

Alexandra ignores him.

Suddenly, Adria gets up from my lap.

"Where are you going?" I say, holding onto the tips of her fingers.

She looks down at me and softens her expression. She's trying so hard not to appear depressed or troubled by what happened with Aramei, but even for her it's not an easy thing to hide.

"I'm just going to be alone for a while."

I get up from the table, worried.

She kisses the edge of my mouth. "You worry too much—I'm fine." She puts the palms of her hands on my chest and gently guides me back into the wooden chair. "Stay here and do what you have to do."

I sigh deeply and let her go.

I notice Alexandra start to go after her, but she stops when her gaze meets mine. My eyes alone tell her that her sister just needs time and Alexandra quietly approves.

After the meeting is over and we've established what needs to be done, I leave everyone to find Adria where I knew she would be, alone in the room where Aramei used to sleep. A few candles have been lit throughout the space, giving off just enough orange light to see her lying on one side of the bed.

She's been crying. I notice her covertly wipe the tears away from her eyes.

All of the immaculate pillows and sheets and other extravagant things my father kept for Aramei are gone. All that is left is the stone slab that made up the bed's frame and the giant pillow that had been used as the mattress. The claw foot bathtub has even been removed, along with the old wooden desk that I split in half and into a hundred pieces when I brought Adria here with me that night. Funny how my father would have the remnants of an old desk cleaned out of Aramei's room, but leaves the corpse of the man he killed out in the wide open for all to see.

"I'm proud of what you did," I say as I make my way across the dimly-lit room towards her. I sit down next to her on the edge of the mattress pillow. "It took a lot of courage and compassion to do it."

She stares at the dancing flame cast upon the wall next to her; the candle it comes from is nearby on the floor.

I reach out and brush a lock of hair away from her face.

"I know it had to be done," she says, her voice distant. "And I feel that even though she's gone, she's grateful."

Finally, she turns her gaze on me; the flickering light of the candle flits across her irises making the blue of her eyes appear faintly golden. She sniffles away a few lingering tears. "It's just something I have to get myself through. And I will. In time."

It never ceases to amaze me the amount of strength in my girl. She's been through so much and is going through so much more that sometimes I can't comprehend her strength, like it's something entirely foreign to me.

She should be Alpha. She's stronger than I could ever be.

I crawl over and move around to lie behind her, my knees fitted into the backs of hers, my arm draped over her arm where I knit my fingers between hers to hold her hand against her side. Her free hand comes around to touch my face. I shut my eyes and kiss her fingertips.

"If we die," she says and my eyes creep open, "do you think we'll still know each other in the afterlife...if there is an afterlife?"

I nestle my face into her neck and squeeze her hand. "I believe that no matter what happens, or where we go, or if there's an afterlife, that we'll always be connected. Not even death can make me forget you, or forget that I love you."

I feel her smile. I don't have to see it.

A quiet few seconds pass between us and then she turns her body just enough to see my face.

"Promise me that if we die, you'll look for me," she says and kisses my lips.

Her words wrench my soul, but I hold my composure and nod gently, looking into her eyes. "I promise."

I take her into my arms and kiss her. And then I make love to her as if it were the last time.

~~~

Half of us leave the cave by midday. Alexandra, Rachel, all four of my sisters and Harry stay behind with Adria. At first, the girls were offended, mainly Rachel and Alexandra who didn't hold back their opinions about how 'leaving all the girls in the safe cave' was 'totally sexist' and us guys should 'really pull our male egos out of our asses'. But Daisy spoke up to diffuse the situation:

"You really think my brother feels that way about you?"

"Umm, yes?" Rachel said with a venomous sneer. "We're the ones told to hide in the stupid cave while they—" her hand shot out beside her to point at us, "—get to go out into the danger zone. It's bullshit."

Daisy smirked and rolled her eyes. "Think about it for a second: Isaac would never leave Adria with the weakest of the pack."

Adria smiled. "We're all female. Doesn't that tell you anything?"

Rachel's sneer melted into a proud grin.

"Yeah, I guess you're right," she said, changing her tune. "Okay, maybe he's not so sexist, after all."

Women. The rest of us gladly left the cave and them to their girl power.

~~~

We arrive back in Hallowell before dark and head to The Cove on the Kennebec River to meet up with the other packs. Fortunately, we didn't have to make the trip to New Jersey to find Treven and his pack. After calling three of Treven's last known phone numbers, by the fourth, his mate, Isis answered.

Treven told me that day he brought one of his pack members, Darren, to challenge Nathan for control of the Maine territory, that if I ever needed him for anything that he'd be there.

And he held true to his word.

"Isaac," Treven announces enthusiastically as Nathan and I get out of the Jeep in the Cove parking lot.

He's a tall, broad-shouldered black guy almost as huge as Big Raul.

Treven grabs my hand into a fist and we pull toward each other, patting each other's backs with our free hands. He does the same with Nathan and then Xavier and Sebastian as they get out of Xavier's red and black Dodge Challenger.

"So it's finally going down?" Treven says, turning his attention back to me.

I nod.

He drops the greeting smile and joins the rest of us in the serious moment, shaking his head in that knew-it-was-coming sort of way.

Isis, Treven's girlfriend, waves at us from their car.

Six more vehicles pull into the lot; all of them from Treven's pack by the way they greet each other when they get out.

"Look, man," I say to Treven, going right into the inevitable, "I just want to say up front that I won't hold it against you if you don't want any part of this—you know what my father is capable of and I don't want to leave anyone with any delusions."

Three more vehicles arrive.

Treven's big, toothy smile returns. "I wouldn't miss this, man," he says and his voice rises so that everyone, even those walking toward us can hear him. "Over six hundred years of fucking tyranny—I may not have been here for most of it, but…man, did you know that your father killed *my* grandfather?"

No, I did not know that….

Treven goes on, still smiling, "I've never held anything against you or your brothers—been kinda' waitin' on this day, to be honest. I think everybody knew it would be one of his own sons who would dethrone him."

"The only thing about this that I don't like," someone from the growing crowd says, "is that it took so long!"

A tall, blond-haired guy speaks up, "Your father scares the shit outta me," he says with his hands buried in his pockets, "but count me in."

"So why now?" Treven says and all of the voices carrying around on the air become still.

Nathan and I glance over at one another, knowing the answer might not be what any of them are prepared for.

I take a very deep breath, "The truth?"

"Yeah, out with it," Treven says.

"Adria killed Aramei."

The smile drops from Treven's face and every other face staring back at me just freezes in a shocked mosaic of wide eyes and open mouths and immobile limbs.

It takes Treven all of twelve seconds to blink. "You're fucking serious?" He turns his chin in a sidelong glance.

Isis gets out of the car and struts over in her high-heeled black boots. "What did you just say?" She's not smiling anymore, either, and her heavily-ringed finger points upward at me.

"Isis, baby, don't do this," Treven says, taking her by the waist.

"No, Trev," she argues, pushing his hand away, "if he said what I think he said, this won't be a battle, it'll be a massacre—the Sovereign is crazy enough without this, but it bein' about the murder of his wife?" She draws in a deep, abrasive breath and shakes her head over and over.

"It doesn't matter how or why it's happening," Nathan speaks out beside me, "because it's going to happen no matter what and you all can either fight with us, or die fighting with him."

It sounded like a threat to me, but I'm not going to rebuke it.

"Look," I say, putting up my hand—(Isis hates me now; if looks could kill)—like I said, I won't hold it against you if you don't fight, but Nathan's right: if you choose his side over mine, we will *treat* you and *kill* you as one of them."

Isis pushes herself angrily away from Treven and walks back to the car. "Lunatics," she hisses just before the car door closes off her voice.

Two more cars enter the lot and one giant monster truck.

"We're with you," Treven says with a solid, devoted nod. He reaches out his hand to me and we shake on it.

In the next couple of hours, the other packs and their Alpha's arrive and we go through the same riotous defense as we did with Treven. Rhode Island decided to back out when they heard that it was because of Aramei's 'murder'. But I won't call them cowards for it. The truth is, they're right to back out. Nothing like this has happened since my father killed my grandfather for the throne over six hundred years ago. Some have tried. All of them have died trying.

If it were me in Rhode Island's shoes, I couldn't back down. But I still can't bring myself to hold it against them.

Maybe this just proves they're the sane ones.

HARRY

31

WOW. FATE THREW ME a friggin' curve ball, that's for sure. But y'know what? I have to admit that I'm glad it turned out the way it did.

Yeah. I'm glad....

I love Adria; she's like a sister to me, and being what I am has never been easy, especially when it comes to the humans we become involved with, Charge or not. It's one of our biggest weaknesses: the relationships we develop. We're born into the human world the same way as any other human, we go through diapers and those kick-ass baby swings that play music—my mom swears by that contraption; said it knocked me out in under a minute whenever she'd put my screamin' ass in one. We bond with our 'foster' families like anybody else and when that day comes that we go through our Becoming and learn all over again what we really are and why we're here, it rarely makes us less human emotionally. Those bonds with our families and friends never go away.

This is why Zia turned Dark.

I feel bad for Zia, I really do, because I can totally relate and understand and emphasize with her.

It almost happened to me once. I was fifteen-years-old, the bastard son of King Edward VII and Lady Susan Pelham-Clinton. In *that* life, I was born in 1871. My mother, Susan, died when I was four, but I didn't know she was my real mother until much later. The midwife who delivered me was who cared for me and commissioned to act as my mother. I loved her deeply. She was later murdered—it was very hard for me. But that was just one of my many pasts, the only one where I almost went rogue, myself. So yeah…like I said, I can understand Zia's pain.

If only we weren't cursed to be what we are, we could live one life like everybody else and not be subject to a thousand lifetimes of pain.

Just picture it; you go through life watching people you love die, you go through unimaginable hardships and grief, you grow old and inevitably tired of living because that's what humans do. They live one life. *One*. Not me. When I Become, when I 'wake up' in each new life, I don't have the luxury of forgetting all of the past lives that I've lived, all of the horrific deaths that claimed me and thrust me into the *next* life so that I can just die all over again. I remember *everything*. Every last infinitesimal detail: the guillotine that took off my head in 1794, my lost battle with tuberculosis in 1906, Amelia Winters, the girl I fell in love with in 1919. We were as young as I am now though I long outlived her. And I outlived the daughter I had with Sarah Marie Devereaux about fifty years ago. Of course, I was someone entirely different then, at least on the outside. And my birth certificate, which I earned, by being born, said: Edmond James Belrose. And my hair was *blond*! Hey, I like my girls blond, but it's definitely not my personal hair color of choice.

Anyway, a person, a *Soul*, even one as powerful as mine, can only take so much.

And a lot like Evangeline, I'm getting tired of it.

Sometimes, a small part of me kinda wants to hop inside one of Minna Abrahamsen's jars, or speak aloud the name of my kind so one of the others will find and reap me once and for all.

But I have Daisy now and things don't feel so lonely anymore.

But back to the whole fate-threw-me-a-curveball thing; Adria was supposed to sire Aramei. I didn't lie to her when I told her that Aramei was special and would live through the transformation despite her mother being killed by it so long ago. Aramei would've become werewolf; the most powerful Black Beast their secret world would have ever known.

Unfortunately, she would've also been a hundred times more unstable than she had been for the past two hundred years, and unpredictably dangerous beyond imagining. Trajan would not have been able to control her and inevitably, that would've been the cause of the war.

But this...wow...I never thought that Adria could actually *kill* Aramei. I saw her future, the way it was *supposed* to be, the way my kind *needed* it to be. But the fate of our Charges are never written in stone. They can easily take another path and it's our duty to make sure they don't. Because my kind have an agenda and our Charges are the keys to fulfilling it.

It's why Minna Abrahamsen and the rest of the Harvesters hate us so much, why it's their lifelong burden to reap us all and to stop us....

"Harry?" Adria says standing over me. "You seem really tense." She lowers herself into a squatting position in front of me.

I sit on the cool stone floor with my back against a jagged piece of rock and my knees drawn up, my wrists propped on the tops of them. I force a goofy smile that I know isn't fooling her.

"I'm nervous, too," she says and then sits down fully, crossing her legs.

"I—." she starts to say, but holds onto the thought for a second longer, "—I feel like I should be apologizing to you, but...I'm not sure if I should. I don't really understand any of this. What you are and what I, being your Charge, has to do with...well, anything. I-I, well—."

"I know, Adria, and it's not your fault. You're right; you shouldn't apologize."

"But I didn't do what you wanted me to do."

She looks genuinely sad, but not necessarily regretful.

I smile and nudge the edge of her shoe with the toe of my boot.

A faint grin cracks in her face, but then it dissolves quickly.

"Harry," she says carefully, "do you really think Aramei would've lived if I infected her?"

She's seeking more justification for what she did and I feel like, as her best friend and setting my issues with the outcome aside, I have to help her come to terms with it.

I raise my back from the rock and cross my legs the same as her. "She would've survived it, yeah, but that life would've been worse than what you did for her. And either way, the war couldn't be stopped."

She's studying my face, not sure yet whether to believe me. For all she knows, I could just be telling her what she needs to hear.

"I'm serious," I say. "I think you did the right thing in giving Aramei peace."

Her eyebrows harden a little. "But why?" she says. "How can it have been right if I was supposed to infect her?"

Because I'm straying from my kind, Adria, I say to myself. Because if you would've succeeded, you would've opened another gateway into my world and that's not something any human here would want.

"Because it was your decision to make," I say instead, "and no matter what you were destined to do, you did what *you* felt was right and so that *makes* it right."

She smiles vaguely and looks off to the side.

"But what about you?" she says without meeting my eyes. Her hands fidget restlessly within the ring of her lap.

Me? Ah, yeah, me. I'll be punished. If I'm caught. But I won't be caught, for a while anyway, because I intend to make a break for it after this is over and get the hell outta here.

"Nothing that sucks too much," I finally answer her and let the goofy smile spread broader across my face. "They'll just rip away a few stars from my jacket and slap me on the wrist, but you're not the first Charge I've failed. It's nothing I can't handle."

The punishment is brutal. I won't go through it again....

She had started to smile, until the f-word.

"You didn't fail me, Harry. Maybe they, whoever *they* are, consider you a failure because I didn't do what I was 'destined' to do, but don't you ever say you've failed me. I'd be a psychiatric patient if it weren't for you, or I might be sniffin' too much stuff from underneath the bathroom sink like crazy-ass Cecilia acts like she does. Damn, Harry, I could be a slut if I ended up best friends with Tori. I could have glittery hoe-bag clothes hanging in my closet!"

I laugh.

"I doubt you could ever be a slut," I say and then wrinkle one side of my nose and glance upward playfully, "but I dunno...you might look hot in glittery hoe-bag clothes."

Her foot pops out from underneath one knee and kicks me in the boot.

She gets serious again. "There's something else that I've been meaning to ask you."

"Shoot."

"How long am I supposed to be your Charge exactly?"

I didn't see that one coming.

I smile a close-lipped smile across at her. "Well, I can say that you're officially off the hook."

"What?"

I nod hard once. "Yep! You haven't been my Charge technically since you...well, you know."

"Oh...," she doesn't know really what to think about this news.

"If Aramei were still...alive," I say and just cut to the chase rather than trying to tiptoe constantly around the dismal truth, "then I'd still be trying to influence you to infect her."

Actually, I wouldn't be doing that anymore. Because, like I said, it looks as though I've recently made the decision to stray from my kind. But Adria doesn't need to know about any of that.

She seems lost in thought for a moment. "So, you're here because of Daisy?"

My smile widens, showing now more in the corners of my eyes. "Yeah, I'm here because of her, but you're still my best friend and I want to do what I can to keep you safe."

Adria returns the smile.

I guess it's also a good thing she doesn't know that because she didn't fulfill her so-called destiny that I'm supposed to kill her.

Yeah...another damn good reason that it's time for me to become one of the renegades.

Renegade. Hmmm, I kinda like the sound of that. I could get a motorcycle and a big ass gun and ride around in Death Valley with a new tattoo.

Or, maybe I should just stick to skateboarding.

Daisy, Camilla, Shannon and Elizabeth come back inside after spending some time outside the cave, casing the area.

"Nothing out of the ordinary," Daisy says. "Adria, I think picking this place was a good idea."

Damn, I love that English accent of hers. I grin up at Daisy and she blushes. I can always get her to blush.

"Well, I'm not worried about us here," Adria says, turning at the waist to look up at Daisy, but then she just stands up altogether and crosses her arms. "I'm worried about Isaac and the others. The longer we stay in here, the more I believe he intentionally left me here to keep me out of the fight."

That's exactly what Isaac did, but I'm not about to admit it to her and neither is Daisy. Daisy and I share a knowing look.

Adria notices.

"That's what he did, isn't it?" Her face hardens disapprovingly.

Daisy smiles reassuringly and says, "No, he'll come back and when he does he'll have a small army with him."

Alex and Rachel emerge from the dark, dank stone hallway that leads farther into the cave; a blazing torch moves along the wall, glowing against the rock ceiling from Alex's hand. When they step back into the large area where the rest of us are, the darkness swallows up the passageway behind them. Alex places the fiery torch into the mount on the wall nearby, leaving a bath of new light to spread across the room. Alex hops onto the stone table and sits on the edge with her legs dangling off the side.

"This place is so medieval," Rachel says, sneering and looking edgy as she scans every inch of the area with an ugly wrinkled-up nose. She hasn't done much since she got here except complain about how musty the cave is and talk about how that skeleton is creeping her out. "Really, like Black Plague, behead-a-Boleyn-girl medieval." She visibly shudders, crossing her arms.

"They didn't typically live in caves," Alex says, swinging her legs back and forth.

"Whatever, girl. You know what I mean!"

Alex rolls her eyes and turns to Adria.

"How are you doing over there, sis?"

"I'm fine."

"Liar."

"Well, of course I'm a liar." Adria raises her hands in surrender. "How do you expect me to be?"

Adria regretted the attitude right after she'd snapped at her sister, but given the circumstances Alex understands and doesn't take offense.

Adria begins to pace and she's growing more restless every passing second.

Daisy sits on the tabletop next to Alex and pulls her legs onto it, Indian-style. "Well, Sian and her group are all outside, scattered all around the cave to keep watch—not that I think we need it, but just in case."

Sian is the red-headed leach that used to follow Rachel around like a lost puppy, until Alex came along.

"Daisy," Adria says, "be honest with me; can Isaac defeat your father?"

The room becomes quiet.

Daisy steps up and takes Adria's hands into hers. This is what Daisy's great at: easing the troubled with that infectious smile of hers.

"I think that if anyone can, it would be Isaac or Nathan," she says honestly.

Adria's not so easily comforted this time. She turns to me brashly, as if she'd just thought of something with the potential to give her hope.

"Can you see it?" she says. "My future? Can you see anything that might tell me that Isaac is still in it?"

I hate to ruin that hopeful light shining dimly in her eyes, but I can't lie to her, either.

"I can't see anything anymore," I admit. "You're no longer my Charge and because you changed the course of your destiny, everything I did see in my visions of you really doesn't apply anymore."

Adria's shoulders and chest inflate and she lowers her head. Alex hops off the table and walks around to stand behind her, draping her arms over each of Adria's shoulders and crossing them over her chest.

She kisses her hard on the cheek. "Dria, I don't know Isaac—except that he's smokin' hot, but that's beside the point—but I don't think you have anything to worry about."

"What makes you say that?" Adria says.

"I'm not sure…a gut feeling, I guess."

Adria actually smiles and for a split second I can hear her thoughts: "Wow, Alex and Isaac really do have a lot in common."

Rachel makes use of the spot on the table where Alex just left and she lies down fully on her back against it, looking up at the low rock ceiling, her raven-black hair spread out around her sloppily. Camilla takes the wooden chair at the head of the table, while Shannon and Elizabeth start walking toward the cave exit.

Shannon looks across at Daisy. "We're going to take watch with Sian," she says.

"Yeah, it's stuffy in here," Elizabeth says and they both leave together.

Camilla has been quieter than usual; even now she just kind of stares off at the wall. I've tried to get into her head a few times, but she's been difficult to break. I don't know, but it's odd, like she's been using every shred of mental strength she owns to keep anyone from getting inside of her mind. She even looks exhausted.

Alex let's go of Adria and leans against the table's edge.

"Something's not adding up," Adria says at no one in particular. Then her face shoots up and she looks right at me and then at Daisy with burning worry in her eyes. "Don't you think Trajan would've found out by now?" She doesn't give anyone a chance to answer. "I mean think about it; he's been connected to her for over two centuries, even though Viktor was the one she was bonded to, still, Trajan has been inside her mind. He had a link to her because she drank from him for so long—shouldn't he *know* by now?"

She makes a valid point, but I want to think more on this before I agree openly with her.

Unfortunately, Daisy doesn't:

"I've thought about that, too," she says. "You know, it's been quiet, almost *too* quiet—I've opened my mind to my father, just to see if I could sense any emotion in him, anything at all, but I haven't heard or felt a thing."

"Thought you said he closed himself off to all his offspring?" Rachel says from the table, now sitting propped up by her elbows. "How would you know anything at all?"

"Well, he did," Daisy clarifies, "but with something like this, it just seems like we would know when he knew."

"Yeah," Alex says, "I would think the second he found out, not only his kids would know, but every werewolf in a hundred mile radius that wasn't telepathically connected to him, would know. This is like the ultimate scream-at-the-top-of-your-lungs scenario. Goat herders in Mongolia should hear Trajan howling from the mountainside."

Adria's nervousness has amplified intensely over the past minute, which is what I was trying to avoid by not putting in my two cents. She has started pacing, back and forth along the length of the enormous table; one arm resting across her stomach, the other hand over her mouth with her fingers curled nervously over her lips.

What little calm was left in the air is suddenly forced out when Camilla starts screaming and bursts into tears. She plunges her head forward harshly and stops just before making contact with the stone and buries her face in the palms of her hands. Her body rocks as sobs send shockwaves through her chest. Rachel shoots up the rest of the way on top of the table and turns around.

Daisy runs over to Camilla, pulling her up from the chair and taking her into her arms. Camilla wails, tears streaking down her face. She tries to speak through the sobs, but her words are choked and garbled.

The rest of us move closer. Adria watches in horror and something about Camilla's display sends a streak of encrypted panic through us all.

"I'm so sorry!" Camilla finally gets the words out and Daisy continues to hold her. "I-I tried so hard...b-but I couldn't—."

ISAAC

32

IN A FEW MORE hours, the sun will be rising and I'm growing more apprehensive.

Something's off and I can't put my finger on it.

We've been joined by nine different packs mostly from the northeastern states; a few—Arizona, Oregon and Nevada—are also on their way, but it will take them a couple of days to get here if they don't catch a plane, but they always travel with their pack, so finding a short-notice flight with twenty to fifty empty seats, isn't likely.

And we still haven't heard anything from or about my father, so I'm sure he still doesn't know and hasn't even left Serbia yet. We still have time.

I think....

No, this isn't right. *Damnit!*

I jump down from the hood of Xavier's car and walk quickly over to Nathan who has been talking to Treven most of the night. There are dozens of little groups mingling in and all around The Cove, some down by the river not far away.

I lost head-count after one hundred twenty.

"Nate," I say, taking him by the arm, "I need to talk to you."

"Alright."

Treven turns his attention on the others standing nearby, but I get the feeling he'll listen in on us if he can. I would.

Nathan and I walk to the edge of the parking lot and stop.

"What?" he says, "Are you ready to get them all out of the town?—was thinking it might be best anyway; too populated this close in."

"No, listen," I say leaning in further toward him, "don't you feel it?"

"Feel what?"

I glance downward in contemplation and back up at him again. "That's just it, I feel *nothing*, Nate."

He catches on fast.

"You're right, bro," he says and covertly glances around at everyone and keeps his voice low. "Yeah, I think he should know about Aramei by now and *we* should be fully aware of it."

"What was that you said?" Treven says, walking up. "Come on, man, we're here to stand with you, don't put us at the kiddie table."

Others nearby hear Treven's words and the wave of conversations going on all around us ceases.

I look at Nathan and Treven both; Treven standing two full inches taller next to him. And then I go to elaborate more, just so maybe I can make some sense of it myself, and I hear Isis' voice from somewhere behind:

"The dogs," she says, "They've stopped barking." She comes up next to Treven and loops her arm around his giant bicep; her face is imbued by unease.

We all stop to listen and she's right; all night they've been barking sporadically, though nothing out of the ordinary, and now they are utterly silent all over the town.

Panic envelops Nathan's face all of a sudden and his nostrils flare. He takes in a deep, aggressive breath and catches the scent on the wind. He always knows before any of us when others are nearby because of his powerful sense of smell. We all have it, the enhanced sense of smell, but Nathan's ability is extraordinary.

The muscles in his arms harden and his dark eyes widen so quickly that it alone sends a jolt of panic through my bones.

"What is it?" I say, trying to look at him and keep my eyes peeled all around me at the same time.

"They're here," Nathan answers as his eyes shift black and his lips curl into a hard, bitter display. "Holy shit, they're...*everywhere*."

Instinct kicks in as Nathan's announcement rolls through like a thick fog carrying grave news on the air and everyone becomes alert.

Xavier steps up, wiping sweat from his face, which in itself is strange. "It's my mother," he says with foreboding in his voice. "She just spoke to me."

"What did she say, Xavier?" I'm too impatient. "Xavier, tell me what Nataša said!"

His eyes are so panicked that it puts me more on edge and I didn't think by now that could even be possible.

"They're at Adria's aunt's house," he announces, "and so is Father. My mother demanded that we bring Adria to them now—they think she's with us—or they're going to kill everyone in this town."

I start to pace furiously over the broken blacktop. My senses are going into overdrive as all of the beasts around me begin to go into an inner frenzy, each one of them preparing themselves mentally for what's about to go down.

Focus. I have to stay focused on the plan which has just been shattered, and I'm realizing that with the unexpected turn of events, can't be restored. The plan was to gather as many packs as we could and then take them into the mountains farther northeast into the Appalachians and away from Adria, station there for as many days as it took before my father found out about Aramei and then lure him and his army to us. We were going to be waiting, with an army and a plan.

But the plan has gone to shit. The plan has gone to shit....

"Isaac!" Treven says, bringing me back, "We can't do this here. In the town."

Isis glares heatedly at me next to him, but fear is dominant in her face. Fear of my father and not of me.

"He's known all along," I say vacantly; my intent stare absorbing the asphalt. "Why didn't I *know* this? He knew the second that it happened—." My head jerks up to see Nathan. "He *knew*, Nathan! He did everything we didn't expect him to do, stringing us along to believe that he didn't know when the whole damned time he was preparing and on his way back here—HE KNEW!"

Nathan steps toward me. "This isn't the time to start blaming yourself, or questioning your position as Alpha." He forces his hands on my shoulders, shaking me to. "This is our *father*, Isaac." He pushes the words on me aggressively so that I'll let the truth of his words sink in. "This isn't some neonate half-breed Alpha, he's the *Sovereign* and all of us—," his gripping fingers fall off my shoulders and he points to himself with both hands, "—*all* of us made the same mistake, bro. *None* of us saw this coming!"

But I was the one supposed to be able to see it coming. I'm Alpha....

"Let's go," I say without another word and I make for my Jeep, jump inside and slam the key in the ignition.

Nathan gets in on the passenger's side.

Everyone follows us out in a chaotic procession of squealing tires and bouncing headlights illuminating the dark trees out ahead.

In under a minute, when the first house comes into view along the dimly-lit road, I see them.

Nathan was right. They are everywhere, hidden in the shadows of every yard. Some are perched atop the roofs and in the trees. I can see their preternatural eyes glinting off the moonlight in the darkness like owls hidden in the branches.

The dogs are too afraid to bark anymore.

"Holy shit, bro...," Nathan looks nervous and excited as we drive by that first house and see two brooding werewolves, still in human form, standing on the side of the house at the garage.

Our procession of vehicles slows down almost to a crawl. I feel like one of those kids sitting in the backseat as his parents drive him down the brightly-lit streets of a Christmas wonderland. Except this is much darker and the figures scattered about the lawns of all of these houses aren't giant inflatable snowmen or nativity scenes.

Every. Single. House. From Water Street, to 2nd and Litchfield and Smith and finally to Vaughan. All my father has to do is flutter his eyelids and every person as far as two towns over from Hallowell will be dead.

I open up my ears to hear the residents inside as we pass, but no one so far seems to know that they're in danger. Thankfully, most of the town's residents are still asleep.

Finally, I pull off the road and onto Beverlee and Carl's long dirt driveway leading to their house. I pick up the speed now that I've got a better idea of what we're up against all over the town and come to a hard stop outside the Dawson house. The only car parked out front is Beverlee's old gray

Chevy Malibu. But I sense those inside and I can hear Nataša's voice slithering through the room.

We get out cautiously and more than a dozen vehicles pull in behind us, clogging the driveway all the way out onto the main street; some park *along* the main street.

There's only one light burning in the house, downstairs in the den. Shadows move across the windows of the downstairs floor and so far I can tell there are at least six different figures inside. The tall light pole that stands between the old barn and the house casts a buzzing grayish-white light across a large portion of the west side of the yard. Movement stirs inconspicuously at the side of the barn. Two werewolves. And then on the top of the roof. Two more werewolves. The house is surrounded.

But I don't sense my father.

"Nathan?" I say without looking away from the house. "I don't think Father is inside."

"I don't, either," he says in a low voice.

A large crowd walks in behind us and I turn around to see Treven standing at the head of them all; Sebastian is next to him.

"Treven," I begin, "I need you to take everyone with you, spread out throughout the town wherever you see an enemy and do whatever you have to do to keep them from Turning in front of the humans and, more importantly, keep them from killing or infecting them."

I look to Nathan and Xavier. "I'm going inside and it's probably best that I go alone."

Xavier shakes his head in refusal. "Oh, no way, brother," he says, "my mother is in there and I'm going with you."

"That's why you shouldn't go," I say.

Xavier grits his teeth.

"I'll do whatever you want me to do," Nathan says, "But I don't think it's a good idea to face them alone."

"You doubt me?" I say, offended, but quietly doubting myself a little.

"I don't doubt your strength, Isaac," Nathan says, "but I do doubt your heart."

"My heart?" I say blankly.

Nathan nods. "Humans are involved; Adria's aunt and uncle, which makes it worse. Nataša isn't here holding them hostage so Beverlee will show her how to scrapbook—she'll use them against you."

"So, you doubt my ability to make hard decisions."

He's right to doubt me, but I remain outwardly firm.

Nathan gives up and says, "I'll go with Treven. There are at least one hundred of her beasts out there and unless we want a whole town infected in one night, Treven needs as many of us as we can spare."

I nod in agreement and then I turn to Sebastian. "Are you alright in this?" I think because he's still so new and a half-breed, I feel a sort of responsibility to him.

"Hey, man, I'm good," he puts up his hands,

I give Treven and Nathan one last nod and all of them take off running through the trees in a flash of scattering figures.

Xavier is still standing beside me.

"Maybe I can talk to her," he says about Nataša. "I know she's a hardass, but…I hate to say it, but she's not like Sibyl."

His comment about my mother didn't sting as he apparently thought it would; I got over my mother's betrayal a long time ago.

"Nataša is loyal to our father," I say and then from the corner of my eye, I catch a glimpse of the figures inside the house moving across the front window. "She will do whatever he's told her to do, Xavier, and that includes taking you down with me if it comes to that."

Xavier tries to act as if the truth doesn't faze him, but I know otherwise. He rounds his chin and says, "At least let me talk to her. Give me that much. If she chooses her orders over her own son, then you do what you have to do and I won't interfere."

So then it's not just me and Nathan and Daisy who want things in our society to change. Even Xavier understands the importance of freedom and revolution. All of us, my brothers and sisters and I, have lived among humans for too long, inadvertently exposed to human nature and have experienced the differences in their nature and ours. We have come to realize that the ways of our generations-old totalitarian government and lifestyle is wrong, and that it doesn't have to be.

Change begins with us.

I inhale a deep breath and say, "Okay, I'll give you the chance."

And without wasting any more time, we head toward the front porch together.

~~~

"Eet ees about time you joined us," Nataša says in an accent, standing in the den in the center of the room. "Xavier, I am surprised you have involved yourself in this...atrocity."

There are six other beasts standing in the room with her: one near the stairs leading to the upper-floor, two in the den with Nataša, one in the kitchen looking out the window at the front yard, one at the large den window and now one right behind Xavier and I.

I still don't see my father. Could he be waiting upstairs? But why?

I realize that he isn't here. I felt it earlier, a heavy feeling of absence, but now I'm *sure* of it. So many things are shooting around inside my head.

Right now the most important thing is what's in front of me: Adria's aunt and uncle, terrified and in grave danger.

Beverlee sits in her nightgown on the center couch cushion with her back straight and rigid; her trembling hands are pressed against her thighs where she wrenches the fabric of her gown in her fingertips. Tears streak down her face and I know she wants to look at me, but she's too afraid to move her eyes. Her brown hair is matted and ravaged; strands are stretched messily across her face, stuck to her skin by tears and snot and sweat. Carl Dawson is in his favorite chair, but the way he sits there in an unnatural position with his back at an angle, tells me he had been tossed there by violent hands. Carl is shirtless and wears a pair of navy pajama bottoms. There's a trickle of blood running down the under part of his neck and instantly I fear that maybe he's already been infected, but I'm relieved when I notice the blood came from his busted nose. There is no emotion in his face except the fear I see in his eyes. Unlike Beverlee, he does make eye contact with me and I know he's hoping that I'm here to help them, but can't understand how someone like me, a twenty-year-old guy seemingly harmless, could possibly help in a situation like this. He keeps glancing covertly over at Beverlee, wanting only to reach out and hold her even if in his arms she truly isn't safe.

Xavier speaks up first:

"Mother," he says carefully, "this isn't right. They have nothing to do with what happened to Aramei." He doesn't feel confident with his own words, but he's trying. He swallows and takes a deep breath, stepping forward just a little. "Only rogues do this; take human hostages and risk exposing our society to theirs. You know it's wrong."

Nataša would probably smile wickedly right about now, but she has never been one to smile even for mocking sake. She stands there for a moment, studying her son. Her dark red hair is pulled back tight into a ponytail, stretching the skin at the corners of her eyes and making them appear tight and slanted. As always, she wears her signature skin-tight black leather bodysuit and tall black boots with the shit-kicking kind of heels.

She walks across the room to stand in front of Xavier and I step up beside him boldly. She reaches out and combs her fingers through Xavier's messy blond bangs, but says nothing to him in return.

She looks right at me, getting right down to business, bypassing the ridiculous monologue that we all know would make absolutely no difference.

"Where is your foolish, blasphemous little mate?"

I stay calm. As calm as I can, considering. "Not here, obviously."

"That is unfortunate." She turns only her head to see one of her men and he moves in behind Beverlee. I tense up and Beverlee's tears rush heavier to the surface as if someone had turned on a faucet behind her head. The man's shadow looms threateningly over her. His black claws are at the ready down at his sides.

Carl struggles in the chair, his face contorted into a livid and frightful expression, but he can't move. I notice a flicker of hatred for himself pass over his eyes, hatred for being paralyzed and feeling completely useless when Beverlee needs him the most.

I ready myself internally, keeping one eye on the one behind Beverlee so I'll see when he goes to make his move and one eye on Nataša who stands inches from me, waiting on *me* to make *my* move.

"Where is my father?" I say.

Nataša licks the dryness from her lips in a slow, concentrating motion, never taking her eyes off me.

"Not here, *obviously*," she mocks without having to let it show in her face; maybe just a little in the depths of her piercing dark eyes.

Something urgent is digging away at the back of my brain and then I realize...it's Adria.

Thrown completely off balance and my game, I stagger backward, knocking over the small console table Beverlee used to display family portraits; the frames crash onto the floor, the glass shattering.

"He's here! Isaac, he's—." Her voice cuts off in my head.

My heart feels like it's about to explode! The people in the town. Beverlee and Carl. Adria, who is over an hour away....

"I take it you know where he is," Nataša says so coldly that I react in a flash, shifting into my mediate form and lunging for her.

All I see is furniture and picture frames and sheetrock wall zip past my line of sight so fast that it all blends into a seamless streak of color. Nataša's back hits the fireplace mantle and the stone it's made up with crumbles into a thousand pieces. The walls of the house shake and rumble. A white-hot pain spreads across my face and over the back of my head when Nataša jerks back and bashes her head into my face. I land in the center of the glass-top coffee-table; my legs and arms splayed, hanging over the top of the wooden frame the glass had been held in by. Nataša is on top of me before I can jump out; her black eyes swirling like a violent storm; her long, black razor-sharp claws cutting pieces of flesh from my face as she slashes at me over and over and over. I do the only thing I can do and pay her back with a violent knock to her skull with my forehead and it's just enough time to stun her out of her advantage. She rises up from me and in that split second, I manage to pull back both of my knees toward me and plunge my feet outward into her chest. Her body flies across the room, but she catches herself before hitting the wall and rolls once back into a crouched position.

Carl and Beverlee are trying to crawl across the carpeted floor, Beverlee practically dragging Carl by his arm because he can't move his own legs.

I defy gravity and leap up, latching onto the high ceiling to get out of Nataša's way when I notice her barreling towards me. The second my hands and knees hit the ceiling, Xavier's figure blurs right past underneath me and he spears his mother and they're both sent crashing into the giant television. A bright spark flashes and a searing *pop* and fizzle hisses through the room as the screen is destroyed by their bodies.

I fall from the ceiling perfectly on my feet right in front of Beverlee and Carl; Beverlee yelps and cowers lower against the floor.

"I'm going to get you out of here," I say and just as I go to grab them both from the floor, the other six beasts, also in their mediate forms, rush me from all sides.

I lose my grip on Beverlee's hand and see her face fall away from me as my body is hurled through the den; a crunching sound reverberates from my ribs and into my head as one foot slams into my side. And while Xavier fights his mother, I see that I'm left to fight six on my own. Blood slips into the corners of my mouth, my arms are prickled by shards of glass littered all around me from no telling what all has been broken in the struggle. As the brooding figures advance on me, I faintly hear the sounds of the other beasts in the town rise into a frenzy.

I spring and bound across the room straight for the ones coming at me and I take two down. I sit straddled on top of one, slashing away at his face and neck and chest much like Nataša had done to me just moments ago, until I'm dragged off him by the back of my shirt.

No…I can't shift here.

I'm trying everything in my power to keep my beast inside, because I have to. I can't become what I am here because I could very easily mistake Beverlee and Carl for the enemy in that violent, destructive, blood-thirsty form. I feel my ribs cracking as I'm dragged across the room, the pain in my skull starts at a tiny point right between my eyes and is beginning to spread towards the back of my head and widen as if a fissure is splitting right down the center of my skull.

I scream out in pain, trying to hold it back; not the pain, but my beast.

There's a *crash* nearby and it jolts me momentarily back into my senses, making me more alert than crazed and on the verge of changing. I see Beverlee's bare feet slipping around the side of the couch and Carl's limp, heavy legs being dragged with her.

But the crash, I realize, came from the large bay window overlooking the front yard. Two familiar figures stand inside the den while two more burst through the front door, knocking it clean off its hinges.

It's Viktor and Ashe, the two we shackled with them back at our house and a handful of others I've never seen before.

Viktor races over to me with burning anger and intensity in his eyes. I prepare for impact, to be in battle with my father's greatest enemy, but he stops just inches from my face. His mouth is twisted into an unbreakable scowl; his black eyes bear down on me as if they contain all of the world's hatred in their depths. "You remember, Isaac Mayfair, when you see my face again it won't be to help you." I only allow him to get away with grabbing my shirt and pulling my face towards his because I'm confused by what he's saying. I feel his hot breath on my skin; so rank and deadly. "I want the Sovereign dethroned," he goes on like the madman he knows he is, his voice low and harsh, like the most extreme sort of whisper.

And as he slowly leans away and releases my shirt, I understand why he's here: he feels he has a better chance at Sovereignty defeating me than my father. He's not here to help me; he's here to help himself.

I accept it and move quickly to the side as he and Ashe and the others with him clash with the six who were about to tear me a new one. I race through the den and into the back room where I saw Beverlee finally manage to drag Carl. I scoop them up, one in each arm and propel myself through the room and to the back door, bursting through the screen and out into the night. Beverlee screams against me even though I'm trying to help her and I feel the dead weight of Carl's paralyzed legs swinging all around me since he has no control over their movement. I run as fast as my not-so-human legs will take me until I make it far away from the werewolves scattered and fighting throughout the town.

I set Beverlee and Carl down behind an abandoned building that smells like water damage and old air. With my bare hand, I rip the rusted padlock from the door and the door creaks open.

"Get inside and hide," I say quickly, "don't come out."

Beverlee, still in shock and staring up at me from the ground wide-eyed, finally understands and goes to help Carl inside.

I leave them there and watch the lights of traffic and stars and houses flash by me as I speed toward Sugarloaf Mountain. I'm fastest in my mediate form and know that if I have any chance of getting there in time, that this is the only way I'll make it.

But already I feel my heart breaking because I can't hear Adria or feel her emotions. She has been blocked from me and I know....I know that in a time like this she would never do it on purpose....

HARRY

33

"YOU COULDN'T *WHAT*, CAMILLA?!" Daisy screams, but I know she already knows what Camilla is having a hard time getting out. We all know it. Daisy roars at her, "DOES FATHER KNOW?"

Camilla nods furiously, tears shooting continuously from the corners of her eyes. "I-I tried to keep him out of my head, but I couldn't! I couldn't concentrate; his link is too strong for me."

Daisy told me when we were alone in our room one night that Camilla was the weakest of them all when it came to controlling and safeguarding her thoughts. It was why she had always sought other means of mental and emotional discipline by practicing Yoga and all sorts of other human activities.

I start to lower my head in defeat, until I think better of it and try to shape up, suck it down and figure out what I'm going to do.

I start to pace.

"Oh you can't be serious!" Rachel cries out, popping completely off of the table like a snapped rubber band.

"WHERE IS HE, CAMILLA?" Daisy shakes her body violently by the shoulders.

Camilla sobs even louder, her cries shuddering out of her pathetically. When Daisy sees how freaked-out Camilla is, she pulls her toward her chest and holds her there, cradling the back of her head. "We'll figure it out, Cam, don't worry."

Adria is the opposite of Camilla. Camilla's hysterical display nearly made me forget that Adria was even in the room. She stands off to the side, staring down at the floor and no visible part of her body is moving.

I think she's in a sort of shock and Alex rushes over to her, wrapping her arms around her.

Daisy and I look at each other.

"What do we do?" Daisy says to me telepathically as Camilla sobs into her shirt.

I was going to ask her the same thing.

And as is if God, or whoever it is up there watching all of this unfold, hates us, Shannon and Elizabeth burst through the entrance, screaming: "THEY'RE COMING! FATHER'S HERE! THEY'RE COMING!"

I can't tell which of them said what, maybe they both said it at the same time, I don't know.

Adria finally looks up.

"I'll face him," Adria says suddenly, scared but as calmly as I've ever heard her say anything. "I know he'll kill me, but we all know I'm the one he's here for and I'm not afraid to face him for what I did."

"SHUT *UP!*" Alex roars in Adria's face; clearly she's petrified of Adria getting killed. "Screw that! Don't pull that dumb movie hero drama bullshit!" She tries to grab Adria, but Adria pushes her away.

"What do we do now?" Shannon screams at the exit; she's bouncing around nervously like she's trying to keep from peeing on herself.

"We fight him," Daisy says and her gaze falls solemnly on me.

"You know what Isaac said, Harry," she says in my mind, *"Don't let Adria out of this cave. Don't let her shift."*

"I'm not letting you fight him without me," I say.

"Harry…you have to stay in here with her. PROMISE ME!"

I grit my teeth and hold back my dispute.

I'll think of something….

Daisy looks around at everyone and they all know what to do. In a blaze of movement, they burst through the exit and head down the long, narrow tunnel that leads outside; the sound of their bones snapping and teeth gnashing and screams of pain ricochets off the cave walls and fills my ears with terror.

I stop Adria before she gets around the stone table.

I shake my head carefully, regretfully. "I can't let you go. I'm sorry."

"MOVE OUT OF MY WAY, HARRY!" She goes to push past me, but I grab her by the arm and swing her body around crushing her back into my chest and I hold her here.

I feel her start to shift under the weight of my arms.

"Calm…," I whisper into her ear. "Calm, Adria."

"NO! DON'T DO THIS!"

My lips move along the arch of her ear and softly I shut my eyes to better delve deeply into her mind. "Just calm down," I say, letting each word roll seductively off of my tongue and into her mind, letting my power to dictate her emotions overwhelm her.

"HE'S HERE, ISAAC, HE'S—HARRY…please…."

And she's practically comatose, except that her eyes are wide open and she stares up at me with a drunken look on her face. I lift Adria into my arms and run with her through the tunnel behind me, which snakes around and deeper into the mountain, far past the room where Trajan once hid Aramei.

And I hide Adria there, in the pitch darkness of the cave, behind a recess in the stone just spacious enough to fit her body.

I run fast back toward the main room and dash past it, covering as much tunnel ground as I can with my long longs and I don't stop until I make it out of the mouth of the cave and into the early morning air. The sun is barely rising over the top of the mountain, bathing the gray morning in pale light. I smell smoke. I inhale deeply to catch the scent and practically choke on it, only now realizing how thickly it moves through the forest. As far as I can see through the dense trees, the smoke leaves a heavy blanket of gray lingering in the air. I look up to see the first searing flame crawling up the trees on the hillside.

They're setting the forest on fire. They're trying to smoke Adria out!

A series of thunderous howls rips through the atmosphere and I take off running toward the sound. Trees and bushes whip by, snapping me on the face as I run. But I don't stop; I have to get to Daisy and I don't give a damn that she'll probably never forgive me for leaving Adria alone.

But Adria will be fine; this is the only thing I'm sure of. At least until Isaac can get here and I know he's coming because I saw him in Adria's mind just before her link to him was severed. She can't hold a mind link when her thoughts and emotions are being manipulated and controlled. But I don't know how long I'll be able to sway her…or how long I'll be able to do everything else I'm about to do.

I run right through a blazing flame ten feet high devouring the landscape. The flames are spreading outward around me in a horseshoe shape. I see Daisy and her sisters out ahead, not too far off in the distance, surrounded by dozens of other Black Beasts. And there are more…at least eighty or ninety, appearing over the top of a ridge and from the tree-filled hills and some even from the trees. My head is spinning with indecision! I know Daisy's beast form to an extent and can pick her out of the crowd, but I can't tell the others apart. I can't tell us from the enemy.

A forceful roar tears through the air. And then another. And another, until all of the Black Beasts are standing tall with their heavily-muscled arms pulled back and their teeth-gnashing heads are pointed upward toward the sky. Their howls send chills all over my body.

In a split-second that feels like slow-motion, they charge one another and I instantly lose sight of Daisy. I can no longer tell her apart from the others. The ground shakes beneath my feet as another large group of werewolves come charging over the burning hill, some dive right through the flames and come out the other side, on fire but unfazed. I can smell the burning and singed fur all around me mixed with the burning trees. I can't control fire. Air is my element and that power is as useless against fire as water is to a flood. I feel so powerless!

There must be more than one hundred beasts fighting below and on every side of me; enormous, beastly bodies charging and crashing into one another like bulls with demonic growls and roars more terrifying than a lion or a grizzly. One beast swats another one across the forest like a fly. The body crashes through dozens of small trees before hitting a wall of rock embedded in the side of an incline. A huge beast in my peripheral vision lunges at a smaller one and takes off its head with one deadly swipe of its massive, razor-sharp claws.

I stumble backward into a tree, gasping for breath. My eyes are wide as they can be in the sockets; my strained lips pulling away from my teeth in recoiling terror.

The severed head thumps against the leaf-covered ground and rolls several feet away from its body. I don't have it in my heart to see whose head it is. I just can't do it, even though I can tell that the head and the body both have shifted back into their human form.

I can't do it. If it was Daisy….

The tree behind me snaps off just above my head and crashes to the ground. I'm left instinctively crouching, covering my head from the falling branches. Finally, I look up to see a colossal beast bearing down on me, blood dripping from its teeth.

I can't use my powers or Adria will be unprotected!

I start to crawl away on my ass and my hands and just as I hit the top of the hill and find myself falling down the side of it, another beast comes in behind the one after me and backhands it past my rolling body. As my body rolls once, I see it flying across the space and the other beast lunging out after it. I manage to break my fall the rest of the way down the side of the hill when I hit a rock jutting up from the ground. Pain sears through my back and I cry out. The smoke is choking me now; it's so thick closer toward the bottom of the hill. But beasts are everywhere and I can't figure out which danger is more pressing, them or the raging fires. I just sit here and watch the slaughter, holding on dearly to Adria in my mind and hoping that by some chance I can figure out who is who out there so that I can help them. Even if I can only make out which one of them is Daisy.

I should've known not to leave the cave and that I would be making everything harder on Adria and Daisy and myself.

I watch in horror as more beasts are taken down, as more are killed and their beastly bodies give way to their naked human forms as they succumb to death. Tears coat my eyes, but I can't actually cry. I'm too much in shock for tears and my power over Adria is diminishing. My mind keeps going back to her, seeing her body lying helpless behind the rock. I feel her struggling against me, pressing her mental hands into the deepest recesses of my brain.

Suddenly, Adria's face snaps out of my mind as my body is sent hurtling through the air. At first, I think I've been hit in the stomach because there's so much searing pain there, but then I realize I'm hurtling because I'm being carried and the pain is coming from a beast's massive arm tight around my waist. It feels like my ribs are pressing down on my lungs, the beast is holding me so securely.

But it's not Daisy. I would know if it were her being this close.

I start to panic.

"It's Raul," a voice says in my mind and I realize it's coming from the beast racing with me through the forest. *"Protect Adria!"* And that's the last thing I hear as he drops me hard on the ground several feet from the cave entrance and hurries away just as quickly, out of sight.

They've switched sides...Raul and his men have sided with us!

The realization numbs me, but gives me hope.

I crawl on my hands and knees closer to the cave and all along the way the ground rumbles and shakes as beasts bound through the forest violently like a stampede of buffalo. Trees—full-grown scaling trees—fall all around me, crashing down against the earth from both the fires and the violence. Plumes of smoke rise high into the sky and smoke crawls its way across the forest bed, making it harder to see even six feet in front of me. But it's also starting to rain and if I believed in God, I would think it was a miracle because the rain couldn't have come at a better time to help put out the fires. No lightning and no thunder, just a steady, heavy downpour of cold rain. Already my clothes are soaked and my hands are muddy as I continue to push myself toward the cave entrance, but now that the rain is taming the smoke, I can get to my feet and run again.

I push myself up and just as I reach the cave entrance, Trajan appears in front of me and embeds his boot in my chest, knocking the breath from me and me on my ass many feet away. My back hits something; it could be a tree or rock, I don't know, but it snaps Adria almost completely from my power. I hold on to her as tightly as I can. I can't let her fight him. He will kill her.

Trajan says nothing to me as if I'm as insignificant as an insect, and his tall, menacing figure clad in an old leather trench coat and leather boots, disappears into the darkness of the cave.

My head is spinning. I can hardly breathe or see straight or think straight, but I know I have to do something.

I shut my eyes and let my head relax against whatever it was that I hit and I calm myself. The sounds of the battle go on all around me: the growls, the roars, the howls, bones breaking, flesh ripping, teeth gnashing, and beasts dying. I hear the fires sizzling as the rains pound on the flames and I hear Trajan's footsteps echoing off the cave walls as he makes his way inside. Every little sound is amplified in my head as if I'm a werewolf, too, and somehow have their magnified sense of hearing.

But I can't focus on anything anymore, not when I have to localize all of my efforts into Adria's mind, using all of my power to tame her beast and keep her from Turning.

My God…she is *so* powerful….

My chest shudders to a halt and I take one more deep breath and do the only thing I know to do: I envision Adria's death. I picture Trajan finding her out in the wide open because my power is no longer strong enough to hold her back and keep her hidden behind the cave walls. I picture her facing Trajan in her last moments.

And then I see him kill her....

ISAAC

34

TRAFFIC AND STOPLIGHTS AND light poles rocket by me like long, rods of light snaking through some infinite space beyond. Buildings and houses and churches and gas stations look like nothing more than one-dimensional structures sprawled out across the landscape; those closest to me I don't even see, I'm moving so fast. I have to get into the mountains. I have to get to Adria before my father does.

And when my heart tries to tell me that I'm too late, I have to stop myself from reaching inside my chest and ripping it out just to cease its sacrilegious cries.

I push on harder and faster, feeling the earth grind beneath my feet each time my boots thrust against the ground. We rarely get tired and we rarely ever feel the effects of exhaustion when running, but right now and for the first time in my life, I feel it. I feel every muscle in my body tightening beyond their capabilities in this form. I feel my bones heavy with enervation and excruciating pain. I feel the blood surging so hard through my veins that I wonder if my heart might explode.

But I just push harder.

Every town and small city I run through is nothing but a blur, a stain seared into the back of my mind. Several parked cars I know I destroyed when I covered their distance, using their hoods and tops as a means to propel me farther into the air as I leapt onto a train bridge just beyond them. And from the bridge, I find myself dashing into the outskirts of the mountain as I speed lightning-fast through the first layers of trees.

Deeper into the mountain I run, only picking up speed instead of slowing down when for any split-second my mind attempts to tame my legs. I defy all reason; cast aside anything that might hold me back from getting to her in time.

I smell smoke.

And by now I'm running so recklessly fast that it is by sheer luck that I don't run smack into something and crush my skull flat. Because I have tossed away my reason and supernatural instincts and have traded them for full and uninhibited speed.

I smell death.

My heart sinks like a stone and tears choke me. But I keep running and the closer I get the more death that I smell.

But I can't run that fast anymore.

The world funnels back into my sight all around me as my pace begins to slow. Bodies. There are bodies lying naked and bloody and dead, everywhere. I try not to look at their faces, because I can't bear it. My fists tighten at my sides as I run past them; blood oozes from the palms of my hands. My mouth is open, seeking breath that my lungs aren't getting anywhere else. My eyes burn from searing tears and choking smoke and the reality of the death surrounding me. My vision is fogging.

Smoke rises from the blackened earth where a fire had recently burned. Pockets of burning brush are still aflame here and there, but quietly going out as the rain continues to lick them. My eyes glimpse the extent of the damage stretching father than I can force myself to see in this moment. I press on, stumbling through scorched trees and past more bodies and I inadvertently see that one of them is my sister, Elizabeth. She lies naked against the wet ground, her body twisted horrifically as if her back had been snapped in two and the only thing holding it together is her flesh.

I push past her, trying to hold down the wailing scream that wants to force itself from my lungs.

I stumble to the front of the cave and fall against the opening, thrusting my hands against the slick wet rock as I try to hold my body upright and the pain and exhaustion catches up to me.

I sniff the air and I can smell Adria inside.

I can smell my father....

I stop long enough—two seconds—to catch my breath and I run into the cave and through the snaking tunnel until I burst out the other side and into the main room.

When I see the two of them there, I feel my body trying to move, but my mind is trapped between my conscience and my will. I can't move and I can't find my voice or my heart. My blood has become like acid in my veins. My heart has stopped. It utterly died the second I saw Adria lying dead upon the massive stone table.

My father sits at the head in the high-back chair and he looks across at me with absolutely no emotion in his face.

I'm shaking from the inside, but I still can't move. Tears are burning down my face. My voice is still caught somewhere within me.

Adria lies with her legs hanging over the side of the table, one arm twisted behind her head, broken, the other curled up near her chin. Her eyes are open and lifeless. Blood seeps from her nostrils and her partially-opened mouth, pooling into a puddle below her lips. The lower-half of her body is warped as though my father's hands had been around each end of her and he twisted her like a dishrag until every bone and muscle in her body snapped.

It feels like my eyes are trying to shut, but they can't. Shock and anguish have completely numbed my body and my mind. I feel like all that I can move are my eyes and even those I don't think I'm actually moving myself.

"You would have done the same," Trajan—because I can never again call him my father—says from the chair.

I look up, though I never recall actually moving my head, to see him from the chest-up over the top of Adria's body.

"Now you know the true complexity of the kind of pain that love can cause."

I can't speak. I'm still shaking from the inside-out; my bones feel like metal, my muscles like burning hot mush, tightening and constricting in some inner struggle to keep me on my feet.

Trajan reaches out his hand and touches a lock of Adria's dark-brown hair. I watch his bloody fingers move slowly through the length of it.

I still can't move. Am I even really here? Is this real? This can't be real...I-I can't be without her. She can't be dead....

Trajan stands from the chair and looks down upon Adria.

I fall against the rock wall behind me, finally gaining some sense of control over my own body. Tears rock my chest and for a moment, crying is all that I can bring myself to do. And then I scream out amid the cave walls and my vision turns very dark as my eyes shift color.

Trajan looks across the room at me still showing no signs of emotion. Nothing. I could fully shift right here, right now and something tells me that he wouldn't react to it at all. He doesn't care. The only thing, the only person in this world that he cared about is dead and gone. Aramei is dead and gone. And Adria, the one who took Aramei away from him, is dead and gone…he has nothing else to live for.

No…I can't be without her!

I scream out again, pulling my fisted hands back against the stone and hitting it with such force that it quavers loosely from the surrounding wall and falls in pieces around me. "BASTARD!" I cry and rise to my feet; my voice booms around the walls of the cave.

And then from the corner of my eye, I thought for a moment that the room…blinked. The sheer strangeness of it catches me off-guard. It happens again, but this time even Trajan notices. He looks up from Adria's body and at me with a vague sort of curiosity in his eyes.

Then suddenly, Adria's body…disappears, leaving us both dumbfounded and scrambling inside our minds for something to make sense of what just happened.

It hits us both at the same time as our wrathful, vengeful eyes lock from over the table and across the room.

And the world blacks out in an instant as our beasts are unleashed.

HARRY

35

UNABLE TO MAINTAIN THE illusion any longer, my body is hurled backward and away from the cave as the power explodes completely out of me. I land hard on the ground and skid a few feet before I come to a stop, gasping for air. My head is spinning; the trees above me are moving around so fast that I double over forward and puke my guts up, my back arched in an embarrassing display. I even manage to puke on my hands.

A thunderous *crunch-crash* resounds through the forest as Isaac and Trajan, in full-fledged Black Beast form, burst through the cave entrance, sending shards and chunks of rock outward in every direction as if dynamite had been set off inside the cave. And when they slide across the landscape, their massive bodies take a few remaining trees down with them.

I get my head together and run behind them as they fight their way viciously through the forest and towards the opening in the trees that leads to the top of the hill.

I don't even care to stop long enough to turn around and see who's behind me, but I know that others are following. I had heard more than two dozen sets of legs sprinting in after Isaac and coming from the same direction.

Enemy or foe? In this moment, it doesn't matter to either side.

Trajan, obviously the larger of the two, grabs Isaac up by his mammoth neck and batters him against the ground.

Isaac hits with so much force that I'm knocked from my feet as though a small earthquake had just shook the ground beneath me. I get up just as quickly and follow still, running out over the top of the hill where the fires had scorched the ground to blackness and tree stubble and I see them roll down the side and into the opening.

Others are watching from the top of the ridge where I stand.

I glimpse Daisy's naked form, staring at me from the other side and I'm momentarily overwhelmed that she's still alive. But right now, neither of us moves to go to one another.

I hurl myself farther down the blackened hill, sometimes having to break my fall by pressing the palms of my hands against the slope and I skid the rest of the way down practically on my butt and my hands. I get about twenty feet away from Trajan and Isaac and decide this is as far as I should go.

Isaac, seven-feet of blade-like teeth and a massive beastly head, charges Trajan in the wide open. In two seconds, he's crashing into him, plunging them both onto the ground. All the way down, Isaac slashes his father, hand after hand; blood splattering with each and every blow. Their demonic roars ricochet off every tree and every rock. But Trajan manages to hurl Isaac off him and he leaps up so quickly that I barely see him move. Trajan swings around full-circle and comes at Isaac, crushing his skull with his giant iron clawed fist. I hear the blood-curdling *crunch* when it makes contact. I never even noticed when my hands came up to cover my ears from the sound. Isaac hits the ground hard and falls on his side. Slow to get up, his body twitches horrifically as though the force of the blow had connected with the neurons in his brain. A God-awful grunt rumbles out of Isaac's chest as he jerks his head side to side, trying to shake it off.

Trajan charges him.

I brace for the impact, every bone and muscle in my body rock-solid, rendering me motionless and unable to breathe.

As Trajan's giant foot comes down to finish the job on Isaac's skull, Isaac rears back and out of the way, swinging out his arm to catch Trajan in the lower stomach. His great claws rip through the black fur and thick flesh, leaving five crimson fissures slashed across Trajan's abdomen. Blood trails behind Isaac's hand like liquefied ribbons of red floating on the air and Trajan's colossal form stumbles back several feet to catch his balance.

Standing five feet apart from each other, Isaac and Trajan pull back their arms; their hands balled into fists. Their chests protrude outward as they crane their thickly-muscled necks in a display of dominance. And at the same time, their heads come down to face one another and two horrific, wrathful roars bellow out; their full set of razor-sharp teeth unsheathed by their wide-opened jaws.

The roars shock masses of birds from trees several miles away and for a strangely quiet moment all that any of us watching can hear are the cries of the flocks and the flapping of hundreds of wings as a swath of black dots move through the gray, cloud-filled sky in the distance.

And then a gruff grunting cry ripples through the air.

Trajan has Isaac in a lock; his deadly teeth clamped around Isaac's throat and right shoulder-blade. The snapping of tendon and the crushing of bone fills everyone with frenzied dread. I see Daisy and many others watching from the top of the ridge, all in their mediate forms, climbing the sides of the trees. Some are trying to contain themselves, to tame their beasts by gripping their heads in their hands. Daisy is one of them. I want to run back up and across the expanse of the ridge to get to her, but I can't move....

Isaac roars painfully as Trajan lifts his body from the ground—Isaac still trapped within his jaws—and shakes him back and forth violently like a fight-dog would its prey. Isaac falls from Trajan's teeth and hits the ground hard.

Struggling and clearly in tremendous pain, Isaac still gets up.

Trajan goes to deliver one last blow to Isaac's skull and just as his claws come down within inches of him, Isaac's arm projects outward and he buries his hand inside Trajan's chest cavity.

Trajan freezes in a shocked tableau and all of the others watching from the ridge suddenly cease their movements and stare out at the scene wide-eyed.

As Trajan begins to fall to the ground with Isaac's hand still inside his chest, his form begins to change.

In seconds, both of them are human.

Without hearing my own feet shuffling through the burnt leaves, or my breath wheezing as I run, I make my way closer to them and I stand just feet away in the wide open, watching with absolute relief and sorrow as the rain mists down around their seemingly unmoving bodies.

Isaac lies over his father, peering deeply into Trajan's dark blue eyes glazed over with moisture. His naked body— like Isaac's—is covered in mud and blood and cuts and gashes and black-blue bruises. His long, dark hair lays disheveled about his head; tiny pieces of leaves and burnt twigs are tangled in the mess. He gazes up into Isaac's eyes and for the first time in probably hundreds of years, there is a true sense of love and regret and respect in those eyes. I think death has given Trajan back his sense of being and his memories of life before he met Aramei and became the madman that he became.

Tears pour from Isaac's eyes and fall upon his father, but there is still anger and retribution in his face. He looks down at Trajan with an unbreakable stare; his lips are twisted into a teeth-grinding mass, his eyes pulled together harshly and his rigid eyebrows twitching as the tears shudder through his body.

"Forgive me for all I have done…," is all that Trajan can force out of his fading body.

Isaac tries to hold back both his anger and his forgiveness, but in the end he can't hold either of them down.

In a quiet and peculiar moment, Isaac leans over and places his lips against his father's forehead and holds them there for a devastating moment. And then he pulls away. The air is rife with emotion and darkness. Not even one like me would be able to repress these emotions on this day. Isaac stares into his father's eyes and wrenches his hand firmly inside his chest, crushing Trajan's heart. Trajan's body locks up, his eyes flaring horribly as he peers upward at the sky, and then as the last breath escapes his lips, his body goes slack.

No one moves or breathes or makes the minutest of sounds. I believe that for a brief moment, their thoughts even freeze in time. I don't hear anything except for the rain.

Covered in blood and mud, Isaac raises his body farther away from his father's. He sits there, held up by his naked knees, surrounded by rain and filth and blood; the ground beneath him is as black as coal. He stares longingly at the face of the man who gave him life, the one who Isaac had always loved and admired and sought to impress and please. But also he stares at the face of six hundred years of tyranny and death. But he was still his father and that part of Isaac that loved him can't be hidden away.

Isaac throws his head back and looks upward at the sky, letting the rain mist lightly upon his blackened and bloody face. And then he wrenches back his arms and screams out into the atmosphere, letting the pain and the truth of what his life has become to course through him.

All becomes quiet again as he lowers his head back down. He only looks up when he hears Adria's footsteps running through the puddles of water and towards him.

"Isaac!" she cries out as she gets closer. She can hardly speak, the tears are suffocating her.

She falls to her knees beside him, wrapping her arms around him. She kisses his head and cheeks and his filthy hair and finally, his mouth. When the painful moment finally runs its course through him, Isaac slowly looks into Adria's tear-filled eyes and then he grabs her, forcing her into his arms.

Neither of them can speak; it's as if the moment has stolen all the words from the air, but they cry and laugh and embrace each other knowing that it's finally over and that a new beginning has just begun.

ISAAC

One year later…

36

THE DARK, SECRET WORLD of the legendary Black Beasts embraced my emergence as Sovereign with open arms. Alpha's all over the world heard of the fall of my father, Vukašin Prvovenčani—Lord General, Sovereign; he carried many titles—and celebrated me proudly with grand festivities and ceremonies in my honor. Of course, I didn't attend even a fraction of them because it's impossible to be in a hundred different places at once, but I know about each one in heavy and vivid detail. Deep in the mountains of Serbia, a statue of me was erected and I've heard rumors of my Name being protected by law within the first three days of my reign.

Seth, my younger brother is Alpha there now, appointed by me. And his cruelly devoted mother, Nataša, was grateful for that. In an uncanny, yet not-so-unexpected twist, Nataša declared her unwavering allegiance and loyalty to me as her leader. It was not-so-unexpected because Nataša is and always has been eternally loyal to any Sovereign. She has lived her entire life to serve the One leader of our kind and she will die serving him, whether it be me, or someone after me.

Nataša was the one rumored to have passed into law the protection of my Name in such a short time.

And I believe the rumor to be true.

My name...I should probably explain how I got the name 'Mayfair' seeing as how neither my father, nor my mother, Sibyl, carried it. When we were brought into the

United States, the Elders found it necessary that we blend in as smoothly as possible and so we were given a name that resonated with humans—and Americans—more than the name of my father. Mayfair was chosen by the Governess, the Elder werewolf who raised us and taught us the ways of our politics and heritage. I could have chosen to take the name of my father, or any other powerful name that I wanted to carry in my reign, but I decided—also because of a very contentious Adria, who refuses to carry a last name she can't pronounce—to keep the name simply: Isaac Mayfair. I don't carry a title and I would never ask or expect my brothers and sisters and friends to bow to me or to call me Lord. Outsiders? That's a different story. But I am still Sovereign and I am still Lord General and I will be until the day I retire, or when my own son comes along and decides to dethrone me.

But Adria puts her metaphorical fingers in her ears whenever I bring up the whole heir-to-my-throne topic.

I find it hilarious, but one day….

For now, she has so happily agreed to accept my offer giving her certain rights as a female Alpha. She passed into law that all females are given the right to be financially independent if they so wish, but she was more adamant about changing that Lord title to something less… chauvinist. Nataša is still trying to adjust to being called Lordess. I think she hates it, but she'll get over it.

I intended to appoint Nathan as Alpha of the Maine territory, but he had to decline for reasons that I am fully aware of, but am not at liberty to reveal.

I will say, however, that it has to do with a girl.

For now, Nathan is still my Right-Hand and he will always be within my reach whether by phone or any other means of communication, but he will be leaving Maine soon. And so Xavier, next in line, I happily appointed as Alpha of

Maine just four months ago. Xavier gladly accepted and I know he's capable of pulling it off, but I also know that he's unpredictable and as Adria might put it: a man-whore. So far he has done well as Alpha, but I think sooner than later, his wicked rebel ways and his tumultuous past with women will be his undoing.

I travel all over the world, doing the things that my father did before me, but with more respect from those who follow me. They fear me, but they respect me because I don't rule with intimidation and cruelty and an unforgiving heart. And the one who travels with me everywhere I go is Raul. Big Raul, Adria calls him. I think he could kick my ass if he ever wanted to, but we're like brothers and even during my father's reign, Raul had always been partial to me. I named Raul the General over my entire army. If I ever go to war again, Raul will be at the head of my army where he belongs. He is as old as my father was at the time of his death and the battles and wars that Raul has fought in and often led, are too many to count.

But despite the many packs that honor me and are devoted to me, there will always be those who seek to take everything out from under me. Viktor Vargas will always be my greatest enemy and as the months wear on, I do see more and more signs of his inevitable uprising.

I will be prepared for him when that time comes. And he knows it.

I never heard from or saw my mother, Sibyl, again after the last time I saw her. More rumors have reached my ears that she was at the battle in the mountains when I defeated my father and that she was killed. Some say she went into hiding, while others claim that she committed suicide after Viktor betrayed her with intentions of siring Adria.

No father. No mother. But I don't need them because I have a real family now and they fill every part of me that ever wanted to feel human love and experience human life. Adria completes me. We complete each other. It was fate that we met, both parentless and broken and confused. We both lived very different, yet very similar lives and we fell in love fast because we were meant to be together, because destiny pulled our lives every which way to make sure that our paths crossed. And when they did, the rest just fell into place.

Sovereign Isaac Mayfair

HARRY

Two years ago, I was just a seventeen-year-old skater living happily in Hallowell, Maine with pro-skater aspirations and too many plaid shirts (hey, the stereotypes are true for *some* people). I can't say I never would've imagined being here, where I am now, because in the grand scheme of things and being what I am, saying something like that would be pretty damned redundant.

I asked Daisy to marry me last month.

She squealed and said yes—I think—in some half-excited, half-crying weird voice that kind of scared me a little. I mean, sure, she could've been crying because I'm such a pushover when it comes to her, and maybe laughing because the thought of being married to me is entertaining. But I'm pretty sure she said yes. I guess picking out colors of bridesmaid's dresses and something about a theme and whatnot, constitutes as a yes—(God, someone *please* conveniently drag me off at the right moment when she starts shoving patterns and color palettes in my face because I don't know my ass from my head when it comes to that stuff).

So I'm good.

I guess I just have a hard time believing that a girl as beautiful and as sexy as Daisy Mayfair—English accent and all!—wants to be married to *me*. Not that I have some sort of self-esteem issues or anything, but Daisy is far from being your typical girl-next-door. And guys like me usually only get the girl-next-door types.

In darker news, Daisy and I had to move from Hallowell shortly after Isaac defeated his father in battle. Minna Abrahamsen, the Harvester, was hot on my trail. Harvesters are my kind's worst enemy and nothing can be said, no bargains can be made for even the most innocent of us. They have and always will hunt us until we've all been reaped and are no longer a threat to this world. I wish I could just meet with Minna and try to convince her that I'm on her side now and that I could never do anything to hurt the ones I love.

I've been hurting those I love for generations because of our 'agenda'.

But you can say that I've gone rogue now. I mean, not in a Zia sort of way, but I have officially, after living so many different lives, turned my back on my kind. I've even gone as far as committing the single most treacherous act that one of us could ever commit: I told Daisy *everything* about me, about *Us*. I told her our agenda and what will happen if we succeed. I told her about the gateways that have already been opened throughout the world: The gates in France, Alaska and China, all whose Charges fulfilled their destinies, unlike Adria who was supposed to help Aramei open a gate right here in Maine. And then the most famous gate of all: Sorrento, Italy, opened by Victoria Hizri's Charge, Pelicia-Cinnia once known in her human life as Josephine.

But that's another story....

Yeah, Daisy and I are still living in Maine, but I won't say where until after we leave again. I feel like we're always kind of on the run even though we've been pretty stable in this apartment for a long time. But we'll move again, I know, because I'm not only running from Minna and other Harvesters like her; Genna left knowing where to find me and I'm fair game even to her now. But I'm also running from my own kind, those who aren't exactly the same me, but who are above me and who I can't hide my identity from. I fear what they will do to me, which is more than anything Minna or Genna could ever do. Punishment for failing to manipulate my Charge into fulfilling her destiny to sire Aramei will be severe enough. But the punishment for going rogue….

I miss Adria. I miss her a lot. But we still talk and we still share our deepest, darkest secrets (she hysterically brought up to me on the phone just the other night something about Isaac trying to sweet-talk her into giving him an heir. I laughed my ass off on the other end of the phone. She didn't seem to like that much. "You frickin' jerk!" she snapped into the receiver. "Aww, come on, you know I love you," I said. "And I'll still love you when your two hundred pounds, waddling around the house and barely able to fit your fat ass through the front door." No doubt, she hung up on me. And of course, she called me back an hour later acting like the conversation never happened.)

Adria may no longer be my Charge, but she'll always be my friend and I'll always do anything for her.

How long I live in this life, it's never something one can tell. I could get run over by Mack truck tomorrow and be reborn into…Oh God, Adria and Isaac's brat werewolf child. That would be my luck! Not a guy destined to be a billionaire, or the next Prince of Whatever country that still has princes and such. No, I'd end up snot-nosed little brat with a more hair than I want to imagine ever having to buzz off.

But in reality, the chances are that, like always, I'll outlive even Daisy who is almost immortal herself.

Yeah…I always outlive them.

HARRY LUCAS GRAVES

ALEXANDRA

There's a knock on my bedroom door. I've been living in the Mayfair house ever since my now best friend, Rachel, beat the crap out of me in the basement that night. Other than my sister, no one is closer to me than Rach.

"Who is it?" I shout across the room and when no one shouts back at me, I get up from the bed and waltz over to open it.

Xavier stands there holding a bouquet of white roses, smiling from ear-to-ear.

Flowers? *Really*? What is this, *1940*?

"What?" he says, noticing the repelled look on my face. "C'mon, what girl doesn't love roses?"

I smirk at him and let the door swing shut in his face.

Just one more day of torture. Just one. I mean hell, it's been a year and the guy is still trying to get in my pants.

And it's incredibly hot.

Just one more day....

NATHAN

"Baby, are you ready?" my girlfriend of over a year says sitting across from me at our favorite table at the bar.

Our relationship has been a secret...for many reasons.

I drink down the last of my beer—I drink it for taste; werewolves can't get drunk easily, unfortunately—and stand up, holding out my hand to her. She smiles up at me with those sexy bright green eyes, framed by jet-black silky hair. I could so easily force her ass up out of that chair and have my way with her in the back of the bar, but we really do need to get on the road. Got about a seven hour trip to Providence ahead of us.

She grins up at me, already having read the sexual frustration written all over my features, and that grin of hers knows no bounds. She knows how to push my buttons and force the beast inside of me just a little to the surface. She loves it. But I often have to put that girl in her place. She loves that, too. She takes my hand and stands up, pressing her body playfully against mine, triggering a deep growl rumbling through my chest.

"We have time," she whispers and then tugs my earlobe with her teeth.

I shut my eyes and inhale abrasively.

"No," I say and she looks up into my eyes, "I want this taken care of. When you're not with me, I feel *her* in my skin. It's like an infection—Genna, I-I can't take it anymore." I clasp my hands around her upper arms and peer down into her ethereal face.

"I know, baby," she says and her soft fingers move up my arms and take hold of my wrists. "Minna Abrahamsen's time is almost up and you'll be free of her for good."

I kiss her savagely, lifting her petite body into my arms; her legs straddle my waist. I grip her butt in my hands and growl into her neck. The music funnels around us through the bar and there's no shortage of conversations and the occasional pool stick making contact with a ball, but all I can really hear is Genna's rapid heartbeat pumping through every corner of my body.

The kiss breaks reluctantly and she gazes into my eyes; her fingertips lingering upon my lips. "So are we sticking with the plan?" she says and kisses me softly one more time.

I kiss her back in the same way and answer, "Yes, I'll take Minna out while Saiulee does her thing in the basement with the Praverians in the safe."

Genna pulls my lip back with her teeth.

I go in this time hungrily, wrapping my arms so tight around her small form that I could crush her ribs if I'm not careful.

Alright...so maybe there's a *little* time to spare before we leave for Providence.

438

ADRIA

37

I JUST FINISHED PACKING the last of my stuff from my room at Aunt Bev and Uncle Carl's house. It's going to be hard saying goodbye, but I'm entering the next chapter in my life and chapters are never easy in the beginning.

Hearing Isaac's Jeep pulling into the drive, I head down the stairs with a duffle bag over one shoulder.

Aunt Bev and Uncle Carl are standing at the foot of the stairs waiting for me. Yes, I did say that Uncle Carl was *standing*. About seven months ago, he started moving his legs on his own and they pushed his physical therapy sessions into double-time. He took his first new steps five months ago and is making progress every day. He'll never walk like he used to and he'll always have an obvious limp on his left side, but to Uncle Carl, a limp is a miracle. He smiles a lot now and has taken to talking so much these days that it's scary. When I first moved here, he hardly ever said anything at all. Now, Aunt Bev can't get him to shut up!

"We're going to miss you!" Beverlee says reaching her arms out wide to me as I come off the last step.

I hug her tight and she kisses me on the temple. Uncle Carl smiles like a dopey little boy and he pulls me into a hug. I work my way carefully between his crutches, trying to avoid knocking him off balance.

"You'll call us at least once a week?" Uncle Carl asks with some innocent demand tossed in there.

"Of course I will; *twice* a week."

"And whatever you need," Beverlee says, "money, food…a ride back."

I smile at her, knowing what she really means by a 'ride back'.

"This will always be my number one home," I say, "You know that."

Beverlee beams proudly and I notice her eyes watering up.

Isaac knocks on the front door and then let's himself inside; this is just as much his home as is it mine. Aunt Bev hugs him the moment he steps up, jangling his keys in his hand.

"Isaac, I know you're responsible," Beverlee says, looking slightly worried, as usual, "but I just wanted to make sure you checked all your tires, got an oil change; y'know, the basics."

She always asks this when we drive anywhere more than an hour from home.

Isaac smiles and nods. "Yes ma'am. She'll be perfectly safe with me on the drive down."

Uncle Carl and Beverlee exchange glances.

"That, I *do* believe seeing as how you're a…, well, you know." Beverlee swallows the word 'werewolf' down. She and Uncle Carl still aren't used to saying it out loud.

Isaac grins.

They know everything now. It was kind of hard to lie about what happened that night Nataša and her pack held my aunt and uncle hostage. I'm really kind of glad that I wasn't here to witness it myself, but there was no hiding the fact that my boyfriend and just about everyone I know and hang out with, aren't exactly human. I could've asked Harry to help with letting them 'forget', but he did explain that a mind can only take so much manipulation and that his power wouldn't last forever. Eventually, they would start to remember bits and pieces. Genna helped erase their minds of the time I had disappeared when I was going through my transformation and that was enough messing around with their heads. So, I figured why not just tell them the truth about everything?

And so after that night, Isaac and I sat down with them and pretty much turned their quaint little life as humans upside-down with the information. But we spared overwhelming them with anything other than werewolves. They still think Harry is as human as they are and it's probably better that way.

The story throughout the rest of the town was that a huge gang had come in from somewhere—there's a lot of rumors flying around about what happened that night—and fights broke out all over the place. Thankfully, no one, not even Nataša's pack, let themselves Turn in front of the humans. The fighting going on in the streets and in people's front yards and even on their roofs, was blamed on gang violence. Some of Hallowell's residents claim they saw some of these 'gang members' actually jump onto second-story roofs and others say they saw men leaping from one building to another. A group of students from Hall-Dale—including bitchy Tori and Cecilia, who became best friends, believe it or not—have started rumors about there being 'vampires' in Hallowell (because of the black eyes and claws we have when in our mediate form). Of course, no one really believes that, or they're just not openly admitting it. Harry found Cecilia shortly after the night we trapped Zia and definitely had to use his Praverian powers to manipulate her memories.

But she's crazy by default and so whatever she says is almost always brushed off as mental illness, anyway.

It could've been worse that night Bev and Uncle Carl got the shock of their lives; this whole town could be one big werewolf infection on the map.

"Call as soon as you get there," Beverlee says, taking me into yet another hug and I'm starting to think she's going to cave and try to hold *me* hostage inside the house.

"I'll call you even *before* I get there, I promise!"

Still smiling as brightly as ever, a few tears finally roll down Beverlee's rose-colored cheeks. She lets go of me and I say goodbye for now. I'll be back sometime on break.

~~~

Six hours later and Isaac is helping me carry my bags up to the third floor to my college dorm room in Hudson Valley. I didn't have to fill out paperwork and I got to bypass all the basics of getting in. It was like one night Isaac asked me if I wanted to go to college and when I said yes, everything was prepared for me in just a few days' time. All I had to do was show up today.

I guess it helped too that Isaac is who he is; I'm sure that sped things up a lot. This isn't your average college; at least not our section of it anyway. There is only one requirement: you can't be 100% human. Of course, there are humans in this school, but they're oblivious to what we are.

Isaac and I walk down a short stretch of hallway toward my dorm room and already I feel eyes at my back. It feels a lot like it did when I first stepped foot inside the Mayfair house as the new girl, except there's something more comforting about this.

A blond-haired girl wearing a pair of black skinny jeans and bright red lipstick walks up barefooted and smiles mesmerizingly at Isaac. She bows awkwardly, first and then says, "Ooooh my God…you're the Sovereign." She looks exactly like an obsessed fan-girl of any new lame boy band, minus the grabby hands, tears and screaming: *I love you!*

Isaac nods, but doesn't give her any more attention than that for fear of instigating her.

She eyes me now and her giddy smile turns into a scary, hopeful look that I'm already beginning to recoil from.

"And you must be Adria," she says, hardly able to contain herself.

We keep shuffling down the hallway toward my room, but she keeps up pace right beside me. By now, more heads are poking out of the doorways as we pass. Most of them wearing the same awed faces as the blond girl.

"Yes, I'm Adria," I say, "And your name is?"

She looks blankly at me for a second as though so awestruck by us that she didn't understand the question. I notice she can't seem to stop sneaking a drooling glimpse at Isaac, too.

"Oh!" she says, finally realizing, "I'm Nora Cunningham, your roommate."

My face falls, but I suppress the full strength of it before she notices and takes offense. I roll my shoulder so that my duffle bag strap will slide back in place and then I stop to reach out my hand. Nora shakes it vigorously, still smiling.

"Next room up," she says pointing and then she moves out ahead of us to escort us the rest of the way.

"Oh my God," she hisses a whisper to a girl standing in the doorway of the room next to ours. "It's Isaac Mayfair. I'm roomin' with his *mate*!" She jerks her head back around to face us, her cheeks flared up with color and she can't seem to stand still.

Why couldn't I get the typical bitchy roommate that could care less who I was and only wanted to be sure I never touched her stuff?

We slip inside the spacious room and I see that the rest of my stuff is already here—we shipped it ahead.

"I'll uhhh…leave you two alone for a minute," she says with a carnal grin spread across her tanned face. She ducks out and slips out the door, shutting it behind her.

Isaac drops the two suitcases he carried up and stands in the center of the room checking out the place, his hands buried in his pockets.

I immediately start to unpack.

"I'm glad you're doing this, babe."

I reach into a box sitting on the floor beside my twin bed and start to pull out a few of my favorite things which always help me feel more at home no matter where I happen to be living.

"Me too," I say, looking over at him once. "And it'll be good for me to be here learning what I can about all this werewolf stuff—." I point at him momentarily. "—I don't just want to be 'the girl with the Sovereign', Isaac. I want to earn my place and learn everything about the politics and…whatever else."

I catch a faint smile tug one corner of his delicious mouth.

Diving back into the box, I tug out my small cork bulletin board I like to tack photos to and move toward my desk to mount it to the wall.

"You're already more than just the girl with the Sovereign," he says. "And you don't have anything to earn or to prove. You know that, right?"

I push the tack in with my thumb and lean away from the wall, turning at the waist to smile across at him.

"Yeah, I know, but just the same, I want to learn everything because it will make me feel better to know."

I go back to the box and as I reach into it to pull out my roll of posters, I feel Isaac come up behind me and he slips his hands around my waist. I lean up and take in the scent of him, closing my eyes and savoring the moment...because it'll be the last for a little while.

"You're avoiding me," he says, frowning, but he knows the reason why.

I stop what I'm doing and step up to him. "I don't know if I can go without seeing you for three months. I've been dreading this day, to be honest."

I feel the tears trying to push their way to the surface, but I hold them down the best I can. Gah! I hate this!

Isaac pulls me toward him with his hands on my hips. He leans over and presses his forehead to mine. "I've been dreading it, too, but the first place I'll visit when I get back from Romania will be here with you."

I smile and a tear escapes down my cheek. He wipes it away with the pad of his thumb and smiles in at me. "And you've already made a friend," he says, grinning.

I pull away and scrunch my nose playfully at him, sniffling away my tears. "Yeah, I guess you're right," I say, focusing on the positive things about our separation. And then I turn back around to my posters and start unrolling them.

Isaac is still standing in the same spot behind me and I know he's not finished with the things he wants to say, but I'm still trying to delay the inevitable. I don't want him to leave.

"Baby, you know I didn't mean now or soon when I brought it up…I was just curious about your reaction."

My whole body locks up and I suck in a quiet breath.

I turn around to face him with one poster, still rolled up tight, hanging from my fingertips.

He's trying so hard not to smile, but he's not exactly making fun of me, either. He's talking about the day he mentioned light-heartedly about me 'giving him an heir'. He tried to make it sound like a joke by saying the word 'heir' instead of 'baby', but I know deep down he really meant it. In *both* senses.

Isaac leans in and kisses me softly on the lips. "You've got a lot to do: college, having fun, marrying me—you know, stuff like that."

I think I stopped breathing altogether, but I can't tell. I never saw that coming. Really. I've pictured it, being married to Isaac, I mean like with a ring and a pretty vintage-style dress bought at a second-hand store, but I think hearing him say those words out loud make my simple thoughts of it actually come to life.

My heart is beating so fast I feel it in my knee-caps.

But I'm not ready for that, either. I love him and would say hell yes if he ever actually asked me to marry him, but right now I'm so nervous I feel like I'm going to be sick. I'm just not ready….

"I heard that," he says, grinning.

I didn't even think to close my mind off to him. My cheeks flare up with warmth.

He cups his hands around my upper arms and peers in at me with a devoted, beautiful smile. "At least I know in advance that you're going to say yes when I ask you." He kisses my forehead and leans up, letting his fingers trail down my arms as his hands slide away. "But I'll give you some time." He looks down at his pretend watch and then purses his lips. "You'll never know when it's gonna be—it could be after you leave this school, or three months from now when I come back to see you, but at least you have a warning."

His grin just gets deeper.

I fail miserably at keeping a straight face. I'm blushing and smiling and still trying to hold in laughter *and* tears all at the same time!

Finally, I just let the tears pour from my eyes, but they are happy tears and as huge as my smile is right about now, no one could mistake them for sadness.

Isaac pulls me into his arms and holds me tight, pressing his lips into my hair. I never want to leave these arms, but I better get used to it and so I kiss him deeply once and reluctantly move away from him. He understands my need to get this over with and I think he probably needs to do the same thing.

I move over to the head of my bed and unroll my *Supernatural* poster—which I've had hanging on my wall since before I moved to Hallowell—and I smooth it out against the wall.

"Babe, *really*?" Isaac says with a hint of humor in his voice. "You've got *me* now; why do you need posters like that looming over your bed?" He's totally playing with me; he can't stop grinning.

I let the poster fall to my side and I put my free hand on my hip. "Baby, I love you, but it's *Sam and Dean Winchester*?" I say as if I can't possibly grasp any reason for why he doesn't understand that.

He smiles and says, "Well, they can keep you company while I'm gone I guess, but when I get back...," he points his index finger upward and shakes his head slowly in warning,

"...they'll have to go; they can't be looking down at me when I'm having my way with you in here."

"Understood," I say, grinning.

~~~

I watch Isaac from my window as he walks down the sidewalk and away from the building. He hops in a cab at the end of the parking lot. The Jeep is mine now. And then I watch him pull away as a few tears stream down my smiling face. Three minutes without him sometimes feels long, so I can only imagine how long three months will be. I'm going to miss waking up curled up next to him and the way I always laid my head on his bare chest and listened to his heartbeat while he was sleeping.

I miss him already.

So, that's how my life turned out. I went from abuse to happiness and heartbroken to being in love and human to werewolf. Rollercoaster doesn't even *begin* to describe it. But I wouldn't trade any of it for anything in the world.

And I would do it all over again.

Adria Dawson...Mayfair :-)

To see more of The Darkwoods Trilogy, visit the author's Pinterest page:

HTTP://PINTEREST.COM/JREDMERSKI/THE-DARKWOODS-TRILOGY/

~~~

OTHER BOOKS BY J.A. REDMERSKI

***

-THE DARKWOODS TRILOGY-

#1 – THE MAYFAIR MOON

#2 – KINDRED

#3 – THE BALLAD OF ARAMEI

-STANDALONE NOVELS-

DIRTY EDEN

THE EDGE OF NEVER

-COMING SOON 2013-

THE DARKSOULS TRILOGY

ABOUT THE AUTHOR

Jessica Ann Redmerski was born in Little Rock, Arkansas on November 25, 1975. She lives in Arkansas with her three children and a Maltese.

www.jessicaredmerski.com

Made in the USA
Lexington, KY
27 December 2013